Little Grey Mice

LITTLE GREY MICE

Brian Freemantle

St. Martin's Press
New York

Library of Congress Cataloging-in-Publication Data

Freemantle, Brian.
    Little grey mice / Brian Freemantle.
        p.   cm.
    ISBN 0-312-07625-8
    I. Title.
PR6056.R43L58   1992
823'.914—dc20   92-838
                                                                              CIP

First published in Great Britain by Random Century Group.

First U.S. Edition: May 1992

10 9 8 7 6 5 4 3 2 1

For
John and Gloria Shearer,
with great affection.

Europe has entered a new promising era. Central and Eastern Europe is liberating itself. The Soviet Union has embarked on the long journey towards a free society. The walls that once confined people and ideas are collapsing. Europeans are determining their own destiny. They are choosing freedom. They are choosing economic liberty. They are choosing peace. They are choosing a Europe whole and free. As a consequence this alliance must and will adapt.

The London Declaration of
NATO leaders, 6 July 1990

Our alliance is no threat to anybody. We do not see ourselves as a bloc in a confrontational situation. We are moving beyond confrontation and becoming a partner in a new Europe.

Manfred Wörner, Secretary
General of NATO, 8 June 1990

We could agree to a United Germany's NATO membership provided the US accepts associate membership and the principle of the *rapprochement* of the two blocs in the reunification process, during which the security obligations of West and East Germany would not change.

Mikhail Gorbachov, President
of the USSR, 12 June 1990

Little Grey Mice

Chapter One

A minor accident on Adenauerallee, just after she'd left the Chancellery, had delayed Elke Meyer. It was hardly an inconvenience, but it unsettled her, just as being summoned on a Saturday for a minor security infraction had unsettled her. Elke liked ordered routine and disruption offended her, even something as small as arriving slightly later than usual for her established Saturday morning visit to the Bonner Café, in the corner of Bonn's flower market.

She tried to hurry, tugging at Poppi's lead to urge him on, but there seemed to be more people than normal, crowds milling aimlessly around the stalls, blocking her way. Poppi, with the inbred nervousness of all miniature dachshunds, became frightened among careless feet and legs and began to resist, so finally Elke bent and scooped him up. As she eased her way through the alley from the larger vegetable market Elke started to worry that her usual table might be occupied. There was fresh annoyance at the possibility, but she tried to suppress it: it was absurd to invent difficulties in advance. She wasn't normally so tense: once a month, sometimes, but from her careful calendar note that wasn't due for another two weeks. Maybe, after all these months, the workload at the Chancellery from the coming together of the two Germanys was causing too much of a strain. She didn't really think so. She was very sure about her ability to do her job: it was the only thing she really did feel sure about.

Nearer the café, beyond the vivid glare of the flower displays, the crowds thinned and she lowered the protesting Poppi to the ground again. The pampered dog tried to scramble back into her arms but Elke refused him. She considered women who carried their pets in their arms to be drawing attention to themselves. All the outside tables at the Bonner *were* already occupied but it was a sparkling early spring morning, warm yet without the oppressive, valley-trapped heat that in the summer turned the West German capital into the 'Bonn kettle', so she'd guessed the pavement would be full. And anyway Elke never sat outside, on display. Her place was inside, where it was quieter and more proper for a woman to sit alone. She hesitated at the doorway, momentarily unable to focus against the inner darkness, before seeing her accustomed table was vacant with her accustomed waitress in

1

smiling attendance. The girl, whose name she knew to be Clara although Elke never addressed her with such familiarity, gestured towards the waiting chair, as if she had reserved it for Elke's arrival. Elke smiled back gratefully and sat down. Poppi settled with a satisfied sigh beneath the chair and Elke had a matching relief at the re-establishment of routine. She was in surroundings she knew, where she was safe, and it didn't matter at all that she was late or that there were too many people swarming around outside. She *had* been stupid, letting silly things distress her. She hoped, belatedly, that no one had been injured in the Adenauerallee collision.

The waitress allowed a few moments for Elke to go through the pretence of studying the menu before taking the order for coffee and apple cake, which was what Elke had every Saturday.

What was she going to buy for the children? She had to take something, because she always did when she went to Ida's for lunch, so they expected it. But it wasn't easy any more, not at the age they were. At fourteen Georg drove her sister to distraction with his pop music, so a tape or a record was obvious, but Elke knew nothing about pop music: choosing the right one would be difficult. Doris, just a year younger, was slightly easier. Her niece was just becoming aware of herself, concerned about her appearance, and Elke decided upon a pair of hair-slides. The size or cost of the gift was unimportant, after all: it was the gesture.

The waitress offered cream with the apple cake and Elke smiled the anticipated refusal. The cake was fractionally burned at the bottom but Elke didn't complain: people who complained in public places embarrassed her. She cut away the charred pastry and chopped the remainder into neat, easily eaten squares. Maybe she should have ignored the cake as well as the cream today: the increase on the scales that morning wasn't too bad, less than half a kilo, but it definitely registered and Elke was careful about her weight as she was careful about everything involving her appearance. She hoped Ida hadn't prepared anything too heavy for lunch: on a day like today she'd prefer something cold, maybe with a salad. She could lose the weight over the next few weeks, without any difficulty. She knew herself capable of great determination: she'd learned, bitterly, from past experience.

'You should have said something.'

Elke raised her head, startled, to see Clara standing beside her table: the girl was looking down at the discarded, blackened pastry. 'It's not important: it doesn't matter.'

'It's a problem, with apples. They cook hot. It's the sugar, I think.'

2

'I know,' agreed Elke. 'It was very little.'

'I'll bring you another slice, without charge.'

'No!' said Elke, quickly. 'I couldn't eat any more. Really.'

'Next week then,' promised the girl.

How predictable she must be to people, thought Elke. She said: 'Maybe next week,' not wanting to make an outright refusal.

'Would you like your second coffee?'

Predictable again, thought Elke, who always had two cups. 'Please.' She leaned slightly forward over the table as it was served, twisting her arm to read her watch. She occasionally went from here to the cathedral in the Münsterplatz, but after the delay Elke didn't think she had time today if she was to get to Bad Godesberg promptly at one. The self-accusation came very quickly. She had more than enough time, if she wanted. But for what? She'd lighted all the candles for Ursula, and said all the prayers in all the side chapels, that she ever could. And Ursula was the only person she prayed for, no one else. She could always go to church tomorrow. Or the day after. Or next week. Or next month. Or the month after that. She had all the time she could ever use. Too much. She wished she could give it away: give almost all of it away. The musing drifted, aimlessly. Today's novelty gift, for Georg and Doris, she thought. *Here you are, my darlings: empty time, to fill as you wish, like a sand bucket on a beach. A week, a month, take what you want. I don't need it. I've too much to occupy already.*

Elke jerked away from the table, as if she were physically trying to slough off the self-pity. It had been forgivable with Ursula and everything that occurred, but finally Ida had told her to pull herself out of it and Elke imagined she had, long ago. She didn't want to slip back into the trough of easy despair: didn't want people talking and shaking their heads, not again. That period of her life was over: locked away and forgotten. All except Ursula. Ursula wasn't forgotten. Never would be. *Couldn't* be.

Wanting further movement to break her depression, Elke called for her bill, carefully concealing the crimson security pass in her handbag as she counted out the exact money, with an additional two Deutschmarks for a tip. The waitress wished her a happy week and Elke wished the girl the same in return and re-entered the bustle of the flower square. Poppi tugged for attention but Elke decided it wasn't necessary for the dog to be carried again.

She crossed the square directly to the Kaufhalle store and found the accessories section on the ground floor. The ribbons and scarves and economy jewellery blazed brighter than the flower stalls outside, a

Technicolor of decoration. Doris had white-blonde hair so Elke selected the slides in contrasting harsh red and because it matched, forming the complete set, she also took the brooch shaped in the face of a lugubrious clown. Ursula's hair was blonde, although not so pale, and for several moments Elke fingered a second set, fantasizing how they would look in her own daughter's hair. Abruptly she replaced the slides, offering just the one set to the assistant to be wrapped. Small ornaments or jewellery, particularly anything fixed with a sharp pin, were dangerous for Ursula. Elke had to go back along the linking alley into the Markt to find a tape and record outlet in one of the permanent shops bordering its edge. A bored assistant perfunctorily recommended a tape by an American artist named Springsteen, which Elke bought without question.

Elke had parked her car, a Volkswagen Golf, among others on a meter bank just off Brudergasse. As she approached she automatically checked the gleaming blue bodywork for damage from another parking motorist less careful than herself, relieved there wasn't any. Poppi's blanket, protecting the rear upholstery, was neatly in place but Elke fussed it into further neatness before lifting the dog in. He settled into immediate sleep, seemingly exhausted by his enforced walk through the city. In the driving seat she fastened and checked the seatbelt against its lock, made a minute adjustment to her rear-view mirror and ensured both wing reflectors still gave the necessary back view. Satisfied, she edged out into the traffic stream to join Adenauerallee from Belderberg. The earlier accident had been at the junction with Hofgarten. The congestion was cleared now but one of the involved vehicles was still there, hauled off the road on to the pavement. One of its front wheels was buckled, making it impossible to drive, but the car itself seemed intact. None of the glass was smashed, either, so Elke guessed there had been no serious injury. Everyone in Germany drove far too fast: she'd heard the Transport Minister complaining about it to Günther only the previous week, as if it were somebody else's responsibility other than his own. Elke only ever used her superior's Christian name in her thoughts. In discussion or conversation with anyone – and certainly when talking directly to him – she always referred to him respectfully as Herr Werle or Herr Doktor, just as he with equal respect – but more importantly, great consideration – always addressed her as Frau Meyer. He was one of the few people outside her immediate family who knew about Ursula.

Elke got to Bad Godesberg early, and that allowed her to drive around Bonn's dormitory suburb to a safe car-park instead of risking the vehicle on another meter, where she'd read hit-and-run damage was most likely. It was some way from Ida's home on Stümpchesweg but the walk gave Poppi the opportunity to relieve himself: it was a nuisance – and a vague embarrassment – if he began demanding to be let out as soon as they got there.

The house Elke was approaching was a large but slowly decaying structure, three storeys high and with a basement in which her brother-in-law maintained an inferior wine cellar he couldn't afford, just as she suspected he couldn't afford the house itself. The paint was fading in odd, discoloured patches and in too many places had cracked away from the wood beneath, which was twisted and warped by exposure to the weather. That much of the front garden Elke could see was weed-strewn and overgrown because there was no regular gardener and he never got around to tending it himself. An outer fence sagged as if weary of trying to contain the mess. Horst Kissel had bought the house within a year of his promotion to Personnel Director of Federal communications, shortly after marrying Ida sixteen years earlier, and Elke could not recall his doing anything about its upkeep from its day of purchase. Occasionally she wondered what her sister, who was impatiently vibrant and sometimes over-demanding, had ever seen in the man. But only occasionally: Elke did not consider herself qualified to criticize another's choice in men.

Kissel was at the drawing-room window when Elke pushed through the creaking, path-scuffing gate, so he was already at the front door when she reached it. That creaked too. Kissel was a large, fat-bellied man whose hair had receded to the middle of his head and was rapidly retreating further. When he gave her the duty family kiss, Elke detected a cologne she hadn't smelled before.

'Beautiful, Elke!' enthused the man, expansively. 'Every time you look more beautiful. And that suit is superb: I haven't seen it before. Always so elegant!'

Elegant for what or for whom? wondered Elke. The suit was a green tweed, a British import: Kissel had admired it when she'd worn it to lunch two weekends before. Playing the expected role, Elke said: 'How's the world of big business?'

Kissel took her hand, which she wished he hadn't because she didn't enjoy physical contact, and led her into the drawing-room from which he had seen her approach. He said: 'Terrible: you couldn't believe the pressure. I arrive at eight and sometimes I don't leave until after seven. And I never look up, not for a moment. I don't remember the last time I left my desk for a proper lunch.'

'You shouldn't let them work you so hard.' Where were Ida and the children?

Kissel raised his shoulders and held them high, in a gesture which made him look oddly froglike. 'That's the dedication expected from senior executives. You should know that, surely!'

Elke hoped her sister would not be much longer. She said: 'The Chancellery has certainly been very busy, with so many changes in the East.' There was no indiscretion there.

'Yours are still the pampered lot,' dismissed Kissel. 'All glamorous trips and free lunches. They don't know what hard work is.'

It was a frequent sneer and Elke didn't respond. She didn't imagine her brother-in-law knew what hard work was, either.

'Let's drink some wine,' suggested Kissel, the anxious host. 'I've got something special: some excellent red from the Drachenfels slopes. You'd be amazed at the bargains there are if you know what you're buying, like I do.'

While the man was pouring, Ida thrust into the room with her usual exuberance, trailed by the children. Elke was kissed and hugged and kissed again before bending to be further kissed by the children, first Doris, then Georg. Elke presented the gifts and got more kisses in return. From Georg's reaction to the tape it seemed the assistant's recommendation had been a good one: the boy asked at once to go to his room and hurried out with Doris at his heels. Ida accepted the glass from her husband, sipped the wine and pulled a face.

'What's the matter with it?' demanded Kissel, defensively.

'It's beautiful, darling,' said Ida, easily. 'I just wish I had the palate to appreciate it like you do.' She led Elke towards a worn couch set in front of the windows. The light showed how badly the upholstery had faded.

Kissel frowned, suspiciously. To Elke he said: 'What do you think of it?'

'It's very good,' lied Elke. The wine was thin and sharp, souring her throat.

'You've got better taste than your sister,' smiled Kissel, gratefully. 'I'll open some more, for lunch.'

Ida waited until her husband left the room and said: 'It's your fault now that you'll have to drink this horse piss.' She squeezed her sister's hand, which she still held. 'You're looking good.'

From anyone else the remark would have sounded insincere, but Elke knew her sister meant what she said. It had always been this way between them, a deep closeness that neither bothered to define as love

6

but which Elke supposed to be the only description: a genuine, unassailable, unbreachable love that no one else could understand or intrude upon. There had never been any jealousy or resentment or eroding, lasting anger, not even when they'd been children and might have been expected to fall out, as all children fall out. Older by two years, it seemed Ida had always been with her, always protective, always comforting. Just as there had never been jealousy or resentment or true anger, neither had there ever been criticism or judgement. And there'd certainly been the opportunity for critical judgement. Remembering that morning on the bathroom scales, Elke said: 'I'm putting on weight.'

'It doesn't show,' assured the other woman. 'You've no cause for concern. I'm the one who should be worried.'

Elke was aware for the first time of a rare plumpness around her sister's waist and hips. She extended the examination, recalling the long ago but frequent, flattering comparison of others between them in their teens and even later: constant surprise at their close similarity, going as far as repeated insistences that they had to be twins, not just sisters. Elke supposed it was understandable. Both she and Ida had the same luxuriant white blonde hair – the colouring Doris had inherited – and deep blue eyes and had never had to worry about growing-up spots or blemishes, each equally lucky with clear, unmarked skin that still only required a minimum of make-up. During those teenage years, although never with envy, they'd matched and measured each other's femininity: because she was older Ida's bust had been bigger, but Elke had caught up to be just as heavily breasted, their measurements eventually identical, just as they were identical in those other parts and places which had seemed so important then.

But Elke knew there *was* a difference between them. Not physically, not even now, but in other ways. She sought an explanation of the dissimilarity, wanting to get it right. Attitude, perhaps. Demeanour, although that sounded too stiffly formal. Personal ambience? Some way towards what she was trying to find. Ida had always seemed to possess more internal enthusiasm, about everything. She bounced rather than walked. Laughed more easily. Cried, too, unashamed of showing emotion. Elke thought back to her impression when her sister had first entered the room: how exuberance had immediately come to mind. *That* was how it had always been. Ida filled a room when she entered it: people looked at her and were drawn to her, wanting to be enclosed in the charisma which surrounded her and in which she moved.

Elke knew she didn't have charisma. She might look the same and feel the same but there was one comparison that didn't exist at all between them. She didn't so unconsciously, so effortlessly or so attractively project herself, as Ida did: side by side, coiffured the same, dressed the same, it had always been Ida to whom people – to whom men – looked, never her. Quickly, aware of the extended silence, Elke said: 'We should go on a diet together.'

'Does it show?'

'Yes,' said Elke, with the honesty there always was with each other.

'Shit!' said Ida, but without too much feeling. 'Sometimes I wish you'd lie a little.'

'What's all the news?' asked Elke.

Her sister shrugged. 'Georg got a commendation, for his mathematics. Doris finally started her periods, last week. I told her she was a woman now. She seemed quite proud. There were hardly any cramps, thank God. Horst tried to increase his loan from the bank, to get a new car, but they deferred a decision so it looks like we'll have to struggle on with that bloody old Opel, although I'm frightened to risk a trip even to somewhere as close as Bonn any more . . .' The woman stopped, grinning. Then she announced: 'And Horst's deputy made a pass at me.'

'What?'

'Made a pass at me,' Ida repeated, still smiling.

Elke realized with surprise that her sister wasn't at all upset. 'How? When?'

'It was a boring retirement dinner for someone in the Finance department,' Ida recounted. 'I was sitting next to Horst's deputy and just when the speeches started I felt a hand upon my leg.' Ida smiled again. 'Actually under my skirt.'

'You're not serious!'

'Of course I'm serious.'

'What did you do?'

'Nothing.'

'Nothing!'

'Darling,' said Ida, patiently. 'He was sitting more or less upright beside me. There was no way he could reach the interesting parts, was there?'

'You mean you just sat there and let him do it!'

'It was more interesting than all the mumbled crap about what a fine man the Finance Controller had been.'

'You're mad,' declared Elke, genuinely shocked. Was that what Ida intended? If it was, her sister was succeeding.

8

'Where's the harm?'

'Your husband's deputy was running his hand up your leg, under your skirt, and you ask me where the harm is!'

'He wasn't really running his hand *up* my skirt. He couldn't because the skirt was quite tight.'

'Mad,' insisted Elke. She wanted better words: stopping words.

'Then he asked if he could call me.'

Elke shook her head in disbelief. 'What did you say?'

'Of course.'

'So what are you going to say, when he does?'

'I'm not sure, not yet.'

Elke twisted on the lumpy couch. 'You're surely not going to do anything about it! Have an affair, I mean?'

'I don't know. He hasn't telephoned yet.'

'Ida!'

'His name's Kurt. He's got soft hands . . .' Ida smiled at the outrage on her sister's face. '. . . And a stutter.'

'What are you going to do?' insisted Elke.

'I already told you, I don't know.'

'What about Horst? And Georg and Doris?'

'Darling! Nothing's *happened*.'

'It sounds as if it's going to.'

'No one's made a pass at me for years.'

'So you're flattered,' accused Elke. 'That's juvenile!' No one had ever put their hand on her knee under a dinner table.

'I told you, the speeches were boring.'

'I know I shouldn't give warnings . . . that I'm the last person to give warnings . . . but don't be as stupid as I was.'

Ida's face seemed to dim, as if a light had gone out. 'You didn't have to say that. I've never once thought you were stupid. Just unlucky.'

'It's just . . .' Elke waved a hand, without direction. '. . . You're worrying me!'

'I'm *playing*!' said Ida.

'You mean it never happened?'

'Of course it happened. I mean I'm not going to do anything about it, even if he does call. His prick's probably smaller than Georg's.'

'That's disgusting!'

'No it's not. Don't you ever look at a man and wonder how big his prick is?'

'No!' said Elke, tightly and at once.

9

'You told me you did once,' accused Ida. 'About the geography teacher at college.'

'I don't remember,' said Elke, who did.

Ida used her free hand to measure from that holding the wine glass. 'You said you thought it would be that big, at least. That you'd like to see it.'

'I didn't,' denied Elke. She knew she had coloured.

'You don't have to worry!' said her sister. 'I'm sorry I told you now.' She straightened herself abruptly, which had always been a signal that any discussion between them was concluded, like the closing of a book. 'You seeing Ursula tomorrow?'

'Of course.'

'Would you like me to come with you?'

'There wouldn't be any point. I've told you before.'

'I'd still like to come, one weekend. It's been a long time.'

Elke listlessly raised and dropped her shoulders. She didn't like anyone coming with her, not even Ida, which was why she always tried to avoid company. Ursula belonged to her, no one else: anyone else was an interloper. She said: 'That would be nice, sometime.'

'One weekend soon,' pressed Ida.

Kissel came back into the room, rubbing his hands like a workman who had completed a hard day's labour. 'The wine's open,' he announced. 'I've called the children down: Doris has taken the dog out to pee.'

The child returned from the garden as they were sitting down. The lunch was veal, with sauerkraut and dumplings, not what Elke had earlier hoped it would be. She refused potatoes and only ate half a dumpling, looking quizzically at Ida, who ate a whole portion of each while ignoring the accusing stare. Elke congratulated Georg on the commendation and listened politely to an interminable story from Kissel that had something to do with the difficulty of installing the necessary electronic links throughout Europe to accommodate the incredible demand for facsimile machines. The man made it sound as if he were personally installing every line. Elke was ready when Kissel insisted upon the inside stories of high-level government and what was really happening in East Germany and in all the other former communist countries, because Kissel made the same demands at every visit. She replied as she always did with what had appeared in every newspaper and been broadcast on every television channel during the preceding week. Kissel appeared not to recognize some of the stories, which was a frequent reaction, and Elke wondered if the man ever

10

repeated what she said, trying to convey some special knowledge. She hoped not: she wouldn't have wanted to expose him to ridicule.

The wine at lunch was worse than the aperitif: Elke only drank half the first glass. Ida drank less. Kissel finished the first bottle and consumed half of a second and immediately after the meal announced he was going to bed for an afternoon siesta, as all true gentlemen were supposed to do. It was a customary conclusion to a Saturday lunch.

The garden at the rear of the house was not quite so overgrown as the front, so there was enough room for two lounging chairs and the women could relax, read newspapers or magazines or doze. Doris played with Poppi, tiring him out, and Georg disappeared again to his bedroom and his tape deck. Throughout the afternoon Elke was continuously aware of the dull throb of pop guitars and drums and synthesized keyboards. She thought it all sounded like the heartbeat of some huge animal: maybe something prehistoric, on the point of death.

Kissel was still in bed when Elke was ready to leave. She asked her sister to say goodbye and thanks and Ida promised she would.

'I think I'm happy with Horst,' declared Ida, unexpectedly. 'He's full of bullshit and I don't listen to a lot of what he says, most of the time, but I do love him, which I guess might be difficult for a lot of people to understand. Not blind, fucking-every-night kind of love: more like a contented, satisfied feeling. Knowing all the time where he'll be, if I want him. So you mustn't worry.'

'I hope I don't have to,' said Elke. She was uncomfortable at her sister's swearing.

The Volkswagen was untouched in its safe car-park and the traffic back along Adenauerallee was comparatively light, so there was no delay in Elke getting back to her apartment. She did not want to eat again. She settled Poppi and decided there was nothing to watch on television. She had four new books, two in original English. She tried one of the German novels, a Günter Grass reprint, but she was not in the mood, so she abandoned it. For an hour before she went to bed she listened to a radio recital by the Vienna Philharmonic Orchestra, although Bach was usually too strident for her. Her final act, before going to bed, was to enter her diary. She did not, of course, record her sister's confession. Elke wrote: *Lunch with Ida and family. A pleasant day.*

She'd made the identical entry the previous week. And the week before that.

The two men who had followed Elke Meyer throughout the day were part of the initial surveillance squad, in place for more than three months. The weak joke between them was that by now they knew more about Elke Meyer than she knew about herself. It was an exaggeration, of course. But only just.

As the light went out in the identified flat, the driver of the car said: 'I never thought at the beginning we'd have to keep the observation up as long as this.'

'Moscow's certainly taking a lot of trouble over this one,' agreed the observer, from the passenger seat. 'It's understandable, I suppose.'

'It's difficult to believe that professionally she holds down the job she does,' said the first man. 'Have you ever known anyone lead such a boring private life?'

'Yes,' said the second man at once. 'All the other *grauen Mäuse* in Bonn.'

Grauen Mäuse is the slang term in the West German capital – and in every espionage service – for lonely, unattached women employed in government service.

It means grey mice.

Chapter Two

It was Elke's unalterable practice to set out early to make allowances for the Sunday traffic, deciding as she drove south along the valley road that the precaution would be increasingly necessary in the coming weeks, now that the better weather was coming. It wasn't always possible to see the Rhine looping and curling to her left but when it was the water glittered silver in the pale, early sunshine: several times she saw holiday ferries fussily churning to the pick-up points for the first excursions of the day, down to Remagen or Linz or Neuwied or even as far as Koblenz. Elke had gone on river outings in the past, but not for a long time, and she resolved to do it again soon. If she went all the way to Koblenz and back it would occupy a whole day: activities that occupied a whole day were important.

The home was just short of Marienfels, set high in the mountain foothills in its own park. Because of her early start Elke approached long before the scheduled visiting hours, which she invariably did, climbing part of the way towards the higher ground before pulling into her accustomed layby, to wait. She urged Poppi from the back seat, to sniff and leave his mark, able on the little used road to let him wander without a lead. She leaned against the side of the car, waiting for him to return, gazing down upon the waterway she could see completely now. She was just able to pick out people moving around on Nonnenwerth island and squinted further, fully across the river towards the Drachenfels and the wine slopes from which Kissel claimed to get his sour wine. Elke doubted it had come from Drachenfels at all.

Elke remained unsettled by Ida's account of being fondled under a dinner table, not wholly satisfied with her sister's easy assurances that it meant nothing. Ida had always been the more impulsive – another difference between them – and Elke could not lose the fear that in a certain mood on an aimless day Ida might respond to a telephone call in a way she shouldn't. It was unimportant that she would not regard it seriously: that she'd think of the entire episode as an experiment or an adventure or simply just fun. Because it wouldn't be any of those things. It would be a deceit – the way Ida had talked yesterday had been deceitful – and Elke had not known her sister be that before.

Would Elke have flirted if she were married to someone as

pretentiously dull as Horst Kissel? Immediately her mind grew more unsettled. Fantasies about marriage, what sort of man her husband would be and what sort of home they'd have and how they would live and what they would do had long ago been shut out, like giggled speculation about how big some men were in certain places. And she didn't believe she knew properly how to flirt anyway, a further trait unshared with Ida: it was something she had never been able to learn or develop, as she supposed most girls did. What about. . . ? Elke began to think but quickly stopped, positively refusing the reverie. She was no longer unsettled – no longer considering Ida – but hot with anger at herself for letting such a thought even begin to grow. She *never* allowed herself to remember that, not as she had been doing then. It was nothing to remember. Just to forget: as best she could ever forget, that is. She could not, of course, feel any annoyance or irritation at her sister, but there was regret: regret that Ida had so casually talked about a hand on her leg and of doing nothing about it. The greatest regret of all was that the conversation had eased open, just a little, doors that Elke had believed forever closed and bolted in her mind.

A Mercedes she recognized, carrying the parents of another afflicted child, swept by on its way up to the home. Elke called Poppi and lifted the obedient animal into the back of the car when he returned, hurriedly setting off to follow. Although there was no way Ursula could ever possibly know, Elke always needed to be one of the first to arrive. It was a tiny ritual but it mattered to Elke: Elke Meyer was a person of tiny rituals.

It was not a high-security institution but there was a moderately tall surrounding fence and a manned gatehouse for the patients' own safety. Quite unaware of what they were doing, some inmates, in the past, had tried to leave: the fear was for the suffering if one did wander away, particularly in the sub-zero winters, before being located by concerned searchers.

Elke was known but still checked at the entrance before being allowed to continue along the lazily curved drive towards the main building, a hugely square, stone-built mansion erected more than a hundred years earlier by a banker who made his fortune financing the Prussian royal family at exorbitant rates of interest. The extensive grounds remained as they had been originally landscaped, full-skirted firs and conifers and trees she could not name now grown to towering maturity. There were several groups of patients in those grounds, walking or sitting in chairs, always with an attendant within a few metres. Elke strained hopefully, trying to locate Ursula among them,

14

but couldn't see her daughter. She turned familiarly into the designated area to the left of the mansion and parked alongside the Mercedes. From the social gatherings arranged from time to time – and which Elke hated for their artificiality and false happiness, as if there was something to celebrate – she knew the man who owned the car to be a wine exporter, from Cologne. Passingly she wondered what his opinion would have been of Horst Kissel's wine selection.

The system was for senior members of staff to greet visitors just inside the surviving entrance hall, a high-ceilinged, chandeliered vault only minimally converted into a functional vestibule, which consisted of a glassed-off office and a separate receptionist's desk. The desk was dominated by an elaborate display of vivid orange gladioli: Elke remembered it as the predominant colour in the flower market, the previous day.

Dr Schiller, the principal, was standing in front of the desk, white-haired and cadaverous and stooped forward, shoulders hunched, as if perpetually ready to listen considerately to everything said to him. For no obvious reason, because Elke always brought the dog – carrying him in her arms because she never felt she was drawing attention to herself here – Schiller looked curiously at Poppi before smiling a yellow-toothed smile towards Elke. 'Ursula is in her room.'

'I thought she might have been outside, on a day like today.' Poppi awkwardly began to wriggle and yapped to be put down, but Elke shushed the dog into silence.

'She was, earlier. She came back herself. We wouldn't force her to do anything she didn't want to do. We don't, ever.'

'How is she?'

'No change, Frau Meyer,' said the man, serious-faced. 'There never will be, you know that.'

The principal always courteously addressed her as 'Frau', like her superior at the Chancellery. 'I was wondering about any deterioration, not improvement,' said Elke.

Schiller shook his head, in reassurance. 'There's still the music: she's soothed by that. It's a very common manifestation in autism.'

'Soothed?' queried Elke, at once. 'Have there been many outbursts?' It was because she had no longer been physically able to restrain Ursula when the child erupted into those irrational, unexpected rages that Elke had finally been forced to commit her into the care of professionals. Elke still felt guiltily inadequate at having done it, although it had been the only possible decision.

Schiller pursed his lips. 'No more than we expect.'

15

'She hasn't caused herself any injury?'

'We take care of our patients to ensure that doesn't happen,' said the man, stiffly.

'I'm sorry . . . I didn't mean . . .'

'I know you didn't.'

'Can I take her for a walk, back out into the garden?'

'Providing she wants to go: don't force her.'

'I know better than that.'

More families and friends began to arrive behind her and Elke moved away, climbing the encircling stairway to Ursula's room on the first floor. The door, the third on the right along the west corridor, was closed and although she knew it would not register with the child – was as much of an affectation as those embarrassing social gatherings – Elke knocked instead of immediately entering. She did *not* regard it as a pointless affectation. Although it was a gesture – a satisfaction – for her own benefit, Elke considered it gave Ursula some dignity and some respect, even if the child was unable to appreciate the love it conveyed.

Elke actually waited a moment or two before pushing through the door, which was fitted only with a press-stud closure because locks were not permitted, on any patient's room.

Ursula was almost fully turned from the door. She was sitting on a chair but bent forward over her bed and rocking back and forth to the music coming from the enclosed and securely bolted tape machine on the wall shelf above. Elke thought it was a Mozart violin concerto, but she was not sure. Ursula's movements did not coordinate with the music. Ursula wore her newest red skirt and a beige sweater, which seemed tight. Her hair, blonde and so very much like Doris's, was neatly brushed but loose, practically to her shoulders, and Elke thought how prettily bright red slides would have held it in place.

'Hello Ursula.'

There was no reaction at all from the bent, rocking girl.

'Darling?'

Still nothing. Elke clicked the door shut behind her but stood just inside, unsure as she was always unsure what to do next. The heavy easy chair was in the corner of the room and Elke grated it forward, to bring herself nearer to her daughter. She reached out to the girl and said: 'Ursula? Hello, my darling.' There was a response at last, to the physical contact. Ursula turned to her mother, without the slightest recognition, and made a sound, which was quite unintelligible. The disjointed, unconnected movement to the music lessened, just slightly.

'Hello Ursula,' said Elke again. Still with her hand outstretched Elke

16

moved to stroke the child's face, to push back a skein of straying hair, but Ursula pulled sharply back, not wanting to be touched, and Elke immediately dropped her hand.

'Nice,' said Ursula, unexpectedly. The voice was harsh, coarse-sounding, not like a child's voice at all.

With no idea to what the child was referring – if she was referring to anything – Elke said: 'Yes, darling. Nice. It's Mummy, darling. Mummy's come.'

Poppi began to agitate in Elke's arms, and the girl looked towards the dog. It had actually been bought for Ursula, the year before it had been necessary to commit her into care, a forlorn hope of Elke's that in some way it might penetrate Ursula's enclosed world, as the music did. When it had been a puppy there had occasionally been something Elke tried to believe was affection, some sort of tenuous bond, but now she knew it hadn't been, not really. 'It's Poppi,' said Elke, to the girl. 'Poppi's come, too.'

Ursula put her hand towards the dog, a straight-fingered, exploring gesture, not a caressing one. Poppi flinched but then came back, moving to lick the extended fingers. At the first contact Ursula gave a surprised cry, neither pleasure nor fear, and jerked her hand away. Then she said: 'No!' and paused and said again, more vehemently: 'No! No! No!' and slapped out. Elke easily pulled the dog away but the swipe was a heavy one, reminding her of the strength Ursula possessed, the strength Elke had ultimately found impossible to manage.

Without positive intention Elke began comparing her child to Ida's daughter. Although only a year older, Ursula was far bigger than Doris, her feet and hands ungainly and nearly out of proporation to the rest of her body. She was much fuller lipped, too, her eyebrows were heavy, more masculine than feminine, and there was more hair than Elke would have expected on the child's arms and legs. *Doris finally started her periods . . . she seemed quite proud.* Ida's announcement of the previous day sounded in Elke's mind. Ursula had started much earlier, just after she was eleven: Elke knew from Dr Schiller how carefully they had to keep a calendar note because there was no way to explain it to the child and Ursula was terrified, every time it happened. She suffered a lot of discomfort, too.

Practised from the years they had lived together, Elke offered her hand again and this time Ursula didn't flinch away from her face being touched. Elke began smoothing her cheek, back and forth, as she'd coaxed her to sleep when Ursula was young, and after a while Ursula bent her head towards the caress and began making a guttural sound, humming without any tune.

17

And Elke talked.

She knew there was no purpose: that there would be no understanding or comprehension. But she talked nevertheless, forever hopeful of entering a window not even Dr Schiller suspected to be open, hopeful of a word – her voice alone – meaning something, of somehow reaching Ursula. Most of all, forever hopeful of the child realizing, knowing, that the person who came every Sunday was someone who loved her and always would love her. Elke talked of the winter going away and how the sun was shining now. Of Ida. Of Georg and Doris, who had always been very kind to her when Ursula had lived outside, never treating her as if she was in any way different from them. Of the river ferries and the trip she'd decided to take that morning, on her way here. Until there was nothing more she could think to say. Throughout it all, Ursula sat head to one side, enjoying the contact, the deep-throated murmur rising and falling.

The only other sound in the quiet room was the violin concerto. Elke thought she recognized a repeat of the movement that had been playing when she entered and guessed the machine reversed automatically, for the music to be continuous. Ursula's room was sparse but very neat. The bed was crisply made, the edges and the sheet folded and tucked to a hospital pattern. There were some picture books lined correctly upright on a shelf, as if they were important tomes. Ursula's dressing gown hung from a hook beneath which her slippers were placed tidily side by side. The drawers of the dressing table were all closed: nowhere did clothes lie casually discarded. At the head of the bed was an array of summons buttons: Elke knew the red one, attached to a cord, to be an emergency bell.

Ursula suddenly straightened her head, shaking it, as if irritated now by the caress, no longer comforted by it. Elke withdrew her hand again.

'Shall we go outside for a walk, darling? Take Poppi for a walk? It's a lovely day outside. Sunshine.'

The child gave no indication of having heard. Elke took her daughter's limp hand and pulled, very gently, for Ursula to stand. The girl moved as if to do so but then snatched away and settled back in the seat.

'All right,' said Elke. 'We won't go out then.'

Ursula felt towards the dog again, not a prodding move as before but with both hands, to receive it. For a moment Elke was too surprised to respond but quickly passed it over. Poppi, a lap dog at ease on any lap, immediately settled. Ursula cuddled him, both arms around him, and started rocking back and forth as she had been when Elke arrived, crooning tunelessly again. Elke smiled, delighted, always eager for the smallest omen: Ursula had never before shown such recognition, not even when she had been living at home. Dr Schiller might insist Ursula could never improve, but what was this if it wasn't improvement, a child doing something perfectly normal and natural, like loving her pet? Briefly she was tempted to call the man, to call someone at least, to see if they regarded it as a sign of anything, but held back. If this was the slightest emergence from the shadows in which Ursula lived the sudden, maybe flustered, arrival of the medical staff might upset her, wrecking everything. Elke decided to wait. Wait just a few minutes. Just in case. Then call someone.

So immersed was she in the hopeful reflection that Elke was slow to recognize what was happening: later, seeking some little excuse, she remembered at the beginning there was very little sign of *anything* happening. Her initial impression was that Poppi was just shifting himself, to a more comfortable position on Ursula's lap. But the movement increased, becoming panicked, and Elke saw the dog's legs scrabbling for purchase; his head turned frantically to snap, but Ursula was holding him in such a way that the dog couldn't reach to bite. He began to yap, terrified: it was not a loud sound but a gasping one and Elke realized, appalled, that Ursula was holding him so tightly that the breath was being crushed from his body.

She grabbed out, clutching Ursula's arm, tugging to loosen the grip, but the arm was rigid, too strong for her to move.

'Ursula!' said Elke, trying to remain calm. 'Let the dog go, darling! Let Poppi go!'

There was no movement from the girl, not as much as a head turn in Elke's direction. Elke was sure the sounds from the animal were growing fainter. He made another futile effort to bite his way free, tongue lolling. Elke pulled again at Ursula's arm and the dog tried to bite her, grazing her wrist.

'Let go!' yelled Elke, ignoring the long ago warning never to shout at her daughter.

There was still no response, no relaxation of the crushing grip.

Elke grabbed for the red emergency button, pressing it again and again, seeing Poppi's eyes roll up into his head. Careless of being bitten she tried again to loosen Ursula's hold. The dog was past snapping now, but Ursula looked up. There was no focus at all in her blank eyes. She kept crooning, monotonously.

Elke wasn't aware of the attendants' entry, only of being pushed aside. It was a man and a woman, both white-coated. Their

19

understanding was instantaneous. They ignored the dog and any direct attempt to free it. The woman cradled Ursula's head against her chest and began to rock back and forth in unison with her, even appearing to match the croon. The man increased the volume of the tape player and stroked the arms that held the now unmoving form of the dog, all along her arms at first but then just where the dog lay. Finally he got his fingertips against the child's finger ends but still smoothing, not trying to force her hands apart. Elke stood with her arms across her body, holding herself against a collapse: she blinked to clear the blur from her eyes, lip bitten closed against any sound. She could feel herself shaking.

It seemed a very long time before Poppi was released, and Elke was sure he was dead. When Ursula did let go it was sudden, a simple parting of her arms: the dog stayed where he was, unmoving, although a final gush of air came from him, making his tongue loll further from his mouth. The male attendant moved the body slowly and calmly from the child, putting it on the conveniently nearby bed. As he did so, Dr Schiller came into the room. The principal did not waste time asking for explanations. He said: 'Bad?'

'No,' said the male nurse.

'Is she in spasm?'

'No,' said the comforting woman. 'She's quite all right.'

Schiller looked at last to Elke, who shook her head without knowing why and said: 'The dog . . . it was the dog . . . she wanted . . .'

'It's breathing,' reported the attendant, from the bed. 'I thought it was dead, but it isn't. It's breathing.'

There was immediate confirmation from Poppi. The animal whimpered, still short-breathed, then raised and dropped his head. He remained lying where he was.

'It was awful . . . terrible . . .' blurted Elke. 'She just sat there, crushing him.'

'She didn't know she was doing it,' said the principal, patiently. 'Won't ever know. It has no meaning . . . no importance . . .' He hesitated, to correct himself. 'Only to the unfortunate animal.'

'I thought it meant something,' admitted Elke. 'She reached out for him, as if she recognized him. I'm sorry . . . very sorry.'

'There's nothing to be sorry about . . . no blame,' insisted Schiller. 'It was an accident, that's all. A regrettable accident.'

'The dog might have died! Look how he's lying there: he's probably injured!'

'An accident no one could have anticipated,' said Schiller, still with patient insistence. 'Here we care for people. Maybe it would be a good idea to take the dog where they care for animals, to see if it is hurt.'

Which was what Elke did, eventually, after further reassurance from Schiller and failing to say goodbye to an unknowing, blank-eyed Ursula and finally letting the male attendant help her to the car with Poppi cradled, alive but softly complaining, in the centre of a towel carried hammock-like, held at both edges. That was the way she supported the dog into her apartment to telephone through the veterinary surgeons listed in the directory. The fifth agreed to see her on a Sunday: fortunately he was in the city, in the centre quite close to the cathedral.

The man, who was short and thin and had body odour, listened frowning to Elke's truthful explanation of too forceful an embrace from an unthinking child. He X-rayed the dog and made him yelp pressing and feeling. The X-rays showed no bone fractures, but the man diagnosed severe bruising. He administered a muscle-relaxing injection and made up a further relaxant prescription, both pills and powder.

'Tell the kid to be more careful next time.'

'I will,' promised Elke, emptily, wishing she could. She returned the dog still hammock-fashion to the apartment and settled him, sedated and unprotesting, into his wicker basket in the kitchen. Elke always created a newspaper surround to the basket to avoid night-time accidents, but tonight she extended the protection and added more paper to that already set, as an added precaution. Throughout Poppi stayed on his side but open-eyed, looking at her. Knowing it to be an absurd impression, Elke nevertheless thought it was an accusing look, blaming her for what had happened, although no one else had.

'I'm sorry,' she said. She tried to avoid talking to the animal, because only tragically lonely people – old maids growing weak-minded – conducted conversations with their pets. That night, in bed, the shaking was worse than it had been at the home, in Ursula's room, and Elke held herself again until it quietened. It didn't go, not fully: occasionally she shivered, as if she were cold, which she wasn't. But she didn't cry. There'd been a lot of crying, in the early years: and would have been, then, over today's episode. Was it a failing – like so many other failings – not to be able to cry any more?

It was a working group, not a properly formed committee, three men with the specific authorization of the Executive President himself to co-opt anyone they considered necessary or demand any resource from any Soviet ministry.

'I think there should be other, independent attempts, apart from this,' protested General Stefan Cherny, the army chief of the Soviet General Staff. His appointment more than any other reflected Moscow's suspicion, despite all the public assurances, of the military dangers of a re-united Germany.

'This is the way,' insisted Dimitri Sorokin. He considered that his position as First Deputy of the KGB gave him ranking superiority but didn't expect Cherny to recognize it.

'Too much depends on chance,' protested the soldier.

'It's a well proven espionage technique,' said Sorokin. Pointedly he added: 'I'm always prepared to consider alternatives.'

'Our man was chosen from a profile comparison of twenty likely candidates,' said Nikolai Turev. The third member of the group was the head of the KGB's foreign espionage Directorate and expected to be the most closely involved in actual fieldwork.

'Too uncertain,' insisted Cherny. 'And too dependent upon psychological bullshit.'

Chapter Three

As personal assistant to the Permanent Secretary to the West German Cabinet, Elke Meyer had a spacious corner suite office overlooking from two sides the park in which the Chancellery is situated. There was a large main desk, with a smaller one at right angles completely occupied by an extensive bank of telephones: all calls to Günther Werle were controlled through Elke. There was a small and rarely used conference area beyond the desk, with a low table ringed by modern leather-and-chrome easy chairs and along one wall a two-tiered bookshelf for the official records of Bundestag debates over the preceding twelve months. There were no filing cabinets. Those were in the outer offices that accommodated the rest of Werle's staff, secretaries and archivists and researchers. There were no personal photographs on Elke's desk and the three prints on the walls – historic reproductions of some of the Rhine castles – were those provided by the government supply ministry. The two perennial, polished-leaf plants were also officially supplied and tended by a government maintenance employee. One door from Elke's suite led to the outer offices. The other connected directly to Werle's private domain.

Elke had risen earlier than usual, concerned about the dog, but Poppi had got unaided from his basket, managed their morning walk – although not as far as usual – and appeared to eat as much as normal on their return. She'd considered bringing the animal to the office – she did so very rarely, although Werle did not object – but finally decided he would be more comfortable in surroundings he knew.

She was still in the Chancellery at her regular time, before everybody else on Werle's staff. The promptness was unnecessary – she could have left lesser staff to prepare the day – but this routine was the most important of all to Elke. A person unsure of everything in her private life, she was, professionally, superbly efficient and assured, and proudly guarded that reputation. She maintained a diary identical in entries to Werle's. She checked it generally for the week and then in detail, for the forthcoming day: when the outer offices began to fill she had already dictated a series of tape-recorded memoranda ordering all past records, current forecasts and statistical information Werle might possibly need for every meeting and scheduled appointment.

23

Werle's correspondence was delivered promptly at nine with the customary resentment from a hard-faced, grey-haired senior secretary named Gerda Pohl. The most obvious cause for the persistent attitude was that Gerda disliked taking instructions from someone younger than herself: from the personnel records to which she had access Elke knew the other woman to be almost twenty years her senior. Elke also suspected that Gerda considered she should have gained the promotion as Werle's personal assistant: she'd been on his staff much longer. In the first few months, almost a year in fact, Elke had tried to break down the antipathy but had always been rebuffed. Now she no longer bothered, although she remained always politely civil.

Gerda had already opened and sorted the correspondence not governed by an official security restriction. Elke waited until the other woman left her office before going through the pile again, rearranging three of the relegated letters to greater importance in Gerda's order. On those and several more she attached hand-written reminders to Werle of previous exchanges on the same subject and dictated further memoranda into her tape machine for the earlier letters to be retrieved from records and lodged with her in readiness, should Werle call for them.

Material governed by security restrictions had not, of course, come through the normal postal service. It had been delivered by hand to a central security receiving bureau in the basement of the Chancellery. There each item addressed to Günther Werle was logged against the name and identity number of the courier and that of the receiving official before being assembled all together in a sealed pouch for final delivery to Werle's department. Elke possessed the security clearance authorizing her to open the package. Inside were six separate pieces of correspondence. Three were marked at her level of clearance: the remaining three were not. One she could open was a request from the American embassy for policy guidance on the settlement of the constantly arriving East German refugees, another was a position report on the estimated number of original émigrés returning to the East, and the third an assessment of the difficulties the original, massive crossing continued to impose on relief agencies.

Elke scanned each paper intently, making reminder notes to herself on a separate jotting pad, then formulating further hand-written reference notes to be attached to all three for Werle's guidance. These she placed uppermost on the correspondence file, with the three envelopes she was not allowed to open at the very top.

By the time Werle's buzzer sounded, Elke also had ready all the material she had earlier requested from the other staff, topped by a typed schedule of everything the Cabinet Secretary had to do that day.

Werle was seated at his desk, smiling up, when Elke entered through her connecting door. There were similarities in the furniture and décor between the two offices, although Werle's was much larger, the conference room actually set aside in a separate, adjoining chamber. The area of the park was the same, but with a view of the Rhine which Elke didn't have, and Werle had his telephones on the principal desk. There were also framed but separate photographs of his wife and son. Apart from an unmarked blotter and a double row of pencils and pens, the remainder of the desk was bare. Werle was a meticulously neat and tidy man, in everything: he rarely left work over from one day to the next, neither did he like cluttering his desk with papers or documents. His system was to answer or respond to items as they were presented, for them to be cleared and moved on at once by Elke. He was also personally very neat. He was slightly built and comparatively thin, with no middle-aged thickening around his waist. He was always dressed in black or grey, his shirts were always white and his ties never loud. His hair was barbered very short and Elke could never remember it being disarrayed, any more than she could recall him losing his temper or even his composure, whatever the frustration or crisis. His voice was so quiet it was easy sometimes to imagine he was whispering, although after so long working as closely as she did with the man Elke never had difficulty in hearing what he said.

Although Günther Werle never boasted, because he was far too modest, Elke knew that throughout the upper echelons of government he was regarded with far more admiration and esteem than his official title might have suggested. He had occupied the position for nearly twenty years and achieved the status, although unofficial, of adviser and confidant to ministers and senior officials in every ministry of goverment during every coalition and administration.

From hurriedly terminated laughter when she entered a room or from occasionally half-heard remarks Elke was aware of sporadic and quite ungrounded conjecture among the rest of the staff about a personal relationship between herself and Werle.

Elke had tried to analyse it herself. There was a deep and profound mutual respect. A perfect professional working understanding. And an instinctively defined friendship. At Werle's request Elke suggested presents at anniversaries and at Christmas for his wife, whose name was Sybille and who needed daily rest and frequent visits to health spas to ease a lassitude for which doctors and specialists could find no medical explanation. Elke bought the gifts, too. And those for the son. On Werle's own birthday and at Christmas Elke only ever offered a commemorative card, which she noted he never took home but always left in his office. On matching occasions he, usually shyly, gave her perfume or chocolates. The gifts were always quite small and relatively inexpensive, as was proper from a superior to a supportive personal assistant.

'An enjoyable weekend, Frau Meyer?' The query was a familiar beginning to their week.

'Thank you, Herr Werle,' replied Elke, on cue.

'Ursula?'

'As always.' She wouldn't tell him about the incident with the dog: she wasn't sure yet she would tell Ida. She hadn't been able to record the incident in her diary, the previous night, either: she'd left the entry blank, which was how it would stay. 'How is Frau Werle?' She always felt it necessary to include the man's wife in the ritual.

Werle gave what could have been an impatient lift of his shoulders. 'Indisposed once more, I'm afraid. She's considering a spa she's heard about in Bavaria.' He moved, as if to speak further, but then stopped. He was absolutely sure of what he was recommending for Elke – privately hoping it would be beneficial on more than one level – but there were still too many procedures yet to be completed for him to be able to tell her. It would be good, when he could. Businesslike he straightened and said: 'Shall we start?'

Werle's side-table, assigned for Elke's use, was as clear as the main desk. She sat at it primly, her skirt covering her tight-together knees, offering first the three sealed security envelopes and waiting while the man went through the contents. He looked up, having done so, and said: 'Can you imagine after all that's happened that America is seeking private discussions on short-range nuclear missiles!'

Absolute trust, thought Elke, adding to her mental list of what they shared. Strictly according to regulations it was a breach of security for Werle to have intimated what had been in the sealed messages, but neither regarded it as such. She offered the three documents she was cleared to open and said: 'This is all fairly predictable.'

'I'll need everything, from the time of the Hungarian open door decision in 1989. Keep the reunification file constantly up to date.'

Elke indicated the notation attached to the top three letters. 'That lists what I've already called for: they'll be with me in an hour.'

Werle smiled again, a white, even-toothed smile. 'I rely upon you so very much,' he said. And would soon prove how much.

Elke was momentarily confused. She felt hot and wondered, further surprised, whether she was blushing. Hurriedly she said: 'The amount of material will be substantial. It might be better if you told me the references most likely to be needed: I could go through everything and create a discussion index. I'll assemble the missile material separately.'

'Just get me the statistics,' ordered Werle. 'Numerical strength between NATO and the Warsaw Pact, dates of decisions in the past and a résumé of the arguments put forward.'

Elke nodded, indicating the remaining mail. 'Everything else is routine.'

'Diary entries?'

Elke offered the typed list of that day's engagements. Werle looked at it, but only fleetingly. 'Two hours before I'm due anywhere. Send Frau Pohl in first, to start. I'll switch every thirty minutes, to clear it all before I go. Usual vetting, by you.'

Elke returned to her own office and dispatched Gerda Pohl, who responded with a grunt but said nothing. At the same time Elke told the secretaries that upon completion everything had to be returned to her to be checked and approved. This system for non-classified and routine correspondence enabled Werle to sign at the end of the day without having to concentrate upon every word, fact and phrase, confident it had been approved by Elke.

After instructing the secretaries, Elke carefully briefed two researchers upon what she anticipated Werle would want on the continuing refugee movement from East to West Germany. Finally she outlined the request to the third researcher on the more easily assembled missile information Werle demanded.

Having established the activities of the day Elke turned at last to Saturday's security summons. It only took a few minutes' study of the late night personnel log of the preceding Friday. Elke sighed, heavily, at the identification of Gerda Pohl's name: the carelessness would have to be challenged and Elke disliked confrontations.

She was rehearsing it in her mind when Ida came on to her private line. Even on a mechanical instrument like a telephone her sister's ebullience, a liveliness, was tangible. It began as a disjoined social chat but quite quickly Ida asked about Ursula the previous day and insisted that she'd meant what she'd said about making a visit. Elke accepted, suddenly knowing the need for companionship the next time. She positively decided against telling Ida of the previous day's episode. It was very unlikely that Dr Schiller or anyone else at the home would refer to it in front of Ida. Schiller had dismissed it as something without importance. Elke ended the conversation agreeing to the usual lunch with her sister and worked for an hour collating Werle's briefing notes before returning to his office to ensure he left with sufficient time to make his first appointment. She left soon after Werle.

It took her less than fifteen minutes to reach her apartment, which was on the third floor of a pre-war, five-storey house in a cul-de-sac off Kaufmannstrasse. She entered calling the dog by name. There was no answering bark – no sound of him scurrying to meet her – and Elke practically ran into the kitchen. Poppi lay in his basket as she had left him, but he must have moved at some time because he had been sick, very slightly, out on the protective paper. Anxiously Elke called his name again. The dog lifted his head and got stiffly up, emerging with staggered unsteadiness towards her. Elke knelt to pick him up, but quickly stopped, not wanting to hurt the already bruised animal again. She fondled his ears instead, deciding she could not take a chance over the sickness.

'Can't have you . . .' she began, addressing the dog, but didn't finish. Despite the determination not to do so, she increasingly found herself talking to Poppi. It really had to stop!

The veterinerary surgeon came curtly on to the telephone, clearly irritated at being interrupted during a lunch period, and just as curtly insisted it was nothing to worry about. As she cleared up after the dog, relaid more paper, and deodorized that part of the kitchen with a disinfectant spray, Elke decided that if Poppi was ill again she'd take him to a different animal specialist.

As she washed her hands, first with liquid disinfectant before switching to normal soap, Elke wondered about making herself something to eat. At once she remembered the reading on the bathroom scales. Today – occupying her lunch-hour attending to Poppi – was as good a time as any to begin the intended diet. She wasn't hungry anyway. She slowly walked the dog, although more briefly than in the morning, resettled it into its basket and set out fresh food and water.

'I'll be back soon,' she said, at the door, and wished she hadn't.

There were three telephone calls listed for her attention when she returned to the Chancellery and she easily resolved each without the need to consult Werle. Before she finished doing that the researchers delivered everything she'd ordered that morning, giving her the opportunity to consider it and ensure the file on the missile query was in proper chronological order before the appointment with Werle.

Elke was fully prepared when the buzzer sounded, promptly at three o'clock. Werle accepted the folders without opening them, confident they would contain everything he wanted, and nodded agreement to Elke's brief account of the telephone queries she had handled in his absence. Elke had anticipated with the exception of possibly three past reports all that the man needed.

Pleased with herself she said: 'I'll have most of it indexed by tonight: everything completed by mid-morning tomorrow.' If she had not had to get home to Poppi she could have worked late and completed the task that night.

Werle smiled. 'I don't think I could function without you.'

'It'll give you an opportunity to review everything: to decide if you want anything else.' Elke wished he hadn't made the remark, just as she wished he hadn't said what he had that morning. It wasn't how things normally were between them.

'All this afternoon's meetings are here in the Chancellery,' he said, looking casually at his typed schedule. 'I'll get back before the last appointment to deal with this morning's correspondence.'

'It will all be ready,' Elke guaranteed.

Again Werle felt the urge to tell her what he had set into motion. Instead, lamely, he said: 'I know it will be.'

Elke ordered the extra missile research at the same time as asking for all the secretarial work to be delivered to her within thirty minutes. She'd already indexed three files by the time it came.

Her immediate concern just as quickly became anger. There were mistakes to be corrected on four of the letters she first read and even more serious errors in two much lengthier reports she had wanted duplicated for overnight ministry distribution.

Gerda Pohl had prepared every one.

Elke's first consideration was to minimize delay. She searched hurriedly through the pile, separating everything upon which the woman had worked and putting it to one side. There was no correction necessary on anything the other secretaries had prepared. Elke went back to the isolated pile and found two more wrongly typed pieces. She made a further separation, leaving herself with only the erroneous material. Patiently, utterly absorbed, she scrutinized and corrected everything before finally summoning the older woman into her office.

'Do you have a problem?' Elke demanded. The anger helped, but she always found it difficult to convey authority.

'Problem?' Gerda's attitude was insolent.

'I was called here on Saturday by security. A classified reference file released to this office, into your custody, was not recorded as having been put in your own safe.'

29

'I put it in the safe,' insisted Gerda, at once.

'But didn't log it!' said Elke. She pushed the rejected letters across the desk. 'Now this! Seven items with figures wrong and facts wrong and places appallingly mistyped!'

'I can't hear what he says,' protested Gerda. It was the established defence to any correction or rejection.

'Difficulty in hearing doesn't excuse mistyping or misspelling. And there are addressee and destination faults that are clearly – and correctly – printed on file,' retorted Elke.

'Must have made a mistake,' said the older woman. The insolence was becoming childishly petulant.

'I'm *telling* you that you've made mistakes!' said Elke, in an exasperated effort for sarcasm that didn't work. 'That's why I want to know if there's some problem, beyond this office.'

'No,' said Gerda. 'I haven't got a problem.'

'So why did it happen? Seven times! And why didn't you complete Friday's security log?'

The woman shrugged, carelessly. 'Unavoidable mistakes.'

'They're not unavoidable.'

'Are you accusing me of doing it deliberately!'

Elke recognized the first direct challenge. She had to take account of the unions. She said: 'I'm asking, not accusing.'

'I've explained.' Gerda looked disappointed at Elke's answer.

'Not satisfactorily.'

'What do you want me to do?' demanded Gerda, still challenging.

There were several answers. Elke chose what she considered the easiest. 'I want you to take them back and do them all again. Correctly. Tonight.'

'That would involve my working overtime,' said Gerda, at once. Invoking the enshrined work rule, she added: 'Overtime has to be by mutual agreement: I can't work tonight.'

Elke's anger flooded back, but she refused to allow Gerda the satisfaction of realizing it. Instead, with attempted reasonableness, she said: 'Why are you doing this?'

'Doing what?'

Elke sighed, fearing the dispute was slipping away from her by the sheer nonsense of it. Stiffly formal, she said: 'I consider this work grossly incompetent. I shall record that assessment upon your personnel file. You will receive a copy of that assessment, which is your right: so will your trade union representative, which regulations require.'

30

Striving to retrieve the earlier insolence, Gerda said: 'Is there anything else?'

'Quite a lot,' said Elke, considering herself completely in charge now. 'I want every rejected piece of work properly completed upon my desk by noon tomorrow. If it is not – or if there is the slightest mistake in anything – that further incompetence will be added to your file. And that complaint also forwarded to your union representative . . .' With a sudden determination to get some concession from Gerda, she said: 'Do you completely understand?'

'Yes,' said Gerda, tight lips barely moving.

She *had* won, decided Elke, knowing a relief greater than the victory justified. And she could go on, dominating the secretary further. She didn't. Indicating what lay between them, Elke said: 'I will lodge it all in my safe overnight, for security. They will be on your desk, waiting, in the morning.'

There was no drop in Elke's anger as she entered Werle's office for the final encounter of the day. By inference, as the person in ultimate charge of the Cabinet Office Secretariat, some of the incompetence reflected upon her. And *never* being professionally incompetent was so very necessary to support what little other, outside confidence she had. 'I am afraid there is a problem,' Elke announced at once.

She had to list the replies that could not be dispatched that night, according to their regular practice, because he clearly had to know each individual one. When Elke finished he said without needing to be told: 'Frau Pohl was the stenographer.'

'Yes,' agreed Elke. Security would automatically inform him of the Saturday episode, Elke knew. She said: 'There was a weekend difficulty, as well. She quite properly returned a classified file to the office safe, but failed to log it. The classification was minimal, but she should have registered it, according to regulations.'

'Have there been any other occasions?'

'Some clerical errors,' admitted Elke. Why should she have any reluctance to criticize someone who had been as obstructive as Gerda Pohl?

'What have you done about it?' There was nothing relaxed between them now: Werle was extremely serious, stern-faced and demanding. Elke recounted the interview with Gerda, without mentioning the other woman's permanent resentment, and Werle said: 'She can be moved if she is causing disruptive difficulties, without your having to consider union objections. Dismissed entirely, if necessary.'

Elke was shocked at the unexpected ruthlessness. From the

personnel file from which she'd learned Gerda's age Elke knew the woman to be a widow, with only a small pension from the Federal railways which had employed her husband. Even a move from this department could affect her seniority and salary scale. Urgently Elke said: 'Please don't arrange a transfer. Or consider dismissal. I'm sure it won't happen again.'

'I won't allow it to happen again,' insisted Werle. 'I won't ever have this a department in which mistakes occur.'

When Elke entered the Kaufmannstrasse apartment Poppi made a slightly wavering approach of welcome, his tail barely moving. There had been no further sickness. Normally it would have been sufficient to elevate the day into a pleasant, relieved ending, but this night Elke felt unusually depressed. The argument with Gerda had left her dejected. And Werle's abrupt and totally surprising hardness towards the woman had distressed her. Elke didn't know how to deal with the unexpected. Her narrow life had a pattern and a pathway and she didn't like it being disarranged, minuscule though that disarrangement might have appeared to anyone else.

It was another day she did not want to record in her diary. She left it blank, as she had the day before.

'There's only one further matter to discuss, before you begin,' announced the Russian psychologist. His name was Yuri Panin, although of course he had never been identified, always remaining anonymous throughout the months he had acted as the chief psychologist at the most unusual of all KGB academies. 'What about your wife?'

'We were given permission to discuss it.'

'What was her feeling about the entire operation?'

'A professional one.'

'No reservations whatsoever?'

'She regards it as an assignment, nothing else. Nothing personal.'

'Do you believe that's an attitude she'll be able to sustain?'

'Of course. She is a very controlled, objective woman.'

Panin frowned. 'How would you describe your personal relationship?'

'Very good,' the man insisted.

'There are no children?'

'My wife is a very dedicated woman. For several years now everything has been subjugated to her career as an intelligence officer.'

'In West Berlin she was officially your superior, the cell leader,' reminded Panin. 'Did your having to be subservient create any difficulty between you?'

'I never regarded it as subservience. What degree of authority there was only applied to our professional activities.'

'What about your feelings at what you are going to have to do? Do you have any doubts or reservations?'

'None.'

'You don't fear your marriage could be endangered?'

'Most certainly not!'

'Good,' nodded the psychologist, approvingly. 'There is to be a recognition for the dedication you have shown. Your wife is being flown here to join you for a brief holiday.'

'I am very grateful,' said the man.

His name was Otto Höhn, although he had already completely adopted the legend name of Otto Reimann, under which he was to work. His intended mission was to make the lonely, abandoned, locked-inside-herself Elke Meyer fall so hopelessly in love with him that she would tell him every secret with which she came into contact.

Chapter Four

Otto Reimann was not a blatantly sexual man, as a gigolo is blatantly sexual, because to have been so obvious in either appearance or demeanour would have been dangerously wrong. He had, in any case, been chosen because of a remarkable resemblance to another man, so his selection was in some ways imposed upon the KGB. His hair, predominantly deep brown, was greying slightly at the sides, which conveyed the impression of maturity but not age, because his face was unlined and his skin very clear, a clear indication of health heightened by the physical exercise that was a part of the curriculum of the training academy at Balashikha, on the outskirts of Moscow. His eyes were brown, too, and he had been taught how to use them since his arrival. He was naturally broad-shouldered and slim-waisted, but the physique had improved from the same exercise that had given his skin its tone: the stomach had tightened and there was no longer the slight excess that had shown over his waistband in the beginning. He had undergone extensive dental treatment, to fill two cavities and whitely to scale all plaque, but the slightly protruding eye-tooth on the left had not been corrected nor the remainder capped into perfect evenness, because few men apart from matinee idols have exquisitely even teeth. His hands, which he had disregarded with the casualness of most men, were smooth now, softened by the prescribed creams he had been ordered to administer nightly, and the nails were faultlessly manicured, not irregularly clipped as before. After so much instruction he no longer automatically thrust those hands into his pocket in the stance of the majority of men who stood waiting, as he was waiting now, as if they were embarrassing attachments at the end of either arm, which his psychological lecturers had defined as inherent nervousness. Instead he stood with them by his sides, calmly relaxed and supremely confident.

The confidence, measurably short of either conceit or arrogance, would probably have been the most noticeable difference to anyone who had known him before, but Otto Reimann was never again going to encounter any of the few people who had known him before, apart from his wife for whose flight from East Berlin he was waiting at Moscow's Vnukovo airport. So good had been his tuition, however, that Reimann was not obviously conscious of the changed attitude: for him to have had such awareness would have made it all a pose and therefore recognizable to others. Nothing that marked him out could ever be recognizable to others. From the moment of his graduation, a man reborn like a Frankenstein experiment that this time had brilliantly succeeded, not created a physical monster, Otto Reimann had always to be perfect, never making the slightest error.

Jutta was one of the first through the arrival gate looking around her not with the anxiousness of a stranger in an unfamiliar airport but with the imperious command of an assured woman in complete control of herself. Reimann did not move to meet her and at first she failed to see him. She wore a belted raincoat he had not seen before and guessed she had bought for the visit. She carried only one small weekend case. Her pale brown hair was as she always wore it, combed severely back from her forehead and collected into a tight bun. The lipstick and eye-colouring were light and perfectly applied. He decided she was quite different from any of the professional women with whom he had trained. But then, he supposed, she should have looked different: Jutta practised another profession altogether.

The smile when she finally located him was brief, quickly followed by a frown. When she reached him she didn't offer a kiss but waited for him to move. There was hardly any contact between them when he did.

'You were standing, watching me,' she said, accusingly.

'I wanted to see you first,' Reimann admitted.

'Why?'

'To decide if you'd changed.'

Jutta frowned again. 'How could I have changed?'

'It was stupid of me.' It had been a very intentional experiment, providing him with an answer. Jutta certainly hadn't changed. She wore autocratic authority like an article of clothing.

She was already looking around the terminal, as though eager to be moving. Confirming the impression, she said: 'Shall we go?'

'There's a car waiting.'

Jutta's controlled demeanour weakened slightly at the chauffeur-driven Zil and then further when he led her into the apartment which spanned almost an entire floor of a high-ceilinged, pre-revolutionary mansion in Neglinnaya Ulitza. Those high ceilings were corniced and moulded and most appeared still to retain the original gilding. The furnishings accorded with the apartment and the period. The drapes for the full-length balconied windows were heavy velvet and the carpets, although faded, were clearly antique and probably Persian.

35

The table in the separate dining-room had seats for twelve, although leaves had been removed for their visit, to make it smaller. It was satinwood, as was the serving sideboard already set with silver salvers and silver serving cutlery. The two settees and an array of easy chairs in the main lounge were brocaded and heavily padded and there was actually a canopy, complete with more quilted brocade, over the bed. To one side, arranged into a vast window alcove in the bedroom, was a claw-legged breakfast table, bordered by four chairs, and a chaise-longue nearer a dressing table display of cream jars and lotion and perfume bottles. The modern, contrasting bathroom led off. Every-thing – the bath, the double wash-basins, the alcove-recessed toilet and bidet – was in black-speckled white marble: reflected by an assortment of mirrors, chrome glittered everywhere.

'You live here!' exclaimed Jutta.

Reimann laughed, enjoying the rare experience of Jutta being impressed with anything. 'We're allowed it while you're here. I normally live at the school.'

'It's . . .' Jutta straggled to a halt. '. . . amazing.' Jutta visibly jumped at the appearance of a fat, sag-breasted woman.

'You don't have to bother about cooking,' assured Reimann, who had been given a tour and had the apartment facilities explained to him by the chauffeur before being driven to Vnukovo.

'I didn't intend to.' On their previous assignment in West Berlin, they'd eaten out most days. When they'd stayed in, Reimann had done most of the cooking. And become good at it.

'We'll eat early,' decided Jutta, ahead of Reimann, to whom the housekeeper had put the question about what time they wanted dinner.

Reimann served white wine with the fish, fresh salmon, and changed to a mellow Georgian red for the stroganoff, opening a second bottle by the middle of the course. Throughout, his attention was entirely upon Jutta, encouraging when she spoke, deferring to any interjection she made. When Reimann held the conversation almost everything he said was light, amusing: he actually made jokes about the Balashikha women, insisting upon his initial apprehensions and exaggerating his embarrassments. Jutta listened attentively, although occasionally her eyes strayed around the opulent apartment.

Jutta went into the bedroom ahead of him, which Reimann allowed her to do under the pretence of his dismissing the housekeeper. Jutta was already in bed when he entered. She kissed him properly for the first time when he got in beside her, but again waited for him to come to her, not initiating it herself.

Reimann didn't hurry.

He played his lips over her neck and shoulders, momentarily mouthing her nipples before kneeling over her but not close enough for their nakedness to touch, diving and darting with his mouth, to her gorged nipples and belly dimple and at last into the anxious thatch. He entered her as he'd always done, from above, and she locked her legs familiarly around his waist. Reimann remained utterly controlled, feigning the reaction to her quick urgency, and only partially climaxed with her. Almost immediately she squirmed under his weight and when he rolled off she leaned at once to the bedside table for tissues. She dried between her legs and handed him tissues to dry himself.

'That was good,' she said, edging away.

Reimann thought she sounded like a schoolteacher praising a homework project. Jutta *really* hadn't changed. Why had he expected – or hoped – she might have done?

'How many others have there been?' she demanded, suddenly. It was an objective question, with no sexual interest. Or jealousy.

'Six,' he answered at once. All better, he thought.

'Singly? Or sometimes more than one?'

'Sometimes more than one.'

'Why an orgy?'

'To see if I could sustain it.'

'Could you?'

'Not at first.'

'Now?'

'Yes.'

'What's it like?' She was still objective.

'Mechanical.'

'Do you enjoy it?'

'No.'

'Do you come?'

'Of course.'

'So you enjoyed it!'

'A man has an orgasm with a prostitute: he forgets what she looks like by the time he walks out into the street. The entire act is meaningless.' He was almost surprised she was bothering with the questions.

'Is that what they all were, prostitutes?'

'What else?'

'You could have caught something! Given it to me!'

'They're special girls, retained exclusively by the KGB: subject all the time to medical tests and examination.'

37

'What's special about them?'

Reimann sighed. 'Aren't you bored with this conversation?' He was. Sex had never been important to her, in their marriage.

'I want to know!'

'They're special in what they do: particular tastes.'

'Tell me.'

'Some like pain: to hurt. Others need a woman, as well as a man. Some do nothing, not at first: they like to watch others.'

Jutta was silent for several moments. 'Why so much?'

'I have to know everything. Never be surprised.'

'Why! You're not going to seduce prostitutes! Perverts!'

'I don't know *who* I'm going to have to seduce.'

'What I . . .'

'Stop!' said Reimann, loudly. 'You want to talk sex, I'll talk sex: I've been taught how to do that, too. But I don't want to.'

Her indifference was immediate. 'Tomorrow we'll sightsee.'

Which was what they did. They went to Red Square, although not to Lenin's tomb because the queue was too long. They toured the cathedrals and the Kremlin museum, Jutta lecturing with a guidebook in hand. Because the weather was so perfect Reimann took her on a half-day cruise on the Moskva River. And every night they made love, always in the same position, always with the tissues waiting. Twice Reimann didn't climax at all. Jutta never realized.

In the intelligence parlance of the KGB, men trained as professional seducers of women, versed in every type and aspect of sexual expertise, are officially called ravens. Women are also trained, to that same degree of expertise, to entrap men. They are known as swallows. Thus a room or an apartment in which a swallow seduces her prey is called a swallow's nest. The sometimes suggested term honey-trap is not a professional description. Sexual blackmail is, of course, the objective: swallows' nests are fitted in every room and vantage point with recording equipment and self-focusing and adjusting cameras, both still and movie. Mirrors and apparently framed pictures which from one side appear genuine are frequently two-way glass screens from the phoney side of which observers can sit and witness everything that takes place.

The apartment on Neglinnaya Ulitza in which Otto Reimann was reunited with his wife was one of the best equipped swallows' nests existing in the Soviet capital. Everything that occurred there, in any room at any time, was recorded or filmed, usually on more than one machine, as a fail-safe. On this occasion, however, blackmail had not been the objective.

'Well?' demanded the psychologist, Yuri Panin. With Nikolai Turev he had spent two days reviewing and assessing all the film footage and tape recordings. Both had actually sat, quite unmoved, on the other side of the main mirror in the bedroom to watch the sexual activity on the day of Jutta's arrival.

'I didn't think much of his performance,' said Turev. He was chain-smoking American cigarettes, Camels, clouding the room with the odour. Turev, who was a full ranking colonel, was apprehensive at being chosen as Reimann's field control, which would anyway have been far below his position but for the Politburo and Executive President monitor on the operation. Everyone associated with Reimann's mission survived or fell by its success.

'It was absolutely brilliant!' contradicted Panin, at once.

'Brilliant?' frowned Turev, wishing he understood.

'Think how he's been trained!' urged the psychologist. 'He could have shown her the sort of sex she's probably never even heard of: gone through every trick there is. But that's what it *would* have been, a set of tricks. Which she would have realized. They made love as they probably always have. He was actually reassuring her, keeping the tricks for his target. Showing Jutta she's not threatened. Which, as I said, was absolutely brilliant.'

'I suppose so,' said Turev, doubtfully. He was a butter-ball of a man, with heavy jowls and a shiny, pink face. The shortness of his neck was accentuated by a heavy moustache that hung like two question marks from either side of his upper lip. The moustache, like his hair, was pure white.

'He was doing something else, for his own satisfaction,' continued Panin, reflectively. 'He *knows* what he could have done: what he held back from her.'

Turev frowned again. 'Where's the satisfaction in that?'

'Remember the circumstances!' urged Panin. 'He was sent to Berlin, to join the group of which she was cell leader. She was the cell leader when they got married, so she always had the superior authority. Always – professionally – he had to defer to her.'

'So?'

'That's unnatural: completely so, for every minute of their private and working lives. He insisted at our last meeting that it didn't worry him. But now I think it did. I think he was amusing himself with her: feeling superior at last. I think he's resented her superiority all along.'

'Could that be a problem?' demanded the KGB chief, quickly alarmed.

'The fact that he's married has always been a potential problem,' said Panin unhelpfully. 'I've always wished the look-alike could have been a bachelor. But it's Reimann. So we've got to live with it.'

'Isn't there any precaution we can take?'

Panin shook his head. 'Just remain very aware that it is a weakness: something we should constantly monitor. And I think I should sit in when you brief her, on what she's expected to do.'

'How should I handle that?'

'Flatter her.'

Chapter Five

It was difficult to give absolute attention, even for someone as conscientious as Elke, because the security lectures had always been formalized and now seemed more so, nothing she had not heard a dozen (or was it a hundred?) times before. She glanced around the small conference room at the other supervisors, all with a clearance as high as her own, and guessed they all felt the same: boredom permeated the room.

'. . . *continued and unremitting vigilance* . . .' she heard the speaker intone. He was a tall, intense, moustached man who had not addressed them before. She wondered if the speakers were changed in an attempt to keep the talks as interestingly different as possible. It wasn't succeeding with this man: he was as pedantic as the title of the ministry he represented, the Federal Agency for the Preservation of the Constitution.

'. . . *apparent relaxations between East and West do not mean Soviet intelligence efforts have diminished at all* . . .'

Last weekend's visit to Ursula had been much better, although she'd been upset by Ida's last-minute telephone call announcing she couldn't come as promised. It hadn't mattered, in the event. Ursula had seemed much quieter this time, happy to walk in the grounds, seemingly content for them to hold hands. Maybe it had been silly leaving Poppi in the car, as she had: it was a relief he had recovered so completely. And so quickly.

'. . . *anything strange should be reported immediately to your superiors or to the security division here in the Chancellery* . . .'

Gerda Pohl appeared to have been corrected, which was another relief. The meeting with the union representative had become a mere formality, after the slipshod work had actually been produced for him to see. Elke hadn't expected Werle's personal intervention, when he'd heard of the requested interview. All he'd said afterwards was that he'd supported her, in everything, but Elke suspected there had been more than that. The improvement hadn't removed Gerda's resentment, but Elke was wearily accustomed to that.

'. . . *almost every case on record would have been preventable if the proper alertness had been shown, at the proper time* . . .'

41

Ida had been right, about Kissel serving the same disgusting wine because she'd praised it on the first occasion. Poor man.

'. . . *reporting suspicion about other people in a department is not unnecessary interference . . .*'

Elke feared that a woman in the Chancellor's Secretariat whom she did not know by name, only to return an acknowledging smile, was definitely asleep. Elke wished she were closer, to nudge her awake.

'. . . *our secrets ensure our future . . . our security . . .*'

Elke decided the moustached intelligence official was more pompous than any they'd listened to before. She was looking forward to lunching with Ida, and hoped she wouldn't cancel it as she'd cancelled the visit to Ursula. She had to get some more bathroom cleanser. Polish, too. She'd do the bedrooms tonight. Like all things, the arrangement was very regulated, according to days of the week.

'. . . *questions ?*'

Elke began to concentrate, realizing the address was over. She saw, gratefully, that the secretariat official had her eyes open. The intelligence man looked hopefully around the room. No one spoke.

'I want to emphasize the importance of what I've said,' the man insisted. 'It's easy, I know, to believe that talks like this are irrelevant now. They're not: none of you should imagine that. The opening of the borders and demolition of the Wall *increases* rather than decreases espionage activities. Never forget that!'

There was a muttering of assent and some head nodding, throughout the room.

'I hope you do,' said the man, disappointed at the lack of responses. 'I thank you all for your attention. I hope to see you again . . .' He paused, for the prepared joke. '. . . But only in this capacity.'

Everyone smiled and sniggered politely. There was an eagerness to stand and leave. Elke managed to insert herself into the middle of the departing line. There were five logged calls waiting, none from Ida. Elke dealt with them and ensured there were no queries from the outside staff and was at the restaurant precisely on time. Ida, predictably, was late. Elke felt exposed, on view, at the table by herself and wished she had a newspaper or a book. Without either she made the pretence of studying the menu, although she had already decided upon a salad: according to the scales she had lost the weight she'd put on, and she was determined against gaining it again.

Ida flustered in fifteen minutes late, striding assuredly across the restaurant. Elke was conscious of men at two separate tables following her sister's progress: the waiter came immediately, inquiring about an aperitif. Ida said they'd have wine, without consulting Elke. It was offered without question for Ida to approve, which she did. As she sipped from her full glass Ida said: 'Bloody sight better than what Horst serves.'

'I was sorry you couldn't make last Sunday,' said Elke, expecting an explanation.

'Soon, I promise,' said Ida, without offering one.

'We walked, in the grounds. Had lunch in the conservatory. She's growing quite tall. I have to get her some new clothes.'

'Doris might have something she's outgrown.'

'She's much bigger than Doris,' Elke reminded, politely. The offer had been made before and always refused. There was no reason for Ursula to be dressed in second-hand clothes because she was in an institution she rarely left and where her appearance was unimportant, either to herself or to the staff. Like not bothering to knock on her door, it deprived the child of dignity.

They gave their order and as the waiter left Ida smiled and said: 'He called.'

'Who?' said Elke, momentarily forgetting.

'Kurt. He called.'

'What did you do?'

'Talked, of course.'

'About what?'

'He said he hoped he hadn't offended me, at the dinner party.'

'Which was an ideal opportunity to say that he had and put the phone down,' Elke declared.

'Prig!' accused Ida, laughing.

'What *did* you say?'

'That he hadn't.'

'Idiot! You're encouraging him!'

'It's harmless.'

'Don't be ridiculous! How can it be harmless?'

'Nothing's happened!' Ida's lightness was going, although there was no anger.

'What about the risk of hurting Horst? And Doris? And Georg?' Was it another attempt of Ida's to shock?

'No one's going to get . . .' started Ida, and stopped. 'Let's talk about something else.'

'Did you arrange to see him?' Elke persisted.

'Not really.'

'What does "not really" mean?'

43

'The conversation kind of drifted off. I think he lost his nerve. He certainly stuttered more than I remembered.'

'Perhaps he came to his senses.'

'Whatever,' dismissed Ida. 'That was it! No plans, no nothing.'

Elke wondered if her sister was telling the truth. If she was lying it would be the first time: at least the first time that she'd suspected or found out.

'Would you have met him, if he had asked?'

'This is an inquisition!' Ida protested, but still without anger.

'It's meant to be.'

Ida sighed. 'Maybe. Maybe not.'

'That's not an answer. You must have thought about it as soon as you realized who it was on the phone: made up your mind!'

The waiter's return gave Ida a few moments' respite before she conceded: 'I hadn't, not really. Sure I thought about it. First I thought I might and then I thought I wouldn't and in the end I didn't know what to do.'

Again Elke wondered whether her sister was lying and an assignation really was arranged. 'Don't see him!' she pleaded. 'Please don't.' It frightened her to confront how important Ida was to her. She supposed she'd always known it, subconsciously – of course she had! – but now she was positively examining how it was between them and was scared. Embarrassed, too, because she conceded at once and with utter honesty that her concern wasn't for Kissel or Doris or Georg or even Ida. It was for herself. Ida was her security: the only person upon whom she could rely. She'd always felt reassured, knowing Ida was there: knowing ineffectual Horst was there. She didn't want the danger of everything being upset because Ida was bored and flattered by the attentions of another man. By the lust of another man, Elke corrected. How she hated and despised sex!

'You're not eating your salad,' said Ida, avoiding the plea.

'I don't want to eat my salad.'

'I said I'm sorry: I shouldn't have talked about it.'

'Why shouldn't you? We don't have any secrets, do we?' It was as if Ida were aware of the fears, but Elke knew that wasn't so.

'No,' agreed Ida. 'We don't have any secrets.'

Perhaps her sister wasn't lying, after all. Elke said: 'There isn't anything else to say, not without going around in circles.'

'Thank God!' said Ida.

'Will you tell me, if there is?' said Elke.

Ida considered the demand for several moments, again looking very

44

directly and seriously at Elke. Then she said: 'Yes, of course I'll tell you.'

Elke didn't enjoy the lunch and didn't think Ida had either, although at the end she insisted it was fun. They filled the time talking of Kissel and the children and Elke contributed as much as she considered she could about the Chancellery, but there was a strain that was more obvious to them both because it was so unusual for there to be any barrier at all. Elke's feeling of unease, a disorientation, persisted throughout the afternoon and she was grateful that it was relatively quiet, with few telephone calls, no problems from the staff with the work they were assigned and only one request from Günther Werle. That was to arrange the visit of his wife to the health spa close to Munich.

The fully recovered Poppi bustled around her when she got back to Kaufmannstrasse and she went through the greeting procedure before walking and feeding him. Now that she had lunched, the threatening quarter kilo precluded another meal that day. She decided to do Ursula's bedroom first.

It was not complete sentimentality preserving Ursula's pink-washed room as she had, everything in place from the day the child had left to go to the institution. Ursula had come home twice, at Christmas and once for her birthday: during Elke's holiday last year she'd tried to have the girl an entire week and managed four days before Ursula became distressed at the change and had to be returned to the surroundings and the professional care to which she had become accustomed.

There was a bed with a duvet covered with brightly coloured fairy tale characters and over it a mobile of more fairy tale figures and stars and glittering shapes that Ursula had gazed at and seemed to like: certainly she'd gurgled and smiled and followed them with her eyes, when she'd been a baby. When Ursula visited now Elke removed the mobile, on the advice of Dr Schiller, because he thought it might prove dangerous. Perhaps keeping all the baby clothes and the dresses of those first years *was* nostalgic sentimentality. Like the fluffy-furred bear and the beaver toy with the bright red eyes, which also had to be removed during Ursula's visits, against the risk of her picking the eyes off to eat, as if they were sweets. There was a music box in the shape of a gingerbread house, which played a Strauss waltz when the roof was lifted, and more picture books like those in Ursula's room at the home near Marienfels.

It was quite unnecessary for Elke to clean as she had the previous week and the week before that, but the practice was entrenched. She vacuumed and dusted and polished, not simply around the things but taking them down or moving them, with no short cuts. She remade the bed which did not need remaking and as she did so disturbed the mobile, which revolved briefly, tinkling: she stopped to watch and listen, remembering when it had hung over Ursula's cot, not the bed. Ursula *had* liked it: recognized it and smiled at it. Elke was sure she had.

The small dressing table was last. Again Elke removed everything on top, first dusting, then polishing. There wasn't a lot to replace: the lace runner which stretched across its top, a hair brush and a hand mirror, and a pot-pourri dish that Elke regularly changed, and an empty bowl to hold the small things that girls collect, although Ursula had never collected small things like other girls. The china figure of a fawn was last. Elke stood staring at it, held by the reminiscence. It was very cheap and poorly made, the sort of trinket to be discarded the day after it had been picked up. They'd won it together, when Ursula was about nine: at a spring fair with sideshows and stalls. Elke had used a fishing rod with a ring on the line to hook a floating duck to win a prize. Ursula had squealed with delight and demanded it and slept with it for almost two weeks before ceasing to acknowledge or be excited by it. It was the longest the child had ever retained interest in anything, the longest Elke had ever kept the hope that somehow Ursula would ever improve. Elke came mentally to regard the fading brown figure as Ursula's talisman: despite everything, it was how she still thought of it and referred to it, in her mind. Elke held it and wiped away non-existent dust before carefully returning it to its appointed place. Perhaps, she thought, Ursula might recognize it again, on her next visit. She hadn't mentioned the possibility of a visit to Dr Schiller for a long time and he had not raised the idea with her. On her way between the bedrooms Elke glanced sideways into the kitchen and to Poppi, asleep in his basket. Perhaps another visit was something she should discuss in some detail with Dr Schiller, not propose without the fullest consideration.

Elke finished her own bedroom at nine o'clock, precisely the time she expected, as it would be eight o'clock before she finished the kitchen and bathroom the following evening and eight o'clock the night after that to complete the living room – where the bookshelves all had to be dusted – and tiny entrance hall.

She always felt dirty, after a cleaning session. She ran the bath hot, adding salts as well as foam essence, and brought the radio in to play from the far window recess. She was completely immersed, with the radio too far away to turn off, which she would have quickly done if she could, when the music started.

It was Chopin's 'Chanson de l'Adieu' and had been played on their first outing together, when he had taken her to the Cologne concert. Which was still not sufficient reason for its meaning to her. By coincidence, and on a radio again, it had played the night they'd made love, for the first time, the night she'd lost her virginity. Elke luxuriated, felt herself floating, the perfume of the oils and the salts all around her. Her hand dipped beneath the water, as she knew it would, and she moved her legs very slightly, to make it easier, not hurrying, wanting it to last. She shuddered, legs stiff before her, at the final release, anxious for it not to end.

The remorse was instant. She had no grounds for criticizing Ida for lacking control, she told herself.

'What's outstanding?' demanded Cherny. Because it was convenient the soldier had journeyed to the KGB headquarters in Dzerzhinsky Square from a Chiefs of Staff briefing and he'd chosen a civilian suit. He seemed uncomfortable in it, frequently shrugging the jacket around his shoulders.

'Reimann is getting all his instructions tomorrow. The wife within days,' said Sorokin. He was a stoop-shouldered man on the point of going to fat, through middle age. He balanced his increasing baldness with a tightly clipped beard which unfortunately gave him a resemblance to the last Tsar, Nicholas.

'When will they get to Bonn?' said Cherny, impatiently.

'Within a week.'

'I want results, quickly.'

'*We* want results,' Sorokin corrected.

Chapter Six

It was a large building, pre-revolutionary again, just off the main Arbat Ulitza. There was an identity check at the door by officers wearing undesignated uniforms Reimann could not recognize. Inside, the impression was of scurrying but extremely quiet activity: people passed each other in corridors without appearing to exchange any greetings – even to look at each other – and a rubberized coating on the floor minimized the sound of their footsteps. The office into which Reimann was escorted was as sterile as its outside surroundings: it was not a room in which a person permanently worked but a place set aside for this day, and tomorrow someone quite different would be using it. There was just a desk, which was quite empty apart from a telephone, and two chairs, the one behind the desk bigger and slightly more imposing than the other, although both were covered in matching buttoned leather. The telephone was so positioned on the desk that it would have been difficult for anyone in the larger chair to reach out to answer it. To one side was a film projector directed towards an already erected screen: the screen was the sort that collapsed after use around a fan of extension arms to fit neatly into a case, temporary like everything else.

At the moment Reimann entered from the outer corridor a side-door opened to admit another man. He was very fat, white-haired and with an oddly cultivated moustache, also white, against a pink face making his complexion look like an ice-cream concoction. He rocked from side to side as he walked, as if his legs were automatic, operated by motors. He reminded Reimann of one of the constantly chuckling dwarf figures accompanying the Christmas parades along West Berlin's K-damm. He was smoking an American cigarette, a Camel.

'Time for us to meet,' announced Nikolai Turev. 'I am to be your Control.'

Reimann thought the other man seemed vaguely unhappy at not having been in the room ahead of him. Closer, he was conscious of the smell of stale cigarette smoke.

'Sit,' ordered Turev, doing so himself.

Behind the imposing desk the man looked even more like a Christmas dwarf. Reimann sought something to say but then decided

48

against speaking at all. This man was his Control, a Russian and very much his superior. So he had to defer, constantly letting the man lead.

'You have done well, in training,' declared Turev. 'You have been selected for a particular and vitally important assignment.'

'Where?'

'Bonn.'

'Who?'

'Her name is Elke Meyer. She is the personal assistant to Günther Werle, the Permanent Secretary to the West German Cabinet. Get her and you get the key to every secret that passes through every ministry and every Cabinet meeting.'

Reimann felt a physical lurch, in his stomach, almost making him breathless. A considerable period of his training had obviously been devoted to political awareness, concentrating upon the momentous changes of the preceding year in Eastern and Southern Europe. An insistence at those lecturers had been that Bonn and West Germany were the fulcrum upon which all future developments in Europe were balanced. To gain the access indicated by the Russian would provide unbelievable intelligence! If he succeeded, he would achieve an incredible coup. The correction was quick in coming. There could be no question, no if. *When* he succeeded he would achieve an incredible coup. Cautiously, Reimann said: 'It's over a year since all the changes occurred, throughout the Bloc.'

Turev lighted another cigarette from the preceding stub, head slightly bent in his curiosity at the point the other man intended to make. 'Yes?'

'Why hasn't she been targeted before, if she's vulnerable?'

Turev smiled, pleased at the question. 'She has been,' he admitted. 'We flew two ravens past her: both under cover of trade delegations, on official visits. She's so closed-off she didn't appear aware of the attempts. But they weren't specially chosen, as you've been.'

'How?'

'Wait,' ordered Turev. He reached to his left beneath the desk for the controls to operate the set-up projector, then bent to his right, to trigger some other unseen mechanism: at once, to the faintest whirr of machinery, the heavy drapes behind the man closed on electrical runners to put the room in darkness. The projector lights popped on, providing the minimum of illumination.

Reimann was anticipating a video movie, but initially it wasn't. 'Elke Meyer!' Turev introduced the first of the still pictures on to the screen.

Illogically Reimann had secretly imagined the woman to be seduced

49

would be ugly or old or maybe actually suffer some physical disability or deformity. Elke Meyer didn't display any of those disadvantages. The first portrait showed a pleasantly featured woman (soft skinned, he guessed, so she'd have to be careful of burning in strong summer sun) with medium-length, well coiffured blonde hair. She had been half turned when the hidden camera caught her, showing the smallest of bumps on the bridge of her nose, which accentuated rather than detracted from her strongly featured face. The mole just visible above the left eye didn't detract, either. The formal suit was severe and figure-concealing but there definitely *was* a figure. Full busted, in fact, which was fortunate because Reimann liked big tits. The projector clicked, to a fuller-length photograph this time. Reasonable legs, too, judged Reimann before the other man took up the commentary.

'. . . she's thirty-eight years old, a spinster. She has a child, though. Name's Ursula. The girl is autistic: lives in a special institution close to Marienfels . . .'

The photograph now showed Elke walking with difficulty through the flower market with Poppi in her arms.

'. . . Who's the father of the child?' Reimann interrupted. 'How did it happen?'

'We're not complete on that,' Turev concealed. With continuing but necessary honesty, the Russian went on: 'We're speculating here. And this is why you've been selected. It happened long before she obtained the position she now holds, before she became a target. The birth certificate doesn't list any father's name. The date of Ursula's birth is 10 June 1976, which would make Elke Meyer twenty-four . . .' The projector button clicked rapidly, jumping two more shots of Elke by herself, in separate Bonn streets but most likely taken on the same day, because she was wearing the same dress and jacket. The image stopped at a grainy, faded photograph of a much younger Elke with a man of matching age. They were laughing with their arms around each other's shoulders: Elke wore a party hat, which didn't suit her.

Turev smiled at the expression on Reimann's face. 'Well?' he asked.

'A reasonable likeness,' Reimann conceded.

'It's a very good likeness,' insisted the Russian. 'We did a computer prediction of how he might have aged, then ran physiognomy profiles, through computers again, on twenty possible candidates. You emerged the most likely.'

Reimann shook his head, doubtfully. 'I don't see the logic. Why should she be attracted towards someone who looks like the man who made her pregnant and presumably dumped her! She'd hate him, surely?'

'*Him*,' accepted Turev. 'Not necessarily someone who looks *like* him. The psychological reasoning is that it might just open a chink in the armour.'

'*Might*,' isolated Reimann. 'I still don't think it's valid.' It might offer him an escape, he concluded. If he was ignored, just as the other attempts had failed, he had a ready-made excuse.

'I concede the weakness,' said Turev. 'So do others involved. Your orders are to make the attempt: there's no question of it being argued against.'

'I'd like the objection registered.'

'It will be,' promised Turev. Briskly he went back to the projection, pumping the move-on button to show two more similar shots. 'We got these from a Bonn photographer. It was a New Year's party . . . the new year of 1975 . . .' The button clicked again. 'And these came from the wedding of Elke Meyer's sister, whose name is Ida . . .' The screen was initially filled with a photograph Reimann could not properly understand, until he realized it was a greatly enlarged frame taken from a massed wedding shot. Elke was shown, self-conscious in a full-skirted bridesmaid's dress, with a floral headdress matching her small bouquet. At her shoulder once more was the man in the New Year's Eve pictures. '. . . And here and here and here again . . .' recited Turev, moving through the assembly. The Russian coughed, thick-throated, then resumed: 'The records of the photographer at the New Year's party show the photographs were paid for by someone named Dietlef Becker. The cameraman at the wedding took a note of the names, left to right, as they do for these sort of functions. The person shown next to Elke . . .' The button was pressed again, to bring up another picture, the clearest yet of the man. '. . . is identified as Dietlef Becker . . .' Turev smiled, a conjuror producing his best trick. 'Close enough to be your double!'

'Any trace?'

Turev shook his head. 'Certainly there's no one of that name anywhere around now, which might have been expected if he were a family friend. We don't have anything to suggest that he's Ursula's father, either . . .'

'Why's the kid in a home?'

'We haven't been able to discover the stated reason, in Ursula's case,' further admitted Turev. 'Our doctors say autistic children sometimes become unmanageable, as they grow up. We can only surmise that's the reason: you'll have to find that out for yourself.'

51

'Is there much contact?'

'Very regular,' said the Russian, at once. The projector clicked on again: Elke was shown on the approach road to the institution, in a layby beside a car, and the immediate following frame showed her with a tall, well built girl, in what was clearly the institution grounds. They were walking hand in hand. Around them were other groups of people and patients but they were indistinct because the long-range lens had been concentrated upon Elke. 'She visits every Sunday,' Turev continued.

'An illegitimate child could be a pressure point,' said Reimann.

'Agreed,' said Turev at once. 'Definitely something to consider. It's given us a very positive character indicator already.'

'What?' demanded Reimann.

'The regularity of the visits,' said Turev. 'Every Sunday, always at the same time. Always sets out early . . .' The photograph of Elke at the layby, near her car, flashed on the screen again. 'Always has to stop here, because she arrives ahead of time. She's a woman of strict habit, everything according to a routine.'

'That's good,' said Reimann, more to himself than to his Control, thinking back to one of the many psychological lectures. 'There are several ways to manipulate people who need routine. What about Werle?'

Turev smiled, and Reimann thought Christmas dwarfs shouldn't have nicotine-browned teeth. The Russian clicked rapidly through the slides, throwing up the image of the Cabinet Secretary, and said dramatically: 'The goldmine! Nothing has happened in the West German government in the last two decades – but most importantly in the last immediate year – that this man doesn't know about: he has every secret there is. To get him will be to get everything!'

Reimann studied the photograph of the neat, clerk-like man and said, in anticipation: 'So our profile upon him is extensive?'

Turev nodded: 'Forty-five years old. Professional civil servant. Promoted at an incredibly young age, which shows his ability. Wife's name is Sybille. She appears to have made ill-health a hobby after the birth of their son, Frederick . . .'

'. . . Men with difficult wives . . . wives feigning illness . . . often look elsewhere,' cut in Reimann.

'Our first hope!' said Turev. 'We actually expected it. But not this one. Pampers the woman, dotes on the boy, never strays. He plays chess and listens to classical music. We've infiltrated women into his chess club: tried to put them alongside at concerts. There's absolutely no response. Just as there was no response from Elke Meyer to what we've tried before.'

'Could Werle be homosexual?' suggested Reimann.

'An obvious thought,' agreed Turev. 'We've tried that, too. Again, no response.'

'You're sure there's nothing with Elke? She'd be the person closest to him, apart from his wife.'

'Elke Meyer has been under surveillance for just over six months,' disclosed Turev, patiently. 'If there were an affair we would have detected it by now: have compromising photographs, hotel registrations or maybe apartment rentals. Nothing!'

'They don't appear to be very exciting people,' said Reimann, in an aside.

'No one has made a noise in Bonn since Beethoven,' sneered Turev.

'What else about Elke Meyer?'

'Both parents are dead,' said Turev. 'Father was a schoolmaster, excused service in the early days of the war, but conscripted into the Wehrmacht in time to be drafted to the Russian front by 1942. Went through most of the siege of Stalingrad. Was frostbitten – lost two toes – and his medical records refer several times to disturbance caused by shell-shock. He wasn't able to resume teaching, after the war. Lived on a pension and some money his wife inherited and managed to keep intact. He died in 1955, the year after Elke was born . . .' The Russian moved through his projector cassette, seeking a new slide. On to the screen came another enlargement from Ida's wedding, of a stout, feather-hatted woman. '. . . The mother,' Turev identified. 'She died in 1977. Details of the will are on file, of course: the inheritance was divided equally between the two daughters, about 45,000 Deutschmarks each.'

'What about the father?' persisted Reimann, determined to learn everything. 'Was he a member of the Nazi party?'

'No. We searched the archives.'

'What about Elke, now?'

'No details of any political allegiance. We've checked every political party membership list.'

'What's known about the sister, Ida?'

'The married name is Kissel . . .' The Russian gestured towards the screen, which still held the wedding picture of the mother. 'That was in March 1976. Husband is personnel manager for Federal communications. There are two children, a boy and a girl. They live in Bad Godesberg. The precise street address is Stümpchesweg.'

'Does she work?'

Turev shook his head. 'Before her marriage Ida was a beautician. No record of her having worked since 1976. They're very close. Elke goes to Bad Godesberg most weekends. There are lunches, nearly every week. It would seem the sister is Elke's only friend.'

'What hobbies does Elke have?'

'None that we've discovered. She has an account at a bookshop near the cathedral. Reads a lot of review-recommended stuff. Classics, too: Goethe, obviously. Grass, Böll, Krolow. Some of the choices are in the original English, so she obviously reads and speaks that language too.'

'What about money?'

'The gross income is a hundred and five thousand Deutschmarks a year. She pays eight hundred a month for her apartment. She has a car, a two-year-old Volkswagen she cherishes. We can't find any hire purchase details, so we're assuming she bought it outright.'

'Credit cards?'

'We've accessed every company. None.'

Reimann nodded towards the screen, although it did not hold a picture of Elke Meyer. 'She seemed to dress reasonably well?'

'She does,' agreed Turev. 'The surveillance reports are that she is always immaculate but that her wardrobe does not appear excessive.'

'What about payments to the home, for the child?'

'It's greatly subsidized, through her government health insurance: her contribution is eight thousand marks.'

'Have we accessed her bank records?'

Turev shook his head. 'We've tried but we haven't penetrated the computer yet: we're still trying, of course. But there's not the slightest indication of any financial pressures.'

'There shouldn't be, on those figures,' said Reimann. 'Holidays?'

'She took three weeks' leave, during the time we've been watching her. She didn't leave Bonn.'

'Any religion?'

Another cigarette went into the holder. 'A greatly lapsed Catholic, it seems: hardly any church attendance. Once, in fact, since we've had her under surveillance.'

'Habits?'

'On Saturday mornings she goes into Bonn: looks at certain shops, takes coffee in a particular café. Then Bad Godesberg to the sister.'

'The lonely, vulnerable spinster,' mused Reimann. It would be easy. 'When you start work we'll naturally withdraw the surveillance teams,' Turev promised. 'But we'll continue trying to break into the bank computer.'

'I'd like to know more about Dietlef Becker, too.'

'That will also continue,' Turev undertook.

The two men remained looking at each other for several moments, each appearing to expect the other to speak. Feeling it was required of him, Reimann said: 'There is a complete dossier? All the files and reports and photographs?'

Turev nodded. 'It must be memorized completely, here in Moscow. It would be dangerous to consider taking it to Bonn.'

'What is my cover to be?'

'A journalist,' Turev disclosed. 'I would have welcomed something else because it's too well used as an intelligence cover. But it will enable you to make trips out of Bonn if they're required. It also creates an overseas source of income we can adjust always to your needs beyond the immediate scrutiny of the West German revenue authorities.'

'So I am supposed to be working for foreign publications?'

'A group of Australian magazines,' confirmed Turev. 'All are bona fide publications, with our ownership utterly undetectable.'

'Will I have to actually write the articles?'

'Naturally you will have to go through the journalistic accreditation procedures: become part of the press corps. But during contact meetings you'll receive guidance and a prepared format of what you are expected to write.'

'There'll be checks by the West German authorities when I apply for government accreditation,' Reimann pointed out.

'Your legend is established from the United States,' Turev explained. 'You are the only son of Ludwig and Lottie Reimann, who moved to Milwaukee in 1948, the year you were born. That establishes your proper age, at forty-two. There really was a Reimann family who did emigrate. Both the parents are now dead and buried just outside the city, in a place named West Allis.'

'What about Otto Reimann?'

'Dropped out after high school,' said Turev. 'One of the first Flower Power disciples before the Sixties really began. We've traced him to San Francisco, then South America, Bolivia and Peru: where the drugs were, Otto Reimann was. In 1977 he was in Nepal: he died there, a year later.'

'Officially recorded?'

'Not any more,' assured Turev. 'Everything has been removed. There's not the remotest possibility of your ever being exposed. There was no other family, other than the dead parents.'

55

'I'm slightly concerned with the journalistic role,' said Reimann. 'Elke Meyer will have been warned against any such association, because of the sensitivity of her job.'

'That's another valid objection,' the Russian accepted, admiringly. 'As I've already said, I would have preferred something else. But *as* a journalist she'll understand if you want to discuss policy and developments with her. Any other supposed occupation might make her even more suspicious.'

'How am I to know you?' asked Reimann, briskly, trying to recover.

'As Alexandr.'

From the tradecraft that had been deeply instilled within him Reimann knew he could expect no more. 'How will we meet?'

'Two routes,' replied Turev. There was a pause. 'The first – the way you will use for most of the time – will be through your wife.'

'Jutta!' Reimann hadn't imagined such direct involvement: wasn't sure he wanted it.

'This isn't a quick sexual blackmail,' reminded the Russian. 'We want a long-term, ongoing situation. It wouldn't be acceptable for you to visit Jutta only occasionally, would it? So she has to be part of it.'

That was virtually how Reimann had imagined his marriage continuing, although making the visits regularly, not occasionally. He hadn't thought beyond the briefing to consider any association with Elke Meyer being long-term, either. 'So Jutta is to be in Bonn as well?'

'Living separately, of course. Accommodation is already being arranged, for both of you.'

'You said two routes?' prompted Reimann.

'The second will be separate from Jutta: just the two of us. You will receive a postcard, quite normally through the mail. Always from Europe. There will be a date on the card. The message will say "Looking forward to meeting you again." Four days from the date on the card fly to Berlin and come to the East . . .' The Russian paused, sliding a card across the desk between them. '. . . to this address in Johannisstrasse. It's a safe house, just for this operation. I shall always be there, waiting.'

'Why the secondary route, cutting out Jutta?'

'A sensible, professional precaution,' insisted Turev, smoothly. 'Your wife must not know of it, of course.'

Reimann would have liked more time to consider everything that was being outlined to him. Hopefully he said: 'It's hardly a cell, just Jutta and myself. So who's the cell leader?'

'I am,' said Turev. 'But it would be best if Jutta does not consider her

56

past position diminished. She must always believe she is the sole link; the person upon whom you rely and upon whom we rely.'

'I appreciate the arrangement, to keep us together, but wouldn't it be less complicated if I dealt directly with you all the time? And made more than occasional visits to Jutta?'

'Her function in West Berlin is over, after all the changes of the past year. This is the way the new operation is to work,' said Turev, clearly giving an order. Which it was, to avoid any direct, incriminating link with Russia if either Reimann or his wife were identified by West German counter-intelligence.

So they wanted the working arrangement to continue – as it had in the past – with Jutta in control. There was no uncertainty now: he hadn't wanted that, not at all.

'What if a reason arises for me to reach you, without wanting to go through Jutta?'

There were several moments of complete silence before Turev said: 'That *is* an oversight.' The admission irritated him. 'By the time of our first separately arranged meeting in Berlin I will have devised your contact method.'

Reimann felt confident enough to make open demands now. He said: 'The apartment that Jutta and I were allowed, on Neglinnaya Ulitza? It's a swallows' nest, isn't it?'

There was further silence from Turev. Finally he said: 'Yes.'

'So you saw everything? Heard everything?'

'Yes. Does that disturb you?'

'Not particularly,' said Reimann. 'Has Jutta been instructed about coming to Bonn?'

'She's arriving here tomorrow. There'll be the chance for you to be together for two or three days, before you both return to Germany. You have to memorize everything about Elke Meyer. And there will have to be a briefing on your journalistic role . . .' The Russian hesitated, then said: 'Would you like different accommodation from Neglinnaya Ulitza this time?'

'Don't bother,' said Reimann, dismissively.

The room Turev and Reimann occupied at Arbat was also equipped with video and sound recording equipment, and Turev reviewed the results with Yuri Panin directly after Reimann left.

'I thought he was very astute,' said Turev. 'Every point he made was valid.'

Panin nodded. 'I'd say he actually enjoyed performing for you: showing how good he was.'

The chain-smoking man looked curiously at the psychologist. 'Is there something wrong?'

Panin did not reply directly. Instead he said: 'I think Otto Reimann is a much better intelligence officer than he is a husband.'

'Which makes him perfect for the job.'

'I hope you're right,' said Panin.

This time Reimann didn't wait for her recognition when Jutta arrived at Vnukovo. Their greeting was as perfunctory as before. In the car, on their way into Moscow, Reimann said: 'You are to be involved.'

'Of course,' said Jutta. 'You didn't expect any different working arrangement, did you?'

'Not really,' lied Reimann.

Chapter Seven

Nothing went right, from the beginning. Elke left Kaufmannstrasse earlier than normal, anticipating delay at Bad Godesberg, but Ida took longer to get out of the house than she'd allowed for so they were late getting back on the road to Marienfels. Elke had to drive fast, which she didn't like, not even on the autobahns. She rarely exceeded eighty kilometres an hour. Now she had to, and the speed added to her vexation. Ida was unaware of any distress. There were several vehicles already in the car-park and Elke was unable to get her protective space.

Dr Schiller was on duty at his post, in front of the reception desk. Today the flowers were orange tiger lilies. The principal gave his yellow-toothed welcome and agreed he remembered Ida from previous visits, although Elke was not sure that he did. Ursula was unchanged, the doctor reported. She'd had a quiet week. She seemed content.

The child's room appeared crowded with an extra person in it. The two women actually bumped into each other going through the door and got in each other's way trying to sit. Elke felt claustrophobic. There was a tape playing. She didn't recognize the music: violins were much featured. Ursula sat watching their settling-in difficulty. But for its vacancy, the faint smile could have been amusement at their clumsiness. Elke kissed the unresponsive girl and said: 'Aunty Ida's come to see you, Ursula.'

Ursula began to rock back and forth, very gently, but her head moved more strongly, like a nod of greeting.

'Hello Ursula. Hello darling,' said Ida and leaned forward to kiss the child as well.

Elke thought there had been a slight hesitation in the gesture, a reluctance, from her sister but she wasn't sure.

'Poppi's come too.' Elke put the dog on the floor. He briefly remained there, oddly crouched, before going to a corner by the door where he settled down looking in their direction. The corner was the furthest possible from Ursula.

Elke urged her sister to talk about her own children, and Ida did but with visible self-consciousness. She'd bought the toy with Elke's guidance, a long, sloth-like creature made in artificial fur but with no buttons or eyes that could be picked off and swallowed. Ida offered it, insisting it was a present from Doris. After several long moments with Ursula making no attempt to take it Ida placed it in front of the child, on the bed.

'She'll play with it later,' promised Elke and wondered why: it had sounded like an apology and she didn't have to apologize.

Hesitantly, nervous of resistance, Elke coaxed Ursula to stand, which she did quite willingly. Just as willingly she allowed a new cardigan to be tried on. It was red – the colour Elke had wanted her hair-slides to be weeks ago – with a pattern of white flowers etched on the bodice. Ursula actually appeared to examine it, taking the wool between her fingers. 'Pretty,' she said, in her gruff voice.

'Do you like it, darling?' said Elke, hopefully.

'Pretty,' repeated the child.

Elke was pleased that the cardigan fitted so well: she'd guessed the size, without trying to measure. There was a new skirt, too, but Elke decided against attempting to have the girl put that on. Ursula might resist. And it would mean her being briefly unclothed in front of the other woman. Elke accepted at once that she was being absurd: Ursula could have no concept of immodesty. It was all part of according her as much dignity as possible.

Elke felt restricted, in front of another person, unable to talk to the girl as she usually did. Ida tried to contribute, forcing aimless chatter about Georg and Doris, in the unfulfilled hope of some point of contact. For most of the time Ursula sat fingering her new cardigan.

Chancing that Ursula would remain placid, which fortunately she did, Elke encouraged her daughter up again, to walk in the grounds. The women paced either side, each with an arm through Ursula's. Poppi, freed, scuttled and darted ahead of them but never far away.

'Is this how it is, every Sunday?' asked Ida.

'Mostly.'

'Doesn't she ever speak? Properly recognize you?'

Elke wished her sister wouldn't talk over Ursula, as if she didn't exist. 'Not really. Sometimes.'

'That's a contradiction. And it doesn't make sense.'

'Not really,' conceded Elke again.

'You were right, about how big she's got. Much bigger than Doris.'

It was as if Ursula were an object, not a person. Elke said: 'Dr Schiller says she's very healthy, physically.'

They stopped very close to the perimeter fence at a small coppice of recently planted firs, grass-tufted at their roots, and turned back towards the faraway house.

'What happens now?' asked Ida.

'There's lunch,' said Elke. 'Don't you remember?'

The weather was good enough for the meal to be served in the conservatory and they managed to get an individual table, shared with no one else. The catering included families as well as inmates. Ida said she was not hungry. Elke wasn't, either. Ursula ate ravenously and badly: it was pork, with a sauce, which was messy. Elke sat close to the child, napkin in hand, thinking how much better her daughter had behaved at table when they'd lived together at Kaufmannstrasse. It was her first and only criticism against the home. It hadn't seemed to register on any previous weekend. The new cardigan became stained, on one sleeve and on the bodice, where the white flowers were patterned.

Before they left Elke told Dr Schiller about the untried skirt in Ursula's room and the man promised to let her know before the next visit if it fitted or would need changing. Elke had intended discussing the possibility of Ursula making a home visit but changed her mind. The opportunity would still be here, next Sunday.

Neither attempted any conversation during the descent to the major highway. Elke wondered whether her sister was seeking a neutral subject, something for which she was looking.

It was Ida who eventually spoke, sneeringly. 'Horst is writing a book.'

'A book!' In her astonishment Elke risked looking across the car, which she never did.

'It's going to be an international bestseller and we're all going to live in luxury, happy ever after,' declared Ida, still sneering.

'What about?'

'God knows,' said Ida. 'I'm sure as hell Horst doesn't.'

'But I don't understand . . .' started Elke.

'The bank won't extend his loan. We're broke.'

'But a book! . . . Horst!'

'Of course it's bullshit,' agreed her sister. 'He's bought a lot of pads and some pencils and put a table in the bedroom, where he says he's going to work. The kids are forbidden to go near it. I am, too. The children are laughing at him. That's never happened before. I wish it wasn't happening now.'

'I'm sorry, Ida. Very sorry.'

The woman shrugged as if it were unimportant, the theatricality of the gesture betraying the opposite. 'I don't want to go straight home. Let's drink coffee. Or something.'

Elke drove to the Reduttchen and chanced parking on a convenient meter. Because of the weather they took a table outside in the garden instead of going into the raftered stabling from which the café had been created.

'How much do you need?'

'I don't know, not fully,' said Ida. Deep in depression, she didn't understand the point of the question.

'I can lend you money,' Elke offered simply.

Ida blinked at her sister, fully attentive for the first time. She smiled, faintly, and said: 'I knew you'd offer. But no.'

'Why not?'

'Because there wouldn't be a chance of your ever being paid back,' announced Ida, practically. 'Because I wouldn't know how much to ask for, even if I did accept. And because it would make it all too easy yet again for Horst Kissel, for whom there's always a way out as long as he can get just one piece of luck.'

'You've got to do something!'

'Why have I?' Ida retorted, harshly. 'Let Horst do something, for a change. Instead of always fucking up.'

When the waiter arrived Ida announced, without being asked, that she would accept Elke's hospitality and ordered Armagnac. Elke chose coffee.

'Have you talked to him about it?'

'About the bills and the demands that I know of, of course I have. He says he's handling it; that it's going to be all right.'

'What about mother's money?'

Ida snorted a laugh, another bitter sound. 'In the full flush of blind love I transferred it all over to a joint account! What a mistake that was! You know I can't conceive now that I ever admired that man: believed he was an important person with an important job.'

'What's he done with it? The money?'

'In a previous dream world our budding bestselling author was going to become the guru of the stock market: the damned fool actually spent a week in Frankfurt once, studying the market . . .' Ida shook her head. 'He came back claiming he had inside sources so good he couldn't fail! Can you believe that?'

'Did you?'

'Hoped,' said Ida. 'I hoped. Wasn't that stupid?'

Of course concern – genuine, deep worry – was Elke's immediate feeling but almost as quickly came another, of disappointment. 'It makes some things easier to understand, though.'

'Like what?' frowned Ida.

'Why hands under dinner tables aren't offensive.'

Ida shook her head, and Elke wondered if her sister was going to make any further disclosure. Instead Ida bent over her glass and said: 'Christ, what a mess! What a bloody awful mess!' She looked up, damp-eyed and imploring, and Elke was shocked at the despair on the other woman's face.

Remembering her own self-image gazing back at her from the lonely bedroom mirror Elke knew she had looked like that, once. Worse. Hollow-eyed, pale-cheeked, asking why me, why me, why me and beseeching a miracle. Not a miracle! she corrected at once. A miracle was a wondrous event, beyond proper human comprehension, an act of God. That wasn't what she had prayed and begged for, seeking forgiveness and understanding at the same time as asking for escape – nothing more than the normal working of her body – when the calendar date passed and then stayed there, day after day and week after week, mocking her until it came around again the next month still with nothing happening. Quickly there was a further correction. She hadn't been alone, not really. Not after those first few numbed days, those numbed why-me days when she couldn't believe she could be pregnant.

Ida had been the first person she told, long before the most agonizing confession she'd ever made in her life. It had been Ida she clung to, sobbing the words, Ida who couldn't believe it either, not at once, saying there had to be some simple upset, an imbalance, and that it sometimes happened – it had happened to her – and it was going to be all right. And when it wasn't all right it had been Ida who said she knew people because of the job she did and offered the pills, shaking her and shouting at her when she was unable to take them, saying it was wrong. Just as she shouted and said things like damn the Church when, anguished and distraught though she felt, she refused, appalled, to go to the doctor Ida recommended in Cologne as discreet and safe and hygienic. Which was only the beginning. It had been Ida who confronted Dietlef on her behalf, saying there wasn't much time: Ida who made him come to her and promise that of course he would do what he had to, do what was honourable. And Ida to whom she clung again when he didn't come back the following night or the night after that. So many tears: so many times with their arms around each other. Telling their mother. Briefly – happily despite everything when Ursula had been born – with joy. And then in agony again at the cold, clinical medical diagnosis. *Autism is a permanent abnormality . . . loss of contact with reality . . . affects speech and social contact . . . deterioration . . . irreversible . . . no treatment . . .*

'Why a mess?' demanded Elke. 'It's not the end of the world.' Not as what happened to her had seemed at the time to be the end of the world: sometimes, when she couldn't halt the self-pity, still did.

'It just is.' Ida lifted her empty brandy glass to the passing waitress. 'I don't want to lose the house, wreck though it is. I don't want to have to change the kids' school.'

There was more, guessed Elke. 'You've seen him, haven't you? It's gone beyond telephone calls.'

'Maybe.'

'What good is it going to do?'

'I don't know,' said Ida, listlessly. 'It's an escape, for a while.'

The conversation was already disturbing Elke on several levels and suddenly she isolated another. She'd never known Ida helpless before, not like this. Ida had always been the dominant one: Ida the leader, Elke the follower. It was the way it had always been, the way Elke felt comfortable. Safe. She didn't want it to change.

'You'll have to take the money.'

'What about getting it back?'

'I don't care about getting it back.' She didn't, Elke told herself. Just as long as she had some left. She'd always been frightened of not having any money to rely upon: she saved four hundred marks a month, sometimes more.

'Thank you.' Ida spoke with the returned brandy glass to her lips, as if she wanted something to hide behind.

'Wouldn't you do the same for me?' Elke insisted. '*Haven't* you done the same for me, in other ways?' Had Ida sensed, as she had, the reversal of roles, surrendering her customary dominance by disclosing the financial crisis? With further prescience, Elke said: 'You're comparing, aren't you? Comparing Horst with . . .' She waved her hand as if she were trying to grasp the name out of the air.

'Kurt,' supplied Ida. 'Kurt Vogel. I suppose so.'

'So it's no longer fun? No longer just an adventure?'

Ida gave another shrug, without answering.

'Have you been to bed with him?'

'No.'

'Are you going to?'

'I don't know.'

'Do you love him?'

There was another snorted laugh. 'How do I know?'

'This is the real mess, isn't it? Not being broke or losing the house or the upheaval of having to change the children's school?'

Ida smiled across the table at her, a shy expression. 'Wise little sister!' she said.

'Hardly,' said Elke. 'And if this is the way you feel then I agree, it *is* a mess.' There was an unexpected surge of emotion that Elke could not recognize, a feeling she couldn't identify. Just as quickly a thought came into her mind – *not one man but two* – but that had no meaning, either, apart from jealousy, and how could there be that?

Ida straightened, a positive action. 'It's been good to talk,' she said.

'What about the problem we *can* solve?' pressed Elke. 'How are you going to bring it into the open, with Horst?'

'*Make* him discuss it,' said Ida, with further determination. 'Refuse to let it go when he says everything is under control and that he'll handle it.'

It sounded as if Ida was reciting resolutions already made: as if she'd expected Elke to make the offer and decided to accept it, after an initial refusal. Elke felt confused, uncomfortably distanced from her sister, from whom she'd never before had that impression. Had Ida come with her today because she'd genuinely wanted to see Ursula? Or to manoeuvre this encounter? Elke hurried the doubt away, disgusted with herself.

'Let's get it settled as quickly as possible. Get one worry out of the way at least.'

'I'll see that he pays you back. All of it. I promise.'

'Let's not worry about that, not now.'

Ida was silent for several moments, looking down at the table. Then, with the honesty there always was between them, she said: 'It was difficult today, darling, wasn't it?'

'I don't . . .' started Elke before understanding. Showing the same truthfulness she said: 'I don't know why it was like it was.'

'Why do you go every week?' asked Ida, brutally. 'Ursula's not aware of it: it doesn't mean anything to her.'

'It's my . . .' Elke stumbled to a halt again. '. . . what I want to do.'

'Duty? Or guilt?'

'Guilt! That's preposterous!'

'Exactly!' seized Ida. 'How Ursula is . . . how she was born . . . is nobody's fault. It's . . .' There was a splayed arm waving. '. . . I don't know! Genetic fault. An accident of nature. Whatever. But there was nothing you could have done about it. No mistake you made except going to bed with the bastard in the first place, but that's not what we're talking about. So you don't have to feel guilty: exact a penance from yourself, every week.'

Oddly – incredibly – Elke was reassured by the lecture, hurtful though it was. This was how it should be – how she wanted it to be – with Ida back in control. A leader, to be followed. Elke said: 'I don't go because of any guilt. I go because I want to.'

'She's not going to get better, darling,' said Ida, even more brutally. 'She was worse today than I can ever remember.'

'It was a bad day,' said Elke, desperately, the lie like glue in her throat. If Ida hadn't made the visit with her Elke knew she would have thought of today as a good one. Ursula had been placid, unresisting, even aware of her new clothes. Elke wished the cardigan had not been so quickly stained at the lunch table.

'Isn't every visit a bad day?'

'Why are you doing this? Saying this?'

'I'm trying to be kind.'

'It's none . . .' blurted Elke, another false start. 'It's what I want to do.'

Ida reached across the table, squeezing the other woman's hand. 'You know something? I've lost count of the number of times I imagined how much I would have liked to castrate with a very blunt, very rusty knife the bastard who made you pregnant. Haven't you?'

No, thought Elke. She said: 'He just couldn't face it.'

'So he ran away, leaving you to face everything!'

Elke's entry in her diary that night read: *A bad day.*

Reimann was discomfited by the thought of being ill-prepared. He studied the dossiers and the files and clicked his way through the freeze frames and watched the video films – always at Arbat Ulitza, never allowed to remove them to the apartment on Neglinnaya – but Elke Meyer never became a person to him. He was aware of everything about her: how she looked and how she dressed and how she conducted her contained and insular life. He knew, from afar, the few people she knew. Yet she remained as lifeless as the frozen pictures on the projector screen. Because his information *was* frozen. Even the video films did not properly show how her face developed an expression. How she actually walked: held herself. What little signs – body language, the instructors had called it – hinted a feeling or an attitude. The looks and emotions that came into her eyes. He didn't *know* her: not properly know her. But maybe he shouldn't, he reflected, following the objectivity that had also been instilled in training. For whatever mainipulation was necessary, shouldn't he have to learn about her himself, by being with her? Just as he would if he were a normal, ordinary person and their encounter was going to a meeting of normal, ordinary people?

Reimann's general feeling of dissatisfaction was furthered by the unreality of their existence at Neglinnaya and his awareness that they were literally under a microscope. It had been instinctive bravado not to ask for a different, unmonitored apartment: fleetingly he wished now that he had, until he realized that anywhere else they might have been allocated would have been eavesdropped just as extensively.

He was surprised, too, at how Jutta was treated. They had both expected her to be briefed immediately after her arrival in Moscow, but she wasn't. Each day a driver took Reimann to study the Elke Meyer file at Arbat Ulitza, but there were never any instructions for Jutta. And there was no opportunity to question the Control known as Alexandr. After the first extensive interview the white-haired Russian did not appear again. On his following visits Reimann was greeted by a series of hurrying, unsmiling escort clerks who took him to and from the tobacco-stinking viewing room and the dossier tables and responded at once to every buzzer request for more files.

'This has no point,' Jutta protested.

'I would not have been briefed if there had been any change in the planning,' insisted Reimann, professionally. He had said nothing to identify Elke Meyer to his wife and she had not asked. Aware of the microphones and cameras, he would not have told her anything, if she had questioned him about the target.

'Why haven't I been instructed, then?'

Jutta had always reacted with outraged indignation to imagined slights. 'There must be some reason.'

There was, of course.

On the third day of monitoring both the sound and film recordings at Neglinnaya, the psychologist said: 'They've both been extremely professional: she hasn't asked him anything about the mission and he hasn't volunteered anything.'

'He knows the apartment is wired: you told me to admit it if he asked,' Turev reminded.

Panin nodded. '*He* knows. But she seems altogether too confident of herself: there's not the slightest indication of her having any suspicion that we might be monitoring them. I'm glad we staged this test. It's helped a lot to confirm what I'm thinking about their relationship.'

'Time to see her?' Turev suggested.

'Most definitely,' Panin agreed.

67

Chapter Eight

The exclusive and guarded country dachas of the Soviet government elite are dotted discreetly among the hills that surround Moscow. The one to which Jutta was finally taken was actually at the beginning of the ascent, a sort of halfway house between privilege and practicality. It had its own woodland, however, which gave it seclusion. It was a rather stark, square building, with a shingle roof and rough timbered walls. As they approached, Jutta couldn't decide whether it was a completely new structure built to appear traditional or a genuine old cottage that had been renovated. There was another car already parked outside. The driver was leaning against the nearside wing, smoking the cheapest sort of cigarette available in the Soviet Union, the type where only half the tube contains tobacco, leaving the other part like a hollow filter. He watched with smirking interest when a woman got out of the car.

Jutta had prepared herself carefully. The fine check suit was severely cut but also accentuated her full-busted, slim-hipped figure. Her pale brown hair was strained back into its usual style, which she kept because she knew it was fitting for her height, just short of six feet. There was no embarrassment at the chauffeur's interest. Jutta remained by her car, staring back until the man looked away.

Turev, at the door of the dacha, was aware of the exchange. The Russian stood with odd formality, his body stiff, all three buttons of his suit fastened around his bulging body, as if he wanted to look immaculate for an official photograph. 'Welcome, welcome,' he said, gesturing the woman inside.

Jutta entered unhurried and unsmiling. The main room was simply but functionally furnished, with a central table, a couch beneath the main window and two easy chairs, either side of a dead fire. On top of a small sideboard close to the table were bottles – vodka and brandy and wine – and Thermos servers of tea and coffee.

'Sit. Be comfortable,' urged Turev. 'I thought it would be better for us to meet informally like this. We have to become friends.' She had the palest blue eyes he had ever seen.

Jutta decided the white-haired Russian was uneasy as a social host. His discomfort pleased her. 'This has taken a long time.'

'There is much for us to discuss,' said Turev, not responding to the obvious complaint. The Russian had become dependent upon the American cigarettes he'd chain-smoked during an espionage posting to the United Nations in New York, early in his career. He could remember a lot of aloof women like Jutta, on Wall Street and Madison Avenue. He'd seen them described once as 'business bitches'. He'd always been curious about them. Slightly nervous, too.

'I want to know what my responsibilities are going to be,' Jutta insisted.

'Which is why you have been brought here today,' smiled Turev. 'But first let's make ourselves comfortable.' The Russian insisted on personally serving drinks from the sideboard – vodka for himself, coffee for Jutta – wondering if the effort was necessary. The dacha meeting was upon the guidance of Yuri Panin, to convey the ready inclusion of the woman into a special group for a special operation. Only when they were sitting in the easy chairs, their drinks between them, did Turev outline what that operation was to be. He provided only minimal details about Elke Meyer and did not offer any description, beyond her position in the West German Cabinet Secretariat. Neither did he offer a photograph and Jutta did not ask for one.

'I am to be in charge, as I was before?' she demanded, when Turev finished his explanation. For five years, until early 1990, Jutta Höhn had headed a cell of four East German intelligence officers, one her husband, which had successfully infiltrated a West German rehabilitation charity for East European refugees crossing either legally or illegally into the West. It had enabled the KGB, through the East German Ministry of State Security, to create a vast bureau of detailed files complete with addresses and occupations and possibly useful intelligence access upon thousands of émigrés who remained totally unaware how closely their movements and activities were monitored. As the result of information provided by Jutta's cell over those five years, twenty separate émigré men and women had been suborned either through threats against relatives still in the East or through open blackmail into becoming agents for the KGB or the now disbanded East German intelligence.

'You did brilliantly well in the past,' said Turev, again avoiding a direct response. 'Now the focus has to change. Your part in this new operation is extremely important.'

'Am I still to have field control?' Jutta persisted.

'Yes,' Turev lied. 'But you must realize that the situation now is very different from what it was in West Berlin. The division will not be so

69

easily defined. But you will always be the liaison, between your husband and myself.'

There was an expression that could have been doubt on Jutta's face. 'This has been explained to Otto?'

'In great detail.'

'What did he say about it?'

'Nothing specifically,' Turev replied. 'He seemed to expect it. The system worked very well in the past, didn't it?'

'Yes,' Jutta agreed. She seemed contemplative.

'It is obvious why you must maintain separate apartments,' continued Turev, briskly but with a purpose. 'Do not establish any regular pattern with his visits to you, for him to become familiar to neighbours or tradesmen. And *never* go to his apartment, to become established by anyone who might see you as another woman.' He stopped, waiting curiously.

'That would be an elementary precaution, wouldn't it?'

She had responded as the psychologist predicted. 'This could be a protracted operation,' Turev warned.

'I accept that.'

She appeared willing to accept a great deal, reflected Turev. It made it easier to propose the second reason for her inclusion, beyond the ease of abandonment if either she or Reimann were detected by West German counter-intelligence. He said: 'You have proven yourself to be an extremely dedicated and efficient officer.'

'So?' There was a curious suspicion in the question.

'No one knows Otto better than you.'

'So?' she said again.

'Enormous importance is attached to this operation. Nothing can be allowed to endanger it. So we want you always to watch him carefully.'

'For what?' demanded Jutta.

'Anything,' said Turev. 'If anything occurs to you to be out of character – some change you find unusual – you must tell me . . .' He hesitated. Then he said: 'It will not be spying upon your husband. It will be guarding the success of a vital assignment.'

'Of course,' said Jutta, at once.

The Russian waited for her to say more. When she didn't, he said: 'You'll use a different name, of course. Sneider: Jutta Sneider. Your work will supposedly be that of travelling salesperson of office equipment. All the necessary documentation has been prepared for you, in that name. I will decide the date and place of our first meeting after you have both settled into your separate apartments and

70

established yourselves . . .' The Russian allowed a pause. 'Any questions?'

'No,' said Jutta, at once.

That night, at the Neglinnaya apartment, Jutta said to Reimann: 'Operationally we are to continue as we were in West Berlin. I am to be field supervisor.'

'I know,' said the expectant Reimann.

'Good,' said Jutta. It was how it should be.

Turev returned to the Arbat Ulitza to view what had been recorded on the extensive equipment with which the dacha was equipped.

'She's a formidable woman,' Turev assessed. 'I was surprised by her complete acceptance of what was involved.'

'I'm not sure she is a formidable woman at all,' argued Panin. 'I think there's a shell, concealing a lot of softness.'

'She ran the cell brilliantly in Berlin.'

'Which makes her a good organizer. What else?'

Turev used the lighting of another cigarette to cover his difficulty. 'It's not unusual, for a raven to be married. Or a swallow.'

'It isn't just their being married, is it?' demanded the psychologist, with another infuriating rhetorical question. 'She's not just having to accept her husband seducing another woman: at her level of professionalism that probably wouldn't be a problem. But whether she realizes or not at this moment, she's also being asked to surrender that professional superiority in their relationship as well, isn't she?'

'How important is that?'

Panin pulled down the corners of his mouth, in a doubtful expression. 'There's no way I – or anybody else – can assess that, not at this stage. To people such as I believe Jutta to be – people building a shell of apparent superiority around themselves – positions of dominance are very important. They don't like losing them. Or having them taken away.'

'Are you saying we have a problem, before we begin?'

'I'm saying we have an unknown and unpredictable situation with her.'

Chapter Nine

As Ida entered Elke tried to remember the last time her sister had come to the Kaufmannstrasse apartment but couldn't. Extending the reflection, she realized that Ida wouldn't have been there that evening had she not invited herself: Elke had expected them to meet during the day in a restaurant, as they normally did. Ida appeared to have the same thoughts about the length of time since her last visit. She looked curiously around the flat, as if it were strange to her.

'I wish I could keep my place as tidy as this,' she said.

'There's only me,' Elke reminded. 'Me and Poppi.' She thought Ida looked remarkably chic. The light suit, which she hadn't seen before, was a mix of browns and oranges and reds, and there was a matching shawl which Ida wore with careless elegance across one shoulder. Elke was not sure she liked the tightness of the jacket, which seemed to pronounce the curve of Ida's bust. She said: 'Would you like something?'

'Whisky?'

'I'm sorry,' said Elke. She never kept alcohol in the flat because she never entertained. She felt awkward, unworldly.

'What is there?'

'Coffee. Tea.'

Ida made a face. 'I won't bother. It wasn't too much of a rush for you?' Ida had suggested six o'clock and arrived promptly on time.

'Not at all,' said Elke. It would have been, if the workload had been anything like it had been for most of the past year. As it was, she'd only got back to the flat fifteen minutes before Ida.

'I've got an apology to make,' said Ida.

'What about?' As well as the suit jacket being too tight the skirt rode higher than Elke considered it should when her sister sat as she was now, one leg crossed casually over the other. She supposed, from the clothes of some of the younger girls at the Chancellery, that the cut was fashionable.

'That was quite a maudlin little scene at the Reduttchen.'

'You didn't embarrass me,' said Elke. What would Ida have said if she'd confessed the feeling had been fear, for herself?

'It still wasn't particularly edifying.'

'Have you spoken to Horst?'

'As best as anyone can speak to Horst.' There was the sneer in Ida's voice again. Elke wished it hadn't been there.

'What did he say?'

There was a laugh, still with a sneer. 'Lots of bullshit at first. No difficulties, everything fine, he could manage the family affairs, rubbish like that. But I'd collected some of the bills that came in our joint names: final demands, too. Then he had to cut the crap.'

It was as if her sister was intentionally trying to shock her by speaking as crudely as she did. Elke said: 'It must have been awful.'

Ida frowned. 'As a matter of fact I didn't find it awful at all. I enjoyed it!'

'How could you possibly enjoy it!'

'Being honest,' explained Ida. 'For the first time for months . . . years . . . he had to be honest. Admit that he wasn't the big-time executive and that the house was too large and cost too much to run and that he'd lost too much money on the stock market venture.'

'You didn't leave him with a lot of pride, did you?' said Elke.

'I don't give a damn about his pride,' said Ida, angrily. 'For years he's let me go on thinking everything is fine. That he's just a bit of a bumbler but that nothing could really go badly wrong. Don't you think that honesty in a marriage is important?'

'I wouldn't know,' reminded Elke, quietly. 'I suppose so.'

'Believe me, it is!' the other woman insisted. She appeared quite unaware of the hypocrisy of what she was saying.

'How much?' Elke demanded, directly.

'Thirty thousand marks,' Ida replied, just as direct.

'I thought it would be more.' Elke calculated, relieved, that it would leave her with almost the same amount in her deposit account and in insurance investments.

'That's all he would admit to, finally,' qualified Ida. 'And there's the outstanding loan the bank refused to increase.'

'How much is that?'

'Fifty thousand.'

'Can he reduce that, without the pressure of the immediate debts?'

'I've said I want it done properly: a regular monthly amount taken by bank order. And that I want to go to the bank with him to arrange it. That's the only way it will work: he couldn't be trusted to do it himself. At least he'll have to stop buying that pissy wine.'

'You're being very hard on him,' accused Elke, again.

'It's about time someone was.'

73

'Will it help, completely to humiliate him?' Elke was at once astonished at herself. It was the first occasion she had ever come close to openly criticizing her sister. It seemed easy to do so mentally.

Ida shrugged, carelessly. 'I'm not interested in his feelings,' she said. 'I just want to settle this money thing. I hate it! It frightens me! You don't know what it's like, to be frightened like this.'

I do, thought Elke. I know what it's like to be frightened of not having money and I know what it's like to be frightened about a thousand other things, every day of my life. She said: 'I can let you have all of it: the entire thirty thousand.'

They were sitting in opposing chairs. Ida leaned forward, feeling out for her hand. Elke anwered the gesture for their fingers to meet, with difficulty because she had Poppi on her lap. Ida said: 'You're marvellous. I love you.'

'I hope it helps. That everything can be sorted out.'

Ida let her fingers drop. 'I want you to understand we won't be able to pay you back too quickly. I want to reduce the bank debt.'

'I'm not interested in being paid back,' said Elke. Wasn't she? Not quickly, perhaps. But eventually. Money – her savings – was her security, the only positive guarantee of any future.

'We will, I promise,' said Ida. 'And the same way. When we've got the bank debt down we'll make another order, so that you'll be repaid on a regular basis. And I'll have the bank calculate what interest you will have lost and make that up.'

'Stop it!' said Elke, in what would have been irritation if the feeling were possible towards her sister. 'I'm not concerned how or when I'm paid back, or about any interest. What I . . .'

Ida waited. 'What?' she said, finally.

'Nothing. Just what I said. Nothing else.'

There was a further silence between them. Elke filled it by carefully standing up, supporting Poppi to another chair where a blanket was already set out for him to lay upon, and then continuing to the bureau in the corner of the room, for her chequebook. Hunched over the writing desk, Elke said: 'To whom shall I make it payable?'

'*Me!*' said Ida, instantly. 'It's going into my personal account so I know what bills have been paid.'

'Does Horst know? About me?'

'Of course! Where could I have come up with thirty thousand Marks?'

Further humiliation for the man, Elke thought. Despite Ida's insistence to the contrary, Elke was sure the confrontation must have been awful. She completed the cheque and carried it across the room to her sister. Ida took it, folded it carefully, and put it into her small clutch bag. For the first time Elke became aware the bag was patterned in colours to coordinate with the suit and the shawl.

Ida looked up from her handbag, wrist before her, and said: 'Seven o'clock. Still early.'

They could go out, Elke thought, with quick enthusiasm. She didn't know anywhere because she never went out to eat at night, but there had to be a lot of places as close as they were to the centre of the city. She smiled towards her sister, about to propose it, but Ida spoke first.

'My night for favours,' she announced.

'What?'

'I told Horst I was coming here . . .' said Ida and stopped.

Elke said nothing, staring at her sister.

'. . . for the evening,' Ida continued.

Still Elke did not speak: didn't want to speak because she didn't want to say the sort of words she'd never said to Ida before.

'He won't call,' Ida assured.

'This isn't fair!' Elke protested at last. 'Not fair to me!'

'I told you, he won't call. You won't be involved.'

'What if he does?' demanded Elke. 'What if . . .' she stumbled, seeking a reason. '. . . What if the children became ill?'

'Don't be melodramatic!'

'I'm not being melodramatic. I'm being practical.'

'I could call you. Keep in touch.'

'How do I explain your not being here, in the first place?'

'I . . .' started Ida uncertainly, quickly smiling as the explanation came to her. 'I went out for a bottle of wine! We were enjoying ourselves and I went out for another bottle of wine!'

'That's puerile.'

'It's fine.'

Elke was horrified how careless – how absolutely dismissive – Ida had become about everything and everybody. She said: 'Not again. This once but not again.'

'I knew you'd do it for me!' said Ida, rising. 'I have to hurry!'

Of course her sister had known she would do it, supposed Elke. Everyone could anticipate what Elke Meyer was going to do and say: dependable, loyal, supportive Elke Meyer. 'Call!' she insisted, anxiously.

'Of course,' assured Ida, at the door.

Elke remained where she was for a long time after Ida left, until the gathering night put the room into darkness. She rose at last, switched on a light, and reversed and plumped the cushions of the seats upon which she and Ida had sat. She tried her latest Graham Greene acquisition but couldn't concentrate so she put it aside. She prepared Poppi's meal. When the phone sounded stridently in the apartment she gave a small cry of apprehension and started at it, not wanting to pick it up. When she eventually did she said, very quietly: 'Hello?'

'Anything?'

The relief sighed from Elke at her sister's voice. 'No,' she said tightly. There was no sound of activity from the other end to indicate that Ida and the man were in a restaurant or bar.

'I told you it would be all right,' said Ida.

'Call again.'

Ida did, two hours later. There was still no background sound. She said she was on her way back to Bad Godesberg, which was what Horst was to be told if he called. He didn't.

'It's wrong, Poppi. It's very wrong,' said Elke, as she settled the dog down for the night. Elke knew that she had been wrong too, becoming an accomplice. So why had she? Why hadn't she grown angry and refused? Elke wished she knew the answer, just as she wished she knew the answer to so many other questions.

'Wrong,' Elke insisted, to the indifferent dog.

That night, in her diary, Elke wrote: *I. 30,000.* She hardly needed a reminder date for the loan, but it was a neat entry for a woman who liked neatness, in everything. She sat looking at it for several moments. Then, quickly, she scrawled *Fool* and closed the book.

Once more, because Dzerzhinsky Square is so close to the Kremlin, Cherny went to Sorokin's KGB office after their conference at the President's Secretariat. This time Cherny wore his uniform, with all his medals.

'Can you ever see liaison – an association – between NATO and the Warsaw Pact becoming a reality?' queried the KGB deputy chief.

'Of course not!' the soldier retorted. 'Whatever America says the West will cheat, somehow. Or Germany will. History proves it. And the last war cost Russia twenty million lives.'

'Will Germany ever agree to the removal of missiles and troops from its territory?' Sorokin was picking up another discussion point from the Kremlin meeting.

'It has to, for Russia even to begin to be safe. Our negotiators should have insisted upon that before surrendering our occupying Power status over Berlin.'

'I wish to hell we were in a stronger position.'

'The army have wished that for over a year,' Cherny growled.

Chapter Ten

Reimann was disappointed with Bonn. He'd always believed capital cities should *look* like the most important place in a country: overwhelm ordinary people on the streets or on the pavements because they *were* ordinary people and such people had to be overwhelmed into believing that the other sort – the special people – who occupied the monuments of power were bigger and better and more able than they were, properly equipped and qualified to rule. But there weren't any enormous, intimidating structures in Bonn: even Berlin, razed in 1945, still possessed more imposing buildings than existed here, although they were not all utilized for government purposes.

It shouldn't have happened – or been allowed to continue – whatever the immediate post-war history. Which Reimann knew well enough, even before the Balashikha lecturers. He knew – although he cynically did not fully accept – that the first post-war Chancellor, Konrad Adenauer, had chosen his birthplace as the government centre for the divided, Western-orientated country believing that the location would only be temporary and that Berlin would be fully restored, after reunification. For years 'temporary' was the recognized and accepted qualification, preceding every official reference to Bonn as the West German capital. To Reimann Bonn appeared nothing more than a village inhabited by passing strangers who might any day move on, leaving it to go back to sleep like Rip Van Winkle among its small streets and stunted dwellings. He actually discerned a rural, yokel somnolence about the place: people moved slowly and reacted slowly and spoke slowly. It was little wonder West Germany demanded reunification so fervently after the dismantling of the Berlin Wall and the impervious borders between the two countries. Reimann guessed the politicians here would be as anxious as hell to get back to a proper, imposing city. It was certainly not a place where he personally wanted to live or even stay too long. He hoped it didn't become necessary to do so.

He arrived believing there was a great deal of preparation to occupy him before he would have to consider Elke Meyer, but establishing himself was not as difficult as he expected. In advance of his coming his intelligence-controlled media outlets in Australia had written to advise

78

the necessary ministries and departments of his appointment as their Bonn correspondent, so he was expected when he presented himself at the press centre off Adenauerallee with his supporting letters of accreditation.

Reimann was content enough with the Soviet-selected apartment on Rochusplatz. He'd feared a modern, box-within-a-box building. Instead it was most of the ground floor of a converted, late nineteenth-century house. Its age dictated high ceilings and expansive windows and the furniture matched. There were heavy velvet drapes and big, larger-sized cupboards and wardrobes. The claw-footed dining table and chairs were mahogany and heavy, the chairs difficult to shift, and the supposed easy chairs were over-stuffed and not particularly easy to sit in. Although it lacked the outright luxury, the size of the rooms and their furniture, together with the suggestion of ornateness, reminded Reimann of Neglinnaya and he wondered if it had other less immediately obvious fixtures, like those the Moscow apartment had possessed. In fact there were no eavesdropping devices, in case of discovery by West German counter-intelligence if any romance with Elke Meyer should lead to a security check.

The plumbing was ancient, the tiling was white and heavily fissured with cracks, and all the taps were very large, so the unconscious tendency was to use two hands. The bath stood, like a beached boat, in the middle of the bathroom. The toilet seat was mahogany, like the furniture outside. When the water flowed, the pipes creaked and whined, playing their own surrealistic melody. Because of the approaching summer the central heating, provided by gargantuan radiators, was switched off, but Reimann guessed it would have a tune to perform in the winter. His only additions to the apartment were a microwave and electrical fitments – coffee grinder, coffee maker, toaster and food mixer – in a kitchen already fitted with a refrigerator and deep freeze. In the living-room he installed a television, a video and a hi-fi set and attached a facsimile machine, befitting his supposed role as a journalist, to the telephone. Faithfully following the last-day Moscow instructions he bought an expensive Nikon camera and a set of proxile copying lenses, which he stored in the top left-hand drawer of the desk, hoping he would have an early use for them. On the same day as he signed* the lease, paid a deposit and agreed an inventory deduction at the end of his tenancy, Reimann notified the telephone, gas, electricity and rating authorities that he was now responsible for all charges incurred upon the property.

With his settling-in allowance Reimann opened an account at a branch of the Deutschebank on Dohmstrasse. On his way to the bank he passed a car showroom on Flodelingsweg, so in the afternoon he returned and bought a two-year-old 190 series Mercedes. It was black, the bodywork showed no signs of rust and there were only 24,000 kilometres on the clock. He arranged insurance to be covered by the Australian magazines.

And on the appointed day he made contact with Jutta, in a smoked-wood and yellow-tiled inn on the cobbled street connecting the market square with that end of the Münsterplatz where the statue of Beethoven gazed reprovingly down. Reimann arrived early. It was a place of nooks and crannies and coloured-glass partitions between tables. Reimann chose to stand at a decorated pedestal. He ordered a *Kölsch*, a small beer.

Jutta entered precisely on time. She was wearing a cotton summer skirt with short-sleeved blouse open at the neck: it stopped far short of being revealing but was still low enough to show an enticing degree of cleavage. He saw several men openly turn to admire her and guessed Jutta would be aware, too: she was always aware of herself. Jutta chose wine. Reimann stayed with the beer he already had.

'Everything OK?' he asked, returning from the bar with the drinks.

'Why shouldn't it be?'

'No trouble in Berlin?'

She shook her head. 'The landlord demanded three months' severance rent. The office made me a presentation, a flower vase.'

'What did you tell them?'

'That you'd decided on a change and gone to Munich, where you'd got a job with an accountancy firm, and that I was going to join you. I said we'd decided after all against your commuting at weekends.'

It made their relationship sound as if he were the decisive partner, which he hadn't ever been. 'What about possible contact?'

'I said we hadn't got a permanent apartment yet, and I would write when we were properly settled. They gave me the address of the Munich office: asked me to get in touch and consider working there.'

'Did you discuss this in Moscow?' It was a testing question.

Jutta hesitated before saying 'Of course. It was considered satisfactory: a normal, safe explanation for a family move.'

Reimann would have expected a more complicated cover story. It was hardly important. The test had been to discover how forthcoming she would be: he believed he had his answer. 'What about here?' he asked.

'My apartment is a cardboard rectangle: I can hear the next-door neighbour fart,' she complained. 'And I've bought a car, an Audi. What's it like at Rochusplatz?'

So she knew where his flat was, although he hadn't been told her intended address. Part of Moscow trying to build up the importance of her intermediary role? Or did they intend manipulating him and Jutta just slightly against each other, to ensure that each worked properly? He said: 'Old. Big. Not bad really. I've bought a second-hand Mercedes.'

'What do you think of Bonn?'

Now it was Reimann's turn to hesitate. Smiling, to take any offence from the question, he said: 'Is this Jutta Höhn asking her husband a casual question over a lunchtime drink? Or is it Jutta Sneider asking her field officer a professional question the answer to which will be relayed elsewhere?'

Jutta didn't smile back. 'It was a casual question over a lunchtime drink,' she insisted. 'But I suppose I might be asked how you're settling in.' Her voice was flat, matter-of-fact.

'Difficult, isn't it?' Reimann was intensely curious how she would reply.

'Not if we don't let it become so. Which I don't intend.' It was the Jutta of Berlin, autocratic and impatient with doubt.

'As long as we both know the pitfalls.' He didn't have to defer to her, as he had before from professional necessity and expectation. She wasn't the leader any more. He decided against openly confronting her. It was a realization she had to reach for herself: far better that way.

Jutta refused to let it drop. 'So answer the question! What do you think of Bonn?'

Guardedly Reimann said: 'Quite different from what I expected. Very small, compared with Berlin . . . I haven't done anything about supposedly working, not yet, so I don't know how difficult that is going to be. I certainly haven't had any difficulty orientating myself. I already know where the districts are: how to get to Dransdorf from Hardtberg and back again. And I've been across the river, to Beuel and Küdinghoven.'

'Sounds like you've been busy.' There was a mocking, almost critical tone in her voice.

Maybe he deserved it, Reimann thought, unoffended and most definitely unimpressed. His response to her question *had* ended more fulsomely than he'd intended: as he'd reported to her when they worked in Berlin, in fact. Mocking back he said: 'Is that what you're going to report?'

Jutta looked very directly at him with her unusual, glacial eyes. 'You trying to make some point? If you are, it's escaping me.'

'No point,' said Reimann.

'Why this attitude then?'

Reimann thought he detected an uncertainty in her voice. 'I don't think I have any attitude.'

Jutta regarded him with continued directness, for several moments. 'This is going to be different from Berlin.'

Reimann intentionally chose to misunderstand. 'I know,' he said. 'Much more important.'

It was Jutta who backed down. 'I want another drink.'

The tavern had still not filled with a lunchtime crowd. When he got back to her Jutta said briskly: 'Are you properly established?'

'Almost. There are still a few formalities about the accreditation.'

'Can you come back with me?'

Reimann wanted her to supplicate. 'Would it be wise? What about neighbours?'

Jutta beat him and knew it. 'It's a very small block. There's no concierge. The flat opposite mine is occupied by a university lecturer, who lives alone. He leaves around eight every morning and doesn't get back until eight. He also spends a lot of time away, adjudicating examinations. In the apartment above there is a railway executive. He leaves shortly after seven. His wife is a school-teacher who goes out about half an hour later. There are no children. The apartment below is empty. No one has shown the slightest interest in knowing me and I have made it clear, by avoiding everyone, that I have no desire whatsoever to know them. At this time of the day, anyway, the entire building is completely empty: no one will be aware of your entering. Or leaving, if we time it right. Which we will. Satisfied?'

Reimann bowed his head in acknowledgement, an exaggerated gesture, and said: 'I am sorry, Fräulein Sneider! I forgot your expertise.'

'Don't,' snapped Jutta. 'And I'm only Fräulein Sneider to anyone else. To you I'm your wife. And supervisor.'

Enough, Reimann decided. He wouldn't argue any more.

Jutta's apartment was in the Nord-Stadt district and was as she'd described it. The furnishings were cheap and frail-looking and the view from the lounge window was over a patch of threadbare grass towards the backs of more box-like structures. She'd tried to improve it as much as she could. She'd installed a television and a stereo, although not as large or as extensive as those he had at Rochusplatz, and there was a profusion of flowers in vases – one her farewell gift – in the main room and in the hallway. There was also a fairly extensive collection of books and magazines in a rack that overflowed on to a small side-table. The kitchen was cramped, barely functional. Reimann decided it was fortunate she was precluded from coming to his apartment: the difference in their altered status would have been far too obvious. She would have been annoyed.

'Welcome home!' she said, twirling with her arms outstretched to emphasize its smallness.

'It is not an order that you should have this apartment,' said Reimann. 'Why don't you find something else?' He felt enclosed, contained, exactly as he supposed he would feel in a box, parcelled up and wrapped for delivery. Delivery to where? 'This is like living in a railway station, waiting for the train to arrive! You *must* get something better!'

'It's anonymous,' reminded Jutta. 'It'll do, for the time being.'

'You won't be moving tomorrow. Or the day after,' he warned. 'We could be here for a long time. And I don't want you living in a shabby, prefabricated place like this. You're my wife! Do you think I'm prepared to let you stay here, in this shithole!'

'I'll make the decision, if I feel one has to be made.'

'It's ridiculous: inconvenience with no purpose. There must be hundreds of equally anonymous flats, all much better than this.'

'I said I'll move when I'm ready.'

She'd bought pork. There was no discussion who would prepare it. Reimann roasted it with green apples, with a sour-sharp apple dressing.

Trained as a sexual expert – practitioner, innovator, experimenter – Reimann had come to need sex, better sex than he'd ever known with Jutta. That night he went just a little further with her than he had in Moscow, using his mouth and urging her to do the same, which she'd always resisted and broke away from quickly. He was sure she had more than one orgasm. She was asleep long before he was.

His stay at Nord-Stadt developed into a claustrophobic parody of domesticity. Reimann did not leave the apartment at any time when he might have encountered the other occupants of the block, whose every movement – although not actually farting – it *was* possible to hear through the inadequate walls. Jutta shopped for what they wanted to eat, which he always cooked. He told her what wine to buy: she had already stocked vodka, whisky, schnapps and brandy. They watched boring television. Each, from time to time, attempted the books and the magazines but neither was very interested. They made love only once more during his stay.

'The afternoon is the safest time. Around four o'clock,' Jutta suggested on the second day.

'OK.' Reimann was quite ready to leave. Anxious, in fact.

Jutta indicated the telephone. 'You've memorized the number?'

'Of course I have.' They'd arranged a code.

Reimann was relieved to get back to Rochusplatz. The bread was stale, and although not sour the milk was old: he had protectively avoided engaging any trade or delivery men, just as he had avoided engaging a cleaning woman to look after the place, which needed attention. Reimann shopped leisurely for more milk and bread, with time enough before the important task of the day.

He was in place in the carefully parked Mercedes long before he knew, from the rigidly maintained observation files, he needed to be. Elke Meyer returned from the Chancellery precisely according to schedule and parked her very clean Volkswagen exactly where he expected it to go. She entered the apartment without looking either left or right along the street, hunched slightly forward and walking quite quickly, as if she were late, which Reimann knew she was not. He remained where he was, checking further on the earlier, professional observation. It was extremely accurate. Fifteen minutes after entering the apartment Elke Meyer emerged again, with the dog on its lead, and set off in the direction he knew she would take for her evening's walk. Poppi looked like one of those irritating, snappy sort of dogs.

Elke Meyer was taller than he had imagined from the films and the photographs. Slimmer-legged, too. There was a stiffness about the manner in which she held herself: his impression, at first sight, was that she was apprehensive of appearing lacking in something – her stature or her dress, maybe – to anyone she might accidentally encounter. Again she walked without looking left or right, not risking the casual attention of anyone else on the street. Better able to see than when she'd come home, Reimann was aware that she looked down quite a lot, so that she would not meet the eyes of anyone directly ahead, either.

I'm going to seduce you, Elke Meyer, Reimann thought: I'm going to strip you of clothes and attitudes and morals and inhibitions – strip you of absolutely everything – until I can do whatever I want with you. And there's nothing you can do to stop it happening.

*

84

Elke supposed Kissel had to express the gratitude it had taken him three weekends to get around to conceding but she wished he wouldn't: she didn't want his stumbled thanks or foot-shuffling awkwardness, and still less the painful assurances.

'I'm glad I can help,' she said hurriedly, trying to cut him off. They were in the front drawing-room at Bad Godesberg again, waiting for Ida to appear from the kitchen. This Saturday Kissel wasn't serving sour wine as an aperitif and Elke was grateful.

'It'll only be temporary, you understand,' said Kissel. 'It'll all be repaid very soon: with the proper interest.'

'I've talked it all through with Ida,' she said, unhappy that it sounded as if he had no say in any discussion.

'I'm writing a book,' the man announced.

Elke stopped just short of saying she knew that from Ida, too. Instead she said: 'That's fantastic.'

'It's going to be a novel,' he said. 'A political thriller. I think it's going to be very successful. That's why it won't be long before I can pay you back.'

Elke felt herself growing hot with discomfort, more anxious than usual for Ida's arrival. Kissel was looking at her expectantly. Elke said: 'How much have you written, so far?'

'It's at the planning stage,' he said. 'Sketching out a framework: making a character list. That's how a lot of books fail, you know. Insufficient preparation.'

'You're probably right,' said Elke. Poor Horst, she thought: poor innocent, day-dreaming, cuckolded Horst.

Reimann had followed Elke from Bonn that morning but was already driving back, having positively decided how to make his first move.

Chapter Eleven

It had been Elke's suggestion, instantly endorsed by Günther Werle, soon after the collapse of the Honecker regime in East Germany, to divide the official transcripts of Cabinet sessions. Non-classified accounts were distributed for preparation throughout the lower-graded staff, leaving her personally to assemble material which qualified as Secret, to be percolated into the final official records after whatever their designated release period. The days immediately prior to a Cabinet were always the busiest. Leading up to the meeting there was the agenda and the lobbying meetings with individual ministers and their permanent staff, to agree that agenda. Which invariably was not agreed at all, during those initial discussions, despite every indication that it had been. From long experience Elke automatically regarded the initial – and sometimes the second and occasionally, even the third – agenda only as a provisional document. Her sole responsibility after the Cabinet meeting, apart from extremely rare reference decisions to Werle, was to arrange the division of work, which was time-consuming because Cabinet discussions could range from quite mundane, completely non-classified matters, to debates covering the highest security prohibition. Even after the allocation was made there was usually a continuous stream of queries from secretaries who might not, for instance, have a beginning or an end to what they were entrusted to prepare and who occasionally found themselves working in complete bewilderment.

Gerda Pohl waited patiently, seeking maximum advantage, to protest this system and counter-balance the union-referred accusation of incompetence which had occurred earlier. She attacked through the union official, not directly against Elke, producing broken-up and quite disparate tracts of discussion with the demand to know how she or any other secretary could be expected to prepare material which had no logical continuity.

The procedure for such disputes was irrevocably established. The union representative's request for a meeting with Elke had to be channelled through Werle, possibly – and hopefully as far as Gerda was concerned – to get Elke officially reprimanded by her superior.

Gerda miscalculated by assuming that the system had been devised upon Elke's authority alone. Not even Elke was aware, until the complaints procedure began, that the Cabinet Secretary had from the beginning suggested to the Chancellery security division that the work method be adopted as a protective measure by other ministries. As an attempt to harm Elke, Gerda's complaint failed absolutely. Elke provided a hesitantly soft-voiced explanation, which was irrefutable either by the union or by Gerda Pohl herself. And as he had done in the previous instance, Werle insisted upon a separate interview with union officials, on this occasion further requiring security officers to take part, in order to recommend and praise Elke's innovation.

With her customary aversion to confrontation, once again Elke experienced neither satisfaction nor justification at the victory over the other woman. It upset a pattern, and Elke felt too many had been upset in the recent weeks. The most obvious – the most worrying – was whatever Ida was doing. Since the night of the loan Ida had not involved her or even gossiped about the affair Elke was convinced her sister was now having, but the worry and the awareness remained. During the most recent weekends Ida had been disparaging, practically contemptuous, towards her husband. And the man's reaction was a further unsettling change. He maintained a pitiful pretence about a book which they knew and he knew would never be written. But his former forced bravura wasn't there any more: he'd been caught out, shown up in Elke's and his wife's eyes as a failure who couldn't manage his affairs. Now there was a humbleness about him, almost an acceptance that he *should* be disparaged. Elke was deeply saddened by it.

And there was the money itself. Elke was reluctant to concede her true feelings – still wouldn't spell them out, even to herself – but she regretted the loan. It was not that she begrudged the money. It was the feeling of reassurance it represented, sitting comfortingly in the bank. It would be all right if they kept their promise to repay, but Elke couldn't convince herself entirely that she would get it back. And there was nothing she could do about it, not now.

Finally, inevitably, there was Ursula. Except that in her case it was seeing the pattern become more and more deeply established that disturbed Elke most of all.

This, too, had been precipitated by Ida. Which was not in any way a criticism, not like the other criticisms Elke held against her sister. Rather, it was an acknowledgement of the other woman's harsh honesty, after their visit to the home. *She's not going to get any better.* Ida's words. Which, with little variation, was what Dr Schiller had been

87

telling her for months. But somehow, from Ida, the assessment had brought home the truth: illogically, she had found it easier to *believe* Ida than she had the clinic's principal. Not that she had intended to raise it so directly. It had been Schiller who talked about the need to prescribe stonger tranquillizers and quietly recounted the increased tantrums and difficulties they were experiencing with the child, making such dosage essential. *There is a deterioration, Frau Meyer. You must recognize, make yourself face, the inevitable deterioration I have always warned you would occur.*

Elke thought everything was moving too quickly: too many changes were all occurring far too abruptly. She felt buffeted, as if she'd been caught in a strong wind; at the weekend, after Bad Godesberg and then hearing words she did not want to hear from Dr Schiller, she'd been positively breathless. She'd have to prepare against it becoming as bad as that: against almost physically giving way. That would be weakness, and Elke was determined against openly showing weakness, not like Horst Kissel, even if she was churning inwardly.

Gerda Pohl's complaints were dismissed by her union on a Wednesday. The summons from Günther Werle came earlier than normal the following morning, before Elke had completed the customary brief for that day. Her instant anxiety was that she had forgotten a schedule change, which for her would have been devastating. Hurriedly she checked the itinerary which was lying on the desk before her and saw at once there was no change: in fact he had fewer appointments than usual.

She went into the Cabinet Secretary's office frowning, and began to apologize before she reached his desk and her accustomed chair. 'I'm sorry. I was not expecting you. I don't have everything ready yet.' She had not had to make such an admission for years: so long ago, in fact, that she couldn't call the occasion to mind.

'I wasn't expecting it,' Werle dismissed. Nodding towards her place, he said: 'Sit down. I want to talk.'

Elke did so, regarding the man curiously. 'Is there something wrong?'

The immaculately neat man looked down at his blotter, fumbling one of the desk pens between his fingers: with his head bent it was more difficult for the practised Elke to hear the softly delivered words. He said: 'You must not think this is criticism. It's not. It's concern. But I've had the feeling over the last few weeks that you are distracted: that something is worrying you.'

A coldness, a definite physical sensation, engulfed Elke. Her job – her unquestioned ability to perform it – was the only thing about which she *was* sure: the responsibilities didn't frighten her and the daily contact with men in important positions didn't overawe her. The Elke Meyer who worked and operated with competent efficiency in the West German Chancellery was a quite different Elke Meyer from the one who lived alone, apart from a pet dog, in a spinster's flat off the Kaufmannstrasse. Elke consciously considered the two existences quite apart from one another, just as, almost without realizing it, she had come to think of the two personalities as separate – even deciding, without too much difficulty either, which she liked better. Surely that wasn't being taken away from her! Surely, all this time, she hadn't been deluding herself! It wasn't possible: *couldn't* be possible. Stumbling, Elke said: 'I am extremely sorry . . . I didn't know . . . I don't . . .'

The man's head came up. 'Stop it, Elke!' he said, unusually curt. 'I told you, I'm not criticizing: I've never had cause, ever.'

Through her confusion it registered that he had called her Elke and not Frau Meyer, but in that confusion it was not an awareness she wanted to examine. 'I don't understand.'

Werle smiled and said: 'I have thought . . . would like to think . . . of us . . . as something more than merely working colleagues.'

Elke was not sure she understood that, either. 'Yes?' she said, doubtfully.

'As a friend I'm asking you: is there anything outside of here, outside the Chancellery and what you do here, that is worrying you? Ursula, for instance? If there is . . . if there is anything I could possibly do . . . anything at all . . . then I'd be very willing to help. I would like to help.' Towards the end of the offer Werle had looked away again, not meeting her look. He desperately hoped that at this late stage there wasn't going to be an unforeseen problem to upset the plans he had so carefully made.

It would be lowering a barrier, to admit the man into her sheltered other life. Unthinkable, in any circumstances whatsoever, even if he had been a close friend. Elke didn't want intruders: people encroaching on her privacy. Always a division between the Chancellery and Kaufmannstrasse, she thought again. The reflection at once incurred an irksome self-accusation. If the two were compartmented as she'd believed them to be, how had Günther Werle guessed something was wrong, outside? Elke said: 'I appreciate your concern.'

'So?'

With thought pursuing thought in her mind, Elke had difficulty in precisely remembering Werle's original questions. 'There's nothing,' she said: 'Ursula is . . .' She stopped at the automatic lie. 'Ursula is as well as we can expect.'

'You're sure?' he pressed.

'Absolutely.'

Werle smiled across the desk at her again, nodding like a man to whom suspicion had been confirmed as fact. 'I knew I was right!'

Elke's head whirled further. 'I'm not following you here, either.'

'It's this continuing stupidity with Gerda Pohl, isn't it!'

Oh no! thought Elke. She had no reason to protest or defend the woman, but it would be wrong for Gerda Pohl to be accused of something in which she was not involved. Hurriedly Elke said: 'That's all been settled.'

'No,' insisted Werle. 'She's a disruptive influence throughout the department. As well as being inefficient. I allowed you to persuade me before but it's not going to happen again. She'll be transferred.'

How could she stop it happening! She had to try! Quickly, allowing the man his misunderstanding, Elke said: 'It was foolish of me, reacting as I did. And for doing so I apologize. The fault's mine, not Frau Pohl's. She's been corrected once more, by the union inquiry. That's enough, isn't it?'

'No,' said Werle again and just as forcefully. 'And you must stop assuming the blame of others. She is to go.'

'She's a widow,' Elke argued. 'A transfer could mean demotion: create difficulties for her.'

'She created her own difficulties,' Werle insisted. 'And it doesn't automatically follow that she'll be demoted.'

Elke accepted there was nothing she could do. Every complaint about the woman was justified. And objectively she recognized that Gerda Pohl *had* tried constantly to undermine and harm her, in every way possible. So she had no cause to feel guilt if the necessary transfer stemmed from a misconstrued reason. But guilt was Elke's feeling, nevertheless. Resigned, she said unhappily: 'Will you officially inform her? Or shall I?'

'I will,' Werle decided.

Elke was relieved. Gerda Pohl's transfer *would* remove a constant irritation, and that could only contribute to the better working of a secretariat of which Elke was the head, so that it was upon Elke that better working would ultimately reflect. She should be careful – sensible – and not allow the guilt to assume unnecessary proportions.

A silence settled. The routine of the morning was hopelessly disorganized and Elke wanted to excuse herself to re-establish some order. She was virtually moving to do so when Werle resumed talking. He bent over the blotter again, the desk pen revolving and turning between his fingers, eyes averted.

'I was wondering . . .' he started, then stopped.

Elke waited. Finally she said: 'What?'

'. . . Frau Werle has decided to stay on, at the Munich health spa. She feels much improved . . .'

'That's good.'

'. . . before I learned . . . before she told me . . . I had bought tickets for a performance here of the Berlin Philharmonic. They have a new conductor, an Italian. The critics say he's every bit as good as Herbert von Karajan.'

'I hadn't heard that,' said Elke. There was a warmth of nervousness, a dampness upon her face, and she felt ridiculous. She hoped it wasn't as obvious to him as it seemed to her.

'. . . I was wondering . . . you've mentioned music in the past . . . whether I could suggest, ask, if you'd like to make use of the ticket?'

Elke made no reply.

'. . . You probably have another engagement, of course . . .' Werle started, retreating, and Elke seized the respite and said: 'It's extremely generous of you . . . I'll have to check . . .'

Werle's fleeting smile came as he looked up. 'There is no urgency,' he said, quickly. 'No urgency at all. I would be very honoured, pleased, if you were able to accept.'

So what was she going to do? Elke wondered.

'Why not?' demanded Ida. She poured the wine, which once again she had ordered without reference to Elke.

'He's married.'

Ida looked pained at her sister, the expression changing to become quizzical. 'I believe you think more about sex than I do!'

Elke glanced anxiously around the restaurant. 'Why say that?'

'His wife has extended her stay at a spa, right?'

'That's what he said.'

'And he'd already bought tickets for a concert?'

'Yes.'

'Is Günther Werle a liar?'

'Certainly not!' said Elke defensively.

'So why can't it be a perfectly ordinary gesture, with no strings or hidden meaning attached, from a man whose wife is away?'

91

There was no reason whatsoever, Elke conceded. She felt admonished. 'It just seemed . . . not right.'

'It could only not be right if you let it develop otherwise,' said Ida, with relentless logic if difficult syntax. 'I think you'd be a fool, not to go. You like music and it's not often you get the chance to hear it performed by an orchestra as good as that.'

'I suppose . . .'

Ida added to their glasses and said: 'What's the attraction of living as you do, practically as a recluse?'

There isn't any attraction at all, thought Elke: I hate it. She said: 'I don't live practically as a recluse. I just don't get the opportunity all that often to go out in company.'

'So now you have!' said Ida, triumphantly. 'Take it!'

Elke guessed that Gerda Pohl had led the gossip about a relationship between herself and Günther. But now Gerda wasn't in the department any longer: not that there would have been any likelihood of Gerda or anyone else learning of the outing anyway. Still reluctant to make a positive, personal decision, Elke said: 'I'll see.'

'Go!' urged Ida. 'Where's the harm?'

Ida was wearing the suit and shawl she had worn that night to Kaufmannstrasse, and Elke thought her sister looked elegant. 'How's Horst?' she asked.

Ida shrugged. 'He claims to have started to write something. I don't expect it's anything more than "Chapter One". '

'Don't ridicule him all the time,' urged Elke, in a sudden plea. 'I don't want to hear any more about what's happening between you and Horst and anyone else and I think the way you disregard and diminish him as you're doing is wrong.'

Ida sat with her glass suspended halfway to her mouth, openly surprised by the outburst. Elke was surprised at it herself. Ida said: 'Forgive me, if it distresses you!'

There was a brittleness in her sister's voice and Elke thought, further surprised, that it could become an unprecedented dispute between them. 'My distress isn't important,' she said. 'It's Horst's distress that matters.'

'I doubt that he notices,' said Ida, uncaring.

'Of course he notices!' said Elke, exasperated. 'Remember what you accused me of, for visiting Ursula every Sunday? You said I did it because I felt guilty of something. Don't you think there's a lot of guilt at what you're doing with Kurt in the way you're behaving towards your husband?'

'Quite the little analyst!' said Ida.

Their roles were reversing again, Elke decided. She hadn't liked it on the previous occasion but she did not feel so discomfited now: maybe it was because Ida was not collapsing, as before. Whatever, it was probably the time for her to withdraw. 'I don't want to debate it. It was just something I wanted to say.'

'Bravo!' said Ida. The sarcasm did not work and they both knew it. Ida flushed.

Elke decided the lunch was ruined and that it was her fault. Did it matter? It *had* been an opinion she'd wanted to express, rare though such an experience was for her. She tried to think of a subject to raise between them but couldn't: they'd talked about the children before she'd mentioned the invitation to the Berlin Philharmonic concert and there was nothing more to say about Horst Kissel. There was the business of Gerda Pohl, but Elke didn't think her sister would be genuinely interested in that. Who else would be?

Elke imagined her sister was having the same difficulty, but Ida abruptly confessed: 'It's getting pretty serious between Kurt and me.'

'On whose part? Yours? His? Or both?'

Ida considered the demand. She smiled, but only slightly, shaking her head. 'His, I guess.'

'How?'

'He wants us to go away together. Only for a vacation: a week, something like that.'

'How could you do that?' Elke decided, positively, not to be judgemental. If she were the only person to whom Ida could talk then that was the role she'd play. A sounding board. Adviser, maybe, if advice was sought. But not a judge. What criteria did she have to judge morals?

'I don't see how I could,' admitted Ida, at once.

'Do you want to?'

Ida shrugged, uncertainly. 'I don't know.'

'What about him?' asked Elke. 'What family does he have, apart from a wife?'

Ida stretched across the table, taking Elke's hand. 'Use his name,' Ida asked, her face very serious. 'It wouldn't hurt to use his name, would it?'

Elke was dismayed at the anguish on her sister's face. She said: 'What family does Kurt have?'

'A daughter. Twelve. I've seen a picture. She's very pretty.'

'What about the wife you met at dinner? Is she pretty, too?'

'You really think that reminder was necessary?'

'Why not?' Where was the decision not to judge?

'I think you could easily . . .' started Ida, but stopped.

'What?'

'Nothing.' Ida had almost accused her sister of envy: her stomach knotted in horrified awareness of how such a charge would have sounded against someone like Elke.

'What?' insisted Elke, again.

Ida fervently sought a way out. 'I was going to say I think you could easily be risking what there is between us. Which would have been absurd. It was silly anger: not thinking. I'm sorry.'

Elke relaxed, smiling. 'I shouldn't have said it, either,' she conceded. It had, she supposed, been an argument of sorts.

'I don't think I'll do it,' said Ida. 'Try to get away, I mean.'

'It'll just make things even more difficult,' Elke told her. 'Do you really want that?'

'No,' said Ida, sincerely. 'I certainly don't want any more difficulties than I've already got.'

That night, walking Poppi, Elke made the decision definitely to accept the concert invitation. It was positively ridiculous, ever to have had doubts: she simply didn't have the experience.

'Moscow considers it's dangerous,' Jutta insisted. 'You'll have to come into direct contact with the police.'

'That's the whole point!' argued Reimann, frustrated by the objections. 'The police will give me inherent credibility: honest men seek assistance from the police, not dishonest ones!'

'Too much can go wrong.'

'Have Moscow agreed?' Reimann demanded. In Jutta's thin-walled apartment they were both speaking quietly and playing the stereo loudly as an additional precaution against being overheard.

'They want to know if there couldn't be another way.'

'If I believed there had been another, more effective way I would have suggested it instead.' In his impatience, Reimann wondered if the reluctance was entirely from Moscow. To Jutta this would be his moment of contact with Elke, the very moment when his relationship with the woman would hopefully begin.

'You're sure?'

Reimann refused to argue any further. 'Do they have enough men available?'

'Yes,' she conceded.

'And they'll be in place, ready, as I've ordered?'

'Yes.'

Reimann smiled, satisfied. It was good being the person able to dictate the action, after so long being the obedient subordinate. He wondered how long it would be before Jutta recognized the change.

Chapter Twelve

Elke felt inexplicably happy; happier than she had for months. And at the same time calm. She decided that the calmness – the absence of any baseless apprehension or tension – contributed largely to the other more obvious feeling. There were other factors, of course. After the initial instinctive unease, the unwillingness to accept any change in established patterns, she was coming to enjoy the shifting relationship between Ida and herself. It was no longer one-sided. Now Ida needed her, as a confidante and an adviser, and Elke liked the reversal of dependence. She didn't want the cause to last – and hoped she'd correctly detected a cooling of the affair on Ida's part when they lunched – but didn't believe things would ever go back to how they had been before, with herself forever subservient and forever led by her elder sister. They were more equal now. Equal in what? Mistakes, perhaps. She'd made a mistake. And now Ida was making hers. Just as easily Elke found that a sober reflection, a temporary dip in her unusual happiness. If this was the equalizing mistake, she hoped Ida's was not as irreparable as hers had been.

Elke edged the freshly washed and polished Volkswagen out on to Adenauerallee, that highway she seemed to know so well, shrugging the thought away. She didn't want a reason for the adjustment between herself and Ida. It had happened. That was enough. The reason wasn't important: wasn't necessary to isolate. What about other factors? She began to ignore what came to mind but finally refused herself. Why not consider it? She *was* looking forward to the concert, with Günther. As he said he was looking forward to escorting her, when she'd accepted. Soon – within days – they would have to make arrangements. Would they meet at the concert hall? Or would he collect her? Better to meet at the hall. Less complicated. Less . . . just better. What if he offered to pick her up? It would be rude to refuse. If he did she would have to invite him in, either before or after: further rudeness, if she didn't. Most definitely before, if he insisted on coming to Kaufmannstrasse. She would have to get something in to drink, to avoid being as unworldly as she had been with Ida. Basic courtesy to do so. What? She didn't know. What had Dietlef drunk, when they'd been together? Beer, she remembered: beer was all that students and postgraduates ever drank. Günther Werle didn't seem the sort of man to drink beer. Wine, perhaps. It might be wise to get in some whisky or schnapps, as well. Near the centre of the city, Elke smiled abruptly: it was not a problem. She could ask Ida, at lunch. Ida would know. The reliance was still two-way.

The car-parks were full, but today that did not cause Elke the irritation it might have done. She made a protective tour around familiar streets and succeeded with a meter on Engeltalstrasse. Before lifting Poppi from the vehicle she ensured it was parked evenly between the lines of the designated space, paid and then returned for the dog.

It was getting hotter, warming up but not yet boiling like the 'Bonn kettle'. The sun felt comfortable upon her face: she hoped Ursula would feel like walking in the grounds tomorrow. Ursula had not resisted at all on the last few Sundays. It had to be something to do with the newly prescribed tranquillizers.

The produce market was not crowded and although she did not intend to buy anything Elke lingered among the stalls, smiling at traders shouting their wares, shaking her head to those who picked her out openly to offer samples. She hesitated, too, at the flower stalls further on. If Günther came into the flat it would be nice, proper, to have fresh flowers. But they wouldn't be fresh by then, would they? Better to wait, nearer the day: nearer the day they would have decided anyway if they were going separately or together.

Clara, the waitress Elke never called by name, was waiting to greet her by the accustomed table inside the Bonner Café. Elke accepted the coffee and consulted the menu before choosing the apple cake they both knew she would order.

'Cream?' the girl suggested, as she always did.

'No thank you,' Elke refused, as she always did.

And outside but unseen, concealed by the jewellery shop window, Otto Reimann smiled, already convinced that everything was going to work as smoothly as he'd planned it should.

Reimann considered the most difficult part – the part he could do nothing to anticipate – was already resolved exactly as he wanted it to be because there had not been a restricting car-park vacancy when Elke reached the centre.

The expert observation, a lot of which he had confirmed for himself, had given Reimann precisely the time of Elke's regular Saturday morning departure from Kaufmannstrasse. But Reimann had still been waiting early, to allow for any deviation from normal. Which there hadn't been. The short drive into the city had been just as uneventful, so it had only been about the parking that Reimann had known any concern. Engeltalstrasse could not have been better. Knowing Elke's destination Reimann had not needed to maintain any further pursuit. Instead he'd found his own parking place on Spessartstrasse and still been early for his rendezvous with Jutta, to identify both parking positions, aware more than at any time since this new operation had begun how completely their positions were switched.

'So far it's going all right.' A begrudging concession.

'It can only fail if you and the others make mistakes now.' He hadn't quite intended it to sound like a threat.

'I don't make mistakes,' she'd come back at him, defiantly.

'Let's hope there isn't a first time. And that the others aren't careless,' had been his retort, just as forceful.

Elke left the Bonner Café at ten thirty, the recorded time in the observation files. And as the files predicted, she turned left towards the bookshop and the cathedral. Reimann went in the opposite direction, back through the produce market. The already identified telephone was conveniently near the corner of Spessart. He hurried his approach, to create the breathlessness of a supposedly anguished man, and babbled the beginning of his emergency call so that the receiver had to interrupt to make him repeat the report of his car's theft. He did, with an account of actually seeing the crime being committed, too far away to intervene but able to give the direction in which the car had been driven away. He added the location from which he was speaking and promised to wait until the police arrived.

It was very prompt, quicker than Reimann had guessed it might be. He repeated all the details to the two traffic policemen and was sitting in the rear of the car when the first report came over their radio.

'Just a few streets away,' the observer reported. 'You've been lucky.'

'I don't agree,' Reimann said sourly and for the police benefit when they reached Engeltalstrasse.

The KGB active service unit drafted in to Bonn at Reimann's request had staged the crash brilliantly, causing exactly the sort and type of damage he wanted. The nearside wing of Reimann's Mercedes was crumpled and the bumper was buckled into the wheel. But by far the worst damage was to Elke's Volkswagen. The wing furthest from the pavement was crushed along its entire length from the glancing way the two cars had been brought together. The force of the impact had driven it tightly against the tyre, which was punctured. Additionally the wheel had been shattered away from the front axle and lay skewed, making the car lopsided.

98

Reimann went through the head-shaking pretence of examining the damage and gazing inside the vehicle – carefully obeying the police injunction to touch nothing – while one officer sought evidence and descriptions from witnesses and his colleague directed single line traffic around the interlocked cars. The sort of uninvolved people who always stop to stare at traffic accidents stopped to stare, forming a crowd through which it was difficult for Reimann to detect Elke Meyer's arrival. According to his detailed information it could only be minutes.

It was actually three.

Always someone to fear the worst, Elke had the initial twinge of concern as she came up behind the crowd at the entrance to the street where she was parked. At first the crowd blocked her view. She tried, ineffectually, to make her way through, hearing 'crash' and 'runaway' from unseen people and feeling the concern harden into positive worry.

When Elke saw fully, the worry settled into shocked, irrational panic. There was only one thought: my car, my car, my beautiful car. Then she said it, aloud, but it didn't come out as words, more a helpless whimpering noise.

'My car!' she said again, disbelievingly. 'That's my car!'

The people closest to her moved away, like sympathetic mourners. Someone shouted helpfully to the police: 'Here's the owner,' which was Reimann's warning. He looked up from the crumpled vehicles but didn't move towards her.

Elke was never to have any recollection of purposely getting to the accident. In the panic that held her, she was only conscious of the broken wheel, the punctured tyre and the scarred and twisted metal of the obsessively cherished vehicle.

'Fräulein Meyer?' said one of the policemen. He had already obtained the owner's identity from the registration details through the police car computer. 'Fräulein Elke Meyer?'

Elke blinked at the man, not completely hearing the question. 'My car!' she said. 'Someone's crashed into my car. Damaged it. Look how it's damaged . . . broken. . . !'

Reimann judged it the moment to become involved. Despite knowing the care she took of the vehicle, her distress was far greater than he had expected. He was pleased.

'My car, too,' said Reimann. 'The other car is mine.'

Elke's despair, her inability to get control of herself, started visibly to shake through her. 'You did it! You crashed into me!'

'No,' interceded the policeman. 'Herr Reimann's car was stolen. The thieves crashed into you: three men, according to witnesses. They escaped in a Porsche. We've already circulated a description.'

Reimann wondered where the Porsche would be found; by now the Soviet unit would have switched to prearranged and waiting cars at least twice.

'But what's going to happen? . . . my car. . . ?' Elke straggled to a halt, chest so tight she couldn't breathe, made faint by the recognition when she focused at last upon the other car's owner. It couldn't be! No, of course it couldn't! It wasn't. But so similar! Elke was numbed, momentarily close to fainting.

'There are breakdown trucks already coming to get them off the street,' the policeman continued.

None of the carefully prepared files had cautioned him that the stupid woman was given to hysteria, thought Reimann. The stunted animal named Poppi was twisting round their feet, frightened by the crowds and the obvious excitement. And yapping, just as Reimann had guessed it would yap. Quietly, the sympathy sounding quite sincere, he said: 'I'm sorry about your car. It doesn't matter so much about mine: it's owned by my firm.'

Elke made a supreme effort for control, fully aware at last of the number of people all around and that she was their focal point. To Reimann she said: 'Forgive me. It was a shock . . . I didn't expect . . . forgive me.' So similar, she thought again: practically a double.

'It's naturally a shock,' he said, soothingly. More than you know, he added, mentally: there are many more to come, dear Elke.

At that moment the towing trucks arrived and the policemen closed the street completely while they manoeuvred into position. Men in greasy overalls got from both cabs, nodded with the disinterest of experts to both Reimann and Elke, and started at once to fumble between the Volkswagen and the Mercedes. One shouted for a chained hook attached to a crane to be lowered beneath the front bumper of the Mercedes, yelled again and stood back as one car was lifted free of the other with a screech of tearing metal. Reimann saw Elke wince, as if it were a human sound.

'How will everything be paid for?' asked Elke, dazedly.

As I intend it to be, thought Reimann. Instead of replying he turned to the policeman, who represented officialdom and from whom Elke would accept statements without question. The policeman said: 'By insurers. In the circumstances I imagine it will be a complicated situation. It wasn't Herr Reimann's fault.'

Elke isolated the name for the first time. His voice was different, much lower, than Dietlef Becker's had been. The likeness was still uncanny. Unsettling. She still felt weak.

'I'll find out where the cars are being taken,' Reimann offered. From the fixed way she was staring at him he believed she had made the connection. He got two business cards from the breakdown men and returned his in exchange. He said he would come later that day to the garage, accepting in advance of their protests that it was unreasonable to expect a damage estimate so soon.

'What about her?' said one of the mechanics, nodding towards Elke.

'Contact me at that number and address if there's anything to discuss,' said Reimann. He had to try everything now.

With the evidence of the accident disappearing down the road the crowd began to break up. The policeman in charge shepherded Elke and Reimann on to the pavement and said: 'There is some information I want.' He needed only details of their driving licences and insurance, with the addition of a short official statement from Reimann of personally having seen his own car stolen. Reimann insisted that everything had occurred too fast for him to provide any useful description of the men involved.

'The witnesses to the crash here say there was one comparatively tall man: the other two medium height. All casually dressed?'

Reimann shook his head. 'I really didn't see,' he apologized. By now the unit would be very differently dressed.

'We'll contact you, as soon as we hear anything,' the policeman promised. 'I'm hopeful.'

You shouldn't be, thought Reimann. He said: 'You've been extremely helpful.'

'Yes, thank you.' Elke spoke quickly, anxious not to appear ungrateful. She felt none of the earlier, welcomed calm but neither was there panic now. She still wished her thoughts would come in the proper order, so she would know what to do. She felt she was recovering from the other shock, the positive resemblance this man had to someone else whom she still didn't believe she truly hated, as Ida expected her to hate.

'There are a few things we've got to talk about.'

Elke turned to Reimann. He had a considerate, open face and was smiling at her kindly.

'Would you like to sit down? Take a coffee or something?' The damned dog was sniffing around his legs, curiously. Reimann wanted to edge it away with his foot. He didn't.

Elke realized she would like to sit down: she felt drained, physically aching. She nodded and said: 'I think I would.'

The café was crowded and noisy, not at all like the Bonner, but he managed to get a table on a slightly raised balcony away from the main hubbub.

'Coffee? Or something stronger?'

'Coffee, please.' He had a way of looking straight at his companion but strangely Elke was not disconcerted: she had the impression he was concentrating entirely upon her. He had brown eyes. Dietlef had had brown eyes. Dietlef hadn't gazed so directly, though.

Reimann gave the order and said, businesslike: 'Now! Is there anyone we have to contact? Husband? Boyfriend? Anyone?'

'No, I . . .' started Elke, habitually in retreat. Lunch! She was late, practically an hour! And she was never late: they'd be worried, not knowing! Mustn't panic any more; mustn't babble. Think! She said: 'I was going to my sister. They'll be concerned.' She started around towards the door, half rising before realizing how silly she must look.

'We'll phone,' said Reimann, with further calmness. 'I'll do it for you, if you'd like.'

Of course! Telephone: easy! Elke said: 'I'll do it. But thank you.'

Reimann located the telephone and sat watching her hurry towards it: in her anxiety, she didn't walk head lowered, as she usually did. She had quite a tight ass. He considered adding a brandy for himself when the coffee arrived but quickly decided against it: her immediate impression – and every impression after that – was important. *Would* be important, for quite a while to come. Urged by the reflection, aware that she was looking back from the telephone position, Reimann leaned to pat the dog, which she had left tethered by its lead to the table leg. Poppi backed away, with a nervous snarl. Reimann withdrew: fucking animal, he thought.

Ida's alarm was immediate. Elke cut across her sister's gabbled questions, insisting she was unhurt – that she hadn't even been involved – and that she would get to Bad Godesberg as soon as possible: she just had a few things to discuss with the other car owner. He seemed extremely considerate, and there was an amazing coincidence, she would tell Ida later. Talking to her sister about the accident – and being distanced from the man – allowed Elke outwardly to compose herself. No more spluttering confusion, she resolved, as she walked back to the table. She was conscious of his studying her, smiling, as she approached. When she reached the table he stood, politely, for her to sit.

'I wasn't making a lot of sense out there, was I?' It was the right thing to do, to offer an explanation for her panic.

'Anyone would have been upset,' said Reimann. She'd made a reasonable recovery, he conceded. Just.

'You've been very understanding.' She didn't feel at all ill-at-ease. He was a comfortable person to be with.

More understanding than you'll ever know, mused Reimann. He said: 'I think we should meet properly, don't you?' He reached across that table in greeting and said: 'Otto Reimann. Hello.'

She hesitated, then took the offered hand. 'Elke Meyer,' she said. He wasn't being flirtatious or anything stupid or discomfiting like that: he was trying to relax her. Even more considerate.

'Things you have to know,' announced Reimann, formally. 'Here is my card, with my phone number and address . . .' He scribbled quickly on the reverse side. '. . . And my insurers. Here's the name of the garage where the cars have been taken: I've said I'll make contact this afternoon, to see if they've any estimate of the cost of the damage. They probably won't have, but there's no harm in asking.'

'What do you need from me?' asked Elke.

Reimann positively hesitated, at the irony of the question. 'Your address, certainly. Insurers, too.'

Elke began groping through her handbag. She got as far as: 'I don't seem . . .' before Reimann offered her a small notepad and his own pen. Elke wrote down the Kaufmannstrasse address he already knew and said: 'I suppose I'd better get in touch with my insurance company, to tell them what's happened.'

'Don't hurry about that,' advised Reimann. 'They'll need an estimate for the damage repairs, anyway . . .' He gestured to his business card, which lay between them and upon which the titles of the Australian magazines were listed. '. . . My car is covered by the company insurance. It could be they'll accept responsibility for your car as well as mine. There'd be no purpose in your unnecessarily incurring penalties or losing bonuses if they will, would there?'

Elke frowned. 'Why should they do that?'

Reimann shrugged. 'It's a pretty big block policy: covers an enormous amount of company vehicles . . . even delivery vans . . . They're not concerned with individual who's-to-blame-for-what claims.'

'But it wasn't your fault!' Elke protested. 'Why should your company's insurers pay out for something for which they're not responsible! It wouldn't be fair. It wouldn't be honest, either!'

103

Shit! The honest objectivity was important for him to keep in mind, for later. It had been wrong to push the offer so blatantly. He'd achieved a meeting, which at this stage was the only aim. He smiled across the table at her, indicating the card again. 'If they want me, your insurers can find me there.'

Elke pushed his notebook back towards Reimann. 'And that's where you can reach me,' she said.

And I will; be assured that I will, thought Reimann. He said: 'You're very late for the lunch.'

'And will be later still: I have to get to Bad Godesberg.' She wished now she'd asked Ida to drive in to collect her.

'There's the train,' he suggested. 'But a taxi might be quicker: certainly more comfortable. It's no more than a suburb, after all.' He'd shown almost sufficient consideration: to prolong the meeting much further with suggestions of assistance would be a psychological mistake.

He was right: Bad Godesberg *was* a suburb. The idea of taking a taxi still seemed extravagant. 'A taxi would be more convenient,' she agreed. He appeared an assured man.

'Is there anything else we should discuss?' asked Reimann.

Elke was flattered to be offered the dominant role. She shook her head and said: 'Not that I can think of.'

'Anything else I can do to help?' It was not a contradiction of the previous decision. He shifted in his seat as he asked the question, indicating a desire to end the discussion: the offer was the final, obvious politeness.

Elke recognized it for what it was. 'No,' she said, collecting up her handbag and reaching down, to untie Poppi. 'You've really been extremely kind.'

Reimann insisted on escorting her to a taxi. He held the door for her to enter but didn't immediately close it behind her. He bent in and said: 'I know it seems bad, but cars can be repaired to look as good as new.'

'I hope you're right,' said Elke. He'd put the incident into its right perspective, not allowing it to inflate into a major catastrophe, as she had initially done.

Perfect! decided Reimann, triumphantly, as he watched the taxi pull away: absolutely perfect.

Ida had prepared a salad lunch, with nothing to keep hot, so the only inconvenience was the delay of Elke's arrival. Elke was the centre of everyone's attention, the person who had been involved in a positive adventure. It was an unusual and not displeasing experience. She found herself talking in Reimann's tone of voice, treating it as a misfortune but not a disaster, and at one stage Kissel said, with some admiration: 'I think you're being very philosophical about the whole thing.'

It was not until they were in Ida's car, driving back towards Bonn, that the two women discussed Otto Reimann in anything like detail.

'What was the amazing coincidence?' demanded Ida.

'He's practically identical to Dietlef,' Elke disclosed. 'Not in attitude, I don't mean. He's much more charming: kinder. Just like him in appearance.'

'Jesus!' exclaimed Ida, looking across the car. 'How did that make you feel?'

'I don't know,' said Elke, inadequately.

The diary entry that night was fuller than it had been for a long time. She wrote: *Car badly damaged in a hit-and-run accident. The man innocently involved was extremely kind. Very unhappy.*

It was a positive decision not to record the physical similarity to the man who had abandoned her.

Reimann could not have cared less about getting a quick repair estimate for the cars. He went to the garage that afternoon to discover if the police had examined his car forensically, hoping to find fingerprints, for instance. He knew, of course, there would be no trace from such professionals, but it was the sort of question that might possibly be relayed from Moscow and he wanted to have a reply instantly available. The police hadn't shown any scientific interest whatsoever in the Mercedes. Reimann endured the price-hiking discussion with the foreman about the extent of the damage, accepted the insistence that any estimate would take several days and left promising to keep in touch by telephone.

He actually did telephone instead of personally visiting the police headquarters, playing the necessary role of a concerned car owner. He patiently waited through several department transfers before being connected to an officer who regretted there had not been an arrest. The Porsche, which turned out to have been stolen too, had been located within thirty minutes of the Engeltalstrasse collision, abandoned across the river in Limperich. There was a higher than normal number of alerts out for other vehicles reported stolen that day. The officer was sorry. Reimann said he understood.

Because it was the weekend, with the possibility of other tenants being at home in the block, Reimann waited until darkness before

105

crossing the city to Nord-Stadt. As a further precaution, he telephoned ahead to warn Jutta. And despite her assurance that it was safe, he remained cautious entering the building, confident when he eventually did so that he reached her apartment undetected.

'Scotch or schnapps?' she said.

'Scotch.'

Jutta made the same for them both, with ice, and tuned the radio until she found thumping pop-music. 'There's a package on the hall table: it's the format for the article you're supposed to write next week.'

'I'll pick it up as I leave.' There had been two already. It was childishly simply, like colouring by numbers; there was a framework of the article with gaps which had to be filled in with the latest statistics and information. Always, however, there were accompanying briefing notes so that if there was any query or later discussion upon what he had supposedly written he would be able to handle it. Equally efficient, Reimann had always learned the instructions by heart.

'They want a complete report.'

Reimann knew there had been insufficient time for such a demand already to have come from Moscow: it was clever of Jutta to introduce the demand directly after the mundane operational business of how he was supposed to work. Careful against the self-satisfaction sounding too obvious, he said: 'Quite simple. Everything went exactly as planned and expected. There's been an encounter and a definite reason for my making contact with her again.'

'Do the police suspect anything?'

'Of course,' said Reimann at once, showing up the question for its carelessness. 'They suspect thieves tried to steal my car and crashed it in the attempt.'

Jutta coloured, slightly. 'It was quite an ordinary interiew then?'

'Quite ordinary,' he assured. 'Those are the honest facts, aren't they?'

'There could have been problems, getting away from the crash.'

'But there *weren't* were there?'

'What about the woman, now that you've met her?'

A professional or a personal query? Reimann wondered. He said: 'Highly strung. Almost hysterical. Insecure, which is perhaps surprising, considering the responsibility of the job she has. Works hard – and quite well – at concealing it.'

Jutta raised her eyebrows at the fullness of the assessment. 'To our advantage?'

Professional, judged Reimann. Cautiously, he said: 'I don't know, not yet.'

'Did she show any responses?'

'Tell Moscow I think there was a recognition: certainly something.'

'*Tell* them?' questioned Jutta, challenging.

They remained staring at each other for several moments. Reimann said: 'Don't pick fights, Jutta! Please!'

'I don't intend there to be one.'

'Good. You'll tell Moscow?'

'I think we should be careful, don't you?'

'One of us should,' said Reimann, pointedly.

Predictably Jutta refused him the last word. 'Yes,' she agreed. 'One of us. Why don't you keep it in mind?'

Chapter Thirteen

Elke's life away from the ordered smoothness of the Chancellery was suddenly filled with too many distractions and demands, some trivial, some not. She became aware of the obvious, practical problems – trivial to many but not to her – of visiting Ursula the day after the crash. Ida said a taxi would be a ridiculous expense and offered to take her. Elke accepted at once and just as quickly wished she had not. Ida was late reaching Kaufmannstrasse, even later getting them to the home, and on the way announced she couldn't wait for as long as Elke customarily stayed. Returning to Bonn, Elke wondered whether her sister was using the trip to see her stuttering lover: the insistence on providing transport had been hurried, a seized-upon idea. She waited for Ida to start talking about the man but she didn't, which Elke decided was probably a confirmation that Ida was on her way to see him. Elke recognized it as an uncharitable doubt, but couldn't lose it.

Getting to the Chancellery became an ordeal. She tried the train that ran parallel with Adenauerallee, but even though she attempted to maintain her early arrival, ahead of the rush-hour, there were still too many people jostled and packed around her, stifling her with their closeness.

The garage seemed surprised to receive her call, having talked only to Herr Reimann, who'd said he would handle any queries. Elke insisted that was not so, that she wanted to deal with everything concerning her own vehicle, and made them amend their records with her address. The estimate was still being prepared and would not be available for several days: the Volkswagen was the more extensively damaged of the two vehicles: the work was going to be expensive.

Günther Werle was excessively considerate. He immediately offered her whatever time off she needed to settle the formalities, gave her an introduction to his own lawyer if she needed legal advice and, guessing her travelling problems, proposed he should collect her in the mornings and return her in the evenings. It would have meant a considerable detour at the beginning and end of every day because he lived at Bad Godesberg, although in a more expensive residential part than Ida. Elke refused. Apart from extending his travelling time it would also have meant her being unable to prepare everything in advance of his getting to the office. It would also have resulted in their publicly entering and leaving the Chancellery together, which would have been quite improper, despite the true innocence of the situation. So Elke arranged a temporary account with a taxi firm.

She did take advantage of Werle's time-off suggestion when her insurance company spoke on the telephone of complications over her claim. The insurance official she met was an unsympathetic, unsmiling man with dandruff and a squint, who talked too long and officiously of the need to establish responsibility and guilt. There was little that could be done, he feared, until the police concluded their inquiries: certainly no repairs could be authorized to the Volkswagen to incur expense that might be recoverable from another guilty party. The police regretted no final report could be made to any insurance company while the investigation remained open.

Frustrated, and feeling an increasing helplessness confronted by bureaucracy she expertly recognized but of which, until now, she had rarely been a victim, Elke went to Werle's lawyer. The man was unexpectedly young, far more sympathetic, and did not use the cumbersome language of the insurance inspector, but he was matchingly depressing. Of course he would represent her and would press strongly for an early settlement. But these were always slow-moving situations: insurance companies procrastinated until the last moment to avoid paying out and equally to prevent expending a pfennig more than their legal minimum. Like everyone else to whom Elke had spoken, he was sorry.

But not as sorry – or as emptied or exhausted – as Elke.

There had been other, mercifully few, times like this, times when personal problems had engulfed her, as personal problems always did. Occasions she'd needed help she couldn't find: and didn't know where to look – not even to Ida, who had always helped as much as she was capable of helping anyone. The pregnancy and the birth, of course: far more important – the whole episode initially far more catastrophic – than whatever was or was not happening now. That final reluctant acceptance that there was no alternative to Ursula's admission to the clinic. Catastrophic again. And lesser things: the trivial, ordinary, seemingly easy things. Negotiating the long-term lease at Kaufmannstrasse. That had been a torment for Elke, a woman on her own: not knowing – not *completely* knowing, despite the conveyancing lawyer's advice – whether it was a good or bad decision. Even purchasing the Volkswagen (The right car? The wrong car? The right price? The wrong price?) that was now the cause of this new upheaval, this personal earthquake that would have been a minimal tremor on others' Richter scales.

Just as it had seemed a minimal tremor upon the personal Richter scale of a brown-eyed, attentive and strangely recognizable man named Otto Reimann, whose business card described him as the Bonn correspondent for an Australian magazine group. Throughout, Elke found herself thinking a lot about Otto Reimann and supposed it was because of the remarkable similarity. She had expected him to contact her. She recognized there was no specific need, their having exchanged all necessary detail at the scene, but she'd imagined there would be *some* further communication. A wrong expectation? Obviously so. What was there to talk about, apart from commiserating? The only possible interest, tenuous even then, was whether he'd heard if the people who'd stolen his car had been caught. Was there any other reason? What about to apologize? But apologize for what? He hadn't been at the wheel when it had happened; if he had the accident would have been quite straightforward and there wouldn't be all this difficulty.

Elke waited four days, before trying to call him. She had no definite question and most certainly no other reason for telephoning other than the accident. Her only hope was to hear something, to be told something, that would enable her to hurry the procedure up, to get her car back on the road and to settle at least the practical disadvantage of the crash.

Reimann was at Rochusplatz when the call came. He sat staring at the telephone, expressionless and unmoving, curious to know if it was Elke, but with no intention of lifting the receiver to find out. He knew it would not be Jutta. Their identification code was two rings, disconnect, one ring, disconnect, two rings, disconnect, answer on the next dial. And it didn't matter if it was any of the West German ministries or press spokesmen, all of whom now accepted his accreditation and knew his home telephone number to announce a sudden press conference or a news release. He could pick up any of that later from the press bureaux. There was nothing waiting for him when he checked, so he guessed it probably had been Elke Meyer. He was at the apartment when she tried the following day. He didn't answer then, either. Convinced it would be Elke, he thought: I have to lead, you have to follow, even in something as inconsequential as a telephone call. That's the only way it's ever going to be. Wait, Elke: wait until I'm quite ready.

The concert visit with Günther Werle continued Elke's chapter of misfortune. Without a car of her own, he had to collect her from Kaufmannstrasse. She'd bought gin and whisky and vodka, as well as red and white wine. In hallway and living-room she displayed daisies and chrysanthemum and gypsophila. Werle arrived with six short-stemmed roses that were lost against the flowers she already had. Poppi pawed irritatingly, until she had to exile the dog into the kitchen. Werle asked for mineral water, which she didn't have: he only sipped half a glass of white wine. She split the cork into the bottle, opening it. The cocktail snacks she had bought specially were soft and stale. Each floundered for conversation not involving the office. Poppi gave him the opportunity to talk about the wolfhounds he kept at home, which surprised Elke because Günther Werle did not look like the sort of man to have wolfhounds. Elke said a review she'd read had described the orchestra they were going to see as magnificent. Werle said he'd read the same review. He asked about the accident and she said there was no progress. He said he was sorry. She refused a pre-recital or interval drink at the Beethovenhalle, because he didn't seem to enjoy drinking. She would have liked to mingle with fashionably dressed concert-goers, pleased that the dark blue silk dress she had worried over fitted perfectly into the surroundings. Both read their programmes avidly.

The recital was magnificent, and Elke became completely absorbed in and by the music, not permitting anything else into her consciousness – not car accidents or her sister's affair or loans she'd made and hadn't wanted to or whether she was comfortable or not to be sharing the evening with a married man who seemed to be having as much difficulty with the situation as she was. There weren't even thoughts of Ursula, who usually occupied a part of Elke's mind at all times.

The restaurant to which he took her afterwards was in a narrow alley in Süd-Stadt. They ate trout with almonds and pork with apples and apricots, and although Elke said she only wanted a glass Werle insisted upon ordering a whole bottle of wine. It was drier than that she'd served at the flat and he drank two glasses. The excellence of the concert provided the initial conversation, and during it Elke decided it was ridiculous, creating an atmosphere of artificiality between them, not to talk about the man's family. Werle was proud of his son's progress at school and his prospects for eventual university entrance. Elke got the impression he was slightly less enthusiastic when she asked about his wife. There was still no definite date for her return from the spa near Munich. Her perpetual ill-health was a great tragedy.

It was past midnight when they got back to Kaufmannstrasse, and Elke was relieved that Werle kept the engine running. They both sat looking directly ahead.

111

'Maybe it would be possible for us to attend another recital, some time in the future?' he said.

'Maybe.' Elke felt there was no other reply.

He helped her from the car and extended his hand, inclining forward in a suggestion of a formal bow when she took it.

'How was it?' demanded Ida eagerly when she telephoned the following evening.

'Wonderful,' Elke lied.

When the telephone rang again within the hour, Elke thought it was her sister wanting to talk about something she had forgotten on the first call.

'This is Otto Reimann,' said the voice. 'My car was involved in the collision with yours, at the weekend?'

'Yes,' said Elke. At last!

'Just thought I'd call to see that everything's going along all right,' said Reimann brightly. 'The police tell me they haven't caught anyone, though.'

'The police told me that, too,' said Elke. 'And everything is *not* going along all right. It's becoming very difficult.' She hadn't intended to be accusing, as if it were his fault.

Just about the right amount of aggrieved indignation, judged Reimann, satisfied. He said: 'That's terrible! What's the problem?'

'Apportioning guilt or blame.'

This wasn't to be a protracted discussion, Reimann reflected: there had to be a meeting, the two of them face to face again. Pushing the concern into his voice, he said: 'Could we meet, perhaps, to talk about it? As I told you at the time, I'd like to be able to sort it out, if I could.'

'What could you do?' asked Elke, uncertainly.

'I don't know, not at this moment. Something might occur to me if we had the opportunity to talk it through.'

'I suppose we could.' Elke was still uncertain.

She had to be hurried, before there were any doubts. 'At your convenience,' he said, apparently generous.

Elke didn't know what to say. 'I . . . ah . . . I'm . . .'

'How about tomorrow?' pressed Reimann. 'We're trying to move things along, after all.'

'I suppose tomorrow would be all right.'

'I've only been in Bonn a short while. I don't know a place to suggest.'

Neither did she, Elke realized. 'I'm not sure,' she said.

'There's my apartment,' suggested Reimann, deciding he could just take the chance: if she agreed, so much the better.

'I don't think so,' she refused primly and at once.

'I could come to you,' he offered.

She desperately wanted to get everything resolved: to get her car back and be finished with all the inconvenience. 'All right,' she agreed. 'Eight?' She tried to sound positive, a woman in charge of herself.

'Eight will be fine,' Reimann accepted, guessing her effort. He had it! Had her! Now it was important to get off the line, not to permit her to retract.

'Do you imagine you'll be able to think of something?'

'I'm sure I can.' He smiled down at the replaced telephone. He wouldn't answer it again, not unless Jutta made a coded call, until after he'd been to Kaufmannstrasse. He couldn't risk any change of mind, not now. Elke Meyer couldn't be allowed to escape: *wouldn't* escape. It was going well. So very well.

Nikolai Turev was already considering the private meeting with Reimann, before the first of the panics.

The listening devices were permanently installed in Jutta's flat in Nord-Stadt, embedded undetectably behind plaster in the walls and ceilings – even where the telephone connections were fixed – and all automatically monitored from another Soviet-rented and permanently manned flat across the sparsely grassed rectangle separating the four blocks of the complex.

Every activity was initially recorded, including the minimal love-making. Turev listened to it all, not from any deviant reason but to satisfy himself another way, to ensure no personal problems ever arose between the couple. From the master-tapes he had the KGB Technical Division refine a second recording, removing the sexual interruptions and the extraneous evidence of Jutta in the place by herself: the facile music, the tuneless humming, the television soundtrack, the self-conversation. (*What a mind! How can someone with a philosophy as weak as that be described as an expert! Of course America's colonialist! Always has been. Too much relaxation: that's how the satellites broke away. Weakness.*)

To listen to their actual, unwitting, exchanges.

Turev was not overly concerned, not yet. Just alert. Jutta's attitude continued to show resentment. And despite warnings, here in Moscow before he'd been dispatched, Reimann appeared almost to want Jutta openly to acknowledge the secondary, more menial role she now had to fulfil.

113

Had she already unknowingly revealed her awareness of it, to the inherent jeopardy of the operation? The accounts and reports she had so assuredly presented during their two personal meetings in Vienna since everything had been set into motion were just fractionally at variance with what he heard on the recordings. Those recordings showed she was trying too hard to remain the person in charge, the one who imposed the procedures and conditions.

Reimann had to avoid creating an atmosphere of antagonism.

Turev was trying to decide upon a recall, calculating the wisdom of involving Sorokin in the decision, when the first bombshell exploded, although it came in the muted sound of the telephone.

'It looks genuine!' insisted Cherny, anxious to believe because what lay before them could confirm a conviction he refused to abandon – that NATO would always remain a militarily aggressive organization. In his excitement the soldier was hunched at Sorokin's shoulder, gazing down at the document lying on the Deputy Chairman's desk, all the usual antipathy forgotten.

'The Technical Division have analysed the paper,' Sorokin agreed. 'It's definitely of German manufacture and of the type we know, from originals we managed to get hold of in the past, the Bonn government use. And the postmark was from Bonn.'

At that moment Turev flustered into the deputy's suite, nervous at the summons from the First Chief Directorate headquarters in the Moscow suburb. Ahead of Sorokin, the army chief snatched the papers from the desk, offering them to the fat and breathless man. 'An official West German report, a discussion document on NATO troop strength!' he declared.

'What . . . ?' groped Turev.

Sorokin tried to restore his position. 'They arrived, anonymously, by post at our Austrian embassy yesterday. The top and last pages are missing: they will have been removed to avoid any identification of source.'

'A trap: disinformation,' Turev assessed at once. 'Proper intelligence doesn't arrive like this, in the mail!'

'There have been walk-ins in the past,' Sorokin reminded them. 'This would qualify for the description. But I agree: it's unthinkable that we could act in any way upon it.'

'If Reimann could confirm the authenticity, it would be a different matter.'

'I want more than authenticity,' Turev rapped. 'It's not uncommon for a Western intelligence service to leak a genuine document as a lure.'

'For what purpose?' demanded the soldier.

'The obvious one. To test our reaction: see how we jump. As well as authenticity, I'd want positively to know the source.'

'While I don't think we should overreact, we can't possibly dismiss it, either,' said Sorokin, trying for the middle path.

'I want Reimann activated at once.' Cherny was insistent.

Sorokin regarded the soldier sourly before looking inquiringly at Turev. The other Russian said: 'There's a meeting scheduled with Jutta first. The system established to bypass her to Reimann will take longer.'

'Restrict it to Reimann,' ordered Sorokin. 'I don't want him thinking there's a separate operation: that's he's being excluded from something. But keep it away from the woman: she needn't know.'

'You should have devised a quicker method of contact,' Cherny complained.

Sorokin didn't like the soldier's constant impatience.

Chapter Fourteen

Reimann was late, by a carefully calculated thirty-five minutes. He stood in the concealing shadows of Kaufmannstrasse, hopefully watching Elke's lighted window, intent for any curtain flicker or better still the outright look into the street to tell him he had tilted her equilibrium by not arriving at their agreed time. He saw nothing but still hoped she had been unbalanced. If he was completely to succeed – as there could be no doubt that he would – the exhaustively trained Reimann considered it important always to nudge Elke from the centre of every comforting pathway she tried to find. So even minimal lateness would upset her.

Reimann carried nothing with him – not flowers or chocolates – when he finally entered the apartment house, because the gesture would have been wrong. This was not a social visit. It was the arrival of someone trying to help after an unfortunate encounter: as much as anything, a business meeting. The trivial although meaningful love gifts – meaningful to her – could come later.

Elke opened the door to admit him as if she were unsure who it would be: the yapping Poppi was scratching and pawing at some other door closed against it. He decided the dog was going to be a constant irritation: he didn't like dogs of any sort, not at the best of times and certainly not this one.

'You found it, then?' she said, inviting the apology.

'Easily,' said Reimann, not offering one.

The interior of the apartment was everything he had expected from the information he had about the woman: only surgical gowns would have been necessary for it to be used as a sterilized operating theatre. She had still to be jostled off centre, for a while. 'I'm not intruding? Your husband won't mind my being here?'

'There isn't a husband,' said Elke, softly. More strongly she went on: 'And in the circumstances it's hardly an intrusion, is it? I want to get things settled if I can.'

Reimann nodded. She'd avoided looking at him in admitting to being unmarried. 'Of course,' he said. He looked around the flat, seeming to study it. 'Nice,' he said. 'Very nice.'

Elke gestured him towards a seat, vaguely aware of a masculine cologne. She said: 'I was lucky to get it, on a long lease. Did you find it a problem?' It was so easy to make comparisons with the long-ago Dietlef Becker.

'An apartment?' queried Reimann. Before she had time to confirm her question he said: 'I guess I was lucky, too. An old place, on Rochusplatz. The pipes make a noise. But it suits me.'

'Bonn's not easy sometimes.' It was not the most riveting of social conversation but she felt easy with it. So did he, she noticed. He lounged, rather than sat, appearing quite relaxed. It was, she realized upon reflection, the chair Günther Werle had occupied, perched on the edge as if ready to spring up at any moment.

'Lucky,' repeated Reimann. He guessed she'd changed, for his visit. The skirt was uncreased from any daytime wear and the shirt was crisp, the pressed finish obvious. And she *did* have big tits. The blonde hair was carefully brushed in place, benefiting from the care of a good hairdresser. A little different shade of make-up might have helped, but not appreciably. With detached objectivity Reimann concluded that literally upon face value this appeared a much better assignment than it might have been.

Elke moved to talk about the accident, but stopped before any words came. 'Can I get you anything? A drink, I mean?' She felt good, sophisticated, making the gesture.

'Scotch would be fine,' Reimann accepted. He'd wondered if there would be the offer. The files didn't talk about her being a drinker, apart from wine.

'By itself?' Ida had prompted her.

'Ice, if you have it.'

Elke had not thought how to stop Poppi escaping from the kitchen, if she went to get the drinks. The dachshund scuttled by, yapping and snarling, and she twisted back to retrieve him. Before she could, Reimann said: 'Leave him. Let's try to make friends.'

Elke watched as the man offered his reversed hand, muttering inaudibly. It took a long time for Poppi to quieten but he did eventually, finally approaching with a cautious tail-wag, sniffing. Reimann didn't hurry, waiting until there had been several licking movements before putting his fingers behind the dog's ears. When that was accepted he easily lifted the animal into his lap, still rubbing its ears.

'Do you have a dog?' asked Elke, admiringly. Otto Reimann looked more the type of person to have a wolfhound than Günther Werle.

'It wouldn't be fair on the animal, with the sort of job I have,' said

Reimann. 'But I like them, particularly this one. What's his name?' He loathed the slimy feeling of its tongue upon his hand, and the wet warmth of its body against his leg.

'Poppi,' smiled Elke. She'd *known* he'd be a nice man, from seeing the gesture towards Poppi in the café just after the accident that Saturday. 'He's . . .' began Elke, unthinkingly, halting just before saying Poppi was really Ursula's dog.

'What?' asked Reimann.

'Not a puppy any more,' she resumed. 'Five years old.' Seizing the escape, she said: 'I'll get the drinks.'

She didn't know how much whisky to pour. Guessing at the bottle cap as a measure, she put in two, but it didn't seem enough so she topped it up from the bottle itself: when she put in two cubes of ice, the liquid came quite high in the glass. She tried the recorked white wine she had opened for Günther Werle, grimacing when she tasted it. It was like the wine Kissel had served at Bad Godesberg, claiming it came from Drachenfels. Elke threw it away, opened the other bottle and sipped that. It was much better.

When Elke returned to the living-room, Reimann was standing head bent by the bookshelves, the better to read the titles. The dog was still in his arms. He turned at her entry and said: 'This is a pretty intimidating selection. You actually like Goethe!'

Elke smiled at the demand: he *was* an easy person to be with: much easier than Dietlef. Stop it! She said: 'In all honesty, not a lot. But he's one of our greatest writers. I felt I should try.'

'*You must be master and win, or serve and lose, grieve or triumph, be the anvil or the hammer*,' quoted Reimann. It could sum up perfectly how he intended the relationship between himself and Elke to develop.

Elke was impressed that he knew Goethe well enough to recite like that. She said: 'His philosophy always seemed very hard to me. I could never find much that was appropriate to quote.' Or circumstances in which to quote it, she thought.

Reimann came away from the bookshelf, reaching out for his drink.

'I hope that's all right,' said Elke, the uneasy hostess.

Reimann sat again, still keeping the dog on his lap, before judging the drink. 'Perfect,' he announced, knowing she would welcome the praise. Time they got around to his supposed reason for being here. 'Tell me about the problems with the accident.'

As she spoke Elke was aware of his attention being solely upon her, just as it had been in the café immediately after the episode. She finished by nodding towards the small, closed bureau by the book-

118

shelves and said: 'I've got all the documentation there has been so far, if you want to see it.'

'They're just stringing things out,' he said. 'Keeping hold of their money as long as possible.'

'Which the lawyer insists they can do.' Irrationally she had expected him to say something that would solve everything, not repeat what she had already been told. She felt disappointed.

'Unless they can apportion guilt?' queried Reimann, repeating what she had said in recounting her difficulties.

Elke nodded. 'Which isn't going to happen, is it? It was all caused by car thieves who haven't been caught. And aren't likely to be, not now.'

'Maybe it could be resolved in some way, even without that,' suggested Reimann. The whisky was really good: he decided upon another one before he left. Perhaps two. And decided, also, to get the the bloody dog off his lap as soon as possible.

'How?' Elke demanded.

'I didn't lock my car,' said Reimann, in apparent admission. 'And I left the keys in the ignition. That made it easier to steal, didn't it? I would think it certainly makes me more culpable than you if insurance companies are trying to work out the blame between themselves.'

Elke stared at the man, not immediately able to think of anything to say. 'I suppose . . . but . . .'

'But why not?' said Reimann. 'That's what I did. Which was careless. I should admit it, shouldn't I?'

'You're very honest,' said Elke.

Which is *exactly* what you're supposed to believe, thought Reimann. 'That's my profession; being an honest observer and commentator. And a rule I try to follow personally, as well.'

'It makes you quite an unusual person,' said Elke, admiringly. She'd momentarily forgotten his being a journalist.

Reimann lowered the protesting dog to the floor, holding his glass so she could see it was obviously empty. The dog started to paw to be lifted again and Elke said: 'Poppi, come away, come here . . . oh, would you like another drink?'

Reimann smiled his acceptance, offering her the glass. This was the first time he'd properly practised any of the intensive instruction in anything other than a training situation, where people knew what he was doing or trying to achieve. This was *precisely* what all those months had been focused upon his achieving. And Reimann liked it. He liked listening to Elke Meyer's clumsy words and watching her stiff body movements and knowing – guessing, he was sure, to within ninety per cent accuracy – what she was thinking and what she would say next. He liked looking so directly at her and doing things and saying things and anticipating how she'd respond, just seconds before she gave that response. It made him feel supremely powerful, already able to do what he wanted with her. Careful, he warned himself. It would be wrong to think that: he was a long way from attaining that degree of power. It would come though. Disgusted he began plucking off hairs that stuck to his clothes from the filthy dog.

In the kitchen Elke settled Poppi in his basket and stood over him briefly, admonishing him to stay there. She was careful to make her visitor's drink just as she had before, adding the same amount of ice. She hadn't been wrong, she thought, pleased: by showing such incredible honesty, he had suggested a way of hopefully getting things moving more quickly. Was he married? It was almost inevitable that he would be. A man who . . . Elke stopped the reflection, irritated at herself. What possible connection could there be between what they were talking about here tonight and the man's personal, private life? It had been ridiculous to let her mind drift like that.

'I've put Poppi in the kitchen,' she announced needlessly, handing Reimann the refilled glass.

'He's cute,' smiled Reimann. Deciding it was tilt time again, he added: 'He must be good company for you?' He knew he'd succeeded when he saw the flush come to her face.

Elke hoped he hadn't seen her colour. Hurriedly she said: 'He is; very much so.'

'Do you work?' asked Reimann, experimenting further. 'I mean it might be difficult if you've got a full-time job, with a dog to look after.'

'For the government,' said Elke, intentionally vague. 'He's very well house-trained.'

So are you, thought Reimann, noting how she'd avoided any indication of what she did. Pressing to see if she would volunteer more, he invoked the cliché and said: 'The government! That must be interesting!'

'Not really,' refused Elke. 'It's all dull bureaucracy.' She was sure she had no reason for caution, with someone who had shown so much integrity, but he *was* a journalist. And the stock replies were practically automatic anyway.

It's anything but dull bureaucracy, my love, he thought: perhaps it was not going to be quite as easy as he'd earlier imagined. Too soon to have doubts, just as it had been too soon to reflect about the power of anticipation over her. It was obvious she would show reticence with

120

someone she knew as slightly as she knew him at the moment, and important that she did not consider him too curious. 'I suppose I'd better look at that correspondence you talked about.'

Elke hurried to the bureau and produced the file. It was a compartmented dossier, with an alphabetical index inside the top cover. Everything was listed against its numbered slot in her neatly legible, well formed handwriting. Little containers for a little mind, Reimann thought.

Reimann read the letters thoroughly, particularly those from Elke's insurance company, making a note of reference numbers on the correspondence and, most important, the name of the inspector who was handling Elke's claim.

'Do you really think you can do something?' asked the still unconvinced Elke when he handed back the dossier.

'We'll have to see, won't we?' Reimann let his eyes move, as if quickly appraising her body, and the pinpoints of colour came to her cheeks again. Should he manipulate another whisky?

'What will it involve? For you, I mean?'

'Telling the insurance companies I didn't secure the car, obviously. Maybe making a fresh statement to the police.' He wouldn't bother about another drink: he shouldn't do anything at this stage to deter her, and she might be deterred at the thought of his drinking heavily.

'Will you get into trouble?' she asked.

It was such a little-girl question that Reimann openly laughed, although gently, not to offend her. 'People will probably be upset,' he allowed. 'But then it's my fault, my problem, isn't it?'

'You've been very good about this,' she said.

He had to be the person to decide to go: it would be wrong to make her uncomfortable by remaining too long on this occasion. Reimann snapped shut the notebook in which he had detailed her correspondence. 'I think I've got all I need. If I think of something else perhaps I can give you a call?'

'Of course.'

Making another small experiment, to see if she would disclose a fraction more about what she did, Reimann said: 'Shall I telephone here? Or at work? You can take calls at work, can you?

'Here,' said Elke, quickly. 'I'm here most . . .' Her voice faded at the open admission of her empty private existence. With no choice, she concluded: '. . . most nights.'

'Here, then,' said Reimann, appearing unaware of the hesitation, which he noted at once.

121

'I'll wait to hear,' said Elke.

Was she trying to prolong the encounter? It was a quick impression, but practically for the first time since he'd entered the apartment Reimann was unsure of the woman's attitude. Beware over-confidence, he told himself. Even if she was, it would be wiser to ignore it at this early point. He thanked Elke for the drinks as he stood and shook her hand (soft skinned, as he'd guessed from the photographs in Moscow), and out in the street he hurried to the concealing shadow of the Kaufmannstrasse from which he'd watched the flat earlier. He did so again, curious for any curtain flicker to show she was looking for him. There was nothing that was obvious.

He dialled their coded sequence from a street kiosk, warning Jutta when she picked up the phone that he was on his way if she considered it safe. She did. He stopped the taxi two streets short of her apartment block, so that the destination wasn't obvious and in order to assure himself – absurdly unlikely though it was – that there was no surveillance.

The drink that Jutta had waiting for him when he entered her apartment was weaker than the inexperienced Elke had made and there was only one piece of ice. They selected the covering music and Reimann sat directly opposite his wife, dictating the instructions she had to pass on, pausing to confirm that she had correctly recorded Elke Meyer's insurance details.

'Won't the insurers here become suspicious when the Australian company accept liability?' queried Jutta.

'Surprised, probably,' concerned Reimann. 'And then delighted to be off the hook. From the correspondence it was obvious they were twisting every way they could to avoid payment. They're not going to launch an inquiry or argue when they're offered the very escape they want.'

'What was she like?' demanded Jutta.

'I've already told you what she's like.'

'It must have been different tonight. When she was more relaxed: in charge of herself.'

'She wasn't relaxed and she was only just in charge of herself.'

'Were you attracted to her?'

'She's a dried-up, nervous, totally insecure spinster with no sexual attraction whatsoever,' Reimann insisted, and Jutta smiled. Maybe it's easy to manipulate every woman, he thought. Too confident again! *Most* women, then.

*

122

'He sounds too good to be true,' Ida judged the following day. She hoped her overlooked sister wasn't expecting too much. Or that, if something did develop, Elke wasn't hurt again: in her heart of hearts Ida was reconciled to Elke always remaining a spinster.

Elke hadn't intended to sound quite so excited. Trying to pull back, she said: 'He's a genuinely nice man.'

'I can't believe you didn't try to find out if he was married!'

'How could I have done?' demanded Elke. '*Why* should I have done?'

'What else is there to tell me?'

'Nothing,' said Elke. Certainly not how she'd ended the evening, after the man had gone. And this time without Chopin's 'Chanson de l'Adieu' to encourage the fantasy.

The bulging and grossly overweight Nikolai Turev liked luxury and privilege and indulged himself whenever the opportunity presented itself, which was why he chose Vienna for his meeting with Jutta, even before the coincidence of the anonymous West German document being received at the Soviet embassy there. There was no intention of his going anywhere near the Russian legation. He stayed at the Sacher and ate wild boar at the Drei Hussars. His mornings and afternoons were divided between taking chocolate Sachertorte and coffee at the Sacher or chocolate Demeltorte and coffee at Demel's. It was at Demel's, in the old part of the city, that he met Jutta, to learn of Reimann's second, friendship-making encounter with Elke Meyer.

He nodded through the mist of tobacco smoke when the woman finished, accepting from her the insurance company notes to ensure there would be no mistake in what Australia had to do. 'So it seems to have gone exactly to plan?' he said. It had been a wise edict, to cut Jutta out of the inquiries into the anonymous letter: there was little that she could have practically done, and it might easily have created tension between her and Reimann.

'It would seem so,' Jutta agreed.

'You haven't told me how Otto feels about her.' The KGB Technical Division had succeeded in getting a full transcript of the couple's conversation after Reimann's visit to Kaufmannstrasse, despite the loud music. Turev was intrigued at whatever account Jutta might give.

'He said she was dried up: not attractive at all,' said Jutta, honestly.

Turev thought the disinterest was forced. He considered a second Demeltorte. They were delicious and he wanted one, but he was reluctant to ruin his appetite for dinner. 'Do you think Otto has settled in and adjusted now?'

123

'It seems so. He hasn't spoken much about the journalistic cover.'

'Then ask him! It's important that it remains absolute: that there's no professional curiosity or doubt from other reporters or commentators.' This reminded Turev, and he handed the woman the latest story outline and instructions for Reimann's next dispatch. The package was larger than at any previous meeting because it contained one of the Australian magazines with the first article purportedly written by Reimann.

'Not too much progress so far,' said Jutta. She was attempting modesty, but to Turev it implied criticism of her husband.

'But it's *started* well.' Setting the test for the woman, Turev said: 'Be sure to tell Otto how pleased we are.' He *would* have another Demeltorte: dinner was hours away yet.

On the day Turev returned to Moscow, the second anonymous package of what appeared to be West German government communications arrived at the Soviet embassy in Vienna. Again the front and rear sheets were missing. The papers appeared to be a discussion document on Warsaw Pact troop strengths and commitment, after so much Soviet military withdrawal from the now independent satellite nations.

'Germany always thinks militarily!' insisted Cherny. 'They don't know any other way! This is proof, if ever we needed it. Which we don't. Isn't this the very question we're being asked to resolve?'

'We daren't put it forward for Presidential Council consideration until we have positive verification,' said Sorokin. 'And at this stage, not even then. Everything we're getting is incomplete. And I don't mean the missing pages. These are meaningless, without our knowing the context in which they're being created and discussed.'

Chapter Fifteen

Reimann had, in fact, adjusted very comfortably into the journalistic role of a Bonn-based political commentator on European affairs. At least once a day he diligently visited the press building, amused at the irony of its closeness to the Chancellery that was his intended target. He made a point of attending the most important of the announced press conferences and particularly the off-the-record government briefings. He was affable towards the other correspondents to the extent of drinking with them in their chosen bar in Joachimstrasse, even enjoying the political arguments and discussions, but careful not to allow anything like friendship to build with any of them. He found the Moscow-inspired articles comparatively easy to create, provided as he was with such a comprehensive framework to operate from, quickly noting that the detailed guidance always cleverly gave his supposed pieces a right-wing bias, sometimes quite critical of the Soviet Union. He always drafted the articles in note form at the Rochusplatz apartment but wrote them from these notes at his designated desk at the press centre, where he could openly be seen at work. He also used the centre's communication facilities to file to Australia: the completeness of his cover came with the acknowledgements – and sometimes apparent instructions of what they wanted written in future – coming back to him from Australia through the centre.

It was from Australia, although to Rochusplatz, that the letter came, in stiffly phrased legal terms, accepting all liability and responsibility for the repairs to the Volkswagen. He telephoned Elke at once.

'I can't believe it!' said Elke. 'Just like that!'

'I'm glad it's worked out,' said Reimann. She was obviously excited, which was good, because she wouldn't be thinking clearly. And grateful to him, which it was right that she should be. And important that she should be, too.

'What do I have to do?' asked the reliant Elke. Wonderful: it was absolutely wonderful! She'd known he was a nice man, from the very first.

Reimann smiled at the obvious, professional answers that came to mind. 'You'll need the formal letter . . .' He hesitated, momentarily unsure how to continue. Dominate from the beginning, he decided. 'I'll

125

bring it around tonight.' He was sure she would not refuse, but against her doing so he added: 'It'll enable you to contact your insurance company first thing tomorrow: probably order the repairs to be started, too.'

Elke did not respond immediately. He appeared to be inviting himself, but why shouldn't she agree? It *would* enable her to get things moving: there'd been too much delay. She looked around the immaculate apartment that needed no tidying and said: 'An hour?'

'I'll be there in an hour,' Reimann accepted.

Elke felt lifted, delighted. Five minutes ago all the problems with the car had seemed tangled and confusing. And now they weren't. Now it was all over. Solved. An hour, Elke warned herself. She set out the glasses in the kitchen and considered taking the ice from the freezer compartment in readiness but didn't, not wanting it to melt before his arrival. In her bedroom Elke stood undecided before her wardrobe for several minutes, finally selecting a blue linen dress. She took it out and brushed it but did not put it on, to avoid it creasing. She took off the suit she had been wearing, leaning close to the mirror to examine her make-up. Her eyes were fine. Just lipstick then. And her hair. Elke combed it, studied the result and combed it again, wanting it to be right. She put on more lipstick, blotting it with tissue. Perfume would be too strong: toilet water would be sufficient. She sprayed that lightly. Elke turned back to the dress but did not move at once towards it. Instead, from where she stood, she examined herself in just bra and pants in the full-length wardrobe mirror. Instinctively she pulled in her stomach, just slightly, but just as quickly decided she didn't need to: she'd lost that weight and hadn't put it back. Her legs were firm, not bumped with cellulite anywhere. The bra helped, of course, but there was very little sag: better than Ida, she guessed, thinking back to the constant comparison when they'd been younger. She turned slightly sideways, actually feeling her buttocks. No sag there, either. And her face . . . Why? The demand burst into Elke's mind and she saw her reflection wince. Why was she posing like this, parading herself? For whom? Or for what? In her embarrassment she crossed her arms, covering her already covered pubes, hiding herself from herself. Thank God no one had seen her: would ever know what she was doing.

She hurried into the dress, not examining herself at all when it was on, and went back into the kitchen. She broke the ice out into a dish, refilled the tray to make more, and put the prepared cubes into the refrigerator. Poppi, seemingly aware of the preparations, stirred and came curiously out of his basket. Elke smiled down and said:

'Someone's coming. A man who's helped me. Isn't that nice, Poppi?'

Reimann timed his arrival to be late again, not bothering this time to watch from the street for an anxious curtain flicker. When Elke admitted him the smoothness in the skirt of the linen dress showed that she had changed for his coming, as she had before: her cologne – he wasn't sure if it was actually perfume – was obvious. Good, he thought: very good.

'It's considerate of you to come like this,' said Elke. Some people were inherently bad time-keepers: it wasn't important.

'I want to get everything sorted out,' said Reimann. 'I feel responsible.' From the kitchen came the sound of the dog, yapping: thank Christ the door was firmly shut.

'I don't think you are. Not very much, anyway.' Concentrating upon the man, after Ida's chatter of questions, Elke thought how firm-bodied he seemed, like someone who took physical exercise.

'You're lucky my publishers think I am,' grinned Reimann.

She hadn't noticed, either, the slightly protruding eye-tooth: it wasn't ugly. She said: 'It's whisky, isn't it?'

'Please,' accepted Reimann. The grin became a smile of amusement Elke was never to know, at her obvious effort at sophistication.

Predictably Poppi scurried around her leg-blocking attempt to keep him in the kitchen and came up, tongue-lolling, against Reimann's leg. It *was* like a rat, he thought: a long-haired rat with stunted legs. He wondered how far across the room it would travel if he kicked it, stetched up on its hind legs as it was: probably to the far wall. When Elke called out for the dog to come back to her in the kitchen Reimann said: 'Let him stay: it's good to see him again.' It smelled, a damp-earth dog smell, when he picked it up. He remained standing with it in his arms, determined on this occasion not to sit with it on his lap to prolong the time he had to hold it.

In the kitchen Elke made the whisky exactly as she had before: she was much quicker, with the ice ready. The white wine, corked from the previous visit, was sharp when she tried an experimental taste. It would have to do.

With the dog under one arm, Reimann appeared to reach for the letter inside his jacket when she returned, stopping when she offered the drink. 'I think we'd better put him back in the kitchen,' he said. He didn't hand the animal to her but carried it himself to the door, which hid the action of his skidding it across the floor towards its basket. He did take the letter out as he went back to her, with a hand free now to

127

receive his drink. 'The admission of liability that will settle everything,' he announced.

'I'll never know how to thank you.'

No, mused Reimann: you won't. He said: 'It should all be straightforward now. And again, I'm sorry.' Come on! he thought: ask the question I want.

Elke had not encountered anyone who looked so directly at her as he did. She said: 'What do I do now?'

Exactly on cue, Reimann decided, satisfied. 'Give that to your insurance company. Withdraw any claim against them. Tell the garage to go ahead with the repairs and send the bill to me . . .' He let the sentence hang.

'What?' queried Elke.

Reimann wondered if it would be as easy to train the bloody dog. He said: 'Something that just occurred to me, as I was talking . . . whether the garage will accept instructions from you to bill someone else for the work. It might sound odd.'

'It might, mightn't it?' Her concern began to rise.

'No problem!' said Reimann, forcefully. 'I'll do it. I have to authorize the repairs to the Mercedes. I'll simply tell them to fix both and let me have the bill. Simple.'

'You always seem to make it so,' said Elke. The response had been automatic and she wished she'd thought it out before speaking; it had sounded like obvious flattery.

'Anyway,' said Reimann, guessing her regret from her colouring and talking over it as if he hadn't thought the sentence strange. 'It'll save you the hassle of dealing or arguing with garages, won't it?'

'Will there be arguments?' asked Elke, at once.

'There will be, if the work isn't done properly,' said Reimann. Playing his personal anticipatory game, he thought: look Elke, my glass is empty.

'You're extremely kind. I'll never know . . .' She stopped, then finished: 'I've already said that, haven't I?'

Glass, Elke; look at my glass! He said: 'I'm sure I've more spare time than you: I literally decide my own hours.'

'Would you like more whisky?'

'Thank you,' said Reimann. Fractionally slow, stupid woman, he thought. He'd train her, quickly enough.

Elke was more adept at the door, managing to prevent the dog getting past her into the living-room. Alone, Reimann gazed back towards the hallway and the adjoining doors he had isolated as he'd entered. He would have to explore, minimally: edge slightly further into her life. He smiled his thanks when Elke returned with the drink and said: 'You are allowed to receive telephone calls at work, aren't you? There might be something we have to talk about, during the day.'

'I try to avoid them,' said Elke, cautiously. 'But if it's urgent . . .'

'I won't call unless it's absolutely necessary,' promised Reimann, easily. It would provide another encroaching opportunity.

Elke crossed to the bureau and quickly scribbled her personal number on to a reminder pad. As she handed it to the man she said, unthinking: 'That's my private number: it'll come directly to my desk.'

'Private number!' exclaimed Reimann, pretending surprised although vaguely mocking admiration. 'You didn't tell me you were important enough in the government to qualify for private extensions!'

Elke's colour returned. 'I'm attached to the Chancellery,' she admitted.

Reassure her, he quickly decided: make no comment to indicate any interest whatsoever. 'I'll telephone you here, of course: let you know what they say at the garage. And you can tell me the reaction of the insurance company.'

'Yes,' Elke agreed. 'I'll see to it tomorrow.' She knew already that the diary was not particularly heavy. And Günther would allow her time off, if it were necessary. How much more comfortable she felt with this man in her apartment than she had the night Günther had taken her to the Philharmonic concert.

Reimann edged his glass on to the low table between them, fixing what he hoped was a shy smile. 'I wonder if I might use your bathroom.'

Not imagining the need, she hadn't checked the bathroom for tidiness. But it was never *untidy*: she never permitted anything to remain untidy. 'It's on the right, as you go out,' she said, gesturing towards the hallway.

Reimann bolted the door before going first to the most obvious, the mirrored wall cabinet. There was a container of tooth floss, a tube of antiseptic cream alongside a bottle of liquid antiseptic, deodorants – a body stick and a separate vaginal deodorizer – and two flasks of bath oils. Her toothbrush was capped with a small plastic top, to keep the head clean. The toothpaste promised to prevent plaque. The female razor was electric, packed neatly in its plastic case: there was no stubble detritus to indicate its recent use. There were tampons in an already opened box in the cupboard beneath the sink, with two bottles of pain-killing pills adjacent. He moved the bottles and found a third, its label actually promising relief from menstrual cramps: he would have to be particularly solicitous every month. A third cupboard contained bathroom cleaning equipment. Reimann flushed the unused toilet and splashed water noisily into the sink, actually washing his hands to dampen a towel if she checked. So what had he learned? That she was painstakingly neat: a characteristic he already knew. That she was careful about personal hygiene, which until now had been a fairly obvious surmise but not positively confirmed. And the analgesic pills next to the sanitary protection: that alone justified the exercise. He would have liked very much to investigate her bedroom. Where did the remaining door lead? To what had been the child's bedroom, he supposed. He wondered what the woman used it for now.

Elke strained for conversation – for *anything* to talk about – when Reimann emerged from the bathroom. 'I want you to know how very much I appreciate all you're doing,' was the best she could manage.

'The whole silly business has dragged on long enough,' said Reimann. He looked past her, to the bookshelves, realizing how he could manoeuvre another visit to Kaufmannstrasse, even beyond whatever excuse he felt necessary to invent from the car repairs.

'It'll be so good, to get my car back,' said Elke. The taxi to and from Marienfels the previous Sunday had cost almost a hundred and fifty marks.

'I'll get it done as fast as possible,' Reimann promised. 'Don't forget my number, if something occurs to you that we haven't discussed. Any time.'

'I won't,' said Elke. 'Although I can't imagine your forgetting anything.' It sounded overly flattering, like the earlier remark she had regretted: fortunately he didn't seem to consider it misplaced, any more than he had before.

Reimann had the impression – and felt, self-satisfied, that his impressions about her had so far been remarkably accurate – that Elke would have welcomed his staying. Which made it important for him to get out, hopefully to leave her feeling she could not hold a man's attention. He finish his whisky in a gulp and said: 'I certainly can't think of anything at this moment.'

'Would you like another drink?' offered Elke, hurriedly.

Right again! thought Reimann, the self-satisfaction growing. 'No thank you,' he said, rising from the chair. 'There are things I have to do. I'll be in touch.'

The following day Günther Werle said it was good there appeared to be some progress at last over the accident and agreed at once, as she'd guessed he would, to Elke taking time off to visit the insurance company offices. She was glad she did. It only took an hour, and she utilized the inspector's secretary to dictate her withdrawal-of-claim letter.

Reimann telephoned the Chancellery in the afternoon to intrude as soon as possible into another section of Elke Meyer's personal territory, particularly a section where he had no right. But which, if she thought about it later, he would be entering with her permission. It was going to be an essential acceptance for her to develop. He apologized for calling, the excuse already prepared. One tyre needed replacing. The three remaining tyres, undamaged in the accident, would nevertheless show greater wear than the new one, creating a small risk of imbalance on the road. Small though that risk was, he had therefore told the garage to fit a complete new set.

'You're being extremely helpful,' said Elke. It was not a problem she would have known about, to raise with the garage. She doubted whether her evasive insurers would have bothered, either.

'They said the work would take a fortnight,' Reimann lied. 'I told them I would like it done in a week.' A week had been the work period the garage had promised.

'A week! Can it really be done as quickly as that?'

'I'll do all I can to see that it is.' Reimann had given the foreman a hundred marks to ensure the Volkswagen got preferential attention in the workshop, with the hint there would be more if everything was completed on schedule.

'That would be absolutely wonderful!' Excited as she was, Elke realized that the telephone conversation was going on for a long time, and she shifted uncomfortably in her chair. She'd checked all the correspondence and reports, ready for Günther Werle's signature, so the call wasn't keeping her from any outstanding work. She certainly didn't want to cut Reimann short.

The moment once more to tilt you off centre, thought Reimann. He said: 'I suppose I'd better have the letter back, from the company?'

'I have it ready,' said Elke. She smiled, expectantly: for his third visit it would not be out of place to offer some cocktail snacks. But better than she'd got for Günther. And maybe a fresh bottle of whisky. She was not sure if what remained in the existing bottle was sufficient.

'You've got my address, on the card I gave you,' said Reimann. 'Put it in the post, will you?'

There was an almost imperceptible gap before Elke said: 'Yes. Yes, of course. I'll do it tonight.'

'No hurry. Whenever,' said Reimann, dismissively. Even more casually, wanting to finish on his terms, he said: 'I have to go. I'll call, when there's anything.'

Elke's feeling of well-being, the satisfaction she'd known at the ease with which everything had been settled, and which had grown into something like happiness at Reimann's call, evaporated at the curt farewell and she went solemn-faced into Werle's office for their end-of-day meeting.

The man detected her depression at once and said, concerned: 'Didn't it go well?'

Elke, who hadn't told Werle in detail why she was going to the insurers when she'd asked for the time off, decided she shouldn't appear distracted again by things occurring outside the Chancellery. 'Very well indeed,' she insisted. Trying to stress an impression of satisfaction at the outcome, she explained the settlement.

'His firm's insurers have accepted complete liability?' queried Werle, frowning.

'Absolutely,' said Elke. 'The inspector I spoke to this morning thought I was very lucky.'

'I think so, too,' said Werle. He was suddenly worried.

The security officer was the moustached man who had delivered the last warning lecture Elke had attended at the Chancellery. He listened with hunched concentration, making an occasional note. 'Paying her damage entirely!' he exclaimed when Werle finished.

'That's what she told me,' confirmed the Cabinet Secretary.

'I wouldn't have thought leaving keys in the ignition constituted absolute liability.'

'Neither would I. And because of the inquiries I have already had your department make into Elke Meyer I want to be thoroughly sure about this.'

'Otto Reimann, you said?'

'That was the name on the card she showed me. Recently appointed here as a correspondent, for Australian interests.' Werle hoped so much that Elke had not become involved in an embarrassing problem. He'd been about to make the announcement he was sure would have brought about a great difference in their relationship. And he wanted that difference to come as quickly as possible. He felt very strongly about her.

The second bombshell – with the first still echoing – created a positive panic within Sorokin's Dzerzhinsky Square office.

'There was nothing . . . no indication at all from the woman?' Sorokin demanded.

'I would have reported it, if there had been,' said Turev. If the Bonn operation had failed – had even come under the slightest suspicion – almost before it began, then everyone associated with it would be brought down as well. At least there was no provable connection with them here in Moscow, but penalties would still be exacted, privately. The publicly declared changes within the KGB were only cosmetic, for external consumption and belief; internally a lot remained as it always had been, from the time of Beria and Stalin. Turev didn't think the word purge would ever disappear from the KGB vocabulary.

'What can he have done?' said Cherny, careless of a facile question none of them could possibly answer. A man whose world was literally regimented, the soldier was uncomfortable with the constantly blurred situations of espionage.

'When was the meeting arranged, anyway?' asked Sorokin.

'The day after tomorrow,' said Turev. 'This could mean he won't ever make it: that he could be arrested.'

'Or they might let him run. We'll have to be incredibly careful, against hostile surveillance,' cautioned Sorokin. 'We don't control East Berlin any more.'

'Despite that risk, I think you should handle it personally, considering the level at which the operation was ordered,' said the soldier to the KGB deputy. 'We've still got secure military installations on East German territory: one in East Berlin itself. I could guarantee your safety that far.'

Sorokin was very frightened at the risk of detection, but more frightened of something going wrong if he did not personally supervise the encounter. To Turev he said: 'Is it too late to get any sort of warning through to Reimann?'

'Yes,' said Turev.

'We've got to go,' Sorokin accepted, dully. 'Both of us.'

Chapter Sixteen

Quite confident it was an unnecessary precaution, Reimann still travelled by a circuitous, time-consuming route to avoid leaving any detectable trail. From Cologne, the airport serving Bonn, he flew on the opening flight of the morning to Munich. There was only an hour's wait to catch his connection to Frankfurt. There he actually went into the city – by airport bus, so that he could study the other passengers for any particular interest in him – and briefly wandered the streets in the city centre, making absolutely sure there was no pursuit. He was back at the airport with time enough to eat an excellent lunch of goulash before completing the final leg of his journey into West Berlin, arriving in the late afternoon before the following day's appointment.

Reimann felt comfortable, at home, back in a city where he had spent five years of his operational life. There was, of course, not the slightest temptation to return to the old districts, to Lichterfelde or Lankwitz, where he was so familiar with all the bars and restaurants but where there would have been the risk of a chance encounter with an old acquaintance. He stayed instead in the tourist-thronged heart of the place, booking into the Am-Zoo and taking an early evening drink in a pavement café on the Kurfürstendamm. Along here the clown-dwarfs paraded at Christmas, he reflected, remembering his imagery of the Russian he was to meet. What would he have to report from his side the following day? Little more than impressions, beyond what Jutta had already passed on, he decided. OK, his impression was that he had succeeded very well: certainly he believed that Elke Meyer welcomed his presence and would not be averse to his contacting her further, after the car excuse was exhausted. Honestly objective, Reimann further decided everything was progressing at the pace it should. Although he wasn't permitting it to affect his judgement, he thought he had every reason to feel confident.

He crossed through the remains of the torn-down Wall into East Berlin promptly the next morning, remembering the old money-changing, passport-checking hindrances that had been swept away with the communist regime that imposed them. But the scaffolded, half-finished buildings still remained immediately upon the other side, looking as suspended in mid-construction as they had when he had last walked by, months ago. There were still no signs of any workers engaged in any activity.

Intentionally Reimann took a route along Normannenstrasse, past the grime-coated Ministry of State Security, the former East German intelligence service building from which he'd originally worked, before his transfer to full KGB control. The Stasi headquarters was patched with rings of scoured whiteness, making it look strangely pockmarked, a diseased building. At its base – and on the window-ledges too – were thousands of linked but smaller black scorch rings, where the candles, which they had called freedom lights, had been lit by protesters against the regime of Erich Honecker. Even now, Reimann remained astonished that it had been allowed to happen: it should have been stopped, as so much else should have been stopped. The corruption at the top and the protests at the bottom.

There was no obvious security around the safe house on Johannisstrasse, just a plainclothes, grunting attendant who opened the door to admit him, but Reimann was sure there would be hidden but extensive protection. The bubble-fat, white-haired Turev was standing apprehensively in front of a bare desk. Already behind it was a bearded man, tending to middle-aged plumpness, whom Reimann had not met before.

'What is it!' Turev demanded at once, his own panic spurred by Sorokin's brooding presence. 'Do you know the mistake you made?'

Reimann was dumbfounded. 'Mistake? What mistake?' The Russian he knew was grey-faced and sweating, and seemed to defer to the man behind the desk. For once there was no cigarette.

'There's a security check being run on you!' announced Sorokin, deceptively quiet-voiced but inwardly as nervous as Turev. 'By Australian counter-intelligence. But obviously at Bonn's request!'

Reimann felt a sweep of cold numbness, but his training had erased the sort of panic that the other two men were showing, over an unexplained uncertainty. He had to think: find an explanation.

'What exactly – and I mean *exactly* – was the inquiry?'

'Whether the insurers had accepted responsibility for the accident,' Turev disclosed. Bitterly he added: 'It was a bad idea, arranging the encounter like that. That *was* the mistake, in fact!'

Uninvited, Reimann took the only visitor's chair, further analysing and balancing. His arrival route had been confused enough. He looked at his watch. Two hours already in East Berlin. And the nostalgic – now useful – detour to the Stasi headquarters. They'd have made any seizure before now, if they were going to move at all. Reimann felt the confidence flow back. 'Just that?' he asked. 'Just confirmation that the bill was going to be settled by a bona fide insurance company?'

'The inference is obvious!' Turev insisted.

'*Is* it a bona fide, properly trading company?' demanded Reimann. There was an opportunity to impress the bearded man, who clearly had the greater authority.

'Of course it is! Just as the magazines are,' said Turev.

'And they provided the confirmation they were asked for?' Reimann was aware of a growing alertness from the man at the desk.

Sorokin said: 'Naturally they did.'

It pleased Reimann to feel superior to both men. To Turev he said: 'You told me my legend could withstand any investigation?'

'Yes,' agreed Turev. Nervous doubt stayed in the man's voice: at last a cigarette flared into life.

Reimann smiled. 'I don't think there was any mistake at all,' he said. 'I think we've been extremely fortunate.' He had to be wary against appearing over-confident.

'Explain that,' Sorokin insisted. He was glad he had allowed Turev to lead the attack, outwardly preserving his own composure.

'Explain something to me, first,' said Reimann. 'When did you learn of the security check in Australia?'

'Just over twenty-four hours ago,' said the bearded man.

'Yet you're here, both of you. Knowing that I could be under surveillance, liable to be swept up, you kept the meeting?'

'Not blindly,' said Turev, falling into the trap.

'Exactly!' seized Reimann. 'When did your surveillance pick me up?' He realized, as he asked the question, that he was disclosing his own failing, not having identified it.

'When you crossed where the Wall used to be,' Sorokin admitted, almost enjoying the exchange now.

'I wasn't being followed, was I? If I had been, this meeting would not be taking place. There would have been a radio warning, to get you out ahead of any squad trailing me here.'

Sorokin smiled. 'So?'

'We've been extremely fortunate,' Reimann repeated. 'I don't know – and it doesn't really matter – if it was Elke Meyer who reported to security. Let's assume, let's *hope* even, that it was. As I tried to explain through Jutta, the involvement of the police inherently gave me credibility, as an honest person. And if the concealment of the Australian company and my legend is as unbreakable as you insist, we've not got the slightest cause for alarm. Just as there wasn't any cause for alarm about this meeting today. This security check is going to guarantee me completely. And not just to her, if she made the report. Now any further security inquiries won't be necessary, if anyone becomes curious at the relationship I hope to form. I will have been investigated by Bonn counter-intelligence and possess a full clearance.'

It was a formidable, convincing argument, Sorokin accepted. There had definitely been no hostile surveillance during the time Reimann had been in East Berlin. Despite the apprehension about becoming involved at ground level, Sorokin was glad to meet Reimann, to judge for himself the man's ability. Moving to take over the meeting, he said: 'We have to assume that it was the woman who made the security report. Which makes her extremely cautious.'

That awareness had registered with Reimann several minutes earlier. Tidy-minded and birdlike nervous though she was, Reimann would not have guessed at Elke running to counter-intelligence because of what had so far occurred between them. Certainly she'd queried one or two things he'd told her about the car, but those queries had *been* about the insurance, not suspicion openly directed at him. He supposed she might have discussed it with someone at the Chancellery who'd then made the report, but here again he would still not have expected such a degree of sensitivity. He *was* going to have to be careful. A further awareness came to him: the Russians appeared to have conceded his argument to look at the security check as a bonus instead of a danger. Then he *had* proved himself. 'So am I being cautious,' he said.

Sorokin stretched across the desk, offering the photostats of the two anonymous documents received in Vienna. 'Something else you should know.'

Reimann studied the papers unhurriedly, feeling very self-assured now. He looked up and said: 'How?'

It was Turev who explained, and when he finished Reimann said: 'A deception. It's got to be.'

'That's obviously the way we have to treat it at the moment,' Sorokin agreed. 'Unless we can get independent corroboration from you that such matters are being discussed by the Bonn government.'

Reimann glanced back at the photostats. 'Troop strengths and NATO are predictable subjects: it's inevitable that they *would* be discussed.'

'All the public assurances – all the Summit declarations – are that a united Germany will not constitute an aggressive partner in NATO,' said Sorokin. 'That's your assignment, above all else. To confirm that, from the Meyer woman.'

Reimann disliked the other man's attitude of arrogant superiority. He realized they were attaching more importance to anonymous papers in the post than to him: that he *was* being relegated to a subordinate role again, that of authenticating someone else's information.

'So!' demanded Sorokin, almost with the impatience of Cherny, back in Moscow. 'Do you think you can get it from her? That and a lot more?'

'In time and at the proper pace,' said Reimann, refusing to be bullied. 'To push too fast – particularly if she is responsible for the security check – would frighten her away. Be disastrous.'

'But do you believe, eventually, that you will get as close and be able to manipulate Elke Meyer as much as will be necessary?' Turev persisted. 'Necessary for everything we want?'

They were demanding far more than impressions. He determined not to be panicked into an over-commitment, so that any future failures or mistakes could be blamed upon him. He said: 'I am *reasonably* sure. But it is far too soon to go any further than that. We've met. I've shown her a lot of kindness but stopped short very positively of going any further than that. I think she's responsive, but I can't be definite . . .'

'How soon, before you *can* be more definite?' said Sorokin.

My speed, not yours, thought Reimann. He said: 'We have only reached the very beginning.'

Both Sorokin and Turev nodded, but each with visible reluctance. 'Just as long as you fully appreciate the importance,' said Sorokin. 'We have to know the NATO undertakings are genuine: to be able to guard as much as possible against any misunderstanding, or some unexpected diplomatic move being made by the United States or by a combined Europe believing that Soviet weakness is allowing too many changes from which they can take further advantage.'

'I *do* understand that,' insisted Reimann, angered at their lecturing attitude towards him.

'Has Jutta passed my message on?' asked the chain-smoking Russian, much too directly.

'Which message?' queried Reimann, instantly cautious.

'Our congratulations at what you have achieved so far,' smiled Turev.

'That's very encouraging to hear,' said Reimann, the words carefully chosen. His reply neither denied nor confirmed any message through Jutta. Which there hadn't been. Why, out of everything, had the Russian isolated that? There could, of course, be several explanations, but the one Reimann seized upon was that the man already *knew* the praise had not been relayed. From which a number of other conclusions could be reached. One was that Jutta had intentionally withheld the praise. Which meant she was stupidly still trying to retain the old position of dominance. Another conclusion was that his wife's apartment at Nord-Stadt was electronically monitored, like the apartment in Moscow.

'Have any operational difficulties arisen between you and your wife?' asked Sorokin, re-entering the discussion.

'Not in any way that I've been aware,' said Reimann, still with guarded ambiguity.

'I think, however, that these secondary personal meetings are advantageous,' Turev insisted.

'Definitely,' Reimann agreed. His initial inclination had been to persuade Jutta to move away from Nord-Stadt as soon as he got back to Bonn after this encounter. But just as quickly he changed his mind again, recognizing the personal protection the situation provided. It would be virtually pointless to move anyway: the KGB would simply bug any new apartment, in Jutta's absence. But what if he used what already existed in reverse? It didn't matter a damn whether Jutta fulfilled every instruction or not: anything she failed to communicate, in her resentment, would be realized by the Russians and given to him at these private sessions. But by knowing in advance about the hidden ears, Reimann could ensure that everyone who listened to the tapes would hear whatever *he* wanted transmitted. And never guess they were eavesdropping on what he intended them to hear! It would mean, of course, they would listen also to every private conversation and moment between himself and Jutta, but Reimann decided he couldn't give a damn about that.

'Which is why we will arrange today the reciprocal contact procedure,' Turev announced. From an inside pocket he took a small piece of card and extended it to Reimann. 'We'll go on using Rome, where the card came from that summoned you today. Memorize that box number. It's a *poste restante* facility the embassy *rezidentura* uses as a dead-letter drop.'

'But not a postcard,' anticipated Reimann, ever anxious to prove himself. 'People don't send postcards to *poste restante* box numbers.'

Turev nodded approvingly. 'We're sure the drop is undetected, but no, certainly not a postcard. An unaddressed and unsigned card but sealed in an envelope. And never traceably posted from Bonn, against the risk of any interception. Cologne is less than an hour away, by car. The postal volume there is sufficient to conceal any overseas letter.'

'What should the card say?'

'Just a number: nothing to identify it as a date. Five days after the number written on the card, I shall be here, expecting you,' Turev promised.

'We're imposing great reliance upon unreliable postal systems,' Reimann pointed out. 'If I allow three days for the envelope to reach the dead-letter drop and another day for transmission to Moscow we are working with a delay period of at least a week. What if the need is more urgent?'

'Come directly here unannounced,' ordered Turev. 'I can reach here in less than twenty-four hours.'

Reimann decided that from now on, working on the assumption of Nord-Stadt being an open channel, he was operating from a greatly enhanced position. He said: 'I don't expect such an emergency to arise. I just wanted the provision.'

Turev was determined against overreacting to what amounted to a very small failure on Jutta Reimann's part, but passingly he wondered how Reimann would react to Jutta being removed entirely from the operation. It would be premature even to attempt such a discussion. At the moment there was insufficient cause; and there was still the overwhelming, remote-control reason for the woman to remain in place. 'There's been some progress from our end,' he said. 'Our computer experts have finally broken the entry code to Elke Meyer's bank records. As we might have guessed, she's obsessed with detail and order. Not just the monthly payments for apartment rental and services. She never deviates, on her personal drawings, not in the amount or on the precise dates when those drawings are made. She receives her salary cheque on the thirtieth of every month, and the saving into deposit or insurance is made the day after. And she's a creditor's dream; bill presented, bill paid, practically always on the same day.' He paused. 'But there is one intriguing item. Last month there was an outgoing payment of thirty thousand marks. The cheque was presented against her account the day after it was issued.'

'No details of the payee?' asked Reimann hopefully.

'The ledger records aren't computerized: all we can access are the account details, which only gives us a cheque number.'

Reimann sat reflectively for several moments. 'To whom could the frugal, careful Elke Meyer be suddenly paying out thirty thousand Deutschmarks?'

'Which was about half what she had in her accounts,' said Turev, in further disclosure. 'And you are right. She *is* frugal and she *is* careful. So it must have been extremely important. Any ideas?'

Reimann shook his head. 'Not yet. But I'd like to know. That's quite a lot of money by her standards.'

'By a lot of people's standards,' said Sorokin.

'It would be good if it provided some point of pressure.'

'We'll continue to monitor,' Turev undertook.

'I want a poison,' Reimann announced, almost casually. 'It won't need to be particularly strong: it's only a minimal body weight.'

'What for?' demanded Sorokin, bewildered.

'She's very attached to the dog,' said Reimann. 'She can't be allowed another attachment, other than me. I am going to kill it.'

'Nothing!' queried Günther Werle. He was relieved. At the beginning, when he'd first necessarily proposed to the security service what he intended for Elke Meyer, there had been concern at her having had an illegitimate child.

'Nothing whatsoever to concern us,' confirmed the counter-intelligence officer. 'Or you. We've had the fullest cooperation from the American FBI and from Australian counter-intelligence. Otto Reimann checks out everywhere. He's quite genuine. We even had some of our analysts look at articles he had written. They were pretty dull but politically very sound.'

So he could go ahead, Werle decided. He wondered how Elke would respond. In her usual way, he guessed: calm, unflustered, utterly competent. He wanted very much to make the announcement but there were still the final formalities to be completed. Not much longer, though. His mind lingered upon her involvement with another man. Not really an involvement: certainly not in any way that should concern him. Which in itself was a premature reflection. There was nothing in their relationship which gave him any right to be jealous. Not yet. And in any case, jealousy was an immature emotion, one he was sure he did not possess.

Chapter Seventeen

Despite his dismissing the danger of a security investigation, Reimann remained cautious in returning to Bonn, glad in hindsight that he had taken similar precautions at the outset of the journey. He actually stayed a full day in Frankfurt inquiring among financial institutions about the importance of a stable Deutschmark in the European Exchange Rate Mechanism, material he could use in the next article for Australia. Throughout he was nerve-stetched alert for any surveillance and detected none, nor did he relax on his arrival at Cologne that night or during the drive into Bonn. He paid off the taxi two streets before Rochusplatz to approach on foot, but saw nothing to make him fear observation on his apartment. At the press centre the following morning he was greeted quite normally by journalists or officials of whom inquiries might have been made by intelligence officers. He began to feel easier.

After fulfilling his duty attendance at the press headquarters, Reimann went directly to the garage, initially ignoring his own restored vehicle to concentrate upon the Volkswagen. It had been repaired superbly. Reimann handed over the promised bonus and added a personal cheque for fifteen hundred marks to the prepared bank draft to settle in full the original estimate and the excess charges. He had the amount of that provisional estimate receipted to the Australian cover insurance company, with a separate receipt for the additional charges to be attached to his monthly expenses account. He had a second full receipt, which represented Elke's authority to retrieve her car, put into the Volkswagen.

Elke answered the telephone on the second ring, slightly breathless, as if she had hurried to it.

'The car is ready,' Reimann announced. 'It's waiting for collection.' *Had* she hurried? he wondered: he hoped so.

'That's wonderful,' said Elke. It seemed a word she was constantly using in conversations with him. It always appeared appropriate.

'I inspected it today: they've done a first-class job. You wouldn't know it's been in an accident. I'm sorry it took longer than I promised.' The work had been finished on schedule: the Berlin visit had delayed Reimann from completing the financial formalities.

'What do I have to do?' asked Elke, predictably.

'Nothing,' said Reimann, airily. He wished they had been face to face so that he could have gauged her reaction to his clear indifference. But then talking on the telephone instead of personally going to Kaufmannstrasse, which he was sure she had expected, was all part of that dismissal.

'Nothing!' she echoed.

'It's *all* fixed,' Reimann repeated. 'I've left the release forms, all signed, with the car. All you've got to do is pick it up.' She couldn't misunderstand what he was saying now: goodbye, brief acquaintance. Finished.

'Oh,' Elke said. The disappointment was obvious.

'Is there a problem?' asked Reimann, solicitously.

'No . . . I . . . No problem at all.'

All alone with no one to help any more, thought Reimann: just as I planned this moment to be. He said: 'I think the garage expect you to collect it tomorrow, if it's convenient. If it's not, you'd better give them a call.'

'Yes . . . of course . . . I'll get it tomorrow.' Elke strained to think what she had to do, how she had to do it. Ask Günther for time off again, she supposed. Make an appointment with the garage, so the car would be immediately ready for collection. But Otto (she was mentally calling him Otto now?) had already said it was ready. No purpose then. She'd call, though. So that it *would* be waiting on the forecourt when she arrived to drive directly back to the Chancellery. Only be away for an hour. Two at the most. Wouldn't it have been wonderful (that word again!) if he'd collected it for her: driven it to Kaufmannstrasse and come up to the apartment to hand over the keys and whatever a release document was? She had another bottle of whisky. Two, actually, just in case. In case of what? Nothing. Not important. Somehow she'd fixed her mind upon his bringing the car back to her, that's all. It would have finished everything off. It would have been so . . .

'Well, that's it then!' said Reimann, briskly.

'Yes.'

'In future I'll lock my car.'

'Yes.'

It was working very well, he judged. Prolong her helplessness for a moment. 'Sorry we met under such upsetting circumstances.'

'Yes.'

'I'm glad it's finally been resolved.'

'Yes.'

Elke coughed, because something caught in her throat. She was anxious to sound casual, as he was casual, but couldn't find the words: she rarely could.

It hadn't been necessary to be face to face. Or, he thought, widening the reflection, to be as cautious as he had been to the Russians in East Berlin, about his chances of success. Still wise, though, to have behaved as he had. 'Goodnight,' he said.

Where were the words? The proper, sensible adult words that should be so easy for her! She said: 'Thank you, for everything. You've been . . . you've made it extremely easy for me. I'm grateful. Really I am.' A tongue-tied schoolgirl, Elke thought, bitterly: just like a tongue-tied schoolgirl. Ida wouldn't have been like that: Ida would have been talking easily, joking even, making friends. *Upsetting circumstances but now we've met. Why don't we get together again? All's well that ends better. You call me, I'll call you. Whatever.* Ida was never tongue-tied: never like a schoolgirl. Even if some of the phrases were gauche, too obviously borrowed from some imported, American-originated soap opera. Did she want to copy or borrow from American soap opera? No. Just to be able to find words, to feel comfortable, the way the calm, rarely flustered people in soap operas always appeared, smooth-talking and unharassed and in command of everything, themselves most of all.

'So goodbye again. Take care.' And Reimann abruptly put the telephone down, not allowing her a farewell reply. Elke Meyer had to be alone now, think alone, grow further uncertain. Marinate was the word that most readily came into Reimann's mind: meat became more tender if it was allowed a period to marinate.

Jutta's response, after the preliminary telephone code, was as prompt as Elke's had been but without the breathlessness. But then she'd had the forewarning to be by the receiver, waiting.

'I tried telephoning several times,' she accused at once. 'There was no reply.'

'I was out.'

'I called around midnight. And then early: before seven.'

There were a lot of easy explanations for his absence in East Berlin: the most obvious was travelling beyond Bonn ostensibly to research his articles, absolutely to maintain his cover. He'd even gone through the motions, in Frankfurt. Why should he have to bother? It was good not having to explain to anybody but his ultimate Soviet masters. Maybe not even to them. 'I said I was out.'

'I see,' said Jutta.

Hard then soft, remembered Reimann. The exact phrase that one of the more frequent Balashikha instructors had used: the vague-mannered, dyed-haired one who'd invoked the cliché in describing an interrogation technique and who had appeared butter-soft until you'd looked at his eyes and realized they were empty and utterly devoid of any feeling, any pity. Reimann said: 'Why don't we meet tomorrow?'

'What's wrong with tonight?'

'I have things to do.' He didn't: he wanted an evening alone at Rochusplatz, to think and to review things. *One misplaced brick in a foundation can reduce a skyscraper to dust*: another dictum, on the importance of every detail, from a lecturer he could not recall as vividly as the fey man.

Jutta didn't offer any argument. 'What time will you be here tomorrow then?' Her voice was dull.

Reimann did not want to spend every moment of his time with Jutta mentally assessing every word before he uttered it in front of the microphones he was convinced existed in the Nord-Stadt apartment. There was no reason why Jutta should be constantly exposed, either. He said: 'Why don't we get out for the day? It's nearly summer, after all!' The telephone would be tapped, of course. So what? Why shouldn't the two of them spend a day out together?

'Where?' There was a lift to her voice.

Reimann hadn't decided. 'The river!' he said, on impulse. 'Why don't we take a Rhine cruise? There's an embarkation point just south of the Kennedy Bridge.'

'I know it,' said Jutta, more eager still. 'What time?'

'Early,' Reimann insisted: there was as much danger going every day to the press building as there was not going at all. 'Let's take whatever ferry is leaving around ten thirty?'

'I'll be waiting,' promised Jutta. Which she was, by the ticket kiosk. She wore light jeans and a striped cotton shirt, with a sweater bundled over one arm. Reimann thought she was the sort of woman able to look good – beautiful even – in either formal or casual clothes. She hurried forward when she saw him and he reached out invitingly, happy to see her. They kissed and he said: 'Today and tomorrow and the day after! How's that?'

'Good.' Her attitude was light and frothy, for which he was glad: he didn't want the introverted seriousness Jutta had shown since they'd left Moscow. Nor, either, the demanding demeanour that had been so common earlier, in West Berlin.

There was an explanatory map in a kiosk display case. Jutta studied it for several moments and then, without looking at him, said: 'How about Linz?'

'Linz is fine.' Reimann bought the tickets and cupped Jutta's arm to lead her to the jetty. It was going to be hot later, but at this moment, still comparatively early, it was merely pleasantly warm. Out on the river the incredibly long container barges ploughed nose-down in either direction, like cubed alligators made from children's building blocks. Beside him Jutta covered with hers the hand he had against her arm. It was not a particularly attentive action, more something she did automatically, the unthinking movement of the person who had known the other for a long time. A married couple's: I-know-you're-there-and-I-know-you're-mine. Reimann smiled down at her, wishing there were more such gestures, truly attentive or not.

Was she withholding or manipulating things from Moscow to maintain the tiny imagined supremacy that was so important to her? It didn't matter, with the dual system of control that had been devised now: he wished so much that it hadn't always been so important for her to dominate, in everything.

The ferry was a fast-moving hydrofoil, which meant they were entirely enclosed on rows of seats close together, making it impossible to talk of anything they did not wish to be overheard by other passengers. So without discussing it they decided not to talk at all. They sat arm in arm, her hand still covering his, staring out at the landmarks as they sped up beneath a hovering rainbow of coloured spray. They encountered a lot of cubed alligators and some others hump-backed with what looked like coal. With an irony Reimann was not to know for some time, he pointed out the Drachenfels Castle towering over Königswinter, with its wine slopes in between.

At Linz, still arm in arm, they used the pedestrian underpass to negotiate the shore road into the old town, entering through the medieval gate. As they began climbing the cobbled hill, Jutta said: 'There's no reason why we can't have days like this all the time, is there? Even when you're with her, I mean?'

So Jutta had accepted that he was going to succeed in seducing Elke Meyer. 'None at all. She'll be working during the day. I won't be with her every night, either.'

Both spoke quite dispassionately, as if Elke Meyer were a thing, an object, not a person.

'I'd like that.' Jutta halted, so he had to stop too, and looked directly up at him. 'I'm bored,' she announced. 'In Berlin there was something to do, every day: we really *worked*, quite properly, at the agency. Here there's nothing for me to do, except go to Vienna once a fortnight. The rest of the time all I do is read books I don't enjoy, watch bloody awful

146

television, bloody awful films, drive around the countryside or wander around Bonn. You know how long it takes, to walk completely around Bonn? Two hours! I timed it!'

So she was finally realizing her inferior position, Reimann thought. At last! He started climbing again, bringing her with him. It was lucky he'd insisted on the day out instead of going to the Nord-Stadt apartment: he would not have wanted Moscow to overhear the outburst. They would have been furious at the revelation of two contact meetings a month, all apparently in Vienna. If their Control was prepared to cross into the West to meet Jutta, why were his own meetings with the man in East Berlin? Maybe no reason at all: everything did not require a purpose or meaning. He said: 'I don't think it's as bad as you're making out. There were lots of boring times in Berlin. Let's give this operation a chance.'

'I've even thought of approaching the refugee agency in Munich, as they asked me to when I left Berlin,' Jutta disclosed. 'Nothing full-time, of course. I could still make the Vienna meetings if I worked part-time. There could still be useful things to learn.'

She was trying to retreat into the past to recapture her old command, Reimann guessed at once. 'That's nonsense. And I don't want you to do that.'

'*You* don't want me to do that!' she snapped, bridling.

The square, with its red-shuttered, flower-bedecked town hall, ballooned out in front of them. Reimann continued walking, looping to the left along the still-cobbled street towards a tiny oasis in the middle of the road, one tree and a tight round of seats, none of them occupied. He urged her to sit and did the same himself, at a corner where he could see anyone approaching to make their conversation impossible. 'Not me,' he said. 'Moscow wouldn't want it. You're here for a specific purpose. If you're bored, you've got to put up with it, like the trained officer you are supposed to be. There can be no contact, no association, with anyone we knew in the past. You know that.' It was good to feel – to *be* – the person in authority at last.

Jutta's face set hard and Reimann wondered if he had been too obvious. But she didn't fight back. Instead, inadequately for her, Jutta said: 'It was only an idea.'

'Have you said anything like this in Vienna?' he demanded, concerned. It would explain, beyond any recording devices at Nord-Stadt, the East Berlin conversation about how he and Jutta were working together.

She shook her head. 'Not yet.'

'Not yet!'

'I was wondering whether to,' she admitted. 'Not like I've talked about it to you. Maybe just suggest I should get something part-time, to give me a better cover.'

'Don't! It would be a mistake: a very bad mistake,' insisted Reimann, careless of antagonizing her again. What about him! Jutta was showing a weakness that she shouldn't, a weakness he would not have expected from her, and he was surprised. As a professional and dedicated intelligence officer shouldn't he use the newly evolved contact system with the Russians to warn of a possible problem? They would recall her, he guessed. It would be more difficult for him to operate alone, having personally to maintain a regular, twice-monthly liaison, but another cut-out could be introduced easily enough. So what would her withdrawal actually mean? It would ensure the protection and safety of the Bonn operation, the first priority. Free him from her demanding and mostly imagined control. He paused, confronting a further realization. Free him in another way, too. Because it would mean the virtual end of their marriage. He'd been trained to think and act completely without emotion, in those long psychological sessions at Balashikha. And this was a simple, professional choice. Not even a choice. There was only one decision there could be. Jutta had to be discarded, abandoned, for the sake of the assignment.

But he wouldn't, Reimann decided.

He wouldn't abandon her or disclose the unexpectedly emerging weakness. He'd try to do the opposite – do what a husband was supposed to do – and protect her. He'd protect her from making this mistake and he'd protect her as best he could from making other blurted errors in her dangerous apartment.

Would Jutta do the same for him, if the situation were reversed? Reimann surprised himself with the question. And the doubt. Forcing the honesty, he concluded that she probably wouldn't. He'd always recognized that her professional commitment – her career – matched her commitment to their marriage. It was a further explanation, he supposed, for this utterly unexpected conversation between them, her awareness, despite the Soviet attempts to make it appear otherwise, that professionally she had been diminished.

What Jutta would or would not do didn't matter. He'd made his decision. And was satisfied with it.

'I know you're right,' Jutta accepted.

She was deferring to him, Reimann realized, detecting a further change. The beginning-of-the-day lightness between them had gone now, but it had not been replaced by her frequent combativeness, for which he was glad. As insistently as he could, Reimann said: 'Moscow mustn't suspect anything is wrong: that there is any uncertainty at all.'

Two ancient men, stooped and whiskered, emerged bowed from a fronting tobacconist: one already had a pipe lighted, trailing smoke like a cartoon steam engine. Reimann moved before their arrival at the oasis, taking Jutta's arm once more to bring her up from her seat to retrace their way along the cobbles.

'I've spoiled the day,' Jutta apologized. 'I shouldn't have talked as I have.'

'Let's always talk things through: get difficulties out of the way.' But not at Nord-Stadt, he thought, in private warning. Despite his earlier decision, he hoped that Jutta's depression was not going to become an intrusive complication.

She looked up at him again, smiling gratefully. 'I promise,' she said. 'I really do.'

Reimann had noted several attractive restaurants during their ascent from the river valley. He chose one on the steepest part of the hill, angled to seem practically lopsided, an inn of foot-scuffed wooden floors and worn, ponderous carved furniture. They drank wine – Jutta with seemingly urgency, so a second bottle was necessary before their meal arrived – and Reimann restored the professionalism by explaining the increase in the car repair estimate, to justify the expenses he was submitting to Australia.

'What now?' she asked.

'I carefully make the next move,' said Reimann.

'I see,' said Jutta, repeating the earlier acceptance.

Reimann was caught by the flatness in her voice. He wouldn't question it.

As if aware of his thoughts Jutta said, with abrupt forcefulness: 'I'm sorry. You mustn't worry about me.' She seemed embarrassed.

Strangely, Reimann felt embarrassed, too.

Reimann was sure of the schedule, to within five minutes or so, but he was still in position early at the alleyway junction with the Münsterplatz, only just able to see through the intervening throng into the flower market square for Elke's arrival. She was ahead of her usual time, by about three minutes. He allowed her to get settled at the Bonner, completely relaxed, before even moving: when he entered the café Elke was already at her table, her coffee poured, the apple cake without cream or custard set out before her.

Reimann stood blinking in the doorway, someone having difficulty adjusting from the outer brightness, his face opening in surprise when she finally looked up to see him. He smiled and approached hesitantly, as if uncertain of intruding.

'Hello!' he said.

'Hello.' Elke felt an absurd delight at his totally unexpected presence, a numbed, tingling sensation as if she'd knocked into an obstruction and jarred a nerve: maybe several nerves.

Poppi darted from his concealment beneath the second chair, tail fluttering in recognition, yapping up against Reimann's leg. Reimann leaned down, to fondle its ears. He said: 'What a coincidence!'

'I come here quite often,' Elke conceded.

'How's the car?'

'Wond . . .' began Elke but stopped the too familiar word. 'As good as new, like you said it would be.'

She saw him look searchingly around the interior of the café, then fleetingly at the spare chair at her table. He said: 'Well, I'd better . . .'

'Why don't you join me?' Elke invited. She was sure the darkness of the café would conceal any blush that might have come to her face.

'I wouldn't like to impose . . .' said Reimann, in weak protest.

'Please! I'm not expecting anyone.' *Please!* she thought.

Reimann pulled out the chair, shifting the dog out of his way, and sat down. 'I'd like to,' he accepted. Clara, the dutiful waitress, was at his side immediately. Reimann chose only coffee.

'What brings you to the flower market?' said Elke. Clumsy maybe, but good enough in the circumstances.

'Not flowers,' smiled Reimann. He made a vague gesture away from the outside stalls, towards the commanding cathedral. 'I've been browsing in the bookshop. I particularly wanted a Graham Greene compendium: *The Heart of the Matter, A Burnt-out Case* and *The Power and the Glory*. They didn't have it: I know it exists but they weren't very helpful. It's a nuisance. I suppose I'll have to look elsewhere.'

Elke sat with her cup suspended before her. 'This really is a coincidence!'

'I don't follow,' said Reimann, who did, because he was pointing out the pathway to her.

'I have it!' announced Elke.

I know, thought Reimann: that's where I saw it, in your bookshelf. He sat back, in faked astonishment. 'I don't believe it!'

Elke laughed, unsurely. 'Isn't that strange?'

'You must tell me where you bought it,' said Reimann, who knew from the KGB's briefing where Elke Meyer maintained her account.

Now she gestured, in the same direction as he had minutes earlier. 'The bookshop near the Münster,' she said.

Reimann let his face fall into disappointment. 'So much for that,' he said, resigned. Come on, woman! Come on!

'You could borrow mine,' she offered.

Reimann adopted his uncertain, not-wanting-to-impose attitude again. 'You're sure you wouldn't mind?'

'Of course not. I've read it.' There'd be a meeting to hand it over and a meeting to retrieve it.

'That really would be extremely good of you,' said Reimann. 'I'd take the greatest care of it, of course. Greene's one of my favourite foreign authors. He was once a journalist too, you know?'

'I think I read that somewhere,' said Elke. It was all being so easy: so easy and so natural. Her nerves still tingled.

'How could I collect it?' said Reimann. 'I don't want to put you to any inconvenience.'

'I'm doing something today. And tomorrow,' said Elke. It would have been possible for him to come to Kaufmannstrasse when she returned later from Bad Godesberg, or tomorrow, after visiting Ursula, but Elke enjoyed conveying the impression of full days.

Posturing cow, thought Reimann. He said: 'Could I telephone some evening next week? Tuesday perhaps?'

'Tuesday would be fine,' Elke accepted, too quickly. 'Why bother to telephone? Why don't we agree here and now that's when you'll come by to pick it up?'

She was making it simple for him, Reimann reflected. But then he'd never seriously doubted that she wouldn't.

The third anonymous and disguised document that arrived in Vienna was an instruction to West German diplomats in former Soviet satellites for a country-by-country assessment of any remaining allegiance to Moscow. Coupled with it was a request for any available guidance about the likely secession of Soviet republics, and indications of Soviet troop movements to quell such fresh dissent.

'What the hell do they want that for?' queried Sorokin.

'What reason makes any potential enemy force want military information about other countries?' said Cherny. 'Inconclusive and difficult though it is to explain, we've got to forward reports about this information soon.'

151

'No!' Sorokin would not budge. 'It *is* inconclusive. We'd be raising more questions than we can provide answers, which isn't intelligence. It's *got* to come from Reimann.'

'Nothing *is* coming from Reimann,' argued Cherny, equally insistent.

'It will,' said Sorokin. 'In time it will.'

Chapter Eighteen

They each made a consummate effort, and with contrasting irony for the identical reason, to impress the other.

It was acceptable, at last, for Reimann to take a gift. He initially disdained the obvious flowers or chocolates, but everything else he considered, in an attempt to be original, seemed upon examination to be kitsch. In the end he reverted to flowers, imagining a way to introduce them that was gauche but which he believed would appeal to her. And he bought a chewing toy for the dog, which was so appallingly kitsch that he was hot from discomfort as he made the purchase but reassured himself it was just the sort of gesture that Elke would appreciate, and use words like 'sweet' and 'thoughtful' when she thanked him. On Monday, considerately, he telephoned to ask if the following evening's arrangement was still convenient. Elke, stomach tight at the instant apprehension that he intended cancelling, gabbled that it was fine and that she was expecting him. There's so much more you don't expect, thought Reimann: so very much more.

Elke had happily begun disturbing her established routine immediately she got home from being with Ursula at Marienfels on the Sunday afternoon, starting to vacuum and polish and rearrange the apartment. It was not until Monday evening, just before Reimann's courtesy call (so polite, but then what else has she come to expect?) that Elke attended to her own bedroom. It was here that she kept Ursula's photographs, three individual pictures in separate frames and a collage of several different snapshots arranged in one composite group. Elke stood looking at them for a long time, easily recognizing the occasions when each one had been taken. Two when Ursula had been a newly born baby, before they'd known anything was wrong, at her mother's house across the river, at Oberkassel; at birthdays, the second and the third, when the warnings had started but she hadn't really believed them, Ursula still seeming so normal, so beautiful; she'd been eight when the picture had been taken of her near the roundabout in the play park, not smiling like the other children in the background, the blankness in her eyes obvious, as everything else had been obvious by then. Slowly, studying them as she did it, Elke dusted the frames and the glass. Having cleaned them, Elke remained staring down at the assembled images of her daughter. Without any positive, reasoning thought she put them all in the underwear drawer of her dressing table. 'Don't want to share you,' said Elke, in one of her private conversations. 'Just the two of us.' There was no question – it was inconceivable – of the man seeing into the room in any case, but she didn't want Ursula on display: it had something to do with the child's dignity.

There was an unopened bottle of whisky and some still remained in the old one, so there was no need for more, just wine for herself. She found a new and extensively stocked delicatessen where she was able to try the snacks before buying, and waited until the Tuesday night before having fresh coffee ground from Colombian beans that the delicatessen owner personally recommended.

Elke bathed as soon as she got into the apartment on the Tuesday, but left her hair because it looked all right as it was and might not fall as well if she washed and dried it again. She stood undecided and completely naked before the dressing-table mirror, choosing between the cologne and the scented dusting powder. Cologne, she determined, because the smell would last longer. She made up carefully and lightly before selecting her newest skirt and sweater, smiling despite her rejection at the time of Ida's smirked suggestion after the Saturday lunch ('Don't wear a bra, and if you wear a skirt that's just a teeny-weeny bit tight he could see you weren't wearing any knickers, either'). Both bra and pants were new. The waist slip was new, too. Excellent, judged Elke, surveying the finished affect. She looked exactly as she wanted to appear: a relaxed, self-assured, career executive. She wished she were as self-assured as the reflection gazing back at her with her face and her body and wearing her clothes. This was the best she could do: the best she – anyone – could hope for. Ida would have probably recommended something else.

She prepared the snack dishes at the last minute, preserving the dishes in clingfilm in the refrigerator and broke out the ice, recalling the convenience of doing so from one of his previous visits.

'I wonder what's going to happen, Poppi?' she said to the attentive dog which sat ears cocked, head curiously to one side. Probably nothing, she thought, answering her own question. She didn't want anything – whatever anything was – to happen tonight. This was virtually the first social visit: the others had been about the car, so that had been business. But tonight he was coming to call. Tonight she didn't have to read a book or seek a radio concert: didn't have to think. That wasn't right: she had constantly to think, to find subjects to talk about and words to express them, to try to show she had opinions and views and character. That she wasn't dull. But it had been an easy reflection to have, because during the scant association that was how she had come to feel in Otto Reimann's presence: that he would do all the thinking and make all the decisions. It was a warm feeling: one she sought.

Would he arrive as promised? They'd arranged eight, but they'd fixed times before and he'd always been late. She took the Graham Greene anthology from the shelf and laid it on top of the bookcase in readiness. But immediately decided that was wrong – as if she had made too much preparation for his visit, which she had – and put it back. Would he want to discuss the stories? It was a long time since she'd read them, and Elke realized she'd hardly retained any of the plots. She took the book out again, beginning to flick through to remind herself, but stopped. How could he discuss novels he hadn't read yet? Silly mistake: worrying too much. She'd have to guard against doing something like that – saying something silly – when he got here. She was nervous of doing anything that made her appear foolish: frightened of doing anything. She replaced the book again and went back into the bedroom, examining her reflection in the full-length wardrobe mirror. Elke saw she was quite flushed: no need for any further blusher on her cheeks. What about slightly heavier lipstick? Advertise your wares, Ida had urged, puckering her lips in illustration. But she wasn't advertising anything, Elke reminded herself: didn't consider she had anything *to* advertise. She'd let the make-up stay as it was. She looked at the underwear drawer in which Ursula's photographs rested. 'You'd understand, darling,' she said. 'I know you'd understand.'

The doorbell sounded promptly at eight.

Elke was ready, waiting. She moved at once, stopped, moved again. Not too quick: wrong to be too quick, as if she were anxious, which she was.

Reimann counted, guessing. Glad. Like she should have been: had to be. Trying: always trying. One minute, two minutes, three minutes. OK, you've made your pitiful point.

'Hello.' Standing back for him to enter. He looked so calm, so relaxed. His attention, as always, utterly directed towards her.

Reimann offered his gifts and said: 'I want to say thank you in advance. As we met again near the flower market it had to be flowers, didn't it?'

'They're beautiful,' Elke accepted. They were roses, like Günther had bought, but these were *proper* roses – long-stemmed, to fit in a full sized vase, not stunted, lost if they were mixed with other blooms, as

155

Günther's had been. Elke sought the old axiom, for the significance. Red roses for love, white roses for peace: she thought that was it, although she wasn't sure. Reimann's bouquet was pink, noncommittal.

'And this!' he announced, offering a gift-wrapped box.

'What is it?'

'Open it!' ordered Reimann, moving for immediate supremacy. Elke stood disconcerted, with the flowers in one hand and the box in the other, unable to move, held by her own inadequacy, which was what Reimann intended. She wedged the bouquet on to the hall stand with difficulty, unwrapping the dog's toy. 'I. . . ?' she tried, confused.

'For Poppi,' he explained, deliberately sheepish, laughing as if unsure of the idea.

Elke laughed with him, delighted. 'Oh, that's sweet!' she said.

So easy to anticipate, thought Reimann. He hoped it stayed that way: grew easier, in fact. 'I hoped you'd like it: that you wouldn't think it juvenile.'

'How could anyone think that!' said Elke, within distant view of indignation. 'It's sweet and it's thoughtful. You're very kind.'

He'd failed mentally to predict being called kind, Reimann acknowledged. So he'd scored eight out of ten. Good enough. He stayed unspeaking in the minuscule hallway, putting the onus – the social discomfort – upon her.

'Please!' said Elke, accepting it. 'Please come in! Why are we standing here in the hall?'

'I don't know,' shrugged Reimann. Uncertainty encourages uncertainty: one of the first psychological lecturers.

Elke went quickly into the main room, angry at herself: self-assured career executives didn't stand around in foyers when guests arrived at their homes. They accepted the duty tokens and showed proper – although not too much – gratitude and continued as if the gesture was their due, not the gift for which they'd pined since the previous disappointed birthday. Elke made a valiant recovery, even by Reimann's judgement. She went most of the way through the lounge, gesturing around as she did so. Maintaining a flow of disjointed yet connected remarks, she said: 'Sit anywhere. I'll get the flowers in water. I know what you'll drink . . .' At the kitchen door she paused, looking back. 'Do you want to give Poppi his present?'

'You do it,' said Reimann at once, not wanting the animal near him. 'Let's not divide its affections.'

She hadn't put out the canapés! The realization came to Elke as she opened the refrigerator and saw the plastic-enclosed dishes, like fossils preserved for a million years in a glacier. She didn't know what to do. To carry them in with the drinks would make too much of her preparation, draw attention to the effort. Damn! Elke thought: damn! damn! damn! Leave them the first time. Suggest them casually over the second drink – *would you like something to nibble on? I think I have something –* and bring them in then. But not everything, not now. She wouldn't look casual, walking in with six different selections. Damn!

Poppi was at the door, scratching to get through. Elke ripped off the box wrappings: the toy, created from some animal by-product, was in the shape of an old shoe. She hoped Poppi didn't reduce it to a soggy mess to trail across the kitchen floor or worse, the carpets. It must have been infused with some sort of animal stimulant because the dog leapt up against her, snuffling eagerly. She handed it down. Poppi scurried off to his basket, a four-legged miser.

Having come into near contact with the dog's mouth Elke rinsed her hands even before immersing the roses. She made the drinks quickly, aware of leaving her guest on his own too long. At the door, she looked briefly back towards the fridge, unsure, but carried on through. Reimann was sitting in the chair he'd occupied on the previous occasions, legs splayed in front of him, perfectly at ease.

'Poppi likes his shoe. He's trying to hide it.'

'Good.'

'The Graham Greene collection is over there,' said Elke, jerking her head towards the books as if she wasn't quite sure exactly where the combined volume was. Should she say it? She didn't want to appear cocky but she did want to show her intelligence. So why not? 'And it's not what you said.'

'What?' demanded Reimann. Whatever her qualification was it wouldn't matter, but he was intrigued at what she might mean.

'At the Bonner on Saturday you called it a compendium. It isn't. Every story is complete and unabriged.'

Smart-assed bitch, thought Reimann. He smiled and, lightly gallant to show he was not offended, said: 'My apologies, madam. And I'm glad. I don't really like digests.'

He didn't seem upset at all, but Elke was instantly worried at having made the correction. She didn't know him well enough to make a criticism like that. Trying to maintain a casual attitude, she made another hand movement towards the books and said: 'Look through while you're here: borrow something else if you want. You haven't had time to build up any sort of a library, have you?'

'I'll do that,' Reimann grasped the opportunity, although not with the intention Elke wanted. 'I *am* still settling in.'

'How are you finding it?' Those very direct eyes had moved, just for a moment, encompassing her body as she believed he had once before. She was sure of it!

The question paved the way for Reimann to move into the carefully rehearsed and prepared stories, obeying another Balashikha lecture on the aphrodisiac of laughter. All the stories were virtual inventions, exaggerations of the difficulties with his initial accreditation applications, the anecdotes always told self-effacingly, always mockingly against himself. He was extremely funny, and Elke found herself laughing helplessly and without any self-consciousness, which was so rare as to surprise her, because Elke never truly felt at ease even in the tightly restricted and protective social circle she occupied: self-consciousness was a feeling she always had, to some degree.

Having recounted the fictitious difficulties of a stranger arriving in a an unknown town to an unknown job, Reimann parodied different ministers and officials with whom he'd already come into professional contact and some whom he hadn't met but merely seen on television, or heard journalists gossip about in the Joachimstrasse bar. Because she knew most of them and because of his amazingly accurate mimicry the accounts seemed funnier to her than they might have done to anybody else.

'And what about the commemorative head-and-shoulders bust of Adenauer on the pavement outside the Chancellery?' he demanded.

'What about it?' she asked, smiling expectantly.

'Doesn't it look as though it was designed by the man who makes garden gnomes?'

Elke tried to imagine the outrage such a description would cause among the people with whom she worked – Günther Werle, for instance – but agreed, giggling, that it did. She pleaded with him to stop to let her recover, using as excuse the need to get more drinks – and three of the prepared dishes – from the kitchen. She did so refusing to think of anything, to consider anything, completely absorbed by Otto and happy to exist entirely – and only – for the moment. She couldn't remember ever feeling so reposed, so happy, in another person's company, certainly not another person who was a virtual stranger. Hardly, even, with Ida.

He resumed the moment she returned to the main room, this time about problems with workmen and leases when he'd moved into

Rochusplatz, starting her laughing all over again until, finally, she really did physically ache and begged him to stop at once.

'Don't they strike you as hilarious, all these politicians? Each trying to be more serious than the other! Whenever any of them lose an election they could go into business as professional mourners at funerals!' It was going extremely well, Reimann decided. Although he was performing apparently with impromptu ease he remained intently alert upon the woman, trying as always to discern her thoughts and attitudes. He was sure the laughter and the amusement were genuine, with no hidden reservation. It made him doubt all the more that it was she who had initiated the security inquiry.

The politicians about whom he was talking had never before been hilarious to her – not as hilarious as he was portraying them – but the rest of the descriptions were very apposite. She said: 'Is this how you have to write, satirizing it all?'

'Oh no!' seized Reimann at once, welcoming the question and the direction it offered. 'I wish it were, because it would be more fun. I'm supposed to write the inside stories, disclosing the reasons behind the publicly seen decisions: anticipate reactions and attitudes to developing situations. All very dull, I'm afraid.'

'How do you do it?' Elke was glad of the temporary seriousness, although she did not want it to last too long.

Wait until you believe you've found out, thought Reimann. He said: 'By talking to as many people as possible. Making friends with politicians, if I'm lucky. You'd be extremely surprised how much public figures are prepared to talk and disclose on a background basis, providing they're not identified as my source.' He hoped she recognized the inference of unofficial conduct, and picked up his careful choice of 'my source', indicating that he already had many influential people prepared to trust him and his integrity.

'I know it happens sometimes,' allowed Elke, generally. She felt quite comfortable, talking at this level: pleased, even, because she was transgressing no official regulations yet she was suggesting a position of awareness, of being at an echelon where she was accustomed to such indiscretions. She hoped he did not think she was boasting.

Reimann hadn't expected the conversation to reach this stage so quickly, and he was delighted. Vaguely mocking, to fit the earlier banter that had put her at her ease, but in reality staging a further test, he said: 'I'd forgotten! The executive with her own private telephone at the Cabinet Office!'

159

'How did you know it was the Cabinet Office?' demanded Elke at once, the humour going.

Fuck! thought Reimann, aware of the mistake: the number *was* private, going straight to her desk, not through the intercepting switchboard from which he could have got the information. It was an appalling mistake! Unbelievable! He smiled, with forced calmness, and said: 'I didn't. I mislaid the number you gave me, so I rang around the ministries, asking for you by name. They knew you at the Cabinet Secretariat, finally, although you weren't there when I was put through.'

'I didn't get any message about a call,' Elke persisted.

'I didn't leave one,' said Reimann, a heavy-footed man exploring quicksands. 'I wasn't sure what the policy was about receiving private calls. I didn't want to cause any problems. Then I found the number again, so there wasn't any difficulty.' It hadn't been convincing. How could he have been such a fool!

'It would have been all right to have left a message,' said Elke. She was still grateful that he hadn't. 'Thanks for being so considerate, though.'

Had she accepted the explanation, poor as it had been? It looked as if she had but there was no way he could be sure. How could he further convince her? By enlarging on the call he'd never made. Deliberately inquisitive he said: 'The Cabinet Secretariat? That's how the operator answered.'

'Yes,' confirmed Elke, tightly. She wasn't comfortable any more. She still wasn't transgressing any regulations but she wasn't comfortable.

Back off! Reimann told himself, mental alarms jangling. He'd ruined everything this time by his own ineptitude, and now he had to back off before it got any worse. 'Why am I telling you about Bonn's politicians? You must know them all far better than me! Make me a promise you won't tell any of them how I see them. They'll never talk to me again!'

Elke loosened, slightly. 'I promise,' she smiled. She didn't want the atmosphere – the fun – to have gone.

He had to get an indication, a hint at least, to learn if the stumbling explanation had worked. The idea that came was hardly any more subtle, but he couldn't think of anything else. He put his glass firmly upon the low coffee table and said: 'I'm sure I've taken up enough of your time. Why don't I find the book and get out of your way?'

No! thought Elke: the word wailed in her head, as if she had spoken aloud. She did come fingertip close to making too obvious a protest, pulling back at the edge. Instead, proud of herself even as she spoke the please-yourself words, Elke said: 'Take your time. I'm not doing anything tonight. Would you like another drink, while you're looking?'

Reimann calculated that if she'd been unsettled, suspicious, she would have grabbed the offered opportunity to get rid of him. He couldn't be too sure, too soon, but it looked as if he'd got away with it. 'I'm not doing anything either,' he told her. 'So I'd like another drink.'

In the kitchen Elke saw that the dog had already gnawed the toy into an elongated strip that looked slimy: she decided to throw it away, after Otto had gone. The idea of it being dragged around the apartment revolted her. She could always . . . The reflection stopped, braked to a halt. She was automatically thinking of him as Otto all the time, as if she'd known him forever. So what? She thought of Günther Werle as Günther, so why shouldn't she think of this man by his given name? She actually felt that she had known Reimann for a long period: longer than Werle, although that clearly didn't make sense. Knew him better then. That made even less sense. She didn't know Otto Reimann at all. She saw, surprised, that she had already drunk more than half the white wine, by herself. She didn't feel any effect. She'd had to open the new whisky bottle to top up his glass on the previous occasion, and she added generously now. Otto – Reimann, she corrected – remained absolutely sober. Another word came to her mind, joining the others she had sought to describe him to herself. He was sophisticated: sophisticated men could drink a great deal and stay in complete command of themselves.

Reimann quickly found the Graham Greene anthology, knowing from his earlier identification exactly where to look, and located other books he could ask for, if necessary. He was still disturbed by his gaffe. Too confident, he thought, critically. Then corrected himself. Not critical enough. Arrogant was more appropriate: far more accurate. It had all seemed to be unfolding as he'd expected. And he'd sat back, like an actor (which was another appropriately accurate word) watching himself perform a rehearsed role. Quickly the balance between optimism and pessimism adjusted itself. So it had been a salutary lesson. He'd been stupid but he'd recovered (he hoped) and now he knew better than to become complacent again. A complete fool suffers from his mistakes, an occasional one learns not to repeat them. It sounded like an attempt at a wise quotation, but he didn't recognize it. Whatever, he wouldn't allow arrogant complacency again. *Couldn't* allow it. Fool, he thought, still not able fully to forgive himself.

He was away from the shelves, the book in his hand, when Elke re-entered the room. 'I found it,' he announced, unnecessarily.

'Just that one?'

'I don't really feel I should help myself, to too many, although there are others I'd like to read,' said Reimann, clumsy by intent now.

'Borrow them whenever you like,' said Elke. Not completely sophisticated, she thought, with growing disbelief. She isolated the painful obviousness at once – the ploy for a further visit beyond even the return of what he was borrowing tonight – and felt her mind and her stomach, everything, in turmoil at the unthinkable absurdity of someone wanting to see her on a second or a third occasion. Her, Elke Meyer, an unmarried mother who could never find anything to talk about and who always felt uncertain and lost and lonely. Surely this man who made her laugh more than she could remember laughing for years and was attractive despite the jagged tooth, and who had been so truthful and so frank over the incident that had brought them together – surely he couldn't be interested in continuing an acquaintanceship, although newly arrived and possibly lonely, too!

'I will,' said Reimann, appreciatively. He held the book up. 'Like I said, I'll take very good care.'

'I know you will.'

'Can I call, to arrange when to bring it back?'

'Of course.' He was building up to go and she didn't want him to, but it would be wrong to press him into staying longer. He'd put himself in the position of pursuer, so let him pursue. She hoped she was making the right decision. Ida would know.

She went with him to the door of the apartment, unsure what to expect. He turned, still inside the hallway, and said: 'Goodnight.'

'Goodnight.'

Reimann reached out, for her right hand, bringing it briefly to his lips: there was hardly any contact. 'I'll call,' he promised.

'Please,' she said.

That night Elke filled the entire page for the day in her diary, describing everything that had happened and her fears of mistakes or misunderstandings she might have allowed. *Wonderful*, she concluded. *It was utterly wonderful.* She smiled down at the word. After it she wrote: *I mustn't use wonderful any more. I mustn't do anything to bore him.*

The following morning, walking Poppi, she discarded the slimy, chewed-up dog's toy in a public litter-bin. She'd carefully put it in a plastic bag and secured the top to avoid offending anyone else who might use the bin afterwards.

'So you've established the relationship?' Jutta demanded.

162

'I'm sure now,' agreed Reimann, at last permitting the increased commitment.

'With no problems?'

'None,' he assured her. None that anyone would ever know about, he thought. He still couldn't believe the mistake.

'Well done,' said Jutta, professionally.

Chapter Nineteen

Elke tried determinedly to curb any feelings, because it would have been ridiculous to invest the slightest expectation in so short an acquaintanceship, but she didn't find it easy. Ida didn't help towards cool objectivity. She called Kaufmannstrasse with a flurry of questions before Elke left for the Chancellery the following morning, insisting they should meet earlier than their normal mid-week lunch because there was so much to talk about, and she reached the restaurant first, which Elke couldn't remember happening before.

'Everything!' demanded Ida, practically before they were seated. 'I want to know everything! All of it!'

'There's nothing much to tell.'

'Don't be stupid!' Ida rebuked her sister, grinning in anticipation. 'Of course there is!' She ordered impatiently, urging Elke to do the same, and as usual selected the wine without consultation. A wider grin. 'Was he there when I called this morning?'

'Certainly not! Don't be absurd,' said Elke. She knew, with irritation, that she had coloured, as if she had something to be embarrassed about. Maybe her sister's accusation about stupidity was appropriate after all.

'What then? Don't keep me waiting!'

'He stayed for about two hours. We talked. He made me laugh,' said Elke, with forced simplicity.

'I'm not accepting that,' Ida protested. 'From the beginning, from the moment you opened the door to him.'

Elke sipped her wine, wishing it were drier, and started out as her sister instructed, enjoying once more being the person with a story to recount rather than the patient listener. She tried to repeat what she considered some of Reimann's more hilarious anecdotes, the ones she had found most amusing, but they lost their humour in the telling so she stopped, after one or two. Ida only occasionally interrupted, refusing to allow anything to pass unexplained, otherwise sitting with her chin cupped in her hands, listening intently.

'Kissed your hand!' she exclaimed, when Elke finished.

'It wasn't like that: not like it sounds,' said Elke. She'd thought it had

164

been absolutely the right and fitting gesture for Reimann to have made, neither too formal nor too dismissive.

'It sounds cringingly awful.'

'It wasn't!'

'What else did he do?'

'Do?'

'You know what I mean!' said Ida, impatient again. 'Don't be so naïve.'

'He didn't *do* anything. It was an ordinary, pleasant, enjoyable evening.' It had been anything but an ordinary evening for her, reflected Elke. But very definitely pleasantly enjoyable.

'And all he did was kiss your hand!'

Would Ida have been better satisfied if Otto had tried putting his hand up her skirt? Elke said: 'He was – he is – a perfect gentleman.'

'Let's hope he quickly changes.'

'Let's hope nothing of the sort!' said Elke indignantly.

Ida had been gently taunting her sister, pleased at Elke's obvious happiness. But she became serious-faced, worried about that happiness, and said: 'What about that, darling? What *do* you hope for?'

'Nothing,' said Elke, too quickly. At once, seeing the expression on her sister's face, she said: 'Well, that's not really true, is it? It just . . . well I don't know yet what to hope . . . no, hope isn't the right word. I don't know what to expect . . . nothing, I suppose. Why should there be anything?'

'Why shouldn't there be?' Ida came back. 'Don't start running for cover: don't really do something stupid.'

'There are reasons,' Elke pointed out.

'Ursula? Why should Ursula be an obstacle?'

'Don't you think she is?'

'No!' said Ida, almost angrily. 'So you've got a child who isn't well. Who has to be cared for. Where's the problem there?'

'An illegitimate child.'

'Darling!' said the other woman. 'What sort of era are you living in! You really think that is a factor, in this day and age?'

'I think it could be, for a lot of men.'

'What about this particular man?'

Elke shook her head. 'I don't know. He didn't appear to me to be the type who would judge, who would be critical, but I've no way of telling.'

'*Did* he talk about himself?'

'Only funny stories. About becoming established here and setting up an apartment.'

'So he could be married? Separated? Divorced? Have children of his own?'

Elke blinked at the spurt of questions. 'Yes,' she admitted, doubtfully. 'He could be all, any, of those things. I don't know.'

'You didn't ask?'

'Of course not.'

'Weren't you curious?'

'The opportunity didn't arise. It wouldn't have been right.'

'Didn't he ask about you?'

'No.' Not quite true, Elke remembered. There had been the reference to her working in the Cabinet Office, but upon reflection that didn't amount to personal intrusion. She pushed her salad plate away half finished, no longer hungry.

'Ready for the big question?' said Ida.

'What?' It *was* good, being the subject of a conversation: better this time than after the crash.

'How do you feel about him?'

'How can I answer that? Socially, I've only been in his company once: I'm not counting the other times, when we met about the car.'

'You can answer it honestly,' insisted Ida. 'I told you, stop running for cover.'

Elke smiled, shyly. 'He's very nice,' she allowed.

'My butcher is very nice,' Ida complained. 'Let's do better than that.'

'I like him,' admitted Elke, finally. 'He's nice and he's funny and he's quite good-looking and . . .' She struggled to a stop, shrugging. '. . . he seems to be a lot of things, all of which I like.'

'What about looking like Dietlef?'

'I don't think about that resemblance any more.' She thought of Otto as himself, not as somebody else.

'Could this be love!' mocked Ida.

'We met again, by accident,' said Elke, patiently. 'He came to my apartment for about two hours. He borrowed a book. That's it.'

'Which he's got to bring back?'

'Yes,' agreed Elke. 'And . . .'

'And what?'

'There are probably others he might borrow.'

'Did you offer or did he ask?'

Elke hesitated. 'I think I offered, very generally. He said he didn't

166

want to take more than one at a time but there were some he'd like to read.'

'This isn't the swiftest romance that the world has ever seen,' was Ida's verdict. 'But I think it's got possibilities.' Dear God, don't let Elke be hurt again, she thought once more.

'I'm frightened.' The confession had begun as a thought and emerged as words and Elke wished, having uttered them, that she hadn't.

'Step back a little!' Ida spoke soothingly, all joking cynicism forgotten. Believing that Ursula was somehow still the worry, she said: 'She can't be a reason for you feeling like that: really she can't.'

'It's not just Ursula,' said Elke, in partial confirmation.

'What then?'

Elke shrugged, a little-girl-lost gesture. 'I can't put it into words, not really. I do think, despite what you say, that no man is going to be interested in me, with an illegitimate child. But then there's *me*. I don't know how to maintain a relationship: I never had a relationship, apart from Dietlef, and that wasn't one at all, not really: not what I now imagine a proper relationship should be . . .'

It became Ida's turn to shrug, even more helplessly. 'I don't understand . . .'

'. . . I don't know how to behave!' Elke spoke quietly because they were in a public place, but there was desperation in her voice.

'Stop being so fucking wet!'

Elke grimaced at the obscenity and Ida saw and said: 'Like that was wet, as if you've never heard the word before and think you risk going to hell, because it's sullied your ears. OK, you've had some rotten things happen to you: so have a lot of other people. But a lot of other people haven't let it wipe out their self-confidence: haven't wrapped themselves up in an inferiority complex, like a comfort blanket. You've met a man you like: maybe, with luck, he likes you. If you are going to agonize about everything, like you're agonizing and bleating about everything now, do you know what you're going to do?'

'No,' said Elke, dully.

'You're going to fuck it up! There, you've heard it twice, in one day! Snap out of it, darling! It sounds like you've got a chance of something good here.'

'Don't you see that's what I'm frightened of?' said Elke, her thoughts coalescing. 'I really want there to be a chance; and I'm terrified of losing it, through doing something – saying something – wrong!'

'You will!' Ida insisted. 'You'll lose it if you wallow about like this. And it'll be entirely your fault.'

She wouldn't, Elke determined, positively. If Otto Reimann showed any interest in deepening the relationship she'd do everything she could to make it work. Everything? she asked herself, at once. Too soon to start posing questions like that. 'We'll see,' she said.

'I hope we do,' said Ida, always someone who wanted the last word.

'The Soviet Union is disintegrating into chaos!' protested Cherny. 'The Russian Federation is ignoring us! Lithuania and Estonia and Latvia are defying central control! We are going to end up at best a confederation, bowing to the God of Market Forces. Have you any conception how exposed we'll be then, as a country? No buffer states! No protection!' In deference to his rank, Sorokin had today come to Cherny, to the General's personal dacha set among the wooded military complex on the outskirts of Moscow, off the Zagorsk highway.

'I know the arguments. And the fears,' said Sorokin. It was the nearest the General had come since they had been brought together to hinting that he was only paying lip-service to glasnost and perestroika and that he might regret the passing of the old order. Sorokin supposed it was an understandable attitude, particularly for a soldier. He'd had problems adjusting himself. Sorokin held up his thumb and forefinger, allowing the narrowest of gaps. 'Reimann's that close. He made a convincing argument against going too fast and losing her.'

Cherny, who was wearing his uniform but with the tunic undone and his shirt collar open, shook his head. 'You know what worries me? I still can't imagine how we could stop them building up a military machine again, if we discovered it was going to happen.'

'That wouldn't be our responsibility,' Sorokin pointed out. 'That would be the task of the politicians.'

'That worries me, too,' said Cherny. 'It's politicians who have destroyed the Soviet Union!'

Chapter Twenty

It was a morning when Günther Werle had no meetings away from his office, and at the end of their daily diary discussion he asked Elke to return directly after he had given the low-classified dictation to the secretaries. Werle was at the window overlooking the Chancellery park, seemingly deep in thought, when she re-entered the Cabinet Secretary's suite. He was still reflective when he turned to her, the smile coming as an apparent afterthought. 'Congratulations!' he said. He'd tried to rehearse the announcement but remained unsure of the words to convey precisely what he wanted.

Werle was not a man given to obscure remarks, and Elke wondered why he was doing it now. It was as if he was trying to impress her, something she could not remember his so obviously doing before. She said: 'Upon what?'

'Your security classification is being raised, to Top Secret, Eyes-Only rating,' he declared.

Elke was utterly astonished. It gave her access to every grade of classified material passing through the office: it was, she supposed, the ultimate acknowledgement of her professional ability. An honour, in fact, although she didn't think that was quite the right description. Inadequately she said: 'This is totally unexpected!'

Werle's smile widened. 'It was upon my personal recommendation. And for a particular purpose.'

'What is that?' She had to prove herself worthy, whatever the responsibility. And so she could. This was work: she knew what she was doing, always, when it came to the workplace.

Werle seated himself finally, leaning forward towards her at her smaller desk. In his soft, barely andible voice, he said: 'A Cabinet committee is being created: at the moment it is undesignated, although some title will be evolved. Its function is to consider all ongoing and developing aspects of the East German situation . . . the entire situation in the East, if necessary. And more than that. There is our position in NATO, after full unification. There have already been exchanges between the American State Department and our Foreign Ministry: soon there is to be a delegation here from Washington, in advance of a possible visit from the Secretary of State himself.'

'I thought the NATO position had been virtually resolved?' said Elke. She realized that she was going to be privy to the innermost workings and secrets of the government on perhaps the most important changes in its post-war history. What had she to feel inferior about in her private life if this degree of trust and approval could be accorded to her, here at the Chancellery? It would have been good if she were able to tell someone, boast a little, to show how highly she was regarded. She couldn't, of course. Top Secret meant top secret in everything. She suddenly felt very important, a privileged person able to look out from a situation into which everyone else was looking in. Or wanted to look in.

Werle rocked his hands back and forth, in an uncertain gesture. 'The United Kingdom is arguing against any military relaxation. The British attitude is that the changes have all occurred too quickly: that there should be a period of stasis for everything to be properly analysed. Washington has rejected the Russian idea of some link between NATO and the Warsaw Pact.'

'If there were to be a linking, without any military purpose, it would virtually rival the European Common Market,' said Elke, wanting to demonstrate some political grasp.

'That's a point already being made by some Common Market countries,' Werle accepted. 'A lot of analysts consider the Warsaw Pact as already defunct. Certainly it's no longer subservient to Moscow. What's the point – or the logic – of NATO absorbing something that doesn't exist any more?'

'*Is* that an argument?'

'Certainly one that some countries in the Alliance – America particularly – find easy to accept. And then there's the military position of NATO itself. Which is *very* political. The US arms industry is the major financial supporter of the US Republican Party. Without some tension, some suspicion, who needs an arms industry?'

'It's very complex,' Elke responded. What other questions were there to show a political awareness? 'How will a united Germany fit into the European Economic Community?'

Werle nodded, acknowledging her anticipation. 'Another remit for the committee,' he confirmed.

'How often will it convene?'

'Whenever it's considered necessary. At least twice a month, I would have thought. More frequently, if situations arise which need immediate consideration and recommendation, to full Cabinet.' Apart from any personal feelings and hopes he might additionally have, Werle had known he was right in sponsoring Elke as strongly as he had:

her instant acceptance of what he was outlining showed sound political adaptability. Intellect, too.

'And what will my part be in it all?' She *so* much wished she were able to tell someone.

'I shall officially be the committee secretary, of course. But the practical duties of secretary will be entirely yours. You will handle everything, with no delegation whatsoever throughout the department . . .' He hesitated, to make the point, then said: 'It will obviously be necessary for you to attend the sessions, as a support to me.'

The responsibility being put upon her was very great. Immediately showing the practicality about which her chief had spoken, Elke said: 'I am to take care of all records and transcripts, either relayed by you or recorded by me personally?'

'Yes.'

'Researchers?'

'Only in extreme and urgent circumstances. Always to be authorized by me.'

'Otherwise?'

'Conduct your own research.'

'Records?'

'The exact number, from each meeting, has yet to be decided. As far as this Secretariat is concerned, just one copy. Always locked in my personal safe, to which only you, myself and security have access.'

The mention of security reminded her. Elke said: 'I'll have to undergo positive vetting, I suppose?'

Werle smiled again, shaking his head. 'You've been checked, extremely thoroughly, over several months. Your new classification was only possible *after* such checks. The verbal question and answer stuff isn't considered necessary, after all you've gone through in the past.' It had been another of Werle's decisions, to obviate that.

The idea of being spied upon, which she supposed was how they had done it, mildly disturbed Elke. But then there was nothing in her private life that gave her cause for embarrassment or concern. Her security credentials *were* incontestable. 'When is the next meeting?'

'Five days.'

Tuesday, she identified. 'Will I attend?'

'Naturally.'

'Anything else I should know?'

'There will be a salary increase, of course: the security classification automatically carries with it a job description upgrade.'

She'd bank or invest entirely whatever the increase was, Elke decided: it would go towards rebuilding her depleted savings after the loan to Ida. She hadn't expected any repayment so soon – there were the other more pressing debts – but Elke had looked to Ida to mention it occasionally, and her sister hadn't. 'What about preparation?' she asked.

'Nothing that I can anticipate, at this stage. The actual mechanics will be the same as those to which you're already accustomed. There will be official stenographers, supplying transcripts.'

The very *centre* of political power and influence, she thought, excitedly, and said: 'I'm very aware of the trust you've placed in me.'

'It will involve our working more closely together than we have in the past,' said Werle pointedly.

'Yes,' agreed Elke. Why was he stating the obvious? It wasn't necessary to explain operational practice in that much detail.

'Sometimes necessarily late.'

'That will not be a difficulty,' said Elke. There was only Poppi to consider and that was no problem. What about . . . ? Elke refused to let the question form. Ridiculous to invest with expectations a situation that hadn't even arisen, she reminded herself. The workload involved in the promotion, which was how she believed she should regard it, would not be that onerous or time-consuming anyway, not to the exclusion of any private life.

As if aware of her thoughts about her workload, Werle said: 'If there's a need for additional staff, to take over some of your existing functions, just say so. I'm thinking of a personal assistant of your own.'

Elke was cautious. 'I don't think we should consider an early decision on that: let's see how the job evolves, shall we?' It was flattering to be offered a personal assistant – would be an indication to everyone throughout the Chancellery and beyond of her elevated stature – but her immediate thought was to integrate this new responsibility with her present function.

'As you wish,' Werle accepted at once. 'But I don't want you to be overwhelmed.'

This meant he did not want the proven efficiency of his office to suffer by her trying to handle too much, to the detriment of the established standards. Elke said: 'I'll be extremely careful to see that doesn't arise. Before there is a risk of it happening.'

Werle gave another of his shy, reassuring smiles. 'I know you will, Elke.'

Elke, she recognized, uncomfortably. She said: 'I'm extremely honoured. I won't disappoint you.'

172

'I know that, too,' said Werle. He remained looking slightly away from her. 'I have read that the Vienna Boys' Choir are coming on tour. Bonn is one of the cities to be visited.'

'I haven't seen that,' said Elke, knowing what was to follow.

'I was wondering if you would care to attend a performance? I understand they are quite unique.'

She didn't want to, Elke decided, firmly. It wasn't in any way connected with Otto Reimann: she assured herself she was equally determined not to inflate that situation. It was Günther Werle. It did not matter – did not affect any consideration – that his marriage might be an unhappy or unfulfilled one. He *was* married. With a son. It would be quite wrong, particularly in view of her new promotion, to invite any confusion or difficulty between them by allowing their private lives to overlap even slightly on to their working relationship. On the other hand he might be offended by an outright refusal. She anxiously sought an avoidance but couldn't, not one that gave them both an escape from embarrassment. 'Is Frau Werle still at the health spa?' she asked, knowing well enough that the woman had been due to return weeks before. That surely indicated how – and what – she felt?

'No,' admitted Werle. 'She is not much interested in the music I enjoy.'

It wasn't the retreat for which she'd hoped. What else could she do? The working relationship, the amount of time they were going to spend together, *was* going to increase. So that relationship had to be correctly established on complete and honest understanding, from the outset. Still striving to be diplomatic (wasn't professional, practical diplomacy what she was going to encounter in the future?), she said: 'I appreciate the offer but I am not sure I will be able to accept.' That wasn't diplomatic: it was clumsy. Why didn't she simply chance any temporary offence and refuse outright?

'We'll talk about it again, nearer the time,' Werle persisted.

Say no, Elke told herself: say you don't want to get involved and complicate things. Instead she said: 'Why don't we do that?' In the interim she'd be able to think of a gentle refusal, she tried to convince herself.

Jutta entered the Bonner Café curiously, not knowing the precise table, guessed and took one near the back. It wasn't, in fact, where Elke normally sat. Jutta ordered coffee and cake and surveyed the café, dismayed that it wasn't a dowdy place of dried-up, pet-worshipping,

173

behatted spinsters, which was the category into which she had put Elke.

'Is everything satisfactory?' asked the waitress.

'Quite satisfactory,' lied Jutta. The coffee had been disappointing, too.

Chapter Twenty-One

Elke felt the same jangle of excitement as before at the recognition of his voice, smiling to herself as she assured him he was not calling at an inconvenient moment (how could any moment be inconvenient?) and went through the ritual of saying she was well and was glad he was well, in return.

'I enjoyed the . . .' Reimann paused. '. . . anthology,' he picked up. 'That's the right word, isn't it?'

She'd *known* the correction had been a mistake. Pretend not to notice. She said: 'He's a brilliant writer, isn't he?'

Reimann refused a literary discussion. He said: 'And now I'd like to return it.'

'Whenever you like,' Elke agreed. Soon, she thought: please soon.

'I hope you won't think me presumptuous . . .' opened Reimann, grimacing at his end of the telephone at his own feigned uncertainty. '. . . I have accepted a great deal of your hospitality: drunk all your whisky. I was wondering if I could reciprocate?'

'Reciprocate?' She felt her body tighten.

'By inviting you to eat with me . . .' Reimann introduced the false pause, to continue the impression of shyness. 'Dinner, I mean . . .' Another pause, carefully timed. '. . . At a restaurant . . . not here at my apartment. I didn't mean that.' Reimann decided he'd perfectly portrayed the hopeful suitor afraid of rejection.

It was happening! Elke didn't want to appear too eager but equally didn't want to sound uninterested, which was the last thing she intended to convey. Too important, then, to play the blushing reluctant, although she *was* blushing. But certainly not reluctant. She said: 'I'd like that, very much.'

'I'm delighted!' gushed Reimann, in apparent relief. 'I was thinking about tomorrow evening. But I suppose that would be too soon. So whenever is convenient to you.' Jump Elke, jump.

'Tomorrow would be fine,' Elke jumped.

'I'm so glad.' It was the first sincere thing Reimann had said since the conversation began. He'd be spared too much contact with that fucking dog, as well.

'How. . . ?'

'Seven,' Reimann interrupted, tilting the pendulum from uncertainty to demand. 'I'll collect you at seven. The Otto Reimann Mystery Tour.'

Elke laughed, searching for a response. 'Decorations and decorum? Or jeans and jollity?'

Not a bad effort, he conceded: she was trying. Which was what Elke Meyer had constantly to do, always try to please him. His mind focused on decorum: later he would deny her any decorum. He said: 'I've never seen you dressed any other way but perfectly.' Sometimes it was difficult not to be openly embarrassed at saying the idiotic necessary things.

Elke blushed afresh in the emptiness of the Kaufmannstrasse apartment at the compliment but not at the innuendo, which she missed. 'Just a hint?' she pleaded.

She had to stew – continue to marinate, he thought, remembering his earlier analogy – in doubt, about everything: those psychological seduction lectures had been invaluable. 'A mystery tour,' he reminded. 'No help given. You'll have to live with whatever mistake you make!'

'No!' she protested. She was laughing, enjoying an intimacy that didn't exist.

'Yes!'

'Beast!' Too *much* non-existent intimacy, she feared at once, apprehensive of his response. Fool! she thought: fool! fool! fool!

'Except that I know you won't make any mistake,' flattered Reimann. Don't have an orgasm too readily, he thought: I'm not there yet.

Again he was on time, to the minute. He wore a sports jacket and a tie under a button-down shirt: the trousers were immaculately pressed, just as the shoes were immaculately shone. Elke, after three telephone calls to Ida – one immediately after his call the previous evening, two during the day – wore a black, knitted woollen dress with an ornamental belt she could take off if she felt over-dressed on arrival at wherever they were going. On her left shoulder there was a small costume-jewellery brooch of imitation diamonds. She didn't intend a pose, for approval, as she admitted him, but she later supposed that was how it had appeared, from his reaction.

He said, very seriously: 'You look superb. I am going to enjoy it.'

'Enjoy what?' she frowned.

'Being the object of so much envy from so many men who are going to see me with you tonight.'

'You're embarrassing me!' she said, in weak protest. Without any obvious direction or cause – without even thinking! – their association had become very different. She searched but couldn't find the word to describe it. She didn't want a word to describe it. She was happy, whatever it was.

'I'll never do that,' Reimann said, serious still. He would have liked the Kaufmannstrasse apartment to have been bugged, so Moscow could have savoured that remark.

Elke was utterly confused. She gestured further in towards the apartment and the whimpering scratching of the demanding dog and said: 'Do you want . . . I mean shall we . . . what. . . ?'

Reimann took the control he wanted soon to exercise over everything. He cupped her arm, leading her back into the living-room. She realized as he did so that he had a bag in his other hand. From it Reimann produced her book, and said it was returned with grateful thanks, and then immediately a bottle of champagne. 'I shall take no more of the whisky,' he announced. 'Fetch two glasses!'

Elke was glad the banter was back. She got the glasses without releasing Poppi and waited for the cork to explode. It didn't: he withdrew it expertly, with the faintest of sighs, so that the wine was not bruised. 'Your toast,' he ordered, in further demand.

'I don't . . .'

'. . . I insist.'

She'd never had to propose a toast, never in her entire life! Didn't know one: couldn't remember one, from any of the books she had read. 'I really don't . . .'

'Make one up!'

Elke searched her memory, not wanting to fail, knowing only a blankness, as if her mind were filled with cotton wool. She started, with the thought incomplete, 'To . . .' and stopped.

'What!' demanded Reimann, wanted to keep her on the edge.

'You make it!' she begged. 'Please, you!'

Reimann adopted a ruminative pose. Then he touched his glass against hers and said: 'To ending each day in the happiness that it began.'

Elke drank, trying to think how many of her days either began or ended in complete happiness. She shouldn't wallow, in doubt or self-pity, she thought, remembering Ida's rebuke. 'Do I learn now where we're going?'

'No!' refused Reimann. She'd taken a great deal of trouble. Not as sophisticated and assured as Jutta: he didn't think Elke could ever achieve that. But he didn't consider that a disadvantage.

Sophistication and self-assurance could act as a rebuff, and Elke certainly wasn't rebuffing him. The dress was perfect, just slightly provocative, and as always she had held back from too much make-up. She really was quite a presentable woman. Reimann was irritated at the mental reservation. Not just presentable: positively attractive.

'I might hate it!' she said, unconvincingly.

'You won't.'

She didn't. After the champagne, which made her feel comfortable but not drunk, they drove to the smoke-filled, jostling bar off the Münsterplatz alley in which he had met Jutta for their first rendezvous in Bonn.

'A journalists' watering hole!' he announced, which it wasn't. He thought the cliché appalling.

The ebb-and-flow noise and the push and shove of people all around disorientated Elke. He'd been wrong to tell her that she looked superb, because she felt over-dressed and was glad Ida had advised about the belt, which she excused herself at once to take off. People did not react to her ineffectual efforts to get through to the rest-room and she was jostled further, growing hot with frustration. When she returned to their tiled podium she saw he had bought more champagne, but only a half-bottle this time.

'You don't like it!' he challenged at once.

'I do, really.'

'How often do you drink in a place like this?'

'Not often.'

'How often?' he goaded. She had to be reminded of Dietlef – if Dietlef was in fact the father of her bastard child – so there could be a later comparison.

'Hardly ever,' she finally admitted. 'Certainly not for a long time.' They'd drunk beer then, she recalled, conjuring the memories Reimann wanted her to have. She didn't recollect the smoke and the noise and the walls and barriers of tightly packed people. When she and Dietlef had come to such pubs they'd known everyone, as if it were a club admitting only recognized members. They'd sung a lot, all supposedly vehemently anti-Nazi: protest songs, anti-war and anti-oppression. She couldn't believe herself doing it, not now.

'You didn't have to do it,' said Reimann.

'Do what?' asked Elke, further off-balanced.

'Dress down, by taking off the belt. You were perfect as you were. I told you that.'

She enjoyed the compliment, without blushing this time. 'You're extremely observant.'

'I hope so,' said Reimann, a remark for his own amusement. 'You can put it back on, later.'

'If you'd like me to.' Elke found herself answering Reimann's direct stare without any discomfort, conscious of a tension between them, wondering if he felt it too.

Reimann did feel it, because he'd carefully created and then exacerbated it: she was responding just as she should have done. It had to be the control and power a sculptor felt, looking at a block of unformed clay from which he intended to fashion the perfect figure. Reimann broke the tension: it was something she would recall later, for which she would be grateful. 'Another drink here?'

'You're the tour guide: the man in charge,' said Elke. She was *enjoying* herself! She hadn't felt any uncertainty, any awkwardness, when the tension arose between them. Shouldn't she feel frightened of that, with all its implications? No cause, Elke told herself. She'd liked it. Not the complete moment, with all its unstated inferences, which hadn't been hidden from either of them but which of course would never be anything more than inferences. What she'd liked was knowing that for a few brief moments she was completely holding a man's attention, and that he was gazing at her as a woman, thinking of her as a woman. She forced the reflection on, demanding the phrase. *As a sex object.* She didn't find that offensive, either, not the way so many other women appeared to do on television or in newspaper comment. Rather, because it had happened to her so rarely, Elke was flattered. Flattered but safe: there could be no danger, no misunderstanding, from someone who had shown himself to be considerate. Impression built upon impression. It was idiotic, but she felt they were old friends: that she knew him and could trust him.

'Yes,' said Reimann, another remark for his own amusement. 'I'll remain the man in charge, shall I?'

They didn't have another drink. She recognized the direction to Bad Godesberg as they drove down Adenauerallee: by the Chancellery Reimann slowed to a near crawl, to stop completely against the head-and-shoulders monument. He insisted again that it was garden-gnome design, and Elke laughingly agreed once more. He allowed her three chances to guess their destination. She failed. When he announced it was to be the Maternus she came in quickly – wanting to boast – to say she knew it was the favourite restaurant of government ministers and ambassadors. Smoothly Reimann said he didn't know. Of course he did: he'd made the choice precisely to impress her.

Elke *was* impressed, and was glad she'd put the ornamental belt back on when they'd stopped on Adenauerallee. The Transport Minister who complained about speed limits was three tables away. She recognized the ambassadors of France and Spain. She thought a loud-laughing, straw-haired young girl on the far side of the room was an actress, although she couldn't make an identification.

'Silly man,' said Reimann, nodding in the direction of the minister. 'Unless he wants to be discovered – which I can't imagine he does – he shouldn't eat it in a place as public as this with someone who isn't his wife.'

Elke concentrated for the first time upon the man's companion. She wasn't quite as young as the straw-haired actress, but it was close. She said: 'No. I suppose he shouldn't.' There was a quick alarm, although the responsibility was not hers. 'But you're a . . .'

'. . . not that sort of journalist,' anticipated Reimann. 'I don't seek to expose people. I still think he's silly, though. It could too easily happen.' It was an extra to pass back to Moscow, through Jutta, an archetypal destruction or blackmail opportunity; the man was an utter cunt.

Elke allowed herself to think her forbidden word: wonderful, she thought. Everything about Otto – his behaviour and his integrity – was wonderful. She didn't know what to choose and eagerly accepted his offer to order for her. The veal was cooked to a recipe she did not know and was magnificent. He chose a Mosel wine, a Wehlener Sonnennuhr, and said she would taste the honey, which she did. Poor Horst, she thought, in intrusive comparison.

'I'm having a wonderful evening,' he said.

Now he was using the word! 'So am I.'

'Yet I know more about your car than I do about you!'

Elke laughed. How much she would have enjoyed telling him of the importance of her new promotion! Out of the question, of course: although, despite his being a journalist, she surely could have talked about it to him after the discretion he'd just illustrated over an indiscreet government minister! Still out of the question. 'I'm very dull,' she said, inviting the contradiction.

Reimann made it, knowing it was required. 'I don't think so,' he said. 'Tell me about yourself.'

She *was* dull, thought Elke, in faint desperation. But she refused to panic. She began – and continued for some time – to speak haltingly, unrehearsed and listening with critical unease to her own words. She tried to move the focus away from herself, talking instead of Ida and Horst and dismissing her function at the Chancellery as little more than that of a senior secretary. He had fixed her with that unwavering concentration again, sitting at one stage with his chin supported in his hands, his elbows on the table, and Elke ached to say more, to exaggerate even. When he pressed he did so gently, asking about her family without openly questioning about boyfriends or husbands in the past. Elke spoke of her parents and her father's war service, ignoring the more obvious invitation, and Reimann didn't press further.

It all served as a confirmation, Reimann decided, with cold objectivity. Everything she'd said checked out against the briefing he had received in Moscow. All, of course, except Ursula. He'd been intrigued whether she might admit to the child, without really expecting her to do so. *Had* she done so Elke Meyer would have shown herself to be a different character from that he'd already assessed: maybe made him revise his opinion and his approach. He was happier – relieved – that she hadn't. This way it was easier to intercept. She had a secret – believed she had a secret – she wanted to keep from him, frightened of it becoming an obstacle between them. Which meant she was anxious to prevent any such obstacle: that she wanted the relationship to grow.

'Now you!' demanded Elke.

Reimann was conscious of her increased confidence from that initial, bewildered encounter: she was comfortable – felt secure – with him now. He launched into the carefully prepared legend, talking of emigration to America – lying about cities like New York and Chicago and San Francisco, knowing he could not be caught out because she had never been to any of them either – and inventing journalistic escapades in America and Latin America and Australia. Throughout he guessed what she really wanted to hear and so he never offered it.

Elke listened with rapt attention, never interrupting, never doubting. Could she ask? she demanded of herself, when it was obvious he was coming to an end. Ida said she could – had urged her to – but Elke wasn't sure. She supposed it depended on how she phrased the question.

'It's been a busy life? Exciting?'

'I guess so. Although it's not how I think of it.' Not bad, he judged, knowing her effort: she deserved five out of ten.

'All-consuming, too.'

Reimann shrugged, without replying, letting her splash out of her depth.

'Not a lot of opportunity for any personal life?'

After a reasonably good start she was running out of control down the hill, he thought. Coming to her aid, Reimann said: 'I've regretted that, sometimes. Maybe I have committed too much to the job: sometimes I think how nice it would have been, to have got married and had kids.'

'But you never did?' Elke persisted. She had to get it now: get it one hundred and one per cent certain, so there wouldn't be any doubt at all.

Her knickers were practically around her ankles in her anxiety, reflected Reimann. He had to nudge her at the same time as placating her. Looking momentarily away, as if in genuine sadness, he said: 'No, I never did.' His head came around at once. 'And you? Don't you regret never marrying? Never having children?'

Elke's face blazed. She couldn't, immediately, speak. At last she managed: 'Yes. Sometimes. Sometimes, yes,' and realized how foolish she must appear to him. Why had she said it, told such an outright, easily exposed lie? But what choice had she had? She'd been trapped, with no alternative!

Now there's a burden! decided Reimann, happily. She had the supposed secret of Ursula and now she'd denied the child's existence, which was a positive deceit she might have openly to confess to him in the future. *Would* have to confess, determined Reimann. He'd make her do so: make her anxious to compensate. That's what she had to become, ultimately: consciously eager to please and to compensate for mistakes, real or imagined. And that's what she *would* become. Reimann had no doubt at all now that he could mould her – like the clay he'd thought about earlier – into whatever he wanted her to be.

A street flower-vendor entered the restaurant, offering individual roses wrapped in silver foil. The minister beckoned and Reimann groaned inwardly at an opportunity being lost by the absence of any photographer. There'd be other chances, he consoled himself: the man was too much of an imbecile to escape it.

'No!' Elke protested, weakly, when the flower-seller approached their table and Reimann nodded to buy one.

'It's what happens in all those romantic Hollywood films,' he said.

Elke tried to evade the remark. Still in apparent protest, she said: 'You're always buying me roses.'

'I'd like that,' said Reimann, refusing her the escape because he wanted to raise the tension again. 'I'd like always to be buying you roses.' Christ, he thought: how crass! He was sincerely grateful no one else would hear what he was saying, on any concealed listening device.

Reimann selected a wrapped rose he guessed would die within an hour and presented it to her.

Elke accepted it, smiling her thanks, answering the look once more. What would she do later if. . . ? She stopped the question from completely forming, not wanting to confront it. He wouldn't expect it: she was sure he wouldn't. But what if he *did?* No, she decided, positively. Despite the way she felt, about knowing him for a long time, in reality she knew him not at all. Which would be only the first ground for refusal. If there was going to be anything like a proper relationship it had to be correctly – firmly – established. On respect. Understanding. And. . . ? Why didn't she bring the word forward, for examination? Properly established on love, she thought at last. Not on lust or excitement or on Ida's terms, for fun. She hoped so much that he didn't try, tonight. Everything had been so perfect – *he* was so perfect – and if he pressed her tonight it would all be ruined.

'You all right?' he asked. 'You've become very quiet.'

'Thinking,' said Elke.

'What about?' Shall I? Shan't I? Shall I? Shan't I? he guessed.

'What a lovely evening it's been,' Elke evaded, again.

'*Is* being,' Reimann corrected. Wishing to maintain her uncertainty he added: 'It's not over yet.' He was sure that her smiled response was weaker, in her apprehension.

When they left the restaurant he held her arm, ostensibly to help her through the door, but retained it afterwards, detecting the faintest stiffening at his touch. It stayed until just before they reached the Mercedes, where he released her. Inside he offered to help with her seatbelt, which would have brought them close together again, but quickly Elke insisted she could manage, which she did, clumsily hurrying. Reimann stoked the mood, driving back towards Bonn without talking, curious if she would try to break the silence. She didn't.

At Kaufmannstrasse Reimann stopped the car directly outside Elke's apartment building and turned off the engine. He twisted towards her and said: 'It was a good evening.'

'I've enjoyed it too,' said Elke. She should invite him in, for coffee or a nightcap! For something! No! Not for *something*. For a coffee or a nightcap, that's all.

Reimann created the pause, looking at her expectantly: her hands were shifting one over the other in her lap, tiny washing movements. 'Well. . . ?' he said, after sufficient time.

She had to do it! She had to invite him inside: invite him inside and hope he wouldn't do anything to embarrass them both, to spoil everything. She said: 'Would you like to come. . . ?' but Reimann refused to let her finish.

'No,' he said. 'It's kind of you, but I still have some work to do. You're not offended, are you?'

The relief flooded through Elke. 'No,' she said. 'Of course I'm not offended.'

Next time, Reimann thought: next time, little innocent near-virgin, I shall take you to bed: I know you want me to. He said: 'I'd like to see you again.'

'Yes,' said Elke, glad of the darkness inside the car. 'I'd like that, as well.' A man wanted to see her again! An attractive, funny, wonderful man was interested in seeing her, Elke Meyer!

Reimann escorted her to the entrance to the block. There was no stiffness in the arm he held now. At the doorway he kissed her lightly, not fully on the mouth. At the moment Elke realized what he was going to do she came forward, to meet him.

'I'll call,' he said, as much a promise to himself as to her.

'Please,' said Elke, turning to walk into the building clutching her fading flower. She couldn't feel her legs: was scarcely aware of putting one foot in front of the other or of opening the doors or getting into her apartment. Oh please, she thought; please, please, please.

It only took Reimann thirty minutes to reach Nord-Stadt. He made no attempt to make love to Jutta and she did not appear to expect it. Instead they lay in the darkness, talking.

'No doubts now?'

'I don't think so,' said Reimann.

'Moscow will be pleased.'

It really had been quite easy, Reimann reflected. For the benefit of the microphones, he said: 'I'll have to be very cautious, for a long time yet.'

Abruptly Jutta said: 'Does she wear hats?'

Reimann pulled away, utterly bewildered. 'What?'

'Hats? Does she wear them?'

'No!'

'I thought she might,' said Jutta.

'. . . He's very nice, darling. I know you'd like him. Kind, too: very kind. . .'

Ursula sat unaware of her mother's usual monologue, hunched on her bed today, the music soft in the background. There were food stains on the cardigan, both on the sleeve and down the front.

'. . . he makes me laugh. He's done a lot of exciting things because he's a journalist, a person who writes in newspapers and magazines . . .'

The tape machine clicked into reverse, and Ursula's head moved, in awareness. She remained oblivious to Elke's presence, starting to rock back and forth very quickly, quite out of time to the music.

'. . . and he wants to see me again. He seems to like me. Isn't that wonderful. . . ?'

Chapter Twenty-Two

The committee convened in the Cabinet chamber itself, necessary because of the number of members and because it was judged the most secure room within the Chancellery: even so Elke knew that electronic experts had scoured every inch with detection devices before the meeting assembled. There was a security official at each entrance and three at the main door, through which everyone had to channel for a thorough identity check. Elke filed directly behind Günther Werle, taking every lead from him: she'd already decided to do that ahead of his suggesting it, just before they had left their own offices. He'd called her Elke again there. On their way here through the linking corridors there had been no conversation.

The Cabinet chamber was dominated by a large and highly polished table, hedged by a continuous line of chairs in matching wood – mahogany, Elke thought, although she wasn't sure – with ornately carved and fashioned backs and arms. In front of each chair was a simple place setting, just a blotter in a red leather holder: to the right of each were two bottles of spa water and two glasses. On such a huge table and for a gathering of this importance the preparation looked inadequate. Werle strode confidently around the table, stopping three positions short of a break in the orderly pattern, where there was a heavier chair of padded leather, a slightly lighter colour red than the fronting blotter holders, which was bigger than the rest on the table. Werle put his briefcase beside his chair and the position papers that Elke had assembled on the table. Immediately behind his seat was an individual table and chair, both larger and more comfortable than Elke's customary place in Werle's office. From her briefing there that morning Elke knew her function was not to take verbatim notes but to create the official records from the transcripts of others: while they waited Werle pointed out the stenographers in their booth at the far end of the room. In addition there was official but not visible recording apparatus: she supposed it was in the same booth.

Apart from the Chancellor, who was to be chairman, the official committee all came into the room together, as if they had gathered elsewhere to make a combined and impressive entry. The bespectacled, nervously thin Finance Minister, Walter Bahr, led the group. It was unfortunate, Elke thought, that the man was directly followed by the Defence Minister. Hans Mosen was a grossly fat Bavarian whose jowls trembled as he walked: close together as they were now the two ministers looked like the two extremes of a diet advertisement. The Foreign Minister, Gottfried Schere, was the third in the group. Behind him came Klaus Mueller, who held the portfolio for Intra-German Relations. Each was accompanied by support staffs, none of whom Elke recognized.

Once through the door the group split, each going to a position around the table with the familarity that Werle had earlier shown, and Elke assumed they were taking up their usual places at a Cabinet session. From each minister came nods and first-name greetings to Werle. Elke had not considered it before, but she wondered at that moment if the Transport Minister would have recognized her from the Maternus had the man been part of the committee. She doubted it, and not because she was someone people never remembered: in the restaurant the man had been besotted by the girl.

Everyone stood when the Chancellor entered. Gustav Rath was a portly, grey-haired man who did everything urgently – when he walked or talked or issued orders or considered decisions – conveying the impression of someone permanently in a hurry and with insufficient time to fulfil all that had to be accomplished. The impression was utterly misleading: Elke was well aware of his reputation as a prevaricator. Rath bustled around the table, nodding to people he passed. He dropped quickly into his padded chair, making lowering gestures with both hands as he did so to bring everyone else down with him.

Rath cleared his throat, gazed conspicuously around the table, and began briskly: 'Over the past two years we have witnessed a great many historic changes – changes that perhaps many of us at one time could not envisage occurring in our lifetime. This meeting today, the discussions that will emanate from it, is equally of great historical importance. I think it is essential for each of us constantly to keep that in mind.'

The Chancellor spoke quickly but quite coherently, and Elke guessed the man had rehearsed for the benefit of historians: he'd talked mostly with his head turned slightly in the direction of the stenographers who would have been able to hear him quite adequately on the amplified sound system with which the room was equipped.

It *was* historic, Elke reflected, bent over her pad: truly historic, and she was involved in it, at the very heart! She'd been waiting, since the early morning briefing, to experience some sensation, and was surprised – even vaguely disappointed – that she wasn't feeling more. She had an obvious sensation of excitement, although not excessively so. But that was all. It didn't seem enough, just as simple blotters and mineral water on the table at which these momentous discussions were taking place didn't seem enough.

'. . . many, many considerations on many levels and in many different directions . . .' the Chancellor was saying, ponderously.

Elke became sure the man was practically dictating for the history books. Could Rath believe himself the twentieth-century statesman who had unified Germany as Bismarck had brought together the separate German states a century earlier?

As the thought crossed her mind, Rath actually referred to the original creation of the Fatherland. He hurried through the history of the two wars and gave the largely unnecessary reminder that reunification was written into the 1949 Federal Constitution.

Rath paused, looking in the direction of the stenographers' booth. 'I am proud to have been Chancellor at times like these, to have seen the dream of unification become a postive reality.'

Definitely reciting for history, decided Elke.

'But we must not be blinded by euphoria,' continued Rath. 'Unification is a fact. Monetary union is a fact. But unity – proper cohesion between two countries that had been divided for more than forty years – is *not* . .'

'I'm glad that point has been made,' said Klaus Mueller, whose ministry had the heaviest responsibility for caring for the thousands from the East who had already moved and settled in West Germany since the removal of the border restrictions. Mueller was a rumpled, carelessly dressed man who had entered politics from a university professorship and was rumoured to be annoyed at not having been appointed to the education ministry.

The Chancellor looked irritably sideways at the interruption, but then smiled and said: 'Would you like to expand the point?'

Mueller nodded at the offer. 'The thousands who crossed, in the first months, gave a misleading impression. Like it or not – and I suppose we shouldn't like it, not at all – two Germanys *still* exist: with the majority the ideology is still too deeply entrenched after so long for there to be the assimilation we might have expected.'

'Surely only a very temporary thing?' suggested the Foreign Minister, an urbane, silver-haired man whose sartorial flamboyance had earned him the nickname of the Clothes Horse from one of the satirical tabloids.'

188

'I don't think so,' came in Werle. 'I think it will be probably ten years before there is anything like the assimilation we once imagined there would be.'

'What's the answer?' asked Walter Bahr.

'One of the sociological remits for this committee,' identified Rath. 'Probably the most important and probably the most difficult.'

'What about things that are more tangible?' demanded Gottfried Schere. 'I believe unification – even with the difficulties you've suggested – has strengthened us considerably. And we were already the linchpin of NATO and the dominant partner in the Common Market, however much the other member nations like Great Britain and France might have postured.'

'That might be an opinion we hold privately but I would not like it too openly expressed, outside this room,' warned Rath.

'There is – and will remain for a long time – a great deal of apprehension and even suspicion about a unified Germany,' supported Werle.

'And to be honest,' continued the Chancellor, 'after the two examples of our military expansion within living memory Europe – and America – have good reason to be nervous of a re-united Reich.' He turned to Mosen. 'What is your contribution here?'

The fat Defence Minister coughed, clearing his throat. 'I was extremely surprised that the Soviet Union agreed so easily with the other three Allied Powers in Berlin to give up their occupation rights which remained after the Second World War. I expected them to use their international right as they had done for forty years, as a bargaining lever. I think they're frightened of a united Germany being in NATO. And I expect some pressure in the future for a Warsaw Pact linking, although I can't at the moment anticipate it.'

Elke made her notes, her concentration fully upon the discussion. Already, from what she had heard, the difficulties appeared enormous and the assembled ministers were only yet touching the surface.

'Let's get some statistics into the record here,' demanded Rath.

Mosen was able to respond without any reference to notes or files.' 'Our own troops strength is just over 997,000. The United States are already reducing their 321,000 commitment. France's strength is almost 585,000. The United Kingdom have 246,000.'

'What's the comparison with the Warsaw Pact?' the Chancellor demanded.

'East Germany admits to 450,000,' Mosen continued. 'But also based there at the moment are 380,000 Soviet personnel. Poland's army totals 660,000. Hungary's strength is 139,000. Czechoslovakia is still being assessed. In each country, Moscow has agreed to their troops being withdrawn, over various periods of time.'

'Any bargaining manoeuvres?' asked Bahr.

Mosen gave a wobbly shrug. 'America is withdrawing, as I have said, to create for themselves a lever with Moscow on conventional arms reduction. Britain supports the stance. In my opinion France is ambivalent, although we must never forget their inherent historical fear.'

'*If* Poland and Hungary adopt their already declared Western-style democracy there's a powerful argument, surely, that the Warsaw Pact no longer exists. And if that no longer exists, what's the point of NATO?' said Schere.

An argument similar to Werle's, Elke realized. Her notes were necessary – and would always be necessary – but she thought she was getting the arguments fairly clear in her mind: there was nothing so far to make her doubt her ability to create the preliminary report.

'I think we should always bear one anomaly in mind,' warned Werle. 'Although there is going to be widespread demobilisation, the East German army of 450,000 are being integrated with our forces. Which forms part of the NATO military contingent. And at the same time there are 380,000 Soviet troops in the Eastern half of what is now officially a NATO country.'

'Moscow have pledged to withdraw,' pointed out Mosen, quickly.

'Over a four year period, at least,' pointed out Werle.

'You think they're a protective force?' queried Rath, at once.

'I think there are some in Moscow who might consider them to be,' suggested Werle.

Never having attended such a meeting before, Elke had no criteria from which to judge but she imagined that Werle's opinion and views were being called upon far more than was normal for such a permanent governemnt official: it was more as if he were a respected member of the government than its servant.

The NATO discussion was taken up, one by one, by every member of the special committee: Elke, adjusted and quite comfortable now to her surroundings, was conscious how often Werle's advice was sought and how much it was deferred to. The Chancellor insisted upon moving the discussion on after almost an hour, guiding the debate back to the Common Market. For some time Walter Bahr, the Finance Minister, dominated the arguments, reminding them of the previous remark about Poland and Hungary looking westward and adding to that

190

reminder the fact that the two countries – coupled with East Germany – constituted an incredible trading outlet. He set out the billions of Deutschmarks Bonn had advanced in export credits and loans rescheduling to Poland even before this opening of the borders, insisting that Warsaw was already leaning favourably towards them.

'Reunited, Germany constitutes a nation of eighty million people,' said Bahr. 'In what will then be merely an eastern part of an integrated Germany we have vast and comparably cheap labour resources. In time we can absorb into the Community Poland and Hungary, making the potential even more enormous. And we will dominate it, as we do now! Be the leaders!'

'All of which will put the fear of hell up every other country in Europe, West or East,' cautioned the Foreign Minister. 'The inference will be unavoidable: the world the Third Reich failed to dominate by force the Fourth Reich dominates economically.'

'I think that's an exaggeration,' Bahr protested.

'I think the sort of economic community you're imagining is an exaggeration,' Schere retorted. 'I don't believe we should even be thought to be planning like that, not for years! Decades even. If at all.'

'I agree that sort of conjecture is premature,' said Rath, slightly less dismissive.

Bahr retreated, although not completely. He insisted upon more statistics, detailing the financial aid Bonn was already providing to East Germany and adding to it the extra expense of supporting the influx of refugees who had settled but not yet found work.

Klaus Mueller re-entered the debate here, listing, with its cost, the huge building programme necessary to house the refugees.

'There's growing resentment from native-born West Germans who see jobs and housing and privileges they consider rightfully theirs going to those from the East who seem to have arrived yesterday,' cautioned the Minister for Intra-German Relations. 'Already the unions are complaining: some are even talking of a graded system, for jobs going first to West Germans.'

'And those East Germans who cannot get jobs have distorted our unemployment figures, which were nudging two million before the influx: no one has been able yet to compute what the final figure might be, but I've seen estimates of three million,' warned Bahr, in support. 'We've already got monetary union. Before that linkage, the original estimate of the cost to West Germany of total reunification was forty billion Deutschmarks a year for five years. I now estimate it will be at least five times that. The cost is becoming dangerously near to getting out of hand. There is already pressure on the Deutschmark, because foreign financiers and analysts are beginning to doubt our ability to afford it.'

Turning to Werle, but fleetingly included Elke in the look, the Chancellor said: 'As well as a composite report of these discussions I think we want a separate set of position papers, each isolating the individual problems that have been pointed out. I don't want a proliferation of sub-committees: that just creates more and more bureaucracy. But some are going to be necessary to provide us with suggestions to decide upon, in full session.'

Werle nodded in uderstanding and said: 'And maybe some public reassurance? Events have happened too fast. People – other countries – are confused, each one arriving at different conclusions, even now.'

'You're right,' Rath agreed. 'There should be a steadying statement: something on the lines that while favouring a United States of Europe, West Germany will make no unilateral decisions without full consultation with its Western Allies.'

'Might we not want to enter separate agreements with the East *without* discussion with other Market members? Or with the United States, for that matter?' asked Schere.

The Chancellor smiled. 'Possibly,' he agreed. 'In fact, to do so might provide us with another negotiating lever. Let's insert a rather necessary word into the statement: that West Germany will make no *major* unilateral decisions without consultation with its Allies. Which would not preclude us entering *minor* understandings, would it? And which every foreign government will recognize when they dissect the statement.'

There were answering smiles and nods of approval from those grouped around the table. Werle had been busily writing during the discussion, so that when it finished he was ready. He read out the planned statement and Rath invited more debate. The Finance Minister proposed including an assertion that the West German economy could withstand without difficulty the pressure imposed upon it by the exodus. He was out-argued by both the Chancellor and Schere, who were worried about the risk that foreign analysts and bankers might interpret the statement as a verbal smoke-screen laid down to protect a pressured currency. In the end the statement was agreed virtually as the Chancellor had originally proposed.

Back in the Cabinet Secretary's office, where they went immediately to discuss and agree the session between themselves, Werle said anxiously: 'Well! Were you impressed?' He hoped, particularly, that she had recognized his contribution and noted the deference towards him from everyone.

In truth, Elke had not been overly impressed, although passingly she had been aware of Werle's favoured position. Her mind held on to the knowledge that the meeting had been a momentous one, both politically and historically. Yet none of the discussion or the ideas put forward had struck her as matchingly momentous; she'd been disappointed at the lack of dynamism in either the men or their ideas. She said: 'It was fascinating.'

Werle smiled his pleasure, wrongly imagining Elke in awe: he *had* spoken far more than was normal even for him at a Cabinet session, eager to show her his influence and political acumen. 'Any difficulties, assembling what's necessary?' he asked.

Elke replied by reading out the sub-headings for the position reports she had already annotated as the meeting progressed and itemizing the points she considered essential for the overall record. Werle agreed to everything, without addition or correction.

'It's going to be very good, our working together like this, isn't it?' said Werle.

'I hope so,' agreed Elke, cautiously.

He smiled. 'You don't object to my calling you Elke?'

She hesitated. 'Of course not.'

'As I wouldn't mind your calling me Günther.'

Elke shook her head. 'That would be wrong, in front of the rest of the Secretariat.'

'When we're not in front of the rest of the Secretariat, then,' Werle insisted.

'I'm sorry I haven't called sooner,' Reimann apologized. 'You can guess how busy I've been, trying to interpret and comment about everything happening here in Germany.'

'I can imagine,' Elke accepted. She'd been depressed, increasingly convinced that he wasn't going to make any further contact, but it had enabled her to work late several evenings, to get out the position papers and the encompassing report. There had been a congratulatory message, from the Chancellor's office, on both the speed and the composition.

'And it's going to stay that way,' said Reimann. He allowed a long hesitation, to see if she would say anything. She didn't. He went on: 'So I was wondering whether we could do something together on Saturday? During the day, I mean?'

Now the pause came from Elke. It was established – a firm pattern –

for her always to go to Bad Godesberg, to Ida: she'd done so, apart from holiday breaks maybe, for years. The counter-argument came at once. There *had* been holiday interruptions, so the arrangement wasn't inviolate. What was so important about the visit anyway? He'd think she was reluctant if she went on hesitating as she was doing now. 'Saturday will be fine,' she accepted.

'We'll make a full day of it. Dress to spend the day outdoors: jeans if you have any,' Reimann insisted. He was smiling broadly when he put the telephone down.

Chapter Twenty-Three

Reimann prepared with consummate care. The delay in any contact was intentional, to make her nervous. and specifically choosing Saturday was a challenge, to gauge her unwillingness to break a fixed arrangement. There had scarcely been any reluctance at all, which was encouraging, if any further encouragement had been necessary. Sure of himself – and of what was going to happen – Reimann considered Sunday, when Elke always went to Marienfels, to be the definitive test.

He collected her early, kissing her in greeting at the doorway, which startled her. Elke thought she managed to conceal it from him. She didn't. When she got into the car she saw there was a backpack on the rear seat and said: 'Where are we going?'

'Outdoors, like I told you!' he said, lightly. There was an important reason for the outdoor choice.

Elke was glad she'd bought the jeans he'd suggested, although she wished they had not been so obviously new. She was concerned about how she looked in them: she'd spent the previous thirty minutes prior to his arrival trying to survey her rear view in the closet mirror. His jeans were washed and faded, although the light sweater appeared new. She'd taken a chance with canvas shoes: he wore thick, hiking-type boots. Honestly she said: 'I've never really thought of myself as an outdoor sort of person.'

'It'll be quite painless,' he promised.

Elke recognized the approach to the ferry terminal before they reached it. When he lifted the backpack from the car, she heard the clink of glass. As they approached the ticket office he invited her to decide where they would get off, but she demurred, insisting that he should choose. He declared that Koblenz was too far and was tempted to go to Linz, which he knew from his visit with Jutta. He selected Andernach. So close to summer and on a weekend, the ferry was full, but they managed to get seats out on the deck and on the side catching the morning sun. Almost as soon as the ferry set off Reimann began a commentary in opposition to the metallic-voiced public address broadcast about the castles they were passing, on either bank, recounting the legendary folklore of the river but giving it all his own interpretations, always making her laugh. She automatically looked towards Bad Godesberg as they sailed by, smiling not at anything Reimann said this time but at Ida's reaction to her telephoned apology ('Sorry for what? Do anything to hook him, darling! And I mean *anything!*'), and gazed ashore again when they went by Schloss Marienfels, wondering about Ursula, although there was little to wonder about. Ursula might be with an escorted party, outside in the grounds of the nearby institution. More likely she would be in the room where she would be for tomorrow's visit, moving to her music, her poor mind locked and shuttered against any entry.

At Andernach they had to go some way into the tiny township to get a taxi. Reimann strode easily and fast, the walk of someone athletically fit, and Elke had difficulty matching him. She didn't hear the conversation with the taxi driver, but when they got in he smiled sideways at her and said: 'He promises he knows just the place.'

'You still haven't told me what we're going to do!'

'Picnic!' announced Reimann.

Elke decided it *was* a perfect place. It took less than fifteen minutes to get beyond the town, and when they followed the path recommended by the driver it led up a gradual incline to a tree-thatched hill, which until they reached the top was deceptive, because it wasn't a top at all but the lip of an open-ended cleft that cut completely across, creating a deeply grassed and silent hollow. Once inside it any sight of the town – any sight of anything – was lost, except for the Rhine which sparkled and glinted for their pleasure through the open end of the tiny valley. The sun, still not oppressive, was just at the tip of one edge, as if it were looking in curiously: the entire dip was bathed in yellow warmth, with just a small patch of shade, like a blemish, from the tree line.

'This is idyllic!' exclaimed Elke.

'It is, isn't it?' Reimann agreed. He could not have hoped for better.

Although the grass was not damp he produced a thin blanket from the backpack and laid it out for her with a flourish, making an elaborate arm-sweeping bow for her to sit. As she did so, he said: 'Simple fare: quails' eggs, cold guinea fowl, a little bread, a little cheese, some peaches, some grapes. And wine: enough wine to last us through the day.'

Elke decided it was dreamlike: possible, in fact, to imagine herself in a dream instead of in the real, sometimes unsettling world. How good it would be to stay here forever, cocooned, safe, protected. She felt all of those things, with Otto. When he poured the wine – champagne to begin – she realized from its coldness that he had kept it in a freezer compartment. He peeled the eggs for her – carefully collecting the shell

196

in a bag to avoid mess, she noted – and set out the guinea fowl and offered the bread and the cheese selection, an attentive, considerate servant. As the meal progressed he changed from champagne to red wine but went back to the unfinished champagne when they got to the fruit. As he had on the ferry – as he seemed to do all the time when they were together – he talked and made her laugh: telling self-disparaging fantasy tales that fitted the occasion, of being the worst Boy Scout in America and of being a failed hunter in the American backwoods, and totally false stories of cowardly encounters there with wild animals.

'Lies!' she accused, breathlessly. 'It's all lies!'

They were sitting sideways and opposite from each other, each resting on an arm, so that he was facing her. Seizing the opening, Reimann became abruptly serious and said: 'That's something I will never do: I will never lie to you.'

Elke matched the seriousness. 'I don't believe you ever would,' she said.

Reimann tidied the picnic into the pack, leaving the wine bottles easily accessible, made a mock complaint about the heat and asked if she minded his taking off his shirt: he'd discarded the sweater when they arrived. Elke pretended to look towards the distant river but was able to see him as well. The fitness she'd noticed while hurrying to keep up at Andernach was very obvious: he was hard-bodied and tight-waisted, no excess anywhere, muscles ridged across his stomach and shoulders.

Look all you want, thought Reimann, aware of her covert examination: you're going to see that and a lot more. In feigned apology he said: 'I should have suggested you bring a suntop: a swimsuit top, perhaps.' When he'd first seen her photographs in Moscow he'd guessed her soft-skinned, liable to burn in strong sunlight, he remembered. He thought, now, that was a wrong impression.

'I'm quite all right, really,' insisted Elke, who was wearing a long-sleeved cotton shirt. She didn't possess either a suntop or a swimsuit. She wouldn't have worn either in front of him.

Reimann shifted, positioning himself behind her and said: 'Why don't you lie back: use my legs for a pillow. Your arm will go dead, leaning like that. Mine was beginning to.'

Her arm *was* starting to numb, sitting as she was. But to lie as he suggested would bring her very close to his bareness. Fool! she thought. Elke twisted, so that she was at right angles to him, putting her head on his thigh. It was comfortable, as he'd said it would be.

Unseen above her, Reimann smiled down at her hesitation. He said:

'I really was sorry not to have called sooner. But it's been incredibly busy.'

Elke lay with her eyes closed against the sun's brightness, drifting both in its warmth and the warmth of the wine. She said: 'I know. I had to work late every night.'

So there'd been a Cabinet session, Reimann guessed at once: and of greater length or importance, if she'd had to work late every night, because from the observation before his arrival in Bonn he knew her days ran to clockwork regularity. He tried to think of any particular event in the East to link with such a Cabinet meeting, but couldn't. 'I keep forgetting how involved you must be.'

What had she said! Elke stopped herself drifting, recalling the words. No harm, she decided, relieved. 'Hardly at all.'

'I think you're being over-modest.'

How impressed he would be, she reflected, wistfully. She tried to think of something to say that was not banal – to show that she did have an opinion and an attitude – and recollected her impression after the Cabinet committee. She said: 'Which is not a failing of politicians. Don't you often find them disappointing, when you see them in action, supposedly doing their job?'

What the hell did that mean? Being a personal assistant to the Cabinet Secretary elevated her into a fairly high-ranking position, but not high enough, he wouldn't imagine, for her to make a remark like that: as if she had *seen* them in action. So what was the surmise? Whatever the outcome of the Cabinet gathering, she was critical of it. Contemptuous, maybe? No, he withdrew at once. It would be wrong to try to speculate too deeply. In attempted encouragement he said: 'It's how I find them most of the time. Everyone seems to forget politicians are really ordinary people, not the infallible supermen they expect them to be . . .' He paused, to make her think he was joking, then added: 'Dictatorship is the only answer! One man for the job: democracy does not work!'

'It was a series of dictatorships in the East, wasn't it?' retorted Elke, pleased with herself. 'And look what's happened to them! They've all crumbled into nothing.'

It could be a useful avenue, decided Reimann. He said: 'It's changing. I am not convinced that communism has totally crumbled, not yet.'

'*Crumbling*,' said Elke, accepting the difference.

She was unwittingly perfect in providing him with openings, thought Reimann: he hoped, with sexual cynicism, she would go on doing it. He said: 'I hope not.'

Elke twisted her head, squinting against the sun to look up at him. 'Why ever should you hope that?'

'I'm employed as a political commentator, right?'

'Yes,' agreed Elke. She put her hand up, the better to shield her eyes: his features were in darkness, almost concealed against the sun's brilliance, which at the same time made it look as if he were surrounded by an aura. And in between was the hard-muscled body.

'I've made a speculative interpretation,' said Reimann, in apparent admission. 'I spoke to a lot of people, of course: heard a lot of theories. But one of the suggestions that emerged, one that has hardly ever been advanced, is the reverse side of the coin.'

Elke shifted, so that she could focus better upon him. Hot now, she rolled up the sleeves of her shirt: she would have been much more comfortable in something briefer. 'I don't understand that.'

'All the stress in the West has been upon a practically automatic assumption that those living in the East want to abandon the principle of communism, run as fast as they can through holes and walls or open checkpoints and settle in the West. Wouldn't you agree?'

This wasn't going as she'd wanted, thought Elke, her absolute contentment slipping. She had wanted to go on being pampered and cared for in a glade which no one else knew of or could enter, a magic place. But they were talking politics now: argued-for-a-compromise, adjustable-if-necessary, brutal-if-required politics. None of which had any place in her drifting, euphoric, cocooned dream. Her fault, Elke conceded at once. She'd started it, wanting to impress him: definitely her fault. 'That would seem to be the case, publicly at least,' she admitted.

Publicly, isolated Reimann: she spoke as if she had knowledge of a contrary, opposing assessment. 'Who says so?' he demanded. 'OK, so the people in the East want changes. Travel changes, electoral changes. Changes in their standards of living.'

'So?' asked Elke. How could she stop this conversation: get back to what it had been like when they'd first arrived?

'My interpretation,' said Reimann, in apparent explanation. 'I don't believe everything is as automatic and simplistic as it is being analysed, so far. I've acknowledged that the East demands freedom, certainly. But definitely not a loss-of-identity absorption.' The moment to drop the stone into the water and watch the ripples, he thought. He went on: 'And I've had people agree with me, finally: accept that the assumption of a Europe bound together is premature by years if not decades. So that's the article I have written. That the demand is for a special kind of democracy, one that doesn't abandon the principles of communism . . .' The ultimate pause '. . . and that the government here in Bonn privately accepts and recognizes that reality, whatever the public leaks and assurances might be. That despite all the public posturing they go along with the differing ideologies and are willing to make compromises.'

Reimann was worriedly aware that towards the end his invented argument had started to lose direction. Looking down at her – surprised at the awareness even coming to mind – he suddenly saw her as frail and vulnerable, lying as she was. He hoped she'd stay that way: but then how else could she be?

Elke's concerned reaction was that his complete assessment wasn't at all her understanding. Nor that of Günther Werle, with whom she'd discussed it more times than she could now remember, assembling their joint accounts of the Cabinet committee. Not the Bonn attitude, at least: she conceded that his modified communism thesis might be valid, but that was all. So he'd be wrong. This considerate, kind, attentive man who had done so much for her had concluded a flawed judgement: one, even, that might in its turn be commented upon, professionally ridiculing him. She could correct – avoid – that happening, Elke realized. Just a few words, a phrase: *I'm not at all sure about one aspect . . . have you thought out the possibility of . . . don't forget the Constitutional pledges* . . . Forbidden, Elke accepted, reluctantly: positively and unequivocally forbidden. She wanted so much for him not to be ridiculed: she felt helpless. She said: 'It's an interesting hypothesis.'

'Do you agree with it?' demanded Reimann. He wanted to think he had trapped her, into a box.

There was no warmth from the wine now: little, seemingly, from the sun, although outwardly it was still hot. She shouldn't be involved – forbidden, she told herself again – in this sort of conversation, absolutely innocent and safe though she knew it to be with someone like Otto. She'd never before allowed it to happen; and certainly shouldn't, now that she occupied the position she did. She was fortunate that it had occurred with Otto, with whom there could never be any danger. Elke smiled and said: 'You're the expert. I don't have the political awareness or knowledge to agree or disagree.' She lay back against his leg, hoping he would regard that movement as an end to what they were talking about.

Shit! thought Reimann, as he concluded just that. The balance simultaneously adjusted. He'd learned something, although as yet he did not know how to assess it. And it was infantile to expect any more, at this stage. There was still the rest of the weekend, after all. Quickly he said: 'Forgive me?'

'Forgive you for what?' Elke couldn't guess the direction of the remark, so she remained lying as she was, with her eyes closed, sealing herself off.

'Being boring.'

Now she did stir, but only to turn her head towards him once more. 'Boring?' she said, disbelieving.

'Talking politics: shop. You must be bored to death with it, like I am. And this is our hideaway day. So I'm sorry.'   .

They were back where she wanted them to be, thought Elke, relieved. 'Forgiven,' she said. She believed she'd find it easy to forgive him anything. She felt something against her face and twitched away, believing it was an insect, and then realized it was his fingers, lightly upon her cheek. She stopped twitching.

'I didn't mean to make you jump.'

'I didn't mean to.'

'Do you want me to apologize for this, too?'

'No.'

He caressed on, insect-light. 'What then?'

'Nothing.' She felt thick-throated at the intimacy of his touch, although it was hardly intimate at all: she was glad it didn't sound when she spoke.

'Would you like some more wine?'

'I'd have to move to drink it. And I don't want to move.'

'I'm very happy,' he said.

'So am I.' Elke lay with her eyes more tightly shut than ever, because people's eyes were shut when they were dreaming.

'I want to say something.'

Elke didn't intend to speak, but he didn't go on, waiting as if he wanted her permission, so eventually she said: 'What?'

He still didn't speak, not at once. Finally he said: 'It would be simple – the easy word at least – to say that I loved you. But I won't, because that *is* the easy word. A meaningless one, almost: polished smooth, by too much use. So I'll use other words. I'm so completely happy, to be with you. At the moment – and I really don't think it's going to change – all I ever want to be is with you. I don't get through that much of any day without thinking about you. You're beautiful, which I suspect you don't believe but which is true . . .' Reimann let himself clog to a halt: *people are rarely coherent, always clumsy, at sincere moments of emotion*, the Balashikha instructor had taught. He started again. 'I feel a fool: that I

201

haven't properly said what I wanted to say, although I have really. Oh Christ! I'm sorry. I didn't want to make things awkward, like this. If you like we can blame the wine: *I* can blame the wine.'

Elke lay unmoving against his leg, eyes squeezed together just short of making her face positively wrinkle. It *was* a dream: *had* to be. A warm, floating, perfect dream from which she would awaken to find nothing, no one.

'Elke?' Reimann worked the gulping concern into his voice. 'I'm really, really sorry. I shouldn't have spoken like this: embarrassed you. Now I'm embarrassed. Don't know what to say.'

'Stop!' she said, shortly.

They remained as they were for a long time, the emotion moving through Elke so that he could feel a physical, vibrating movement against his leg. Reimann lolled patiently on his elbow. He watched the toy boats on the faraway river and the contrail of an aircraft – a jet airliner he supposed – draw an accurately straight white line across the sky above, so removed from what was happening between him and the woman using his leg as a pillow that he was actually curious where the plane was going and where it had come from and about the passengers aboard.

'Otto?'

'Yes?' The anxiety was perfect, he congratulated himself.

'I'm not embarrassed . . . I'm not . . .' She couldn't continue for several more minutes. 'The only word I can think of is that I'm flattered but that isn't right at all . . . what I'm trying to say is that I . . .'

'Tell me how you feel!' demanded Reimann, the bored impatience easy to be mistaken for the urgency of his emotion. 'That's what I want to know: how you feel!'

There was another irritating hesitation, while she thought. Elke said: 'I don't know, either. Not to use that word. But I think about you all the time, too . . . I'm blissfully happy, when we're together . . . I know nothing – nothing bad or harmful – can happen to me, when we're together . . . but . . .'

'But what?'

'There are things . . . things to talk about . . .' Elke stumbled. She had to be honest, from the beginning: to say nothing at this moment would be another way of lying, and if she had lied everything would be on a false basis, a foundation that would give way under the slightest pressure. She felt his finger softly against her lips.

'I'm not interested in secrets from the past,' he said. 'They're not important.' Psychologically, a belated confession would be far

202

better: she had to think she had to compensate in other ways to make amends.

Elke raised herself, not wanting to but feeling she had to force the confrontation. 'They are,' she said, unhappily.

Reimann felt out, putting his finger to her lips again. 'No,' he refused. 'Not now. Let's leave everything now.'

His decision, Elke accepted, anxiously seeking an escape. A clumsy, tongue-tangled explanation would be as bad as no explanation at all. She needed the chance fully to consider: sort out what she was going to say and how she was going to say it. Not dishonest: sensible. She couldn't chance the slightest mistake to risk a happiness holding her so tightly she felt she would burst.

Reimann poured more champagne, touched his glass to hers and said: 'Here's to us both finding that right word, very soon.'

Elke drank and said: 'I don't think it's going to be very difficult for me.'

'For me, either.' And then he kissed her, fully. But with careful gentleness, not holding her but simply coming forward, putting his lips to hers, nudging an opening with his tongue.

Elke was frightened. She told herself she didn't know why but knew all the time that she did and desperately hoped he wouldn't sense it. She allowed his tongue, wanting it, tasting the sharpness of the wine, thrusting back with hers, exploring him. He wasn't holding her, pulling her against his nakedness, and Elke thought she was glad but wasn't sure. When? His choice. Here? His choice again. She didn't want to, not in the open like this, hidden away though it was, but if he did then she would, she supposed. Why suppose? Of course she would. Quite safe. She'd stopped a fortnight before. Ovulation five days after: she'd even felt the discomfort. So she was safe now: quite safe. If only she knew more: knew things he might like! Might expect. She didn't want to disappoint him: to be inadequate. Please don't let it hurt! He was always gentle, always considerate. So it wouldn't hurt. Why was she so dry? It would hurt, if she was dry.

He parted from her and said: 'You're shivering.'

'I don't know why.'

'You're not cold?'

'Happy,' she said. 'So very, very happy.'

'So am I,' said Reimann, equalling her sincerity although for different reasons. Should he take her here, bare-assed in the grass? She'd probably consider it romantic, like something out of one of those books back at Kaufmannstrasse. Then again, she'd probably be tensed, nervous of discovery. He didn't want to spoil the first time. That had to be special for her: perfect, in her memory. Which was not the only consideration: psychologically he had to do more than invade her body. So not here. Maybe some other occasion, because this tiny valley would have a significance for her and she might like it here some time. But today, for him, there would be more advantage back at Kaufmannstrasse, where he would be intruding into her personal territory. Unfortunate, really: he quite felt like a fuck.

Elke once more didn't know what to do, what to say. Nothing she thought of was right, and she wanted to do and say everything right. She said: 'This is going to sound like something out of a bad film, but I don't want today to end.'

Most of what they'd told each other so far had sounded like something out of a bad film, reflected Reimann. He said: 'It hasn't got to, has it?'

Elke's throat moved, in her uncertainty. Softly, she said: 'I suppose not.'

'We'll go soon,' he decided.

So he didn't want to make love to her here. Elke believed she was relieved but still wasn't sure. 'If you say so,' she agreed at once. Then frowned, abruptly. 'But how? How do we get back into the town?'

Reimann smiled his crooked-tooth smile at her, glancing at his watch. 'I promised the taxi driver a ten-mark bonus if he came back for us at three.'

Elke smiled back admiringly, thinking how completely capable he was in everything. 'How did you know you'd want to leave by three?'

'I did,' he said, decisive again.

'Afraid you might be bored by then!'

He came forward, to kiss her again, and said: 'I was never afraid of that. And don't seek compliments!'

'I like compliments.'

'You're very beautiful.'

'And you're very handsome.'

Just like a bad film, thought Reimann. He stood, pulling on his shirt, with seeming disregard – but in fact with careful intent – unzipping his fly to tuck it into his jeans, hinting an already accepted intimacy between them. He kissed her again when he held both her hands to bring her up from the blanket, refolding it into the backpack. They walked slowly, hand in hand, back to the top of the hill and then easily made the descent. They only had to wait ten minutes for the taxi to return.

They hardly talked on the river ferry but sat close together, thigh against thigh. In the car going to Kaufmannstrasse Reimann said: 'We're hardly dressed to go out again, for dinner, are we?' He'd determined on the picnic for the clothes they would necessarily have to wear to create precisely such a situation, so they could remain in her apartment that night once they'd returned to it.

'I'm not hungry,' said Elke, surprised at her own obviousness.

'I'm not, either.'

'We can simply stay in then?'

She was actually dictating the pace, Reimann realized, amused at her effort. 'I'd like that.'

Poppi scurried and yapped around them as soon as they entered the apartment, and Elke said: 'I should take him out,' the irritation clear in her voice.

He's not going to be an interference for much longer, thought Reimann. He said: 'Why don't I do it, while you settle in?'

'There's no need to go far,' she said.

'I won't.'

Alone in the apartment Elke considered changing but decided against it, after the remark in the car. She remembered Ursula's photographs and put them in the dressing-table drawer as she had done before, although more fully concealed beneath the underclothes. She didn't speak aloud this time, just thought. Not ashamed. Not hiding her away. Simply a question of things being put in the correct order. Tell him first: explain. Then show him the photographs. That was the way: the correct order.

Reimann hauled the dog along at the end of its leash on the street outside, standing impatiently when it tugged to a stop, to relieve itself. 'I've got a surprise for you soon,' Reimann talked down to it, kind-voiced. 'A big surprise.' The dog pawed up against his leg, scratching for attention. Reimann ignored it, hauling it back towards the apartment. He decided it would have to be quite ordinary, basic missionary position stuff, that night with Elke. He didn't want to offend or frighten her. There had to be a gradual introduction into other more adventurous things. He'd make her like it, all of it. She was going to have to become extremely dependent on sex.

'I've broken out some ice, in case you wanted whisky,' said Elke, when he got back to the flat. They stood in the living-room, staring at each other.

'I don't think so,' he said.

'No,' she accepted.

'Can I get anything for you?' It was important he treat the flat as if he had every right from the beginning.

'No,' she said.

'I'm not going home,' he announced.

'All right.'

'Do you want me to?' She had to come close to asking.

'You know I don't.'

Reimann led her to the bedroom and when he kissed her, by the bed, felt the tremble moving through her. He left the light off, sure she would want the darkness tonight, undressing her by feel and quickly, not trying for any erotic slowness. He undressed quickly himself, but once in bed beside her he changed the pace, aware how much she needed to be soothed into soft acceptance.

As Elke was aware. She lay stiff, rigid, and couldn't stop herself doing it, legs tight together, arms glued to her sides. Do something! she mentally screamed at herself. Move! Respond! Go towards him! Do something! She *was* dry: so very dry. It was going to hurt.

Reimann was patient, coaxing. For a long time he did nothing but kiss her, moving his lips to her face and her hair and her lips before going to her neck and her shoulders. There was a shudder and the smallest of whimpers when he gently trapped her nipple, with his lips at first, until it swelled large enough to bite, still gently, with his teeth. He held it in his teeth then, bringing his tongue back and forth and back and forth, hearing a louder mewing from above and feeling her stiffness seep away.

So good! Oh dear God, so good! She felt as if her skin was burning with pain, every nerve stinging and hot. Why didn't he bite harder! She wanted him to hurt her more. His hand was there! She could feel his finger, hard yet gentle and not trying to go in. Moving slowly, deliciously, wonderfully outside on the bud – *her* bud – but better, so much better, than when she did it herself. Different. Harder, please harder. Just a little. That's right. Like that. Perfect.

She was soft, pliable now. Reimann was sure he could do anything with her – to her – but again decided not to, not tonight. She had her hand at his head, forcing him against her breast, and her legs were splayed in invitation. He didn't take it, not yet. He taunted her, taking his finger from her clitoris to her dimple and back again, up and down, up and down until she snatched at his hand with hers, holding it between her legs where she wanted it.

Wet. She was soaking wet, flooding. So it wouldn't hurt. Couldn't hurt. She wished he'd hurry. Should she hold him? Did he want her to do that? Expect it? She had her hand on his, still holding him between her legs: he could show her whatever he wanted. Do nothing: let him guide, in everything. That's what she wanted, him always to *guide* her: tell her what to do. Elke heard herself moan, a low, near-animal sound, and didn't care, all control practically gone.

When he mounted her it was almost too late. They slid together beautifully, no pain, no hurt. She knew every moment of every thrust, erupting up to meet him, never wanting the sensation to end, never wanting him to pull away, trying to contract herself to hold him in, trapped forever. Marvellous – incredibly – he didn't attempt to withdraw but kept moving, not letting her fade. She came again, lifted beyond herself: beyond her body and the bedroom and where she was. Beyond everything.

Much later, after Reimann had caressed her and played with her and finally coaxed her down, exhausted, Elke said: 'I have never been so happy: so complete and so happy, never in my entire life!'

She hadn't been a bad fuck at all, judged Reimann: with training she could become reasonably good.

Jutta, who knew about the meeting, drove several times past the Rochusplatz apartment: once, in between, she actually stopped to eat by herself in a café she chose for no other reason than that it was brightly lighted and stood on the road along which she was so continuously driving and from the cars parked outside appeared popular. The veal tasted like cardboard.

She made her last check on Reimann's apartment at midnight. To get home she went intentionally along the Kaufmannstrasse, picking out the Mercedes long before she reached the parking bay.

So it had happened: was probably happening, right now. A job, she told herself. Otto was doing a job. It meant nothing. So why was she doing this, ignoring every instruction she'd received in Moscow?

'It's got to be a salary increase,' Sorokin decided, looking down at the print-out the Soviet computer experts had extracted from Elke's bank account.

'There's no doubt,' Turev agreed. 'The deposit is on the same day and the sorting code is identical, from the West German Treasury.'

'Four hundred and fifty Deutschmarks is a substantial increase,' said Sorokin, reflectively.

'For what?' Turev asked. 'Why has Elke Meyer been given such a salary increase?'

Chapter Twenty-Four

Reimann had woken during the night and considered waking Elke, too
– (*women like being awakened after the first time and taken again quickly: makes it
seem less of a one-night stand.* The lecturer had been a woman) – but hadn't
because there were so many other ways to convince Elke this wasn't
going to be a passing affair. He came to the second time initially
without any indication of having done so, eyes closed, still breathing
deeply, listening and sensing, sure even before he opened his eyes that it
was morning. He guessed it was still early from the paleness of the light
filtering through the curtains. Elke had moved, while they slept: she lay
on her stomach, one leg sprawled across his, so that his thigh was tight
into her crotch. It was wet. Her hair was tangled and there were several
tiny globules of mascara on her eyelashes: her skin was slightly
translucent, so that he could see the faint blueness of a vein near her
forehead. Now that it was morning it was important he did nothing to
disturb her. She had to wake up herself, momentarily unsuspecting, to
find him in her bed: then remember, at once, holding his hand between
her legs and crying out and pulling him into her. And know she had to
face him in the coldness of day.

Reimann looked away, around the bedroom, curious what personal
secrets he'd find when he looked. Evidence of the child? It was
interesting there was nothing immediately obvious. Perhaps something
connected with the father? He doubted that, in the circumstances of her
being abandoned. Too much – far too much – to hope there'd be
anything remotely official from the Chancellery, but there might be
something – photographs of a government social occasion, for instance,
which could include Günther Werle or a minister – that could have its
use. He'd have soon to manipulate an opportunity to be here by
himself. But other, more pressing things first. He was confident by now
that he was actually correct in anticipating how she'd react, but today
he couldn't guess, not at all. It was going to be a revealing test.

Elke made a sound beside him, a tiny groan, and Reimann closed his
eyes, feigning sleep. She began to move languorously, her leg remaining
across him, still slumbering. At once there was a tenseness at the
sensation of a presence – his presence – beside her. He sensed the slight
lifting of her head from the pillow as she looked at him, and then

209

another urgent movement. She would have turned her head away: be lying so he couldn't see her face, her own eyes wide open though, trying to work out a morning-after manner. Gently, almost imperceptibly when it began, she eased her splayed leg off him.

Be natural, Elke told herself. Don't behave as if she were embarrassed or ashamed to find him there: last night had been the most wonderful thing that had happened to her. But wasn't there a danger, in doing that? If she were too casual he might think she took men into her bed all the time, that she was easy. Somewhere in between then. Not embarrassed, but not dismissive either. There was nothing wrong – she wouldn't be showing any naïvety or weakness – in letting him know how special it had been for her. She hoped it had been special for him. She thought it had but she wasn't completely sure. He could have been pretending. He was considerate enough to do that: pretend it had been good if he was really disappointed.

Almost the moment for the charade to commence, assessed Reimann: the shift of someone coming through to consciousness, the hesitation of surprise, the whispered recognition. He felt her try to edge further away from him to part their nakedness. He turned towards her, defeating the effort, with apparent, sleeping instinct putting his arm over her shoulder to stage his own supposed startled awareness of where he was and who was with him. Wait a moment: one, two three . . . 'Hello.'

'Hello.' Her head was still away from him, her voice muffled.

'You all right?'

'Yes.' Actually she felt slightly sore. Not a positive discomfort, a reminder of what had happened. A delightful reminder.

Reimann moulded his body into hers, cupping her breast fully in his hand. 'No regrets?'

'No.'

'Sure?'

'Why should there be?'

'I'm glad there aren't.' He could have written the words for her.

The fear of disappointing him was still with her. 'What about you?' she made herself ask.

Reimann kissed where her neck went into shoulder and said: 'It was fantastic. And I liked waking up next to you.'

Elke had liked it, too. After that momentary shock, the lingering uncertainty of failing him, there'd been the good feeling: she felt satisfied, complete. It was even better, now that he was holding her as he was. And now he'd said he wasn't disappointed. There was so much to think about, to take in and believe, but she didn't want to think about anything: just stay here, having him hold her. It was *so* good. His fingers began to move against her nipple, which was even better, and she shifted, to make it easier for him.

'Turn over,' he said. Today's experiment had to be after making love to her: a matter of timing.

'All right.' She almost shut her eyes, as she turned, but realized how foolish that would be.

Straight, like last night? He supposed so. The mascara globules were still on her eyelashes. 'You're beautiful,' he said.

His probing finger was where she wanted it to be. A little bolder than before she moved her hand, to hold him: it thrilled her. 'Is that all right?'

'Incredible.' He was impatient to get it over but accepted it would be a mistake to hurry. From the light coming fully through the curtains he guessed it was another bright day. Cologne, he determined: he liked Cologne. He tried to remember the restaurant near the cathedral but couldn't: he was sure he could find it though.

'What are you thinking about?' Her voice was thick, distant.

'You. Just you. What we're doing. How marvellous it is.' He was sure the name had a number in it: the Three Bishops, maybe. Or was it four? The selection of sausage had been excellent. Definitely Cologne. He brought his mouth from her breasts and Elke squirmed and made small gasping sounds. Three Bishops: he was practically sure it was the Three Bishops. He could probably get a number from telephone information.

'Do it now! Please now!'

Reimann moved over her, permitting her a second's control. Leberkäse, he decided: his favourite sausage. But no eggs: certainly no eggs. He was always surprised more restaurants didn't serve it, disdaining it as tavern food.

'Oh, my darling! My darling!' moaned Elke. The soreness hurt, but it was an exciting, sensational pain, a love pain.

'Darling! Darling!' he said. Sauerkraut! That's what he'd have: Leberkäse and sauerkraut. Beer would be best, to go with it, but wine would be better for his weight. He had to stay fit: in shape.

Elke shuddered beneath him and Reimann shuddered in unison.

'Did you?'

'Yes.' She hadn't been as lubricated as the previous night: he shouldn't let that happen again.

'Good!' she said, still nervous of failing. 'Good! Good! Good!' She

211

had her head into the curve of his neck now, arms tight around him, crushing herself into him with urgent hugging movements as she repeated each word.

Five minutes, Reimann estimated. She'd come down sufficiently in five minutes for him to see how anxious she was to hold on to what she believed she had found. He held her just as tightly with one arm, with the other hand smoothing her hair and her face and her back. The wet-smelling dog would need to be taken for a walk, he supposed. He'd let her do it this morning. If he created some excuse to avoid going with her there might be a chance to look through the apartment. She was becoming quiet in his arms, calmer, breathing more evenly.

'I . . .'

'. . . don't.'

Elke stopped, obediently. He was right: they didn't need talk until he wanted to. She'd wait for him: always defer to him.

Reimann wondered, although indifferently, what she had been about to say. Whatever, it would have been fatuous and unimportant. There was only one subject he was interested in hearing Elke Meyer discuss. Starting with last week's Cabinet meeting. She shifted, although not against his weight upon her: he moved away, using the excuse, wanting to get off her. He wedged himself up on one arm, so he remained above her. Pushing the ebullience into his voice he said: 'It's Sunday: we've got all day! We'll drive to Cologne! It's less than an hour away, and it's a pretty city.'

Sunday! Ursula! The awareness – the unbelievable fact that she had forgotten – literally took Elke's breath away, so that her lungs were tight, empty. How could she! How could she have let herself go so completely – abandoned herself so utterly – as to forget what day it was and the schedule that always rigidly dictated it?

From how he'd positioned himself to look down upon her – *why* he'd positioned himself – Reimann detected the realization surging through her. He heard the grunt when it became difficult for her to breathe and noticed the confused, frowning eye flicker, and was extremely satisfied. At his most optimistic he had not expected quite such an effect.

'I'm sorry . . . I don't . . . I mean . . .' Elke began to splutter, nothing clear in her mind, the words falling from her.

'What is it?' he said, pretending his own feigned confusion.

'It's just that . . .'

Reimann tightened his face, visibly. 'I understand!' he said curtly. 'You've other arrangements? I understand.'

'Yes . . . no . . . there's something, but . . .' He'd think there was

212

someone else! That it hadn't been perfect and wonderful and special and that she had not truly felt happier than she ever had before in her entire life!

'I said I understood.' Reimann was content that the tone was exactly right, offended yet politely trying to avoid her getting that impression.

'No, please!' said Elke, recovering and determined that he really should properly understand. 'There *is* something else: a long-standing family commitment.'

'I shouldn't have assumed . . .' he said. Now he was playing the clumsy new lover, embarrassed at having tried to move too fast.

'I would like to spend the day with you: really I would,' said Elke, hopeful of both placating and reassuring him.

Another of her perfect openings. Seizing it Reimann said: 'Why don't you? Couldn't you rearrange the family commitment?'

'It's come to be expected.' By whom? she demanded of herself at once. Certainly not Ursula, who'd sat oblivious for months, unseeing, unhearing, uninterested. Dr Schiller? What did it matter whether Dr Schiller had come to expect it or not? He'd never even told her the visits had any practical purpose; that they might help. And anyway she knew the answer to that herself, didn't she? So to whom was the commitment? Just to herself, she conceded. A commitment to part fill a day, to ease a conscience she was no longer sure was disturbed or needed easing.

'With how busy you are and how busy I am, with all that's happening, I thought this would have been the best day for both of us,' pressured Reimann. 'When we could have spent most time together.'

It *was* the best time: a whole day. 'It would have been,' she said, her determination torn.

He bent quickly to kiss her, smiling sadly. 'It was not something we could have planned in advance, was it?' said Reimann, who'd planned virtually every movement in advance. 'We didn't know this was going to happen.'

She smiled back up at him, sad too. 'No, we didn't,' she agreed.

'You couldn't . . . No . . . I'm being unreasonably selfish . . .'

Who'd genuinely miss her, at Marienfels? No one! So why . . . The telephone sounded, breaking the reflection, startling them both. From the kitchen the dog began to bark, surprised too. Ida: it was only ever Ida who called. Not any longer, she thought at once, enjoying the correction: but he was here with her. The telephone shrilled on.

'Aren't you going to answer it?' He wanted her to: there was no

213

bedside extension, so she'd have to walk naked across the room, displaying herself. It would be another chip of privacy pared away.

'I know who it will be. I can call back later.'

'I *am* in the way, aren't I?'

'No!' she said, urgently. 'It'll be my sister.' Don't let him think there's another man!

'I see,' he said. The doubt was heavy in his voice.

On and on went the telephone.

She didn't want to parade before him: let him see her without a robe! She knew it was absurd, after what they'd done – that she had nothing to be ashamed of, about her body – but she just didn't want to: it seemed . . . Too soon, she decided: that's what it was, too soon. Haplessly she said: 'Her name's Ida.'

'And she won't go away,' said Reimann. He shifted, moving away from her, and Elke correctly interpreted it as his separating himself from her.

Hurriedly she threw back the covers, partially exposing him as well, and jerked herself up from the bed. Knowing again how foolish it must seem she kept her back to him as she snatched a wrap-around robe from her closet, just needing to half turn as she put it on. Only as she went through the door did she turn, to smile at him.

Reimann was already smiling. At her shyness, mostly, but also at the pleasurable realization of how firm-bodied she was: no sag at all to her ass, which she'd kept towards him, and there'd been very little droop to her tits, as she'd turned.

'Were you in the bath? You've taken ages! I wanted to catch you, before you left! How was it?' gabbled Ida, as soon as Elke lifted the receiver.

'No,' said Elke, tasting the moment, proudly. 'I wasn't in the bath.'

'So how was it!' demanded Ida, missing the hint.

'Fantastic,' said Elke. The precise description, she thought: absolutely and utterly fantastic.

'I want to hear *everything*!'

'It's not really convenient, not now.'

'Not con . . . WHAT?'

'You're shouting.'

'So should you be!'

'I have been.'

'I don't believe this!'

'Thanks!'

'I mean I'm pleased for you . . . happy. Christ, Elke!'

214

'I'll speak to you later . . .' She hesitated, enjoying herself. '. . . I'm not sure when that will be.'

'Don't lose him, darling!' urged Ida. 'Just don't lose him!'

'No,' Elke accepted. She remained by the telephone after putting it back on its rest, savouring the conversation. At once, more seriously, definite parts came back to her. *I wanted to catch you, before you left.* And then another. *Don't lose him. Just don't lose him.*

Dr Schiller came quickly to the telephone, when Elke identified herself. Something had arisen which made it difficult for her to visit today. The principal understood. She hardly thought Ursula would miss her, just this once. Schiller didn't think so, either. They agreed they would see each other the following Sunday.

Elke began to move towards the bedroom door but instead, at the last minute, went sideways, to the bathroom, sighing with dismay at the make-up debris around her eyes and the matted tangle of her hair. She quickly rinsed her face and brushed her hair, although not too neatly, as if she had been trying. *Don't lose him* echoed in her head.

When she re-entered the bedroom through the different linking door Reimann was lying as she had left him, the covers thrown off, exposing him.

Reimann saw her look and was pleased because it was another tiny lowering of her shy reserve. Soon, he promised himself, it would be destroyed completely: she had to be virtually wanton, needing him. He saw she'd washed her face and repaired her hair, just a little. 'Everything OK?'

Elke hesitated at her own bed, unsure what to do. She got in, but high, with her back against the headboard, keeping the robe on. She said, 'It was Ida.' The evasion easily to hand, she added: 'And I cancelled going to see her. I'm looking forward to Cologne.'

You have positively to confront the lie, thought Reimann, recalling the psychological instruction. He said: 'It was your sister you'd arranged to see?

'Yes,' confirmed Elke. 'She said she understood.' Not the time or the place to tell him the truth: she still didn't know how to do it! *Don't lose him.* That was all she could think of at the moment.

She was relying upon him to decide whatever they were going to do, guessed Reimann. She'd had enough sex and he certainly wasn't interested any more: it had served its momentary purpose. The apartment, he reminded himself. He said: 'Why don't you use the bathroom – get ready – first?'

'I'll be quick,' she promised.

215

I won't, mused Reimann.

As soon as he heard her bath running Reimann moved, and was lucky at once, locating her diary in the second drawer of her bedside cabinet. He didn't attempt to take it out, frightened of her emerging unexpectedly. The remainder of the drawers held nothing of interest. He found the photographs of Ursula just as quickly but again merely noted where they were, not trying to take them out for a closer examination. Everything, in every drawer – underwear and scarves and tights and sweaters – was stored with incredible neatness, as if it were regulated to a pattern. Reimann stopped searching after the last of the dressing-table drawers and was back on the bed, where she'd left him, when Elke re-entered.

'Casual?' she said.

'I haven't got anything else and I don't want to go back to my apartment,' said Reimann. 'I feel like soaking for a while, though. Why don't you get dressed and take Poppi out?'

'I was going to suggest that,' agreed Elke, at once.

Reimann rinsed himself in the bath while the taps were running – the plug out so the water ran immediately away – and was already dry, waiting, when Elke called through the door that she was going. The taps were still running, as if he had not yet got in. He emerged as soon as he heard the apartment door close behind her, making directly for the diary.

The entries were stultifyingly dull. There were no intimacies, no confessions. Not even the phrasing changed. Saturday was invariably *Lunch with Ida and family. A pleasant day*. It was interesting, though, that Sundays, when she visited her daughter, were never described as pleasant days. There was only one Sunday entry that intrigued him. *A bad day*. What, he wondered, had been bad about that particular Sunday? Reimann was curious how this weekend would be recorded: he'd have to look, somewhere in the future.

After plodding through the monotonous repetition of the first two months of the year Reimann was tempted to abandon the diary as useless, but he didn't, driven on by inherent professionalism. And was glad he'd continued, when he came to an entry different from all the others. *I. 30,000. Fool*. Reimann stared down, sure it was important. But how? And why? Questions he had to answer. Maybe there wasn't a significance: maybe it only looked interesting because it *was* different, a break in the boredom. Worth remembering, that's all. Caught by an idea, unsure why it hadn't occurred to him earlier, he flicked on to the date of the supposed accident. *Car badly damaged in a hit-and-run accident*.

The man innocently involved was extremely kind. Very unhappy. No reference to anyone called Dietlef Becker, he noted: maybe the similarity hadn't been so important after all. She wasn't unhappy any longer, he was sure. Now she was extremely happy. Grateful, too. Quickly he found Elke's entry after his visit to the apartment to borrow the book. How correct his immediate, gloating reflection had been! It was the longest entry he'd come upon. A detailed account of the visit and her every nervousness over it. *Wonderful*, she had written, in her well-formed, easily legible handwriting. *It was utterly wonderful. I mustn't use wonderful any more. I mustn't do anything to bore him.* Wonderful, thought Reimann, taking her excluded word for his own amusement. He'd been quite wrong, thinking the diary was useless. Although he'd believed it had been obvious, from the way she'd behaved, he definitely knew now how anxious she was, how afraid she was of losing him. She'd spelled it out to him! Thank you! Then, aloud, he said: 'So don't bore me, Elke. And I'll get terribly bored if you don't tell me everything I want to hear.'

Reimann replaced the diary precisely as it had been laid in the bedside cabinet, crossing to the dressing table containing the photographs of Ursula. Another point to bear in mind, he reminded himself, lifting the frames from their concealment among the underwear. That very concealment betrayed her shame: showed that it was instinctive for her to lie. He shouldn't forget that point of pressure, either, if it became necessary to impose. Ursula had, in fact, many uses, not all of which he had fully thought through. The early pictures told him nothing, except Elke's obvious delight, with the mother he recognized from those wedding photographs he had been shown in Moscow. To Reimann babies always looked like babies, without any definitive difference, one from another. He would not have guessed, not truthfully, at any mental problem from the later photographs. Ursula appeared quite an ordinary, normal-looking child. Noticeably tall, perhaps: well developed, although Reimann did not really know at what age girls started to develop. Heavy-featured, too, although again there was no hint of any mental gap in those features. She could even have been considered relatively pretty.

Thirty thousand! The figure rushed back at him, in demanding recollection. The amount – precisely thirty thousand Deutschmarks! – they already knew Elke had withdrawn from her account! The dates even fitted, within the acceptable cheque-issue, cheque-cancellation span. It was, partially at least, the first provable, positive discovery he had made: the first time he had been able to make the facts fit so smoothly. So how should he carry it forward, to complete the deduction? A financial difficulty within the family, obviously. Something between sisters, one lending to another? But why *Fool*? Had Ida done something foolish enough to need thirty thousand Deutschmarks? Or family in the wider sense, a general loan? If it was a general loan, it had to involve the brother-in-law (name! name! name! Reimann demanded of himself; then, relieved, it came – Kissel, Horst Kissel), and there might be an advantage there. Personnel director for the postal authorities, Reimann identified, the recollection coming smoothly. Conceivably a *very* definite advantage. Under the proper, necessary duress Kissel, at his level of authority, could be forced to access anything, nationwide. Unlisted, secret numbers; war-footing emergency communication systems; wire-tap applications, from the security services; Chancellery hotlines.

All these possibilities jostled through Reimann's mind as he stood with Ursula's photographs in his hand. He halted the jumbled ideas, aware of the time-lapse since she had left. As he replaced the frames he automatically erased any fingerprints with the bath towel he still carried. Brilliant, he thought, his own confident assessment: he was doing brilliantly.

Reimann used the cue of the outer door opening to emerge from the bathroom, towelling dry his hair. 'Excellent timing!' he declared. 'I'm ready.'

Satisfied with his morning's discoveries, Reimann let the middle of the day in Cologne float by without pressing for any advantage but not neglectful for a moment, either. Guessing at the guilt she would have for not going to see Ursula, and not wanting it to twist in her mind into any convoluted criticism of him for persuading her to do something she regretted, he kept everything buoyant and light, refusing as well to let her develop any remorse for the previous night. They café-hopped in their vague approach to the cathedral square, Reimann urging champagne upon her (*Haven't we every reason and excuse to celebrate! I certainly think we have!*) so that by the time they reached it Elke was quite lightheaded, uncaring. The restaurant *was* called the Three Bishops and his Leberkäse was as good as he'd anticipated it would be.

On their way back to Bonn, Reimann announced abruptly: 'I can't stay tonight.' He spoke as if it were automatically accepted by both of them that he should have done.

'Oh!' said Elke, who *had* expected it and was disappointed.

'I've still got some time, to change the interpretation of German thinking between East and West I told you about yesterday. There are

still one or two things I'm not entirely happy about in my own mind.'
He'd prepared and practised every phrase in his mind.

'What things?' Elke asked, predictably.

'I don't know if I told you,' said Reimann, airily. 'But I've speculated that the Cabinet here in Bonn are completely unified, talking without any dissent or disagreement with each other. But I've been thinking that maybe that's making it too strong: we know the pressures – they've been commented upon in newspapers and on television enough – so there must be some disagreement between the ministers, no matter how committed they are to the basic principle of unity.'

There *had* been an enormous amount of newpaper and television coverage saying just that, Elke accepted: ministers eager and quite prepared to talk, off the record, she supposed. Who'd told her that? Otto, she remembered: and very true, as she'd acknowledged herself at the time. She said: 'I should imagine the department for Intra-German Relations are finding it difficult. And the cost has to be enormous: there have been public statements to that effect.' There was not the slightest indiscretion there.

'You're right!' said Reimann, as if he had been suddenly reminded, uncaring that she was telling him nothing. Get accustomed to it, Elke, he thought: get accustomed to talking to me in generalities so I can sift out the secrets you won't at first imagine you're telling me. Should he try it? Why not? He said: 'What I really need to know, to be sure, is if there has been any real approach from the East. Or whether the movement has been entirely one way, Bonn towards East Berlin.'

'Yes,' agreed Elke. 'That would make any interpretation a lot easier, wouldn't it?'

Sidestepped, assessed Reimann, still unperturbed. She had responded at once, without discernibly preparing her words: at a guess – and it was certainly not a guess to which he would have attached any decision – he would have said she didn't know whether there had been any such contacts or not. He said: 'I'll just have to grope on.'

He didn't make any effort to leave the car when they got to Kaufmannstrasse.

'Are you coming up?' she asked, boldly.

You get rewards for how well you perform the tricks, he thought: that was how Pavlov trained his obedient dogs. He said: 'I really do want to recast what I've written. So not tonight.'

'All right,' she accepted, her tone of voice showing she considered it anything but all right. She shouldn't crowd him: make him feel suffocated. *Don't lose him.* 'Will you call me tomorrow?'

219

'If I can,' Reimann promised, leaning across to kiss her, passionately.

Elke sat for a long time that night, unsure what to inscribe in her diary. Her first impulse was to record everything, even the sex, but she didn't, of course. In the end she wrote, quite simply and with absolute sincerity: *I am in love.*

The following day one of West Germany's most sensational exposure magazines, based in Munich, published a detailed account of the Transport Minister's affair with a twenty-eight-year-old girl whom they proved, by documentary evidence, to be a former hostess at a Bonn escort agency. There were nightclub and restaurant photographs of the man with her, hand in hand and once kissing, and a separate picture of the girl by herself, naked, performing in a Hamburg strip club before joining the agency. There were also photographs of the Transport Minister's wife and two daughters.

The man resigned the same day, forcing a Cabinet reshuffle.

Chapter Twenty-Five

The postcard summons had been waiting for Reimann when he returned to Rochusplatz, which was a convenient coincidence because he had intended using the now established two-way system to ask for a personal meeting and now he didn't have to bother. With the five-day gap built in between the receipt of the card and his expected arrival in East Berlin he guessed they would be able to discuss what he intended passing back through Jutta, which was more convenient still. The trip away from Bonn could also be useful to maintain Elke's uncertainty.

Reimann was curiously apprehensive at Jutta's reaction to learning he had actually seduced Elke Meyer, and was surprised when inititially there was little reaction at all. He was beginning to outline what he guessed to be the Cabinet meeting when she interrupted and said: 'You stayed the entire weekend?' Reimann said: 'Yes,' and Jutta nodded and said: 'Go on,' nothing more.

He concentrated, of course, upon the conjectural Cabinet gathering, about which there had been no public disclosure, and Elke Meyer's apparent disillusion with some of the ministers involved. When Reimann suggested there might be some disunity within the West German Cabinet on how to deal with new freedoms in the other half of the country, Jutta came in immediately to say: 'That's public enough knowledge: it's been discussed in most newspapers and magazines.'

'Speculated upon,' argued Reimann, irritated by his wife's dismissal. 'And I'm trying to convey how delicately I have to go, at this stage: always having to talk as if it's something I know or I've written and asking her to give her views. That's a difficulty I'd like you to make sure they understand.' And if you don't they'll hear it anyway through the microphones, he thought: would he be able to get any indication during the later East Berlin encounter if she failed to convey the message?

'And what did she say?' Jutta demanded.

'That the Intra-German Relations Ministry was over-stretched and that it was costing their exchequer an enormous amount.' Reimann was suddenly caught by an impression of hardness in Jutta, a hardness about her clothes and a hardness about her make-up and careful hairstyle. It was something that had not occurred to him before. Yet he didn't really think she was appreciably different. His lack of awareness, he accepted: before, he had thought of his wife's unbending attitude as professionalism. A steel-like dedication. He'd come, by comparison, to think of Elke as soft: soft and feminine. The self-criticism was immediate: comparison, between one and the other, had no place in what he was doing.

'Christ!' exclaimed Jutta, contemptuously. 'That hasn't been speculated about! That's been spelled out, with facts and figures!'

Reimann didn't like such outspoken opposition, nor the way it would sound on any recordings. He said: 'It was the first time, for God's sake! She's got to learn to trust me more!'

'Wasn't she cooperative?'

'What's that mean?' asked Reimann, who knew. They shouldn't have talked at Nord-Stadt, not this time. He should have taken her out, flattered her: what they were talking about could as easily have been discussed in a public place without any danger.

'What was she like?'

'Boring.' She hadn't been, judged Reimann, although dispassionately. He'd actually enjoyed it.

'Are you staying tonight?'

Given the free choice Reimann would have preferred to go back to Rochusplatz and be entirely by himself. He said: 'Of course I'm staying. I want to.' The experience left him curious. That night their lovemaking was not as predictable as it usually was. She climaxed noisily, and clung to him and said she loved him. Reimann held her just as tightly and said he loved her too. He'd feigned his own climax: she didn't realize that, either. But then she shouldn't have done: it was something else in which he had been expertly trained.

He telephoned Elke in the middle of the week and at the Chancellery, once more intentionally intruding into another exclusive domain. The call came half an hour after she'd learned of another Cabinet committee meeting the following morning: her initial distraction was obvious to Reimann, at the other end of the line. He insisted he was truly sorry but that it was essential he go out of town for a few days, to comply with the latest story request from Australia. Elke put all consideration of the Cabinet session out of the mind, insisted in return that she understood and asked when he would be back. Reimann, prepared for the question, said he did not think until after the weekend, allowing her the opportunity to visit the child at Marienfels and also, hopefully, to compare the dullness of an ordinary weekend against what had happened during the one that preceded it.

'I'll miss you,' he said.

'I'll miss you, too.'

'Be careful.'

'And you.'

'Don't fall in love with any strange man,' he said. On the jotting pad by the telephone, Reimann was distractedly doodling squares within squares.

'Why not?' demanded Elke, responding.

The interlocked squares became a maze-like prison: at its centre he wrote her name. He said: 'Because if you do I'll get jealous.'

'Do you really mean that?'

'You know I do.'

Reimann showed the same caution as before in reaching Berlin, although he took a different evasive routing, staging through Munich and arranging the flights differently, so that there was no need to stay overnight in the west sector. The atmosphere – or rather lack of it – that he'd imagined on the earlier visit was more pronounced this time. Always, when he'd lived and worked in the city, he'd had the feeling of being enclosed, locked up. But not any more: now the impression was of openness: illogically, as if suddenly more space had become available.

A lot more of the Berlin Wall appeared to have come down since his last crossing: as he approached he saw a lorry trundle along the Friedrichstrasse loaded with rubble. It was not destined for any dump, he knew. It was en route to some entrepreneurial yard to be carefully broken into the smallest practical pieces and sold as genuine souvenir fragments that would enter the display cabinets of idiotic memorabilia collectors all over the world. *Look at that, if you will! That's a bit of the original Wall! The Wall! Can you believe it! The very Wall. What about that, then!* Lucky the one – anyone – who got a piece of the real Wall. Pragmatically he recognized that communism had created a permanent capitalistic market, like bits of the Cross upon which their Christ was supposed to have been crucified: enough chips to restore the Brazilian rain forests a million times over, soon to be equalled by enough pieces of masonry to build a mile-high wall to encircle the world. Buy on, idiots: buy on.

There were still lumps, parts of the Wall not yet removed, but no proper preventive barrier. People stood about in groups, being photographed against it or looking at the broken-down remains as they would have regarded the skeleton of some prehistoric monster. Which was what it represented now, he reasoned. Hardly a skeleton, even. Merely a marker, to ancient history, another time now past. Except for a few: a few of whom he was one. They were all stupid, these memorabilia collectors! Didn't understand. So few understood. They would though: eventually they would.

Reimann walked unchallenged across the dividing line: not that there was a line, a division, not any more. There were still grey-suited border soldiers, mostly looking bewildered – guards with nothing left to guard.

His reception at the Johanisstrasse safe house was as smooth as before. The room was the same, but this time the pudgy Russian was alone, waiting behind the bare desk: the ashtray was already overflowing.

'So you've got her!' It was Turev's only greeting.

'Yes,' said Reimann. As before he sat, uninvited, on the only visitor's chair. Where was the other, higher-ranking Russian, the one with the tight beard?

'Excellent!' praised Turev. 'You're sure you can manipulate her?'

'I think so: there's still some reserve.'

'It wasn't a full Cabinet meeting,' Turev told him, a hint of triumph in his voice.

'How do you know?' Reimann felt aggrieved to be receiving instead of imparting the information.

'We've checked the movements of every member of the Cabinet, for the week you say the gathering took place: three of them weren't in Bonn, not at any time.'

It was an obvious elimination procedure and one he should already have followed. Reimann was annoyed at himself, but he would look even more inefficient trying to make an obvious recovery. 'A special group then? A committee, maybe?'

Turev nodded. 'Yet she felt able to comment, about certain members . . .'

'. . . as if she had been there,' Reimann completed, determined to catch up.

'Beyond the authority we believed her to have,' said the Russian, unnecessarily. 'But something else has come up that we can't explain. Her bank records show a four hundred and fifty mark increase. Any idea how that could have come about?'

'None.' Reimann felt completely ineffectual.

'Could she have attended such a meeting?' asked the Russian hopefully.

'I've no way of knowing,' Reimann had to admit. *Why* hadn't he made the deduction himself? He'd become complacent: complacent and sloppy.

'A possibility,' Turev insisted.

'I'll find out,' Reimann promised. I hope, he thought.

'It would make her far more valuable than we've so far believed her to be.'

'If it's true that she does have personal access.' Reimann was still cautious. She had sounded distracted, not as anxious as he'd expected, when he'd telephoned before leaving Bonn: still insufficient for any definite conclusion.

'It's a priority, to find out.'

'I realize that.' Reimann was surprised the Russian had not rebuked him by now: he deserved criticism.

'Anything else?' Turev demanded.

'I know about the thirty thousand Deutschmarks. It was given to her sister.' It wasn't much but at least it was *something*: because Reimann had been told about the access to Elke Meyer's bank account at their previous personal meeting it had not been something he could pass back through Jutta.

'Why should she do that?' said Turev, reflectively.

'There could be a possible advantage.' Reimann was anxious to restore as much as possible any lost respect. 'The woman's husband is an executive with West German telecommunications.'

Turev nodded. 'Leave it with us: I don't want to risk you becoming involved in any way. And well done again, incidentally, about the Transport Minister. The resignation was disruptive.'

Reimann was still annoyed at himself, and the congratulations did nothing to ease it. He said: 'I'm going to try to pressure the woman in a particular way. I don't believe for a moment that she initiated the security check, but just in case I want a communication sent to me from Australia through the Press Centre. It's to be very critical of my last article. Get a phrase inserted about being deeply disappointed.'

'Anything on the documents coming through Vienna?'

'Nothing,' said Reimann, another admission of failure.

Turev stretched to a drawer on the left of the desk and produced a box. Inside was what looked like the type of pump-operated inhaler asthmatics use to relieve breathing difficulties. 'The poison you wanted. It's a gas that causes cardiac constriction. It dissipates within minutes of death. Is it an unpleasant dog?'

'Appalling,' said Reimann. 'And it smells.' He wasn't at all satisfied with how the meeting had gone.

It had been the sub-committee considering the financial implications of the East German exodus, and the report and listed recommendations had not taken Elke as long to prepare as the account of the full Cabinet committee. She still cancelled the usual midweek lunch with Ida to compile it, so it was not until the Saturday that they talked, and even then not until the afternoon, when they were alone in the garden.

'For someone with a lover as good as you say he is you certainly don't seem very happy!' Ida accused, although lightly. She'd listened without interruption to everything Elke had told her. Seizing the rare opportunity, Elke had gone into considerable detail.

'I'm going to have to tell him about Ursula, aren't I?'

'*Don't*, if you're so frightened!'

'It would be worse, when he eventually found out. Why shouldn't I, anyway? I'm not ashamed!'

'That's what I'm saying, for Christ's sake!'

'This week,' declared Elke. 'I'll tell him this week.'

Chapter Twenty-Six

Elke poured herself some wine before his arrival, and was lifting it to drink before she realized what she was doing, behaving like one of the ludicrous characters in those American TV soap serials she'd always disdained. She put the glass down too firmly on the kitchen ledge, spilling some. She was very frightened: empty-stomached, weak-kneed, numb-faced frightened. She'd gone through all the reassurances – too considerate, too wonderful, too long ago, wouldn't mean anything, he'd accept it because he was so understanding – but nothing had helped. Ida had been marvellous, telephoning as she had, knowing he was coming. *You're making a drama where one doesn't exist . . . it can't matter, if he's as good as you say . . . bring him to lunch next weekend . . . if he dumps you, I'll have him . . . you can have Kurt . . . Kurt and Horst, with my blessing.* Trying to make her laugh: unbend. Dear Ida. That hadn't helped, either. She sipped some wine. It tasted sour, although she'd bought the bottle – six bottles, in fact – on her way home from the Chancellery that night. The spilled wine made her fingers wet. She dried her hands on a paper towel, using it to mop up the wet ring.

I want to talk. Too abrupt: too peremptory. *I have a secret.* Ludicrous, like a soap opera again. *There's something I want you to know.* Soap opera once more. *There's something I haven't told you.* Why did everything sound so facile, so artificial? Ida was right. It wasn't the drama she was making it out to be. Something that had happened long ago. Nothing to affect him. Nothing to affect them. She'd had a baby. So what! His choice. He could either accept it – accept Ursula – or he couldn't. If he couldn't then it would be over. Dear God, no! Don't let it be over. Don't let me be wrong, believing him to be so kind and gentle, so considerate, so wonderful! Don't let him be offended or hurt or digusted! She loved him too much: wanted him too much. Maybe that was the way. *I can say it now: want to say it now. I love you. And because I love you I want to be honest* . . . Not quite right, but better. Definitely say she loved him. Because she did. But wasn't that trying to trap him, imposing a burden on him, before saying what she had to say? A possible interpretation. Whatever she said, however she said it, would have more than one interpretation. Not really. Just one interpretation. *I had another man's child. I'm soiled goods.* Soiled goods! They didn't even speak like that in soap operas. She sipped more wine. How then? She didn't know.

She'd thought she knew, when he'd called. Let's not talk about where we're going, what we're going to do, until you've been here first. Very strong, very positive. What's wrong? he'd said, the concern obvious. When you get here, she'd avoided. So he already knew there was something: was warned. *I didn't mean to sound dramatic. It's just that . . .* No! Ursula wasn't 'just that' anything. Ursula was her daughter: her darling, sweet, lovely, sadly crippled daughter. Not 'just that'. Never. If it came to a choice . . . Elke stopped the thought, shocked by it. There wasn't a choice. Never had been, never would be. She would always be with Ursula, close to her, always a mother, as best she could. His choice, then. Hadn't she concluded that already? She thought she had. It didn't matter. Only Ursula mattered. If he couldn't accept Ursula, acknowledge Ursula, there was no future for them. Nothing for them. She'd have to tell him that, make him understand. No! she told herself at once. That was a demand, an ultimatum. She didn't want to present him with ultimatums: wasn't in a position to do so. It had to remain unsaid: unsaid but inferred. *I'm sorry, but if you can't . . .* How did she know – how could she guess – what he could or could not accept?

When she lifted her glass she discovered it was empty, so she filled it again. Poppi fussed around her ankles, but Elke ignored the dog. He had to have had other lovers, from the way he'd made love to her. Maybe he had a child, somewhere. Not a factor. Not possible, either, she decided firmly. If he had fathered a child it would be here with him in Bonn, being cared for as she knew he would care for it, doting on it, protecting it. Definitely not! Otto might have had lovers, a lot of them, but he hadn't had children. *Darling. I don't want there to be any secrets, so you should know . . .*

The bell sounded.

Elke jumped so profoundly that her wineglass spilled again, and for a moment she stood unmoving, staring down at the new ring of wetness, her mind blank of any thought, her body urged by no movement. The bell sounded once more, longer this time, and the dog skittered around, barking. Elke moved at last.

Reimann closed the door behind himself, after she admitted him, but remained in the hallway, solemn-faced. 'No kiss?' Confession time? It could be something else, but he guessed at unburdening herself being the most obvious. Good, he thought: hurry up, for God's sake!

Elke came forward quickly, offering herself, but staying stiff, and knew he would notice. She stepped back, separating them, when he released her.

'It seems serious?' he said, lightly mocking. He'd hear her out, let her flagellate herself, before doing anything to assist.

'Come in,' said Elke, leading the way into the main room. 'You want a drink?'

'Not particularly.' He presented her with the chocolates.

'I do.' She accepted the offering, forgetting to thank him.

'Then I'll join you.'

She didn't worry about the dog, which scuttled in from the kitchen after her when she returned with the glasses. Reimann scooped the animal up, settling it on his lap. He had considered bringing the gas dispenser with him, in the event of an opportunity arising that night, but had decided against it. It had to be done to achieve the maximum possible advantage. But soon. The dog disgusted him. Let the comedy begin, he thought. 'Whatever it was I did, I'm sorry.'

'It's not you! Nothing you've done!'

'Why the gloom and doom?'

'I want to talk.' Her glass was already half empty: maybe she hadn't filled it properly.

He'd been right, Reimann decided, confidently: as he invariably was. He sipped his whisky. The dog *did* smell. He said: 'Definitely serious?'

'Yes . . . no . . . I mean it's important. Important for you to know, now, before . . .'

'. . . before what?'

'We go any further.'

'Do you want us to go further?' Always, in every circumstance and at every chance, she had to imagine they had a future together.

'You know I do!' said Elke, almost irritably. 'You know I love you!'

'I didn't, not until now,' said Reimann. 'It's something I have been wanting to hear.' He wouldn't say it back, not yet. She had to remain unsure for a little longer. Reimann waited, patiently, watching her fidget and fuss in the facing chair. 'Well?' he encouraged, kindly.

She was going to make a mess of it: Elke knew she was. It was all going to come out jumbled and nothing was going to sound right and she was going to drive him away and it would be her fault. 'I have a baby . . .' she blurted. 'No . . . a daughter . . . grown up. No, not grown up . . . fifteen almost . . . wasn't married . . . it was an accident. Well, no . . . becoming pregnant was an accident. Her being born wasn't. I love her . . .' Elke couldn't think of how to go on: of what she'd said, immediately before. 'I wanted you to know . . . now you do.'

'I see,' said Reimann, soberly. He had to treat it seriously, because that's how she regarded it. But not for long. She had to be lifted up, reassured, quite quickly. She'd talked with her face turned away and still wasn't looking at him.

'Her name is Ursula,' added Elke, lamely.

Reimann decided to urge her to talk, to purge herself further: the more she told him the closer she would consider herself bound to him. 'Where is Ursula now? With her father?'

Still clumsily, but with improving coherence, Elke talked about the child's autism and of the Marienfels home and twice, unaware of doing so, referred to the man who had abandoned her as Dietlef, confirming the Russian guess at that long-ago briefing session.

So maybe the physical similarities *had* helped, mused Reimann.

'That was another lie,' Elke admitted. 'The Sunday we went to Cologne. That's where I was going that day: I go every Sunday to see her.' She looked at him at last, trying to gauge his feelings. He was quite impassive, showing no reaction. She wished his face would indicate something: she didn't like it when he was so completely emotionless. It made him seen coldly distant. But then perhaps that was how he did feel about her, now.

What would she want, most of all? His forgiveness, he determined: forgiveness and understanding and to be told it didn't affect or alter anything between them. It didn't really matter in what order it all came: better, even, if it seemed ill-considered, *without* any order. He waited until she looked anxiously at him again and held her eyes when she did, smiling at her. 'Is that it? The big, terrible secret?'

Elke nodded, tight-lipped, her head jerking rapidly up and down.

Reimann moved very fluidly, gratefully dislodging the dog on to the floor and putting his glass on the side-table as he came out of his chair towards her, but never fully standing, so that he arrived on his knees, looking up at her. He put her now empty glass aside with the same smoothness and took both her hands in his and said: 'Oh, my darling! My poor, frightened, innocent darling! Did you *really* think it would mean something? Upset me or . . .' Reimann allowed the pause of feigned difficulty, '. . . offend me even. . . ?'

'I thought it would . . . could . . .' admitted Elke. He wasn't shocked, closed off against her! He was kneeling at her feet, holding her hands, and being sympathetic, as if he understood!

Reimann came even closer, so that he could kiss her, a light, comforting kiss. 'You want to know how I feel? I feel angry, that a man could have treated you like that. And sad, because Ursula is as ill as she is. But happy: selfishly happy, because if you'd got married then we probably wouldn't have met. And I think meeting you is one of the most important things that's ever happened for me . . .' Another pause. There should be violin music, he thought: or a crescendo of drums, building up to a grand finale. He said: 'I love you, Elke. I love you very much.'

Elke came forward against him, clinging to him, too overwhelmed to kiss or talk, just wanting to hold him. He'd said it! He'd said it and she knew he meant it! Someone loved her: a wonderful, perfect man loved her! No more loneliness! No more uncertainty, having to work out and solve her problems of everyday life! Someone to rely on! Someone who would help! She didn't want to cry. Silly to cry. Wrong. She wasn't sad. She was the happiest she'd ever been. How easy it was to feel like that, when she was with him!

Reimann felt her shaking, detected the wetness from her cheek to his and judged the encounter to have gone just as he'd wanted. It wasn't the moment to spring his own little surprise. But certainly tonight: she had to know how tenuous everything was, how quickly it could all come crashing down. He had to get this tender scene over as quickly as possible; his knees were beginning to hurt, knelt as he was. And the bloody dog was sniffing around his legs and his crotch, demanding to become part of whatever was going on. Perhaps, for once, it would have a use. Reimann eased Elke away, going back on his haunches, and said: 'Poppi's getting jealous: I guess he's going to have to get used to me.'

Elke's nose was red and shiny, where she had been crying, and her eyes were red, too. 'I need to go and . . .' she said, leaving the sentence unfinished.

'Why don't you, while I get more drinks?' Going to the kitchen gave him an excuse to get rid of the dog. By the time she came from the bathroom, her face washed, her nose without its shine, Reimann was ready. He asked to see photographs of Ursula, sending Elke into the bedroom to fetch the pictures he had already studied, and remarking how pretty she was, and asked, as if he didn't know, how far Marienfels was from Bonn.

'Could I come to visit?' he inquired, suddenly.

'You . . . but. . . ?' questioned Elke, first surprised, then pleased.

'Don't you want me to?'

'Of course! It's just . . . I hadn't thought about it. Imagined you would like to.'

'I would.'

'Then I want very much for you to come.' She hoped Ursula would not be in one of her difficult moods. Elke wanted him to get the best

231

possible impression: to love Ursula, even, if he could. Maybe that was too much to hope: like her, then.

'What about next Sunday?' Moscow's insistence was on speed, so the quicker he ingratiated himself in everything the better. He was already calculating how to manipulate the situation into superb advantage.

'Next Sunday will be fine.' She knew Ida had meant the luncheon invitation too. But not yet. She didn't want to crowd him with her family. Soon. But not quite so quickly. Elke was very proud, anxious to show him off, to boast at last. *Look! Mine! Isn't he fantastic!* She knew Horst and Ida would love him: admire him. Right that they should. She hoped Horst wouldn't try to inflate his own importance, as he normally did.

Why hadn't she found a man? Reimann wondered, curious at the intrusive thought. She was attractive. Dressed well. Inexperienced in bed, maybe, but that could be corrected. Lacked confidence, perhaps, but so did millions of women, all of whom were married at least, if not blissfully happy. Who *was* blissfully happy? No one: not truly, not deep-down. So what was the answer to Elke? One that slipped through the net, he concluded: someone always in the wrong place at the wrong time. One of the instructors – an American defector – had actually used an American cliché to describe someone like Elke Meyer. *One of life's losers. Can't help it. Whatever happens, they fall back into the shit.* Poor Elke: poor permanent loser. He said: 'We could go out, if you'd like.'

'I don't think so.'

Bring her down: degrade her, he remembered. He said: 'So you want to fuck?'

She coloured, brightly, but she didn't try to look away. 'Yes,' she said. 'I want to fuck.'

Reimann reasoned that Elke had moved the guidelines further, made a declaration, and he was more adventurous, using his mouth much more – bringing her off the first time without entering her – but careful against urging her to match him, not the first time. Later, from the way she convulsed, he was sure from the clinical training and films that she had achieved a multiple orgasm. It was working out to be an extremely successful evening, at every level. It certainly took her a long time to calm. Reimann was patient, unhurried.

She was actually breathing deeply, near sleep, when he said: 'It hasn't been a good few days.'

'What?' Her voice was heavy, weighted with drowsiness.

'It seems the magazines aren't pleased.'

'What?' she said again, but differently this time, concentrating through the fog.

'You remember the piece I talked to you about? The interpretation?'

'Yes?' Elke was quite awake now, listening intently.

'They didn't believe it: thought the political reasoning wasn't sound.'

'So what's happened?'

'They're not using it,' said Reimann, simply. 'The most important, ongoing political story in Europe for the past forty-five years, I'm supposed to be their leading commentator, and they're not trusting my judgement!'

'Is that serious?'

You'd better believe so, thought Reimann: you'd better believe you have to save us both. He said: 'Professionally it's a slap in the face. But it happens: that's what the job is all about. But I can't afford it to happen too often.' According to the psychological teaching she now had to move slightly away from him in the bed, the better to concentrate.

He waited.

She moved.

'I want to understand what you're saying,' Elke insisted.

'If I keep getting it wrong – in their opinion – I'll no longer be the leading European political commentator for the magazines, will I?'

'What would that mean?'

'They'd replace me, I suppose.'

'You'd have to leave Bonn!'

'What else?'

'I don't want you to leave Bonn.'

'I don't want to leave, either.'

Günther Werle was unhappy that so far he and Elke were not personally closer, but professionally she had proved herself superbly. Not that he'd ever had the slightest doubt about Elke's ability to rise to the challenge. It was just that it was never completely possible to gauge how a person would respond to promotional responsibility, and any failure would have reflected upon him, because he was the one who had sponsored her so strongly. But she hadn't failed at all. She'd conducted herself with complete propriety in everything, deferential although not subservient, hardly a single minute or memorandum or report needing his slightest correction. *No* correction, he acknowledged: merely suggestions, a small shift of emphasis here, the simplest change of phrase there. So any – and every – reflection upon him had been favourable.

233

She'd seen him in action, too. Seen how he was included in everything, deferred to by the most powerful men in the country: knew the influence he had at the very pinnacle of German politics. He was sure she admired it all, although she was far too controlled, far too composed, ever to show it. But she knew. He'd expected a much greater change, between them personally. He called her Elke all the time now, but she only called him by his Christian name occasionally, and then rarely unless he prompted her.

He determined to make the outing to the Viennese recital different than before. Better. Their difficulty that first time had been predictable enough. But now they were closer: more personally familiar. He'd get some more recommendations and go to the restaurants first, so that he would know what to expect: behave as if he knew the place well. And order some champagne in the interval, even though he didn't like it himself because it gave him embarrassing flatulence.

He smiled up, as Elke entered for the day's diary discussion. 'I've been lucky,' he announced. 'I've managed to get some excellent stall seats for the Vienna Boys' Choir.'

Elke had completely forgotten. She said: 'I'm extremely sorry, Herr Werle. But I won't be able to join you.'

'I see,' said Werle. He tried to avoid swallowing heavily, in his disappointment, but couldn't. Herr Werle, she'd said: not Günther.

'Please forgive me. I should have spoken before.'

'It's quite all right,' said the man, shortly. His throat moved, as he swallowed again. Why wouldn't she come? he thought, desperately. Why?

Chapter Twenty-Seven

Her period coming that Saturday evening was an advantage to be used. Anticipating her discomfort from his first inspection of her bathroom cabinet, Reimann cancelled the dinner reservation and prepared steak in her own kitchen with an expertise derived from Jutta's indifference to cooking. He refused her help to clear away, settling her with her feet lifted upon the couch while he did it alone. He reappeared with coffee and a supply of analgesic pills, insisting she tell him the moment she felt she wanted more. He sat at one end of the couch, so that she could remain with her feet up, her back against his chest. Pointedly he watched every newscast on television, remarking with apparent casualness that he couldn't afford to miss out on the slightest political development, and particularly not on any interpretation from another commentator. It was understood without it being discussed that he would sleep with her, but that night he let her go into the bedroom ahead of him. When he followed she was already in bed. She wore a high-necked nightdress.

'You don't mind do you? It's just . . .'

'Why should I mind?' said Reimann.

She fell asleep with both his arms around her. It was too uncomfortable to remain that way but he woke up ahead of her the following morning, so he was holding her again when she stirred. Her first act was to feel for his arm, for reassurance.

Reimann made her stay in bed while he made the coffee. When Elke went into the kitchen, there were pills waiting beside her place.

'It's never too bad, the second day.'

'Take them, just in case.'

'Where did you learn to do everything right?'

'I took lessons,' said Reimann, in an unusual moment of truthfulness.

He did not question the time she insisted on leaving Kaufmannstrasse, although he knew it would get them to Marienfels far too early. Elke sat half turned in the passenger seat, looking more at him than at anything outside the car. Please let it be one of Ursula's good days! She'd considered calling Dr Schiller, but had been unable to phrase the question in a way that would not sound strange: perhaps what he regarded as Ursula's good days wouldn't be the same as hers anyway. Reimann didn't seem to want to talk, so Elke didn't either. She was quite content – more than contect – just to be with him, near him.

Reimann recognized the layby on the final ascent towards the institution from the Russian photographs.

'I usually stop here: let Poppi out for a run,' said Elke, so he did. He gazed around the wooded hills, idly speculating where the surveillance team had concealed themselves. They had been long-lens shots: there was adequate tree cover and coppice all around.

'Sometimes Ursula can be difficult,' warned Elke, feeling there should be some preparation. 'Resistant. She's particularly strong: too strong for me, if she's determined to do something. And she's not very communicative.'

Reimann smiled at her. 'It's all right,' he said, kindly.

'I just wanted you to know, before . . .'

'Don't worry.'

Elke introduced him to Dr Schiller as a friend. Reimann stood politely just slightly apart while Elke and the principal talked about Ursula, hearing the doctor say that Ursula had refused to come out into the grounds and seeing Elke's immediate grimace of concern. The flower display in the foyer today was roses.

Ursula appeared to have remained unmoved from Elke's last visit: she was even wearing the same denim skirt and red sweater. One arm of the sweater was stained with food debris, potato maybe. Mozart played on the secured tape machine. Reimann held the chair for Elke, sitting himself upon the bed, which put him closer to the girl. Elke felt the discomfort she always knew, talking to the non-receptive girl in front of someone. She described Reimann as a friend again and talked about Georg and Doris, and, risking the rejection, said the day was beautiful and how nice it would be to go out in the grounds. She tried to hold Ursula's fingers while she talked but the girl pulled away, sharply, so Elke did not try again.

Reimann reached out, above five minutes afterwards. He did not try to grasp Ursula's hand but gently stroked it, hardly making contact at first. Elke was immediately reminded how the male attendant had caressed to free Poppi from the crushing embrace that terrible Sunday. Ursula let herself be stroked. She even smiled and looked directly at Reimann and made a sound that did not make a recognizable word. Then there definitely was a word – 'nice', which emerged as a favourite – and Reimann smiled back and gently brushed the food debris from the arms of the sweater.

'We'll go outside,' he said. He spoke more to Ursula than to Elke, rising from the bed but keeping hold of the child's hand, to bring her up. Ursula rose obediently. Outside she let her hands be looped through their arms, either side, and said 'nice' several times and made a lot of unintelligible sounds. The dog danced and darted ahead of them and once, trying to turn, fell over its own scrabbling legs, yelping on to its back, and Ursula laughed and took her hand from Elke's arm to point. 'Silly dog' was quite clearly understandable. Reimann talked to Ursula about the dog and pointed out birds and played a game of holding up his fingers and making her knock them down as he counted, never going beyond three. When he spoke to Elke, it was never as if the girl could be ignored because of her disability. Elke thought it was all so natural: a couple walking with their child on a warm, bright day. All so completely natural.

They got a lunch-table to themselves, which was how Elke liked it. It was Reimann who cut Ursula's meat and diced the salad into smaller, more easily managed portions, and he halted Ursula before she started to eat, manoeuvring the spoon better for her to hold it and bring the food to her mouth. Elke only had to clean Ursula's mouth twice during the meal.

Afterwards Reimann showed no impatience to leave. They walked in the grounds again, so it was well into the afternoon – later than Elke normally left – before they settled Ursula back in her room and made their farewells to Dr Schiller.

'She was very active today: enjoyed your being here,' assured the doctor, saying what Elke was thinking.

Elke did not try to talk as they descended the hill towards the main highway, knowing her voice would be clogged and uneven, and was glad that again Reimann did not force any conversation. They were heading directly towards Bonn before Elke believed she had sufficient control. She said: 'Thank you. That's not enough but it's all I can think to say. I can't remember the last time there was a day like this, with her. It was wonderful.'

That banned word, thought Reimann. He said: 'There's nothing to thank me for.' He hadn't expected the response from the child to be so positive: he'd been extraordinarily lucky.

'Believe me, there is,' said Elke, with deep sincerity.

Now to present the carefully planned and supposed surprise, he calculated. 'How long has she been there?'

'Five years. Just over.'

'Is she ever allowed home?'

'At first she did come.' The question made Elke feel guilty, neglectful. She went on: 'It's difficult now that she's got stronger. She became upset, on the last occasion: I couldn't calm her. Dr Schiller thinks she's better in a regular environment.'

'When's her birthday?' asked Reimann, who knew from the Moscow briefing and thought the coincidence could hardly be better.

Elke turned in her seat, to look across the car as she had done on the way to Marienfels that morning. 'Next month.'

'Why don't we have her out, for her birthday?' suggested Reimann, smiling quickly across the car at her. 'Those children you spoke about, Georg and Doris? They're Ida's kids?'

Elke found her throat becoming thick again. 'Yes.'

'It'll have to be a weekend, of course, to fit in with both our jobs.' Reimann spoke as if the idea was growing in his mind. 'Why don't we have a small party. Ursula, you and me? And Ida's children? Ida, too. I'm sure I could calm Ursula; control her if she did get distressed. How does that sound?'

'It sounds marvellous,' said Elke, quietly. 'Absolutely marvellous.' How could anyone be so good: so kind!

'Maybe you'd better talk it through with Dr Schiller. We're doing it for Ursula. We'd better make sure there aren't any medical reasons against it, before we plan any further.'

That night, as she lay contentedly in bed, his arms familiarly around her, Elke said: 'Could it really happen? Could you really be transferred if your magazines don't accept your opinions?'

Reimann smiled in the darkness. 'Don't worry about it.'

'I want to know,' she insisted.

'Yes,' said Reimann. 'That's what will happen.'

'No!' broke in Elke, as her sister ordered the wine. 'Bereich Nierstein is drier: we'll have that instead.'

'Forgive *me*!' grinned Ida, unoffended.

'Otto is very good with wines.' She immediately wished she hadn't shown off her growing personal confidence so strongly.

'Is there anything he *isn't* good at!' There was no bite in the sarcasm: Ida was genuinely delighted at Elke's happiness.

'There doesn't seem to be,' Elke giggled. 'And he's particularly good at *that*!'

'You don't have to give me any more details: I'm already wet with jealousy,' Ida complained.

Elke *had* discussed the sex with her sister, and for a reason. She wanted to *know*. She'd never thought of the coupling with Dietlef as being proper sex – not what she should have felt and experienced – although Ursula had been the result. It had not happened that many times anyway, and had always been hurried and usually painful, over in a moment for him, hurting and uncomfortable for her. And Dietlef had been the only one: she'd had no other lover with whom to compare. But now she had Ida's opinion: *Very special*. Completely accurate, Elke accepted. Otto Reimann was very special, not just in bed but in every other way. It was exciting – she felt proud – that he was good in bed, though. Good in bed and all hers. Ida – everyone – had every reason to feel jealous. Wrong to go on as if she were boasting. Elke said: 'What do you think about the party, for Ursula?'

'Splendid,' said Ida. 'Of course we'll all come.'

'Dr Schiller thinks it would be all right.'

'Should we meet first? You and Otto and Horst and me? The children too. Why don't you come to lunch, like I suggested.'

Elke wanted to show him off: display him and think here's my very special man as everyone came automatically under his charm. She said: 'I'll talk to him about it. We speak most days now, even if we don't always see each other. He has to work very hard, you know.'

'Like Horst!' said Ida. This time the sarcasm did have a bitterness.

It had been weeks since the loan, without any reference to it. Elke said: 'How are things?'

Ida considered the question. 'Dreary,' she decided at last. 'I don't have much to talk to him about any more and he hasn't much to talk to me about. Our relationship could be described as polite.'

She had the right to ask, Elke decided. 'What about money?'

'He's given in on that, which I suppose sums up the character of Horst Kissel. At least it's allowed me to take over the finances of the family. We're getting straight but it's going to take a long time.'

So the repayment of the loan was ever distant: the salary increase had come at the right time. Elke said: 'What about the great book?'

'There's what he calls his manuscript, on the table in the bedroom,' said Ida. 'I asked to read it a while back – thought I should show some interest – but he insisted it wasn't ready yet. That it needed a lot of reworking.'

'You haven't spoken about Kurt for a long time,' Elke reminded her sister. She felt no criticism any more: although the circumstances of her affair with Otto were quite different, with no deceit of a marriage, Elke considered that she and Ida were complete equals now.

Ida shrugged, apathetically. 'We meet about twice a week. He tells me how unhappy he is with his wife. I tell him how unhappy I am, with Horst. We fuck. He goes home to his wife. I go home to Horst.'

'That doesn't sound like an awful lot of fun,' said Elke, and wished at once she hadn't talked of fun, which had been how Ida had described it when it first began: it might have sounded as if she were mocking.

Ida didn't appear to notice. She said: 'Believe me, darling, it isn't!'

Elke regretted asking about Kurt at all. It had started as a happy lunch – with herself the focus of it – but now it had become depressive. She said: 'I'd like to be able to do something. Suggest something.'

It was Ida who regained the earlier mood. 'You could gift-wrap Otto and give him to me!'

'No way!' said Elke. 'I don't intend letting anyone else have him! Not ever!'

'If he's as good as you say he is, in and out of bed, I can hardly blame you!' Ida smiled, fondly. 'My sheltered little sister suddenly has a very full and active life, hasn't she?'

After so long believing – and accepting – herself to be invisibly cloaked in Ida's shadow, Elke suddenly wanted to tell her sister everything. And there wouldn't be any danger, she decided. Ida was utterly trustworthy, and she would not be contravening any secrecy if she phrased it properly. She said: 'As a matter of fact it's become extremely full.'

'How?'

'I've been promoted,' Elke disclosed proudly, glad at last to tell someone. 'I've got a particular responsibility, far beyond what I used to have.'

'Why so mysterious?'

'It's got the highest possible security classification.'

'So you can't tell me about it?'

'Not beyond what I've said.'

Ida sighed. 'You don't have to: it sounds terrific. You wouldn't like to swap my life for yours, would you?'

'No!' said Elke, definitely. 'I wouldn't like to swap my life with anyone.' Not any more, she reflected: not any more.

'We've wasted enough time!' said General Cherny. 'If the woman has an increased responsibility, let's take advantage of it, now that he's got her.'

'She isn't passing information, not yet,' warned Turev.

'Because he isn't pressing her for it!' the soldier insisted.

'What would you suggest?' asked Dimitri Sorokin mildly. Any

mistakes had to be provable against the person who made them. Sorokin didn't intend making any, certainly not through impatience.

'A list,' Cherny decided. 'I think we should set out in writing everything we want to know. Everything the Politburo and the leadership want to know.'

'Do you think that's wise?' lured the KGB deputy.

'Essential,' the General insisted. 'And I will personally prepare the military demands. I want to know whether that stuff coming through Vienna is genuine or not! It's been weeks now!'

Chapter Twenty-Eight

It was a logical assumption that if the Nord-Stadt apartment was bugged there had to be listening apparatus attached to its telephone too. But Reimann concluded there was no risk of arousing Soviet suspicion by suggesting they should meet away from the flat and its attentive ears. He proposed a river trip, like the one they'd enjoyed before. And when she baulked at that he talked of going to Cologne (imagining the Leberkäse as he spoke), or of maybe exploring some of the tourist spots along the Rhine conveniently adjacent to Bonn. Frustratingly she adamantly vetoed each idea.

'The weather's too good to be cooped up in an apartment,' he pressed, taking it as far as he believed he dared.

'It has to be here,' Jutta rejected, just as insistently.

Reimann accepted that ultimately he had to comply, which created a small moment of supremacy for her. 'All right.' Why did she have to be such an obstinate fool to gain such a meaningless victory?

Hard, he thought once more, as he entered the apartment. And then made a slight adjustment. Starched was a better word: every crease in her skirt and blouse rigidly in its proper place, every strand of hair lacquered into position. He felt she was standing aside from them, in critical judgement, when he kissed her. Still trying, he said: 'It really is too good a day to stay indoors!'

'Don't keep on!' Her voice was strident, ragged-edged.

'What the hell's wrong with you?' Reimann didn't want to worsen any situation that might be evolving, but equally he refused to be demeaned like some persistently difficult child. He thought she was playing the covering music too loudly.

'*I* decide how orders should be passed on,' said Jutta. 'Today, more than ever before, it's necessary for it to be done here!'

In self-justification Reimann decided that he had tried extremely hard. He wouldn't make any further effort. 'I've learned nothing more for you to pass on.'

'Which is a growing problem, isn't it?'

'Does that remark have some special significance?'

'It's supposed to signify a deep concern that this operation is not progressing as it should: that there seems to be little progress at all!'

'Whose condemnation is that?' demanded Reimann.

'You appear to be getting very sensitive, Otto! It's not a condemnation at all. It's a simple acknowledgement of a simple fact.'

Grossly exaggerated, Reimann assessed. If there had been this depth of disappointment the Russian would have expressed it at their last East Berlin meeting. 'You have been told to say this? Told to demand quicker results?'

'Just results,' said Jutta, drawing back from the brink. 'The order is that having got yourself into the position you have, we now expect real and positive results.'

We now expect, Reimann noted: Jutta was now trying to attain authority by this pitiful association with the true controllers. Disdainfully he said: 'I need no reminder of that.'

'I've got a complete list of questions that need answers. Which I could hardly have discussed with you on a pleasure steamer or over a lunch table.'

Reimann was astonished that a list had been created and brought to Bonn. Although Elke Meyer was not identified by name, he knew it would have aroused counter-intelligence interest, if not a full investigation, if it had been inadvertently lost or intercepted and its contents had ever become known. Referring to Elke only as 'the woman', the first demand was for a complete and detailed definition of her function, with a specific request to know if she had been allocated any special or particular role. Anger quickly followed astonishment. He'd discussed that – gone through it – with the Russian in East Berlin, so the repetition was pointless: otherwise dangerous, too, because he'd passed on the suggestion that Elke might have a greater authority during one of their private encounters and was now being unnecessarily pressed about it through Jutta, risking her suspecting a secondary communication channel! Reimann subjugated the annoyance, driving himself beyond it. These lists – these demands – showed the sort of ill-considered, unthinking anxiety there had been when he had confronted the two Russians in East Berlin. It was an attitude to be resisted, as he had resisted it then. And the perfect means were available: it was fortunate they had stayed at Nord-Stadt after all. He said: 'From whom or what has any indication come of Elke Meyer being anything beyond the Cabinet Secretary's personal assistant?'

The question distressed Jutta, because she didn't have an answer and therefore wasn't able to sustain the impression of being as close to their Russian Control as she so much wanted. 'I wasn't told,' she said. 'Just asked to relay the questions.'

Allowing full rein to his irritation, Reimann said: 'What about everything else? Can we discuss them, you and I? Or were you "just told to relay"?'

Jutta's face flared. 'We can discuss them as much as you like,' she exaggerated. 'Shouldn't you read it first?'

The demands were staggering.

The list began with questions directed at the inner workings of the West German Cabinet. Moscow demanded a named breakdown of ministers openly supporting reunification against any who openly opposed it, and an indication of any possible rift within the Cabinet. There was a request for a time schedule, stipulated in months and years, in which Bonn imagined complete integration would be achieved and for a detailed breakdown of the pressure Bonn believed it could exert to bring about that integration. There was a separate breakdown insisted upon here. The Russians wanted to know about any intention to suspend or change the already existing multi-million Deutschmark aid agreements or payments to East Germany for transport facilities between the separated countries, with an ancillary query for an accurate assessment of the additional cost to the West German Treasury of the refugee exodus. This was accompanied by another schedule, set out to discover how long Bonn calculated it could continue the staggering financial burden.

There was a series of subsidiary economic questions, covering the trade union attitude to the huge influx of labour and questioning whether that influx would vastly increase West Germany's manufacturing capacity or overwhelm its labour market. Included in this economic section were queries on the strains imposed on West German health and social organizations, both government and charitable, and upon Bonn's capacity to provide satisfactory housing. This last question was also broken down, with an insistence for the earliest advice of ghetto or shanty communities becoming established, in the absence of proper housing, together with evidence of hostility arising between disgruntled or even dispossessed West Germans who considered themselves disadvantaged by the East German population movement.

There was a separate, second list, ranging over all the implications of the Eastern freedoms upon the European Economic Community. Priority was given to the EEC attitude towards separate East German admission, with an additional query whether Bonn would accept such a separate entry or insist upon the membership being that of a united

244

Germany. Here the questions widened, asking for the German-led Community attitude to membership within it of Poland, Hungary and Czechoslovakia, and going on to stipulate a financial schedule covering the anticipated trade benefits of having those Eastern countries either within the EEC or kept outside but joined by formal trading links. A connected list wanted guidance, with positive financial estimates, on the amounts the Community as a whole and then individual member countries might be prepared to grant each Eastern Bloc nation in trade aid and 'soft' long-term, low-interest loans. The final request was for a country-by-country assessment, within the EEC, of those who advocated or those who argued against the entry of the Eastern nations into the Community.

Reimann read on, absorbing it all but with growing disbelief, becoming so incredulous that suddenly, unexpectedly, he looked up towards Jutta. And caught her gazing directly at him. He was sure the expression on her face had been a smirking one: whatever, she cleared it instantly. He stared at her. She stared back at him. She didn't speak. Reimann could think of nothing he wanted to say to her, not yet.

The third list – not counting the addendums – was entirely devoted to defence and NATO, and in passing Reimann wondered why the subject had not been introduced earlier. The insistences here, as with everything prior, were distilled to absolute minutiae. How was Bonn going to react now to the unresolved American-urged, NATO-expected upgrading of short-range nuclear missiles based in West Germany? What pressure had there been from Washington to keep NATO intact and not to consider strength reductions, in face of developments in Eastern Europe? What were the individual attitudes of every other member country of NATO? What was the individual attitude of every member country within the EEC? What country-to-country discussions and contact had there been – and at what official level – between Bonn and Washington and what specifics had been made available of troop or weaponry reduction, if any, during those contacts? What Western countries – and more particularly which Bonn ministers – opposed any reduction or relaxation of NATO strength as a result of what had happened in Warsaw Pact nations?

And finally political thinking. This section was headed – and every corollary hinged upon its answer – by one question. Were the changes in East Germany and Poland and Hungary and Czechoslovakia – and again, coming down to finer detail, the nationalist concessions in some of the Soviet Republics – viewed as the virtual collapse of communism as an ideology by which nations could be governed? The corollaries were itemized, country by country again, republic by republic in addition, and there was an attempt to make the divisions even more absolute by phrasing the queries against all the countries within the EEC, the United States of America and finally Japan. It appeared Japan had been an afterthought, because there was an asterisk against it, with an insertion of trade questions which would have fitted better into the EEC part of the questionnaire, even though Japan did not form part of the Community.

Reimann was appalled. So outraged, in fact, that initially it was difficult to speak. Not that he was speechless. The reverse. There was so much fury bursting out that he couldn't arrange the priorities in his mind. Even when he attempted to speak, the outcome was staccato. 'Incredible . . . absolutely fucking incredible! . . . Insane . . . this is insane. Monstrous! I can't believe it! . . . Simply can't believe it . . . lunacy . . .' He stopped himself, clutching at last for control, aware of the recording apparatus. He didn't, ever, want to appear incredulous: not as he had just shown himself to be, in a way that could conceivably be used against him. Jutta *was* smirking: enjoying his confusion, feeling herself superior.

'I didn't quite understand all that,' she said.

She would learn, determined Reimann. So would the bubble-bodied Russian bastard who undoubtedly was trying to protect his back with a shield of bureaucratic bullshit, together with anyone else who cared to listen: he hoped it was a large number. 'Neither do I!' he said, coherent although still furious, his mind working smoothly at last. 'I don't understand this at all.' Knowing the answer in advance, because he would have recognized her handwriting and there were basic German grammar mistakes that Jutta would not have made, he said: 'Did you write this? Or are you genuinely relaying it?'

Jutta's patronizing expression faded at his obvious rage. Quickly she said: 'I'm relaying it, that's all.'

Reimann tossed the sheets towards her. 'Look at them!' he demanded, not finding it difficult to stress the outrage. 'Read them! Think about them! Shall I tell you something! If I were allowed personally to sit in on every Cabinet session and committee of the West German Bundestag for the next ten years I still wouldn't be able to answer half the questions set out here! This is nonsense: utter, absolute, absurd nonsense. If this is the expectation then I might as well walk away from Elke Meyer: never see her again and abort the whole operation. Tell them that! Fix a meeting and tell that joker of a Control of ours he's not living on this planet: that he's living in some fantasy world, quite removed from reality!' Enough! he cautioned himself. He wanted the incensed anger to get back, on the tapes, but he'd come dangerously close to going too far towards the end.

Jutta recoiled, almost visibly, from the outburst. Her voice at once conciliatory, she said: 'They're guidelines, darling! Just guidelines! No one expects you to provide every answer!'

'Rubbish!' stormed Reimann. 'It's a specific list of specific questions. And incredibly dangerous. There are a dozen ways they could have become mislaid: fallen into suspicious hands. Yet you've brought them . . .' Reimann paused, just preventing himself identifying Vienna, '. . . from God knows where into West Germany. Have you any idea what would have happened if the wrong person got hold of them?'

'I was told to,' Jutta insisted, trying to intimidate him by invoking Moscow.

'This operation has been jeopardized,' declared Reimann. 'I've been put at risk and so have you: not a severe risk, I'll concede, but still one that it was not necessary to create in the first place.'

'I'll make it clear,' promised Jutta.

Reimann doubted that she would: he wasn't sure how vehement he would be at the next personal meeting. It was essential he arrange another encounter soon, to repeat the protests, irrespective of anything Jutta might or might not report back. He didn't want the Russians guessing his awareness of their ability to listen to what was said in the apartment. Reimann's mind moved on, reasoning more calmly. He'd keep the list. He didn't know, at that moment, what for but he'd keep it. He carefully folded the lists and put them into an inside pocket of his jacket.

Jutta watched curiously. 'I don't understand what you've just done! When I carried them, it was dangerous: what's suddenly changed to make it any less dangerous for you to hold them?'

Damn, thought Reimann: now Moscow would know. There was an easy solution. He said: 'Because *I'm* the person exposed to that danger. No one else. So I'm protecting myself: I'm taking them from here and I am going to make personally sure that every scrap is completely destroyed.'

'So you don't trust me to destroy them?' the woman challenged, instantly.

'I would have trusted the people for whom we're working not to have compiled them!' Reimann parried, having to feign the anger now. 'There's been enough stupidity! It's my neck – my freedom – that's at risk here!'

247

Later that night, in the darkened bedroom, Jutta said: 'You didn't want to, did you?'

'I'm not a machine!'

'I thought that was what you'd been trained to be, a machine capable of performing any time.'

'Is that what you want, a mechanically operating machine not caring who it is I'm making love to? Or a husband treating you properly, as someone I care for and love?'

Jutta's subservience was instantaneous. 'I'm sorry,' she apologized. 'I shouldn't have said that, should I?'

'No,' said Reimann.

There was so much to be reported and afterwards debated that for the first time the Cabinet committee, which had convened in the morning, overran into the afternoon. The session was entirely devoted to defence, and was therefore dominated by Hans Mosen. Elke, seated in her customary place behind the Cabinet Secretary, guessed that the obese Defence Minister enjoyed his centre-stage position. Today, for the first time, her presence had been acknowledged with smiles and nods from the ministers as they had entered the Cabinet room. There had been a nod of greeting from the Chancellor too.

Mosen declared that the previous week's visit of the United States Secretary of Defence to the NATO meeting in Brussels had been, understandably, one of the most important for years. As well as the fully reported and analysed public sessions, the American had arranged a private meeting with every defence minister of the NATO member countries. Here Mosen smiled, inviting admiration in advance: with him there had been two personal sessions, acknowledging the greater importance of Germany in any discussion about European defence. Without question the man was enjoying himself, Elke decided.

Mosen's jowls wobbled as he surveyed his fellow ministers. 'There are a number of dramatic defence proposals being considered by the current US administration,' he disclosed. 'Some, perhaps, a little surprising in view of the political importance and influence of the US arms industry.'

'Reductions?' anticipated the Chancellor, quickly.

Mosen nodded, creating fresh facial movement. 'There is a suggested cut in the US defence budget of $180 billion over the next five years,' he revealed. 'This is an enormous figure. It will have to be achieved by all three armed services making positive cuts in future weapon procurement. Exactly what is to be abandoned is still to be decided. The most likely is the planned Advanced Tactical Fighter, an electronic warfare missile known as AMRAAM, a whole new class of helicopters that had been planned for development under the code-name LHX, and the intended construction of Burke-class and Sea Wolf submarines.'

'That would achieve the entire saving?' asked Finance Minister Walter Bahr.

Mosen was prepared. 'The prediction is in the region of $20 billion a year. Which leaves other economies to be made. The US Army has accepted it may have to axe at least three of its eighteen overseas divisions. The US Navy has volunteered to eliminate two of its fourteen aircraft carrier groups. The US Air Force, to which state-of-the-art technology is considered vital, is prepared to close up to fifteen bases but is resisting any withdrawal of research and development funds for future aircraft.'

'If all those economies are made, then a substantial US commitment to Europe – to NATO – would inevitably go,' assessed Gottfried Schere, the Foreign Minister.

'You'll recall, from the public debates in Brussels, that the Defence Secretary insisted the American presence within NATO and its contribution to the Alliance would remain as strong as ever,' said Mosen. 'It was an assurance he repeated to me at both of the private meetings.'

'But it doesn't make sense,' protested Schere. 'They *can't*, with cuts of that size and dimension.'

From the seriousness of everyone in the room, Elke recognized the gravity of the discussion: she supposed it was the most significant session of the committee there had so far been.

'Was there any figure – even an estimate – of what the total troop reduction might be in Europe?' the Chancellor demanded.

'Only estimates,' said Mosen. 'We know there are 321,000 American military based in Europe at the moment: 340,000 if we include sailors in the Sixth Fleet, in the Mediterranean. Using the percentages suggested in Brussels, the withdrawal could involve approximately 40,000 men.'

At last Werle, who Elke realized had remained unusually silent, said: 'Only proposals! Everything you've outlined from Brussels is tentative, isn't it?'

Elke noted that the committee was instantly attentive upon whatever point the Cabinet Secretary was about to make.

'Yes,' agreed Mosen, nodding, which he shouldn't have done.

'What about gallery-playing to the Soviets?' Werle demanded. 'Bypassing Europe as Washington has done so many times in the past in the hope of achieving some dramatic, President-boosting diplomatic agreement with Moscow! Expecting us and every other involved country to accept the outcome humbly, like dutiful satellites?'

Elke was surprised at the depth of feeling in Werle's voice.

'There were the assurances, public and private, that NATO came first in any United States consideration,' repeated Mosen, hopefully. 'The Presidents of both America and the Soviet Union have publicly said they would not consider entering unilateral decisions over Europe.' The Defence chief was clearly uneasy at being asked for a political opinion.

'There are always such assurances, public and private,' said Werle, just as clearly unimpressed. 'Did you have any talks about the Vienna Treaty on Conventional Arms?'

The Defence Minister visibly flushed, and Elke guessed that Werle had isolated an oversight. 'Any reduction of United States armed forces in Europe is conditional upon that Treaty being signed and ratified,' Mosen confirmed. 'It was a point I was about to make.'

Elke thought, sadly, that the man should not have attempted such a blatantly empty excuse: neither Bahr nor Klaus Mueller, the Intra-German Relations Minister, bothered to keep the contemptuous expressions from their faces.

'A bargaining ploy,' insisted Werle, simply.

'Not to be taken seriously?' queried the prevaricating Chancellor, in his falsely energetic way.

'Everything has got to be taken seriously, in the climate in which we find ourselves,' said Werle. 'In my opinion it comes down to our correctly interpreting the *degree* of seriousness. How much Washington and Moscow are each genuinely prepared to give up, against how much is bluff to get a properly unified Germany into the Western alliance.'

Interpretation, Elke saw. Always interpretation, for these men here trying to chart the future for the country, for Otto trying to interpret their interpretation to satisfy disbelieving editors in some country on the other side of the world who probably couldn't find Bonn or Berlin on an unmarked map if the challenge were presented. Words echoed in her mind, as her concentration drifted. *Could you really be transferred if your magazine don't accept your opinions?* Her words. And his reply, after that pitiful attempt at reassurance. *Yes.* He couldn't go: couldn't leave her, not now. She had to do everything she could to prevent that even becoming a remote possibility. '. . . taken seriously or not, if your assessment is correct we have to gauge our own responses with the utmost caution . . .' The words of the Foreign Minister intruded into her reverie and Elke snatched for her lost concentration.

'Something else,' questioned Werle. 'Was there any talk about upgrading the short-range nuclear missiles ahead of the agreed discussion date of 1992?'

'None,' said Mosen, shortly.

'Did you specifically ask?'

'Not directly,' conceded the Defence Minister. 'I considered they came under the general heading of existing forces and weaponry based here. And I *did* ask about that. The reply was that all bases and all commitments in Europe were up for examination and recommendation before the American Defence Committee.'

'Defence Committee!' seized Werle, instantly.

'What?' asked Mosen, baffled.

'Is that what he said, the Defence Committee? Or did he say the Administration? There's an essential difference.'

Mosen flushed again. 'The Defence Committee. I'm sure that's what he said.'

'Further manoeuvring,' Werle assessed. 'The Defence Committee is Congressional, not beholden to the Administration. They can bounce the missile upgrading back and forth between Capitol Hill and the White House for months, giving every impression of serious debate and consideration, and when it suits them to do so announce there won't be any upgrading. It'll make Washington appear the peacemaker.'

So much to learn and properly understand, Elke reflected: at this level hardly anything turned out to be as it appeared, at face value. Interpretation, she thought again.

'There should be another official statement,' suggested the Chancellor. 'I propose we recommend for entire Cabinet approval a communiqué welcoming the assurances of both the American President and Defence Secretary that the United States has reiterated its pledge fully to support and maintain NATO. And that we welcome further another American pledge to consult its NATO allies in advance of any disarmament agreements that may be reached with the Soviet Union. It boxes Washington in: greatly reduces their freedom for a back-door agreement.'

Elke watched expectantly for the nods of assent to come from around the table. They did.

'Are we all agreed?' urged the Chancellor.

251

'Something more, to be added,' Werle quickly interjected, before the final approval. Looking directly at the Chancellor he said: 'Why don't we add to it your expectation to go personally to Washington for a series of talks with the President to discuss the whole future of Europe? And initiate approaches through the US ambassador here, today, for such a visit to be arranged? There can't be a refusal and it would further box them in.'

'Excellent!' the Chancellor accepted, not allowing any discussion on the idea.

Günther Werle had shown himself as a strong motivating force in every discussion she had so far witnessed, Elke recognized, as they returned to their own Chancellery offices. Increasingly confident of herself, as she became more accustomed to her role, she said during their analytical session in his rooms: 'Herrr Mosen appeared ill-at-ease, sometimes?'

'He's over-promoted,' said Werle, with unusual candour. 'He was capable enough at State level in Bavaria. He hasn't the capacity for national politics.'

'Isn't that a disadvantage, at a time like this?'

Werle nodded appreciatively. 'A very definite disadvantage. But there again, at a time like this, there can be no thought of his being replaced, can there?'

'I'm finding this fascinating,' admitted Elke, openly.

Instead of continuing the professional conversation Werle said: 'The Vienna choir was superb.'

'Did Frau Werle find it so?'

'She didn't come with me,' said Werle. 'The seat was wasted.'

It was a sanitized tape, all the extraneous inferences edited out. 'There's a very definite antagonism between them,' judged Sorokin. The KGB deputy had insisted for the first time upon hearing a transcript. He was at the window of his office overlooking the square, talking with his back to the other two men.

'I don't give a damn about their personal relationship,' said General Cherny, who took personally a lot of Reimann's remarks that he had just overheard. 'He's an arrogant, conceited bastard.'

'It was insecure, wasn't it? Having the woman carry a document like that?' said Sorokin. Having insisted upon the creation of the lists, Cherny had further insisted that Jutta take them back to West Germany, so that no instruction or request would be overlooked or forgotten. It had made the man identifiably responsible if anything had gone wrong.

'We need results!' Cherny defended. 'And so far we're not getting them. From Bonn we're getting statements about NATO military capability at the same time as expectations of unified German membership. And what do we get from Reimann, to tell us the real picture? Nothing except excuses why he can't move faster than he's doing!'

'The Bonn statements are simply placating,' Turev argued. 'There's nothing new in them.'

'He's your man!' said the soldier, spreading the blame as if he were sowing seeds by hand. 'Drive him harder!'

Turev detected the patronizing look upon Sorokin's face, and decided he had nothing to fear from the General's rage: like Sorokin, he knew well enough that it came from the ridicule on the tape. Turev said: 'I think Reimann is working as well as we could possibly have expected.'

'There'll be an inquiry soon, about why everything is taking so long. Either from the Politburo or the President's Secretariat itself,' Cherny predicted.

Sorokin indicated the machine lying before him on the table. 'We can produce all the tapes, to show we're doing everything possible,' he said.

Cherny stared, purple-faced, at the KGB deputy but didn't respond to the mockery. Instead he said: 'And what's happened to the Vienna source? Why has that dried up?'

It hadn't.

Two days later there was another anonymous delivery. It referred to possible US troop reductions in Europe.

Chapter Twenty-Nine

Once again, as she had before the visit to Ursula at Marienfels, Elke tried to prepare Reimann ahead of the meeting with Ida and her family, wanting to lay the groundwork for him to like them: it was important to her for him to like them. She identified Horst as a high-ranking official in the Post Office and described Ida as beautiful (*I'm terrified of the competition!*) and called them her best and closest friends. He might think the house a little run down, the furniture slightly faded, but that's the sort of people they were, vaguely Bohemian. Horst was actually writing a book. He believed himself to be a bit of a wine connoisseur, as well.

'Good,' said Reimann. Bohemian or short of money? he wondered: a possible explanation for the thirty thousand Deutschmarks. There *had* to be an advantage.

'Bad,' said Elke. 'He isn't a connoisseur at all. You're going to have to be brave.'

It was obvious that Elke was working hard to prepare the most favourable impression in advance, but Reimann also guessed that she was slightly ashamed of them: apprehensive, at least, that he would not approve. He was glad she remained nervous: that always had to be her underlying feeling, about everything. She could never be allowed to be completely confident about their relationship: to believe she could take him for granted. It was Reimann who suggested, ahead of the tentative Elke, that they take gifts, and he who selected them. Having had the children and their interests detailed to him he bought a re-released tape of all the international top-selling songs of the Beatles for Georg, and an inexpensive pop watch for Doris in the shape of a boat: the funnel had to be lifted to read the time. He chose a Hermès silk scarf for Ida and had it flamboyantly gift-wrapped in the shop. For Horst he found some 1975 Château La Tour-Martillac and had three bottles prepared in a presentation case.

'Appropriate for a connoisseur!' he declared.

'You've been far too generous,' she protested.

'I want to impress them,' he said, which was true. To ingratiate himself with them would be to ingratiate himself further with Elke, who he knew relied heavily on Ida and her opinion.

Everyone at Bad Godesberg had tried, too, and Elke loved them for it. The children's faces shone and there wasn't a hair out of place: Georg wore what she knew to be his newest trousers, with a sharp crease, and Doris looked slightly self-conscious in a starched and pleated dress. Kissel was casual, but his trousers were freshly pressed and the new shirt still showed the creases from being packed in its box. By coincidence the predominant colours in the Hermès scarf perfectly complemented those of Ida's silk dress, which Elke hadn't seen before. Ida put it around her shoulders, completing the outfit. Throughout the greetings and the present-giving Elke stood slightly apart, preferring to watch rather than to be involved, aware of the social ease with which Reimann did everything. He did not treat Georg and Doris quite as adults, but neither did he talk down to them as children, so they confidently talked back and joined in with the gathering, without any shyness. He was attentive to Ida, but without the slightest suggestion of flirtatiousness. Elke considered him most successful with Kissel. There could be no doubt of Kissel's uncertainty at encountering someone he knew to be a political commentator for influential overseas magazines; he was loudly welcoming, drowning insecurity beneath noisy bonhomie. Reimann at once entered into conversation with the other man, and Elke quickly noticed how he was deferring to what Kissel said: once she overheard him openly ask for Horst's opinion of the developments in Central and Southern Europe, head bent in nodded concentration on the reply.

They drank sparkling wine in the shabby drawing-room, and Kissel insisted on opening the wine that Reimann had given.

'I love burgundy,' he announced. 'Can't get enough that's worth drinking.'

He'd gradually quietened since their arrival, Elke realized gratefully: she'd become conscious of Ida's growing irritation with her husband.

During the meal Reimann talked animatedly to everyone, going out of his way to include the children in whatever was discussed, drawing them out and amusing them. Never once did he contradict anything Kissel said: neither, when Elke cast her mind back, did he agree. He latched on to remarks from Ida – and even Georg on one occasion – and told stories against himself (none of which Elke had heard before) to make Ida laugh, which she did, genuinely. As did everyone else. Elke stayed proudly on the sidelines, not needing – not wanting – to contribute more than the occasional interjection, although she laughed a lot as they all did. That's all she had to do, she told herself. They were together, she and Otto: to admire – to enjoy – he was to admire and enjoy her. Reflected glory, which was hardly over-stressing it: just a tiny bit. *Have you seen the two of them? God they're incredible! Just so much fun! You can't believe the wit! The humour! But still – I know you'll find this difficult to believe – still so modest! So natural! Like they don't recognize it. Incredible! Absolutely incredible!* Not quite like that, Elke acknowledged, regaining a foothold on reality. Not yet. But close to what it could be if . . . Not a permitted thought: certainly not to be permitted to continue.

The second bottle of La Tour-Martillac was opened. And then, against Reimann's protest that it was a gift, the third. By the cheese course Reimann was sure he had worked out the thirty thousand withdrawal from Elke's bank account and evolved a potential benefit: it was certainly something worth initiating, because there was a simple retreat if one proved necessary. He said to Kissel, through whom he had been careful always to tell his stories: 'Elke tells me you're writing a book?'

'Trying,' demurred Kissel, with unaccustomed modesty in the presence of someone he believed to be a professional writer. 'It is still very rough. Needs a lot of work.'

'Fiction or fact?'

'Fiction. Just fiction.'

'*Just* fiction! Don't denigrate it! It's my ambition to write a book. I'm too frightened to start!'

'*You?*'

'Why so surprised?'

'But you *are* a writer.'

The table was quiet, and Reimann was aware of the concentration upon what he was saying. 'There's an important difference,' he insisted. 'A vast difference. For a journalist, the story already exists: is there. They have to tell it: report what happened . . .' The listening Elke, he thought: he shouldn't forget for a moment the listening Elke. He continued: 'Even for a political commentator, an interpreter like I am supposed to be, the basic framework exists. But fiction is *real* writing: starting with nothing but a blank sheet of paper and creating something that might possibly *move* people: change real events in the world, even. That's impressive.'

'Well . . . yes . . . of course I understand what you're saying . . .' said Kissel, with head-waving modesty.

Cretin! thought Reimann, gazing admiringly at the other man. 'I don't suppose I could see something of it?'

For a few seconds Kissel, the would-be writer, couldn't find his way. Then he said: 'But like I say, it's rough . . . a very rough draft. Needs so much work . . .'

256

'Why so hesitant, darling?' said Ida. 'You've been telling me for weeks how good it is, even in rough draft.'

'Well . . . maybe a sheet or two . . .'

Elke thought Kissel was flushed. It would be the wine; it really was superb.

'Why don't Elke and I clear away and make some more coffee for the garden while you and Otto go upstairs and look at the book . . . or rather rought draft?' encouraged Ida.

Before Kissel could think of any avoidance Reimann said: 'Why don't we do just that: top up our glasses and go upstairs and have a look!'

Which is what they did, glasses in hand, the reluctant Kissel in the lead. On their way up Reimann noted the further signs of impoverishment: the frayed, sometimes cheaply repaired stair-carpet, chipped paint everywhere, heavy, permanently draped velvet curtains that would have collapsed if there had been an attempt to draw them, faded wallpaper so sun-bleached it was hard – sometimes impossible – to distinguish any original design or motif. The bedroom was neatly tidy – no discarded clothes, the bed properly made, the coverlet taut, without creases – but just as it was outside, the overall aura was of shabbiness. The only exception to the attempted neatness was Kissel's put-you-up, baize-topped table. It was a chaotic jumble of disordered papers and pencils and pens and writing paraphernalia: paper-clips and rubber bands and a stapler and a metal-framed, three-decked file holder from which more papers were suspended, jammed from being completely disgorged by those which had escaped and built up below, creating a frozen paper waterfall.

'Writers aren't tidy,' said Kissel.

'I know,' said Reimann, colleague-to-colleague. Fuck me! he thought.

And thought it again, constantly, when he began to read the sheets Kissel handed him. Everything Reimann purported to write was virtually already created for him, so he did not consider himself to be a writer in any respect, but what Kissel had created was appalling, a collection of clichés strung together without direction or point around parody characters.

'This really is good,' congratulated Reimann. 'I agree it needs work. But basically it's very good indeed.'

Kissel smiled uncertainly. 'You really think so?'

'Most definitely,' Reimann insisted, handing the pages back. 'Have you ever written any short stories? My magazine publishes fiction, around five thousand words a time. They pay, of course. You'd have to accept whatever you wrote being edited: altered for style and to fit the space available, of course.'

'I understand the mechanics,' assured Kissel, eagerly. 'Maybe I'll try something: I could do with a break from the novel. Recharge the batteries, so to speak.'

Reimann gave the other man his card and said: 'Let me know when you've got something ready: either direct or through Elke.'

The two women were in the garden, coffee and cups between them on the grass. With typical over-statement Kissel announced proudly: 'Otto says his magazine would publish any short story I might write.'

Ida began pouring the coffee, unimpressed. 'Everyone's getting new opportunities,' she said. 'Elke with her top-secret job, Horst with his short stories. I feel quite left out.'

Elke frowned towards her sister, but Ida was bent over the coffee and didn't see the expression. The remark did not appear to have registered with either of the two men. She made a mental note to complain to Ida when they were alone. Maybe she should not have told her in the first place.

The afternoon passed as perfectly as the lunch for Elke. The men talked with increasing friendliness and after an hour Georg appeared with a ball and makeshift bat and asked Reimann to teach him the baseball he must have learned during an upbringing in America. Reimann escaped easily by saying the garden was not big enough to create a proper baseball diamond but positioned Georg sideways on, as he recollected from television, and pitched towards the boy. After a while he insisted upon Doris being included as well. Kissel fielded clumsily but fortunately intervened and told Georg to stop asking too many questions when Reimann pleaded he couldn't bring to mind all the rules after so long away from the United States.

Watching the haphazard game but out of earshot, Ida said: 'OK, I'll admit it! He's fabulous. Better than I ever guessed, from anything you told me. And he *is* just like Dietlef.'

'He's not like Dietlef,' Elke corrected at once. 'Otto's a good man.' She decided it was not the moment to rebuke her sister for the remark about new jobs and secrets. 'I'm glad you like him.'

'Like him! I *want* him!' Abruptly, despising herself for even allowing the reflection, Ida wondered what a genuinely fascinating man like Otto Reimann appeared to find in Elke, who'd always had so much difficulty with personal relationships. Ida hurriedly dismissed the doubt. All that mattered was that he *did* seem attracted to her.

'Forbidden fruit! I told you before I'm not sharing him with anyone. And nobody's taking him away from me.' They were playing, joking in their special way, Elke told herself. But she hadn't been joking then. Short though the relationship had been – inconclusive though it still was – his not being with her now was inconceivable. She *was* going to keep him: risk losing him to no one.

They left Bad Godesberg later than Elke normally did by herself, just as they'd been late leaving Marienfels. From what was now her accustomed sideways position in the car, so she could look at him, Elke said: 'You made quite a hit. Do you think Horst is publishable?'

He had to be careful, knowing how much she read. 'Some of it is pretty raw: it needs a good editor.'

'It would be marvellous if it did happen. I think they could use the money.'

Reimann was sure he was right about the thirty thousand Deutschmarks. 'Surely his job is well enough paid?'

'Horst isn't a very good manager: postures quite a bit about wine, that sort of thing. That burgundy you bought today was superb, incidentally.'

'It wasn't burgundy: it was claret. It would have been better left to stand and breathe.'

Elke reached across, squeezing his hand lightly. 'You didn't correct him, when he called it burgundy,' she said, admiringly.

'What would have been the purpose of showing up his ignorance?'

'You're concerned at everyone's feelings, aren't you?'

'Yours most of all,' said Reimann, enjoying the irony of the truth. The building housing the East German mission came up on their right: Reimann didn't even look in its direction. He said: 'What's your secret job?' and was aware of the almost imperceptible intake of breath.

'Nothing, really.' Damn Ida! Damn, damn, damn her!

Reimann gripped the wheel tighter, in his frustration. 'Ida seems impressed. Please tell me. I'm interested in everything you do, you know that.'

Elke shifted uncomfortably, turning away from him to stare directly ahead. 'A committee,' she mumbled. 'I'm the official recorder. Nothing, really.'

'A Cabinet committee?'

'I honestly can't talk about it,' pleaded Elke, miserably. 'There's a security classification.'

'I'm not asking any secrets, am I?'

'No.'

'Don't you trust me?'

'Of course I trust you!'

'I'd never let you down, you know. Take advantage of your position: do or say anything to compromise you.'

'I know you wouldn't, darling. You don't have to tell me that.'

'A Cabinet committee?'

'Yes.'

'It's certainly been kept secret, hasn't it? I don't recall anything being published about it?'

'There hasn't been.'

Change approach, Reimann told himself. In an I-know-you-don't-have-to-tell-me voice, he said: 'It's logical, of course. There'd have to be a special committee to consider all that's happening: it's far too much to be handled at Cabinet level in the first place.'

Elke didn't answer.

'That's right, isn't it?' Come on, you bitch!

'Yes.'

'I understand now.'

She came back towards him, across the car. 'Understand what?'

'Why it's been difficult for you some evenings recently: the extra workload. I really thought a couple of times that you might have another friend . . . another man . . . you know. . . ?'

Elke snatched out for his hand, harder this time, so that the car swerved slightly. 'Oh no, darling! Honestly no! There isn't anyone else: believe me! That's all it's been. Work. I'm sorry: really sorry.'

'It just seemed every week. But then I guess there's a meeting every week?'

'That's all it is,' Elke insisted. 'You do believe me, don't you?'

'I know you wouldn't lie! Why should you?'

Elke decided she didn't have anything for which to rebuke Ida. If Ida hadn't blurted out what she had, he'd have gone on misunderstanding, and that might have threatened everything. 'I'm glad we've sorted it out,' Elke said.

'Tell me, so I'll know in future,' urged Reimann. 'So that I won't make plans that conflict. What days are the meetings?'

Elke hesitated. 'Wednesdays, usually. A couple have been convened on a Tuesday, if there's been something particularly important to discuss.'

There was an atmosphere growing up in the car that had to be broken. Cheerfully Reimann said: 'Understood! No plans for Wednesdays in the future.' At last! About fucking time!

That Sunday they discussed the idea of Ursula coming out for the day with Dr Schiller, who agreed although with some hesitation. They spent the rest of the day, after Marienfels, talking about and planning the party, going as far as to make lists of food and treats. And that night, after she had fallen into wetly satisfied sleep beside him, Reimann decided to kill the dog.

It wasn't difficult. He didn't hurry to get up when Elke did the following morning, saying there was no reason for him to get to the press building before ten or eleven and suggesting that he stay, spare her the trouble of taking Poppi for his morning walk, and let himself out of the flat later. Elke agreed at once. He stood at the window, watching her get into the Volkswagen and set off for the Kaufmannstrasse junction. He didn't hurry into the kitchen. Instead he went through her diary again, picking up from the date of his last examination, smiling at the *I am in love* entry, finding nothing else of interest. The gas canister was in the glove pocket of the Mercedes. Reimann left the front door of the apartment on the latch while he collected it. The dog bustled towards him, its rear moving in excited greeting, as Reimann entered the kitchen. He encouraged it back closer to its basket, leaned down and squirted the nozzle directly into the animal's face. It whimpered, backing away, at once staggering. It slumped, shuddering, going quickly limp. There was a small bowel collapse.

Knowing to the moment Elke's arrival time at Kaufmannstrasse in the evening, Reimann was waiting next to the telephone in his Rochusplatz flat when her hysterical call came. He embraced her in the hallway when he arrived and soothed her and said he'd handle it all: she was to stay in the lounge, away from it. The shit had begun to smell. He lifted the dog into its basket, distastefully clearing the mess, and disinfecting his hands afterwards. There was some major building reconstruction taking place at Nassestrase, the road narrowed by the rubbish-clearing skips along one side. Reimann took the basket and the carcase from the boot of his car and tossed them both into the one which had the greater capacity. He took his time returning to Kaufmannstrasse.

Elke was sitting in the main room. Her eyes were wet, although she wasn't crying any longer.

'Where?' she said.

'In the Rheinaupark,' lied Reimann. 'I marked the flower-bed in my mind, if you'd like to see sometime.'

'I know it's silly, to get attached to an animal. But he was . . . I bought him for Ursula, you see. And when she went he became special

261

. . . the person . . . no, not the person, the thing I suppose, who was always here when I came home . . . like a friend . . . I'm being maudlin.'

Reimann knelt before her, so he could hold her, and said: 'You've got another friend now. Don't ever forget that, will you?'

'Oh God, I love you so much!' said Elke. 'I don't know what I'd do without you!'

'You're never going to have to find out,' said Reimann, satisfied.

The room was heavy with the smell of stale cigarette smoke, so Reimann knew the Russian had again been waiting for some time. As he entered Turev was lighting another cigarette from the stub of the last.

'I didn't expect this contact, so quickly after our other meeting,' said Turev.

'I didn't expect the list of demands that Jutta presented me with!' said Reimann. 'It was totally unnecessary. And stupidly dangerous!'

'We've taken note of your protests, through Jutta,' said Turev, irritated by the lack of respect.

'I would not like it to happen again,' said Reimann.

'*You* wouldn't like it!'

'*I* wouldn't like it,' Reimann agreed. 'I'm the one who is exposed: no one else. Everything – anything – on those lists could have been discussed and understood between us, at one of these meetings.' Would these encounters be recorded? Certainly the facilities would exist in a building like this. And it was the sort of precaution they would take, from what he knew – guessed – they had done so far.

The arrogant bastard had to be deflated. Turev said: 'Is this the only purpose of this meeting, to whine? I had hoped for something more worthwhile.'

Reimann was anxious at last to show positive results. 'There *has* been a special committee of the Bonn Cabinet set up to debate every development in East Germany. It considers – which logically entails sub-committees – and debates those developments before making recommendations to the full Cabinet, for decision. There are meetings every Wednesday: just occasionally, if it is decided to be particularly important, on Tuesdays. There have been two Tuesday meetings. It would not be something I could undertake myself, but I suggest every member of the Cabinet is put under tight surveillance: those whose movements can be accounted for on Wednesdays can be eliminated. That way we can establish the composition and named membership of the committee. Elke Meyer has started to crack: she'll crack further, quite quickly now.'

It looked as if Reimann had every reason for the arrogance he had earlier shown, Turev conceded. Subduing his anger, with some difficulty, the Russian said: 'That's good: that's very good!'

'There's more,' said Reimann, impatiently. 'I am certain the thirty thousand Deutschmarks was a loan, from Elke Meyer to her sister's family. They're short of money. The man, as we know, is connected with the Post Office. He's an imbecile: imagines he can write fiction. I have told him Australian magazines will publish his short stories. They'll be rubbish: need completely rewriting. That's not important. I've promised he'll be paid. If he becomes dependent on the money he becomes capable of manipulation: we can gain access to West German communications. Whatever unlisted telephone numbers or addresses we want. NATO emergency codes. Any and all West German government numbers. And all to be tapped and monitored.'

Too conceited! thought Turev, triumphantly: it was going to be good to puncture this man's pretentiousness. 'That won't work, will it? As the introduction is through you, you'll be identified for what you are, once the pressure starts!'

Reimann sighed loudly, hoping there *were* microphones. He said: 'My introduction is to the money available from writing. After he's become used to it, why can't he be approached by a magazine or an organization quite independent of me? It admires his work, it wants to poach him for even larger sums of money. He's greedy and he's a fool. He'll go for it, particularly if we synchronize the approach with a rejection of something he writes for Australia. When the pressure comes it won't be through anything remotely connected with me. I'll actually be the person he's let down, going to a higher bidder.'

'You've thought everything out very carefully, haven't you?' said Turev, defeated.

'Far too carefully possibly to fail,' Reimann replied.

Using their special dialling code to identify herself, Jutta tried unsuccessfully three times during the evening – the last attempt close to midnight – to contact Otto.

He had to be with her. The job, she repeated to herself like a litany: he was doing the job. So why did she feel. . . ? Feel what? It wasn't jealousy. It was inconceivable for her to be jealous. She was far too professional – knew Otto far too well – for that ever to arise. What then? She was lonely, Jutta decided. Miserable and lonely. But definitely not jealous. There was nothing to be jealous about. A job: Otto was just doing a job.

Chapter Thirty

Elke hunted for the words to express her feelings but couldn't find them. No superlative, no hyperbole, came remotely close: she was inflated, blown up, with an incredible happiness. But happiness didn't fit, not properly: it was insufficient for the morning-till-night sensation that was permanently with her. It left out contentment, for instance, and she was absolutely content. Pride, too, because she was fiercely proud of him, and there was a division here: fiercely proud of everything about him but proud also of herself for being with him, a reflected gratification. Hope entered into it: hope that as well as everything was going her relationship with Otto would progress to the ultimate, although she didn't like thinking that far ahead. She still did, of course. Which created another impression, perhaps more important than any of the others. That of security. She vaguely remembered it being an early half-thought, one of no longer being alone: maybe not even that positive, not in the early days. But certainly now.

Loneliness had always been with her, a wearing-down affliction for which there had seemed no remedy, no cure: and like someone with an incurable affliction she had become reluctantly reconciled to suffering from it, always to living alone, always to being alone, to growing old alone and inevitably to dying alone. But not now. Although they'd never talked of the ultimate, of marriage, Elke didn't believe she would ever again be by herself. He would always be with her. Protecting her. Looking after her. Thinking for her. Guarding her. She was safe: secure and safe, cocooned against any hurt or harm. Which encouraged another word. Luck. How unbelievably, amazingly lucky she was that it had happened to her: that *he* had happened to her! Elke considered herself the luckiest woman in this or any other world: euphoric though she was she came near to feeling guilty, at the same time, because no one deserved the luck she'd had.

There was nothing – very little, anyway – to mar it. And there had been so many changes it was difficult to realize it had all occurred in such a comparatively short period of time.

She'd never expected, for example, that Kissel's short story would be good enough to be published: never truly expected the man would get around to writing it at all. But he had and it had appeared in the

264

Australian magazine which Reimann had produced, with champagne and congratulations, at a Saturday lunch. Kissel had complained of bad translation, which Elke inferred to mean heavy editing, but the five thousand Deutschmark cheque had arrived within a week, and Ida had offered the same sum as the first repayment of the loan at a regular weekly lunch. And now Kissel was writing more, the novel abandoned.

Unquestionably the highlight of the most recent weeks had been Ursula's visit from Marienfels for her birthday. Elke had become desperately worried about it as the anniversary approached, checking with Dr Schiller to guarantee that the doctor genuinely considered it was a practicable idea and putting to Reimann the suggestion, which he ignored, during the run-up that it might be advisable to cancel the outing after all. How glad she was that he *had* ignored it.

He'd helped her buy the party dress – red was Ursula's best colour – and it had been one of Ursula's good days: she'd got without protest into the car, his Mercedes because there was more room. It had not been until the main autobahn that Ursula became distressed. Reimann had swiftly turned on to a minor road to stop the car and quieten her. Elke had given Ida a key, so the entire family was already waiting when they got to Kaufmannstrasse. Ursula showed no recognition and became confused again, jerking out with her arms and making guttural sounds which frightened Doris and Georg. As always, Reimann was prepared. He'd supplied the recorder and bought the Mozart tapes and gradually Ursula calmed, although not as easily as she had in the car. There were party hats – Ursula's specially selected without any dangerous, loosely fixed decoration – and jellies and cake and a birthday gâteau with Ursula's name iced on top. She ate badly, smearing her mouth and face, but Reimann had always been at hand to wipe and clean her.

Party games had not been possible, of course, but there were presents, all again particularly chosen not to have dangerous attachments, mostly warm-furred animals: Ursula seemed to get more pleasure ripping the fancy paper from the boxes than from their contents. There was a total of five toys, and because there were so many Elke urged the girl to leave two at the apartment, in her bedroom: naturally she and Reimann had helped, and in the bedroom, for the briefest of moments, Ursula had been attracted by the long-ago fairground fawn, tentatively touching it with an outstretched finger as if she feared it might be rough or hot, to hurt her.

Two days later Dr Schiller had personally telephoned the Chancellery, even though it was listed at the institution as an

265

emergency number, to say he could not recall, during the past year, such a general improvement in Ursula's attitude, behaviour, or comprehension. When she'd told Reimann he'd said it was obvious there had to be more outings. The following Sunday had been one of the rare disappointments in the recent utopian weeks: Ursula had regressed into her shell and been truculently aggressive, shrugging off any caress, and for once Reimann had been unable to get through to her.

Elke had gone at last – and several times now stayed the night – to his apartment at Rochusplatz, with its high ceilings and heavy furniture and tap-tapping pipes. Strangely, so that it was something else she did not confess to Ida, she regarded going there as a further deepening of their affair, his readily taking her into his life and his surroundings, and so she liked it, always eager to go again when he suggested it. During those forbidden dreams about the ultimate outcome of their being together it was always at Rochusplatz, never at Kaufmannstrasse, that Elke fantasized their married life.

The time they spent at Rochusplatz would not have been possible, unless they'd taken him as well, if Poppi had still been alive. Elke was slightly guilty at her lack of grief: she rarely thought any more about the dog which had, until a few months earlier, been her only companion: sometimes the only living thing to which she talked. It had even been Reimann who'd suggested they visit the hand-dug grave in the Reinaupark. She'd been disappointed there was no obvious indication of a grave in the soft-earth flower-bed. It must have settled quickly, since he'd scooped it out: there were a lot of gardeners, tending the park. They'd probably raked it flat.

Saturdays were not automatically spent with Ida and the family: neither did they go every Sunday to Marienfels. Reimann declared himself against rigid routine and Elke, for whom routine had always been so essential, agreed she didn't like it either. Some weekends they went to Cologne, to eat or to the theatre. They flew once to Munich and stayed the Saturday night in an hotel and visited the beer hall in the old part of the city where Hitler had harangued his Nazi disciples. There were river trips: they went one Sunday back to Andernach and their hidden hilltop valley, and this time they made love and when she said she'd wanted it to happen there, because the place had special meaning for her, he said he'd wanted it to happen there as well, for the same reason. She couldn't remember the last time she had taken Saturday morning coffee at the Bonner.

She had even, hopefully, lessened what she'd detected to be a growing atmosphere between herself and Günther Werle. There had been two other invitations, both for concerts, after the rejection of the Vienna Boys' Choir, and both of which she refused again. Before an inevitable third she introduced Reimann into a conversation between herself and the Cabinet Secretary, talking of the man, although not by name, involved in the unsolved accident. She'd been apprehensive of doing so but more anxious for a barrier, and it appeared to have created one. She'd dared to go as far as calling it a deep friendship and referred to the Munich weekend, with its obvious inference of an hotel stay. Werle had remained distantly silent, apart from the absolutely essential talk concerning the Chancellery, for two or three days afterwards. Now they were back on the level Elke wanted, amicable and courteous towards one another, a perfect working team, but with no after-hours social suggestions. He continued to call her Elke. She addressed him as Herr Werle.

She and Reimann often discussed the political situation: during nearly every meeting, it seemed, although Elke had become more comfortable about it now, never considering she was being indiscreet or breaching official security. He always appeared to know so much, and clearly had other sources, every bit as well informed as she was – better, probably. The composition of the special committee was a case in point, proof of his contacts! It was from Reimann himself that the names had come, every one correct: the Chancellor and Bahr and Mosen and Schere and Mueller. Reimann had laughed at her surprise and said she wasn't the only one with secrets, which had to be true. She'd still been careful. She was sure the figures of the Eastern bloc troop strengths had been published before they'd talked about it: those of the US NATO commitment that might be withdrawn, too. The possible financial savings being considered by the American military establishment had been speculated upon, as well, so there had been no revelation in her talking about that in more detail. She was sure they had not been specifically discussing German reunification during the hypothetical debate on the obvious difficulties, sometimes the impossibility, of any government adhering too rigidly to existing treaties when political changes put those treaties out of date. The growing union and labour difficulties created by the East German workers were no secret, surely? Any more than the severe strain of having to provide habitable accommodation for them.

She had been surprised, though, by Reimann suggesting that the numbers were so great there was a risk of sub-standard ghettoes becoming established. It was not infrequent, during the conversations, for him to make an exaggerated statement like that, so that she had to correct him. She was glad she was able to do so, to prevent any criticism or disbelief from his editors, the sort of criticism that had come embarrassingly in an open press cable which he had shown her during an overnight visit to Rochusplatz. *If I keep getting it wrong . . . they'd replace me, I suppose.* And he would have got things wrong – quite a lot of things – if they hadn't talked as they did. Writing that Bonn did not consider it had any leverage, within NATO or with America and in the European Economic Community, was one example that came to mind. But she'd never once been indiscreet: never contravened a security restriction. She was sure she hadn't.

All so wonderful. And although she was still too frightened to think seriously of his asking her to marry him, she had no doubt – after the most recent gift, after all the flowers and scarves and handkerchiefs and books – that he truly loved her.

It wasn't the sort of betrothal ring she would have chosen herself, because the stone was an opal and Elke would have gone for a more traditional diamond. And he hadn't given it to her as an engagement ring. She'd asked, daring as far as she thought she could go, what finger he wanted her to wear it upon, and he'd said she could choose, although he'd managed the perfect fit by measuring a dress ring she often wore on the smallest finger of her right hand. It still meant something, though. She was convinced of it. She was impatient to show it off to Ida, at lunch the following day.

'You don't think another investigation is necessary?' demanded Günther Werle.

'I can't think how we could do more than we did before.'

'So you're absolutely satisfied about Otto Reimann?'

There was the merest hint of a sigh from the security officer. 'There isn't a check that has not been made. Is there something to make you suspicious: something that has arisen since our last conversation?'

'No,' said Werle. 'I wanted to be quite sure.'

'You can be.'

Werle had wanted very much to destroy the man he regarded as his rival.

Chapter Thirty-One

Reimann was quite confident about the East Berlin visits, thinking of them as ordinary business trips, the sort that ordinary businessmen made: so confident, in fact, that he'd confirmed a return flight and promised to take Elke out for dinner that night. Despite the self-assurance, he still hesitated at the doorway of the by now familiar Johannisstrasse room, surprised by the reappearance of the bearded Russian in charge behind the desk. He continued on, recovering, glad to see the man again: it would be different this time than before.

The greetings were quick, peremptory. Sorokin was not introduced, not even by a legend name. Reimann had initiated the encounter. With additional reason to impress now, he announced at once: 'The Economic Community would accept the membership of Poland, Hungary and Czechoslovakia. But Bonn would stand out against it, if there was also a move to include East Germany as a separate state.'

'Interesting,' acknowledged Turev. 'Anything else?'

Reimann was annoyed at the dismissive acceptance, as if what he was saying was unimportant. 'The West German Chancellor's announced visit to Washington,' he continued. 'There are to be private talks about the upgrading of the short-range nuclear missiles, way ahead of the 1992 agreed date.'

Sorokin came forward very slightly in his seat at the disclosure, knowing how Cherny would react to it. And not just Cherny. At every conference with the Secretariats of the Politburo or Executive President, the insistence was forever upon the military intention of a united Germany. More effort had to be made to confirm the anonymous communication through Vienna, to decide whether it could be regarded as a dependable but totally independent source from anything Reimann could obtain. Sorokin said: 'America can't expect West Germany to accept upgraded nuclear missiles!'

'There have been visits to Europe by both the American Secretary of State and the Defence Secretary,' Reimann pointed out. 'During each there were private, unreported discussions with West German officials, but I'm fairly sure the views expressed were not those of the Administration but of the Congressional Defence Committee. Whether that indicates a split between the White House and Congress over

Europe I don't know: I haven't been able to get any guidance from Elke. We know already of the sort of cuts and financial savings the American military are having to make. There might be an argument that improved rocketry can make up for manpower withdrawn.'

'Political argument and rhetoric is very difficult from positively agreed decisions and policy,' insisted Sorokin, welcoming the opening. 'There can never be any question of our acting on the Vienna documents by themselves. They are incomplete. But the military references are of the utmost importance. A united Germany must *never* have any military significance! It's unthinkable, after what has happened to us in the past.'

'I have talked to Elke about everything contained in those documents!' Reimann protested. 'Short of asking her outright, what else do you expect me to do?'

'Get positive documentation from her,' said Sorokin, simply. 'We want provably official papers from the Chancellery, upon which we can make positive judgements and to which we know we can safely react, in anticipation of any move being made from Bonn: we want to be ahead, not behind.'

Reimann felt the exasperation rise within him. 'She's not suborned, knowingly leaking information! I still can't risk confronting her with the fact that I am an intelligence officer, working for Moscow: dependent upon me as she now is in every way, I still don't think she would knowingly betray secrets faced with the threat of my leaving her.'

'Then she's not sufficiently dependent,' said Turev, as irritated as his superior by Reimann's attitude.

'One item!' Reimann argued back. 'Tell me one item I have passed on to you that has proved to be unreliable or at fault! Just one!'

'Everything has been completely accurate,' Sorokin agreed.

'So you trust my information?'

'Absolutely.'

'Then use it, in the form in which it comes,' said Reimann. 'What difference does it make whether it is in the form of a verbal report from me, later assembled in Moscow as a working memorandum, or a document actually from the Chancellery, with a Chancellery seal and a Chancellery letterhead and marked Top Secret? The information is the same: maybe just slightly less detailed, that's all. But still sufficient. This is an unreal demand, like the lists you had Jutta carry were unreal demands.'

The overweening arrogance had as always to be allowed, Sorokin realized, regretfully: more so, in the position that Reimann now occupied with the woman. The Russian stroked his beard and said: 'At the moment the woman isn't suborned, is she? There is no criminal proof that she's passed anything at all on to you.'

Reimann frowned, unable to fully grasp the point. 'So?'

'All it would need is one piece of paper. That's all, just one piece,' Sorokin insisted. 'Then, if you told her who you really were she would know how completely she was trapped. That – the thought of prosecution and imprisonment if it ever became pubicly known – plus the threat of your leaving her would unlock the flood gates. She'd have to give us every document that passed through her hands.'

Reimann recognized at once the final, crushing blackmail, a scenario he had been taught at Balashikha. There he had accepted it, without question. But now he did not, and the reluctance surprised him. It would devastate Elke: show her how she had been betrayed and humiliated and cheated, and he didn't want to do that, not make her into some sort of slave who had to work at his bidding. Slaves were hostile, resentful. Quickly the surprise was followed by an irritation at his own weakness. What did it matter if she discovered her betrayal? Or what her attitude was, when she did find out? That wasn't a consideration; never had been. He didn't think of Elke Meyer as a person, as someone about whose feelings he should in any way be considerate. He should never forget she was an object: a useful object to be utilized for only one purpose. He said: 'At the moment, working the way I do, I *can* get guidance upon *everything* she sees. If we confront her fully – let her know what's truly been happening, all these weeks – we put ourselves in her hands, don't we? What proof would we have, what way of checking, that she was not just passing over material of the very lowest level? And withholding the really important information?'

'Nothing that Elke Meyer hears at those Cabinet committee meetings is low-level material,' rejected Turev.

'Some things are more important than others,' said Reimann, equally forceful.

'You seem very adamant about this,' said Turev.

'I want to get the maximum, nothing less. I think I am the best person to judge how that can be achieved. I don't think, at this stage, that this is the way to do it.'

'It is an order,' asserted Sorokin, ending the discussion with rigid formality. 'Obey it!'

Bastard, thought Reimann. Refusing absolute capitulation, he said: 'I will try.'

Bastard, thought Sorokin. Refusing the man the escape, he said: 'You will do more than try.'

Reimann sat unspeaking but staring for several moments directly and unflinchingly at the Russian who wore his hair on his chin instead of his head. At last he said: 'Have another cable critical of my material sent to me, through the press centre. And something more this time. Let there be a letter from Australia, too, talking of possible reassignment unless the coverage improves. Give a time limit, for that improvement to be achieved.'

Turev nodded, smiling in understanding. 'That'll increase the pressure. Anything else we can do?'

'No,' said Reimann. He was suddenly impatient to get back to Bonn, away from these dour men and from this depressingly dismal sector of Berlin. The desire, like his earlier unwillingness to hurt Elke Meyer, surprised him. Hadn't he once mentally sneered at the West German capital as a village and been anxious to get his mission accomplished and leave as quickly as possible?

'We look forward to receiving some official material very soon,' said Sorokin, believing he had found the way to remind Reimann that he was still very much the subordinate.

Reimann paused at the door, looking back. 'Let's hope it's not the dregs, when it comes.'

Reimann telephoned Elke from the airport, so she was ready when he got to Kaufmannstrasse. They were slightly late at the Maternus, but the table had been held for them.

'Why here?' asked Elke.

'It's another special, first-time place, like the valley at Andernach.' At that moment Reimann decided he wouldn't crush Elke with open blackmail. He'd try for the official documents that seemed so important but he would not absolutely destroy her, as they demanded. It was a ridiculous suggestion. He frowned across the table at Elke. 'Are you all right? You're very quiet.'

'I'm fine,' she lied.

That night there were no indiscreet government ministers dining. And no flower-vendors, either. As they left the restaurant, Reimann recognized an Audi he knew, parked twenty yards away from his own car. He couldn't see in the darkness if it was occupied. He guessed it would be. The anger burned through him.

272

Chapter Thirty-Two

There couldn't be anything wrong! Elke knew there couldn't: impossible. No need at all then for the bygone, please-never-again feeling. They'd always been careful: openly talked about it, mature adults. Always observed the safe period. *Always*. Otherwise he'd used something. Every time. So there couldn't be anything wrong. Mature, she thought again. That had to be it: obviously that was it. She was almost thirty-nine, so she could expect to start to become irregular. It happened early to a lot of women. Probably the reason, too, for those see-saw moods of uncertainty, those confidence dips, before she'd met him. The logical, sensible explanation. Definitely. Only five days. Women her age sometimes went a month, two months, without seeing anything. Not like before. At her most fertile then. Every cause to worry then when she'd missed: shouldn't have been so stupid. But not now. Why the same feeling now, just like before? *Because* of before, that's why. The same disbelief at first, too. *Not me: can't have happened to me!* Except that it had. Different now: altogether different. Not just her age, when she should expect it. Or the caution they'd shown, every time. The most important difference was between Otto and Dietlef. There'd never been any substance in Dietlef. She'd always known that, deep down: the hope of marriage had been because she was pregnant, not because she loved him. Not like she loved Otto. Otto wouldn't run away. Let her down. She knew Otto: knew him completely. He was a good man. Honest. Someone who could be trusted, without question. Wonderful.

Elke felt the apprehension subside, just slightly. She put the calendar back in its place and went to the refrigerator, knowing there was some wine open. She sat at the kitchen table, the glass between both hands, looking down at it. Not the slightest need to worry, even it it had happened. Which it hadn't, of course. Just *if*. No question of their not getting married. Secretly – deep down again – Elke was sure it was inevitable that they would, although he hadn't given her the opal ring in the way she'd hoped. All this would do – *if* – was make it happen sooner. Somewhere quiet. Away from Bonn if possible. Cologne maybe. Cologne was nice. Otto could fix it. Just Ida and Horst and the children. Ursula, too, if Dr Schiller agreed. What she would have wanted anway. It would mean leaving the Chancellery, of course.

273

She'd regret that. Deeply. She'd been respected, admired, there. Known by ministers. The Chancellor, too. Had the top-secret job, a recognition of her ability. She'd miss it. Even miss the hopeful, stumbling Günther. All unavoidable. Frau Elke Reimann. It had an easy sound – a good sound – echoing in her mind.

Elke sipped her wine, positively making the reflection come to mind, another if. What if Otto didn't want to get married? It was an incredible, inconceivable doubt but what *if*? She wouldn't have any hesitation, not this time. No empty, pointless religious misgivings. Cologne again. Some discreet clinic. She'd read it was a simple operation, if it was done early enough. Quite safe. No more than a fortnight's leave from the Chancellery. Ida would help find a place: Ida would always help. What she'd do was . . .

Elke thrust the glass down upon the kitchen table, a noise to break the reflection. Enough! She'd let her mind drift far enough! They *had* been careful, always. So it *was* impossible for anything to be wrong. Which made all the other fears utterly ridiculous. Her age: that's all it was. Early, possibly, but still just her age. No need to talk to Otto about it. Or Ida. Simply wait for it to happen. Probably come tomorrow. Or the day after. What if it didn't? A doctor, she supposed: a gynaecologist. Not because she was pregnant. For the irregularity. A gynaecologist could treat that, advise her what other symptoms and problems she might experience.

Elke felt her eyes fill, clouding, so the glass before her blurred. *Not me: can't have happened to me!* She began to cry.

'Well?' demanded Sorokin.

Yuri Panin did not respond immediately. 'It was always a risk, that he would become over-confident. Instilling that confidence was vital, for what he had to do.'

'I never trusted all this psychological crap,' said Cherny.

'Reimann has succeeded exactly as we intended,' argued the psychologist, not intimidated by the soldier. 'We trained him to seduce the woman and he's done precisely that.'

'With what result?' demanded Cherny.

'It's the other woman who concerns me,' Turev told them.

'The wife?'

Turev nodded. 'I accept the argument that involving her distanced us, in the event of any seizure by West German counter-intelligence: that any arrest could be turned to seem like espionage against West Germany by two provable members of East German intelligence. But

I'm doubtful now of that benefit. Every tape I have listened to indicates some antagonism. And Reimann never wanted her direct involvement: he argued against it from the beginning.'

'Is she creating actual difficulties?' Sorokin asked.

'Distracting irritation.'

'If it becomes anything worse, we can simply lift her out,' said Sorokin.

'She knows about the operation,' Panin pointed out.

'She couldn't cause any problems, here in Moscow,' said Sorokin, simply.

Chapter Thirty-Three

Jutta stood expectantly, hoping for some embrace, but Reimann stalked by her into the Nord-Stadt apartment. 'Why?'

'I . . .' Jutta started, about to lie. Instead she said: 'Why not?'

'You know damned well why not! We should never get close, when I'm with her. It's against every instruction . . . every rule.'

'I'm disappointed you didn't detect me following you all the way from Kaufmannstrasse!' Jutta was attempting to fight back.

'I don't look out for stupidity, not from you.'

'No harm was done,' she insisted.

'Why?' he repeated.

'I wanted to see what she was really like,' she admitted. 'You said she was a dried-up spinster. She's not. She's an attractive woman.'

More than attractive, thought Reimann. Accusingly he said: 'You parked your car where I could see it, didn't you!'

'No,' denied Jutta, weakly.

'Then your surveillance was no better than my observation.' The microphones would be recording everything. If he'd wanted he could have staged the confrontation away from the apartment. So why hadn't he?

'No harm,' she repeated, stubbornly.

'Satisfied now?'

'Why didn't you tell me what she was really like?'

'I described her as she appeared to me.'

Jutta knew she had to stop: there was no benefit from continuing the conversation. He'd seen her car, which she'd intended: that was enough. She said: 'So I followed you and saw you with her, just once . . .' She snapped her fingers. '. . . That's it. All that it is. I don't want to talk about it any more. I want to talk about getting another apartment, away from this rat-hole.'

Did it matter? wondered Reimann, instantly assessing. He'd decided months ago that the KGB would bug any apartment to which she moved, so the ears he wished to hear would still exist. There might even be a professional argument for her changing her home, getting out before anyone else in the block became curious about her. He said: 'Why not? Have you looked round yet?'

276

Jutta wished he had shown more sincere interest. 'Not yet. I wanted to see how you felt about it.' That wasn't true. She'd driven all the way to the Plittersdorf district to look at one place, been shown two at West-Stadt, and had an address to visit the following day across the river at Niederdollendorf, although like Plittersdorf it was further away than she wished to go.

'You've known how I've felt about this place from the beginning.'

That was another reply Jutta hadn't wanted to hear. Hopefully she said: 'I thought perhaps you could help me choose?'

'You know I can't do that!'

Jutta had known but she'd needed to try. Still trying she said: 'I don't think there would be any difficulty in your just coming with me. Just to look.'

'That's as absurd as following me to restaurants!'

'It was only a suggestion,' retreated Jutta, lamely.

'Have you discussed it, with them?'

'I intend to, at my next contact.'

They'd already know, by then: know, too, how she'd wanted to involve him in the move and about her trailing him to the Bad Godesberg restaurant to which he'd taken Elke. 'I think it's a good idea. Maybe find a bigger block next time, where you can be even more anonymous. There's always a danger, staying too long in one place.'

'I can tell them you agree, then?'

He was surprised she needed his reassurance. Or his approval. 'Of course.'

Show more interest! Jutta thought: please show more interest! She said: 'I'd like us to spend a weekend together. We haven't, for a long time.'

'She has the weekends off,' he reminded her. 'That's when there's the best opportunity for her properly to ease up. When she lets things slip.'

'Just one weekend!'

It didn't become Jutta, to plead: he wasn't used to it. He tried to balance the priorities. He *did* have to impose more pressure on Elke. If he spent part of the next weekend away from her there could be an advantage, making her realize that things were still not as positive between them as she imagined. And he supposed Jutta deserved the consideration. He wished he could feel more enthusiasm. He said: 'All right. Next Saturday. We'll spend all of next Saturday together.'

'I want the day to be on the river, like before,' said Jutta, insisting further.

277

'We'll go on the river,' Reimann promised, going along with everything. What would the Russians do, when they heard the tape?

'Do you know what I wish?' said Jutta. 'I wish this could all be over, so we could be like we were before.'

Reimann knew it could never be like it was before, between them: he didn't think he wanted it to be. What *would* happen to them, when this operation was over? Berlin was impossible: had been, before this began. Anywhere else in the former bloc was unlikely, as well. Only Moscow then. But what would he do, what *could* he do, in Moscow? Some headquarters role, in Dzerzhinsky Square or in one of the outlying Directorate buildings? He didn't want that: didn't want to live in Moscow at all. He said: 'It's far too early to think like that.'

'I'd like it not to be.'

Chapter Thirty-Four

Gerda Pohl's arrest came, as such seizures so often do, from routine. Random security checks over three earlier months had disclosed an occasional failure of classified documents to be accounted for and returned at the end of each working day from the division to which Gerda had been reassigned from the Chancellery. The division, responsible for liaison and communication between the Foreign Ministry and the Chancellery, was monitored and special entrapping designations put upon all material passing through it to establish which papers were handled by which clerk or official. Gerda Pohl was identified during the first week: a file check showed within hours that she had been guilty of such carelessness in the past. She was placed under observation for a month, to trace through her other members of any spy cell. During that time she was in possession of papers from three departmental files, all bearing a security rating. Never, however, during that period of surveillance was she seen to make contact with anyone counter-intelligence considered to be a member of an espionage group. Only much later, during intense examination of the surveillance records after Gerda made a complete confession, was the significance of the Post Office visits realized.

In her first, incomplete admission, Gerda Pohl denied any espionage activity or intent. At the age of fifty-nine, she insisted, she found difficulty maintaining the required turn-around of work essential if she were to remain in her department, which she needed to do if she was to be retained. Which it was essential that she should be. As a widow she was entirely dependent upon her salary: she had taken the documents home to complete there because even if she worked overtime at the government building, which she did at least two nights a week, she had still been unable to complete everything according to schedule.

Only later, under intensive interrogation, did Gerda change her story and admit to posting copies of documents to the Soviet embassy in Vienna. She further admitted acting in spite, for the way she considered she had been unfairly treated in her earlier position, actually within the Chancellery Secretariat. Despite a full week of sometimes brutal interrogation, the elderly woman insisted she was unable to remember exactly how many documents she had sent to Vienna or what their contents had been.

Counter-intelligence officers were waiting when Elke arrived the morning after the arrest, and her top-security classification allowed her to attend all the sessions at which Gerda's confession gradually emerged. Gerda's statement never mentioned Elke by name as the person against whom she felt a grudge. Counter-intelligence requested everything upon which the woman had ever worked while she was in the Chancellery Secretariat to be made available to them. The seemingly enormous demand was, in fact, reasonably easy to meet. Another of Elke's innovations had been always to reference documents against the name of the clerk or secretary who prepared them: the first day it only took three hours to produce duplicates of all the material Gerda Pohl had handled in the preceding two full years of her employment in Werle's department.

'A disaster!' judged Werle.

'According to what she says, she didn't start doing it until *after* her transfer,' Elke pointed out.

'There's no way of knowing if she's telling the whole truth,' Werle argued. 'There's a lot of sensitive stuff going through Foreign Ministry liaison.'

Elke was surprised that she did not feel more strongly about what Gerda had done. She actually tried, for shock or anger, but the emotion wouldn't come. Her only tangible feeling was pity for the woman.

Throughout the rest of the Cabinet Secretariat that first day the affair created an air of excitement: almost, bizarrely, a holiday atmosphere, because the presence of so many investigating intelligence officers made it impossible for the usual and normal amount of work to be completed.

Elke, her mind occupied by her other, personal worry, didn't feel any excitement either. She'd actually thought there had been something that morning, hurrying into the bathroom hopefully to feel herself, but there had been nothing. And the stomach discomfort – not the usual cramps but definite twinges of pain, coming and going – had gone completely as she drove to the Chancellery, leaving the faintest suggestion of nausea. But not bad, she told herself, anxiously. The sickness *had* been bad, with Ursula: every morning, during the first months and starting before she'd really known, positively, that she was even pregnant. She could remember – as she could remember everything about that time – how she and Ida initially snatched at it to convince themselves she was suffering from something medical, an ulcer maybe: pitifully going over what she might have eaten, day by day, to upset her.

The publicity was incredible, in both newspapers and on radio and television, and by midday the Chancellery was besieged by cameramen and journalists. That first day one Munich newspaper, linking one scandal to another, reprinted the incident of the Transport Minister and the stripper because it gave them the opportunity to republish photographs of the girl. To avoid being photographed – because everyone either entering or leaving the Chancellery was being photographed running the gamut of the press – Elke left by one of the side entrances and made her way to Kaufmannstrasse along the river road.

That night Reimann suggested they stay in, at Rochusplatz, and Elke was glad, not wanting to do anything else. He offered to cook for her, as he frequently did when she really had her period, and she was glad for him to do that, too. He grilled the steaks to perfection, knowing just how she liked them prepared, but the nausea became worse than it had been all day and she found it difficult to eat, leaving most of it.

'What's the matter?' asked Reimann.

'Nothing.'

'You've eaten hardly anything.'

'I'm not very hungry.'

'And you've been very subdued, all evening.' It was a mood he hadn't experienced: always, before, there'd been the detectable apprehension, a keenness to defer and to please. Tonight Elke was practically introverted.

'The Chancellery is in uproar, over this spying business,' said Elke. She felt guilty invoking a poor, frightened old lady to account for a mood brought about by something entirely different. Elke supposed Gerda would be in a prison cell, under guard, with bars at the window. All alone.

'I suppose it must be,' he agreed. It was an incredible fuck-up, affecting everything he was expected to do. How could he now hope to get her to bring out official papers? The entire Chancellery – but her Secretariat particularly – *would* be in uproar, everyone lectured and reminded of their security responsibilities and how to conduct themselves. Everything absolutely fucked up!

'I feel sorry for her,' Elke admitted.

'Sorry?' Reimann was immediately attentive, curious.

Elke felt the nausea positively rising and had to swallow against it, so she couldn't speak at once. 'I know perhaps that I shouldn't: that she did something terribly wrong. But that's what I feel. Sorry.'

Room to explore here, thought Reimann. He said: 'But she *took* classified documents!'

Enough – practically everything – had been reported in that day's newspapers, Elke decided: there was no indiscretion discussing it at this level. 'Not from the Chancellery Secretariat, I don't think. From the Foreign Ministry. Her clearance isn't particularly high, so it can't have been anything too sensitive.'

'There'll be a tightening up of security at the Chancellery, I suppose?' said Reimann, a question he very much wanted answering.

Elke shook her head and wished she hadn't, because an ache had begun to settle, at the temples and down her neck. 'It's already tight. They'll probably try to evolve some changes in the system.'

Not much guidance there, he decided. 'Maybe you're right,' he accepted, encouragingly. 'Maybe she is a poor old lady.'

Elke smiled, faintly, at his agreeing with her. What would his reaction be to another, more personal disclosure? Not yet. No reason yet. She didn't want to say or do anything to make him feel compromised or trapped. He *wasn't* compromised or trapped. She would never have him be that: still no reason for despair. It would be all right, in a day or two. Didn't matter if it went an entire month. If it *did* go an entire month she'd see a gynaecologist, though. Get something to adjust the cycle. Ingenuously she said: 'I shouldn't bring the problems of work home.'

Reimann came quite close to laughing openly. Instead, grabbing a possible advantage, he said: 'Why not? Problems never seem so big when they're talked through with someone else.'

'There's nothing more to talk about, not really. I can't stop thinking of what might happen to her.'

Definitely the wrong direction! He didn't want her agonizing over penalties for what he had to persuade her to do! He said: 'If it's only low-level stuff, like you say, it won't be too bad.'

'She's all by herself: no one to look after her,' said Elke. Like I had no one to look after me until I met you, she thought, smiling at him. She moved closer to him on the large, soft-leather couch, resting her head against his shoulder, needing the assurance of his arm around her: he'd poured brandy for her but she hadn't risked drinking it, unsure how her stomach would react to the fumes if she brought it close enough to smell.

'I suppose it's going to be something I shall have to write about, this spy business,' he said. 'It's the headline of the moment. It'll be what they expect. How difficult is it going to be, finding out the full extent of what she's done? I mean is there any way it can be proved what documents she did or did not handle? I suppose that will be impossible, won't it?'

It was *so* good, having him hold her like this! She'd have to discover the name of the cologne he used – it had to be either in the bathroom or bedroom – and buy him some, as a present. She said: 'I don't know about the Foreign Ministry liaison. In the Secretariat I can identify everything she's ever seen.'

She was finding it easier by the minute to tell him things! He pulled slightly away and said: 'Everything! You've got to be joking!'

'It's a system I set up. Not just for something like this: so that I would know who had dealt with what.'

'*You*, personally?'

Elke enjoyed the admiration from someone she adored. 'You'd be amazed how important I am at the Chancellery!'

Hardly, my darling, Reimann thought. He said: 'What are they like, these documents? Large, small? Always annotated by Top Secret? Always referenced, as you reference yours, so a check is easy? What about copies? Are they numbered and listed, for security? Is there a log, to record sender and recipient?'

Elke chanced the brandy snifter but her stomach heaved, so she just touched it to her lips, without properly drinking. She said: 'All shapes and sizes. Always designated, at my level, although obviously not every one is designated Top Secret. Some are Eyes Only and they have to be logged. Top Secret, too. Secret and Classified don't have to be recorded that way. They're always numbered: copies, too.'

This was going incredibly well: far better than he had dared hope! He said: 'I wonder if there'll be any produced in facsimile, as evidence, for the eventual trial? Something that can be printed?'

Elke shrugged unknowingly beneath him. 'They wouldn't be the real thing, if it was for newspaper or magazine publication. It would only be a mock-up example.'

'You're probably right,' Reimann accepted, not challenging, not tonight. How much further could he risk pressing? 'The newpapers say she was arrested as she was leaving the Ministry with papers in a bag or a briefcase.'

'A handbag, as far as I'm aware,' offered Elke. She was paying attention to everything she said: she hadn't been indiscreet in any way.

She'd respond to flattery, Reimann guessed. He said: 'I don't suppose you're ever checked, not at your grade? Security must know how important you are.'

'It's always possible,' said Elke. 'Officially the Chancellor himself could be searched as he leaves.'

Reimann laughed, knowing it was expected. 'But he never has been, has he? Not any Chancellor.'

'Not that I've heard.'

'Or you?' he persisted.

'No,' agreed Elke at last. 'I've never been checked. I suppose the security officers do know me.'

Reimann judged it to be a good evening's work: she was loosening up exactly as she had to. He said: 'I'm very proud of you. And I admire you, very much.'

'I . . .' began Elke and stopped. No one had ever said they were *proud* of her before. She said: 'You're embarrassing me. But thank you.'

The critical cable had already arrived through the press bureau, and he was impatient for the more critical letter: he planned to produce both at the same time. Soon, he decided: maybe even as soon as tomorrow.

Later in bed, when he started to move his hand over her, Elke said: 'Not tonight.'

'What's the matter?'

'Nothing. I just don't feel like it tonight.'

The three of them met immediately after the official Soviet statement denying receipt of any German documents at their Vienna embassy and dismissing the claims of the Bonn government as fantasy manufactured to harm hopefully improving relations between the two governments.

'So they *were* genuine!' said Cherny. He felt vindicated.

'Still insufficient as they are,' said Turev.

'In content, perhaps,' the soldier agreed. 'But they prove one thing conclusively. There's a lot of military thinking and military planning going on that isn't being publicly admitted.'

'We've been getting that guidance from Reimann,' Turev pointed out. 'This confirms it.'

'It confirms something more,' said Sorokin. 'It means we can rely absolutely on Reimann.'

'Let's get rid of the distraction of that damned wife.' Cherny had been listening to the tape of the confrontation over the restaurant surveillance, which had arrived the previous night.

'Shouldn't we talk it over with Reimann first?' wondered Sorokin.

Turev shook his head. 'I don't think he'll feel strongly about it. Object greatly, I mean.'

'I don't want her to suspect anything, until we've got her here,'

Sorokin decided. 'I don't want her doing anything more stupid than she has at the moment.'

'The next regular meeting?' suggested Turev.

'Why wait?' demanded Cherny.

'The next regular meeting will be fine,' Sorokin agreed, enjoying his authority.

Chapter Thirty-Five

That morning Elke was sick for the first time. She managed to reach the bathroom and turn on the taps to blur any sound and clung to the toilet bowl, dry-heaving even when she couldn't vomit any more. Several weeks earlier, encouraged by Reimann because of the impression of her greater permanence with him, Elke had left some clothes and fresh underwear at Rochusplatz so that after staying overnight during the week she did not have to get up earlier than usual to stop at her own apartment to change on her way to the Chancellery. She'd liked the idea, accepting it exactly as Reimann had intended, but that morning she wished she could have got back to Kaufmannstrasse to be alone for a while. Elke felt wretched: as if she were going to be sick again, which she knew she couldn't, her head and stomach aching, her limbs heavy and lethargic. To have been alone for only a short while, just until she felt better, would have been such relief.

If she went back to bed he'd imagine she wanted sex, because they hadn't made love last night, as they normally did, just as they normally did in the morning when they stayed together overnight. Often it was at Elke's urging: she knew, unashamed, that under his guidance she had become almost lascivious, enjoying and wanting to do things to each other she'd only half guessed at or not fully understood when she read a cloaked description in a book. She couldn't have had him touch her that morning: didn't want anyone or anything to touch her. She put a plug into the bath to trap the running water and got in when it was practically too hot to bear, telling herself it had nothing to do with the long ago advice from Ida (*a near scalding bath can bring you on*) but that it might ease the ache in her arms and legs. It did. The sensation of nausea receded, too. When she finally got out her body was pink, as if her skin were burned. Her face was pink, as well, although the tearful redness the sickness had brought to her eyes had gone. She decided to wait before making up: there was a lot of time. She felt herself, just in case. There was nothing. He was awake when she went back into the bedroom.

'Why so early?'

'I felt like getting up.'

'You all right?'

'You asked me that last night.' Elke regretted the hint of impatience.

'You were a long time in the bathroom.'

'I'm fine, really.' Dear God, how much she wished that were true! She shouldn't become irritated with him. He hadn't done anything wrong – nothing they hadn't done knowingly together – and he was only showing he loved her, and she was going to need his support and love a great deal very soon. She was going to need a lot of things.

'You'd tell me if there were, wouldn't you?' he insisted. Reimann realized he was genuinely concerned *for* Elke, not for any difficulty an illness or indisposition in a manipulated victim might cause him.

'I'd tell you,' Elke promised, looking into the wardrobe with her back to him, so he could not see her face. There's going to be a lot to tell you, my darling, she thought: I hope it isn't too much.

'Come back to bed.'

'I've bathed.'

'Bath again.'

'I don't feel like it.'

'You didn't feel like it last night.'

'The curse is hanging around.' How fervently she hoped that were true!

'I'm sorry,' Reimann said, immediately contrite. He realized he hadn't kept the careful note of monthly dates he'd once determined to do. It had scarcely been possible, being called more often than he had expected to East Berlin, in addition to the times he'd felt it necessary to be away from Elke. 'Can I get you something? Some pills: I've got some that might help.'

'No. But thank you.' She really was feeling better. She didn't ache any more. Or feel tired, either. She smiled at him as he finally got out of bed. He *did* love her, she knew: truly loved her. She didn't have any reason to fear his reaction. It was pointless to worry: to worry as completely as she was worrying, that is.

The day began working as well as Reimann wanted it to – as most things had worked out on this operation – with the arrival of the morning mail. He recognized the Australian postmark before opening the letter, of course, so he was able to position himself by his desk and prepare the outburst.

'Shit!' he exploded. 'The bastards!'

'What is it!' demanded Elke, alarmed, from across the room.

'Nothing!' Reimann's voice was loud, the rudeness of a man preoccupied with a private crisis. In feigned anger he threw the letter down, open, on his desk.

'Is there a problem?'

'I said it was nothing!' Forceful enough, he thought: no more.

'I'm sorry.' Elke felt crushed.

'I didn't mean that: *I'm* sorry,' said Reimann, apologetically. 'It's . . . maybe we'll talk about it later. Sorry.' Urgently, clearly wanting to change the subject and the embarrassment, Reimann said: 'Are you coming tonight?'

'Yes,' Elke said at once. Unsure how she would physically feel, she said: 'Maybe we could stay in again: I'll cook.' She hoped cooking food wouldn't disgust her.

'Whatever you say,' Reimann agreed. He'd always intended that they should remain in the flat again: she had worrying news to learn.

The normal and established routine of the Cabinet Secretariat was still disrupted by the intelligence investigators. There was a mid-morning meeting that Elke attended with Werle at which the senior intelligence officer reported that Gerda Pohl remained adamant during an overnight interview that she could not remember the contents or the amount of the material she had sent to the Soviet embassy. The man dismissed the Russian denial that they had received anything and Werle again talked of a disaster. At the further request of the intelligence officer, who said it was necessary to make the damage assessment as comprehensive as possible, Elke initiated a further search of her reference system for documents handled by Gerda Pohl two years prior to the period already processed by the investigators. That afternoon Werle was summoned, alone, by the Chancellor to give a personal report of what potentially could have been lost. When he returned Werle was more distressed than Elke had known him to be during any previous government emergency.

'It's impossible to calculate, with any accuracy!' insisted the Cabinet Secretary.

'What will happen to her?'

'Jail, obviously,' said Werle, bitterly.

'At her age!'

'Age hasn't got anything to do with it.'

'What's being done, positively?'

'There's little that *can* be done. The Chancellor has decided to make a statement this afternoon, rejecting the Soviet denial. He's going to insist that the leakage is of low level. There are going to be a series of individual briefings, to Western ambassadors. And to NATO ambassadors. We're hoping they'll accept the reassurance. The problem is that this isn't our first spy scandal, is it?'

'It's difficult to get the Secretariat functioning properly,' said Elke.

'It's difficult to get anything functioning properly.'

Just before she was preparing to leave the Chancellery Ida telephoned, checking on their regular weekly lunch, and Elke used the continuing investigation as an excuse to avoid it. She didn't think she would be able to deflect Ida as successfully as she had deflected Reimann that morning. Ida knew her too well: was too responsive to the almost telepathic sixth sense between them. When the moment came to tell Ida (*if*, she corrected, desperately) there wouldn't be the need to say a lot.

'It must be hell,' said Ida, with unintentional irony.

'It is,' agreed Elke, sincerely.

'The weekend, then? With Otto?'

'I hope so,' said Elke. She was still reluctant to commit him to anything without his agreeing it first. Particularly now.

Elke was grateful she was experiencing no discomfort – no aching, no sickness, no lassitude – when she reached Rochusplatz that night. She had the urge to fuck – mentally using the word he'd taught her to use and which they did together, always – and was sure they would later. She'd only said her period was hanging around, not that she had it: even that hadn't been a bar, a few times. He still seemed subdued, when he admitted her. They kissed and sat without need to talk and he suggested an aperitif which she refused, not prepared to risk any change in the way she felt.

Reimann regretted the refusal, not having intended to begin the production until several drinks had mellowed her into being as receptive as he'd planned. He said: 'I want to apologize again for how I was this morning. It was very rude. Unforgivable.'

'I'd forgotten all about it,' Elke lied. The letter he had so angrily discarded remained lying on his desk in the corner, near the still unfilled bookshelves. It looked strangely upright, held up by the way it had been folded inside its envelope.

If her assurance was true, which he doubted, it wouldn't stay that way much longer. He got up from where they were sitting side by side, picked up the letter and the preceding cable and brought it over to her. 'Look at that!' he said, exasperation replacing the supposed anger. 'What in the name of Christ do they expect! Fucking miracles! I work my ass off for them and that's all the thanks I get!'

Elke read the cable first. It said: *Greatly disappointed your continuing inability properly to grasp and reflect enormity of situation in which you're placed. Yet again unwilling to use your assessment, which unreflected by any other observer.*

The letter was much longer. It began with apparent friendliness, addressing him by his Christian name, but the complaints followed in mounting succession: *Greatly disappointed* was repeated. One phrase talked of *constant embarrassment, compared with our competitors*. He was accused of absence of depth and necessary detail. The concluding paragraph read: *After so much hope and expectation we must reluctantly warn you that unless there is a major and sustained improvement in the next and immediate six months we will have no alternative but to reconsider your appointment as our Bonn-based chief European correspondent.*

Elke handed back both to him, her hands shaking. The feeling of sickness was back, although not the same as it had been that morning. She said: 'I think they're being very unreasonable.'

'Unreasonable! They're being assholes!'

'What can you do?'

'What can I do, more than I am already doing at the moment?'

'You could resign if they tried to reassign you,' said Elke eagerly, pitifully anxious to help but even more anxious to keep him in Bonn. 'Try to get a position here with some other organization.'

Reimann nodded, seeming to consider the suggestion. He said: 'Every worthwhile news outlet has a person here in Bonn, after all that's happened. It's one of the major news capitals in the world, and it will remain so for a long time. So there aren't openings left any more. And Australia would appoint someone to replace me and the word would very quickly get around that they'd dumped me because I wasn't good enough. So even if an opening were to arise, I wouldn't get it. No one wants to employ a political commentator who's been dismissed for not being able to do the job.'

'So you'd have to leave Bonn?' she asked, with defeated finality.

'I don't want to: I'd try not to,' said Reimann, hanging out the slender hope for her to grasp.

'But you might have to, in the end?'

Reimann stirred himself. The effort he had to make for the optimism looked painfully obvious. 'I've got six months!' he said. 'In six months there'll be cables and letters telling me I'm the best commentator they've ever known!'

'What *can* you do better than you're already doing?' insisted Elke, uninfluenced by his supposed assurance.

'I'll think of something,' he insisted, the struggle for optimism still clear to her.

Both agreed they weren't hungry. Elke made omelettes which they scarcely ate. Reimann opened wine but they each took only one glass.

290

Normally he left the bedroom light on, because they both liked to see. That night he turned it off the moment they got into bed. In the darkness he gave an uncomfortable laugh and said: 'The situation is reversed.'

'Reversed?'

'Tonight it's me who doesn't feel like it. I'm sorry . . . it's just . . .'

'I understand . . . I don't want to either . . . I told you this morning,' said Elke, glad of her earlier excuse. She didn't want to any more, either. I can't lose him now, she thought: now, more than ever, I can't lose him.

Chapter Thirty-Six

Elke believed herself to be so close to him now that her initial disappointment at Reimann's apology for having to be away from Bonn for the second successive weekend went beyond being automatic to be almost instinctive. She didn't show it, of course, insisting that she understood the effort he had to put into work, particularly after the cable and the letter he had shown her.

Her disappointment did not last long. She actually became glad they were going to be apart, temporarily relieving her of the strain of trying to explain away the depression she couldn't conceal. Elke clung to her original excuse and came close to collapse when he said it was a long time coming. She almost broke down again when, with the compassion to which she'd become accustomed and which was one of the many reasons why she loved him so much, Reimann later suggested she consult a gynaecologist if she was going to suffer this degree of discomfort every month. Elke said she was thinking about doing so.

The Gerda Pohl affair continued to dominate Günther Werle's attention, so much so that he did not notice any change in Elke, which was a further relief. And a scheduled meeting of the special committee was postponed for the Cabinet to discuss the espionage débâcle, so she was spared the extra burden that inevitably imposed. She nevertheless tried to escape into as much activity as possible. She immersed herself in clearing up the backlog of normal work delayed by the counter-intelligence inquiries and presence, continuing to prepare Werle's daily itinerary but reducing it to the absolute minimum to enable the man to concentrate on the Pohl affair. And with her increased security clearance Elke was able to take over and handle a proportion of the day-to-day business with which Werle would normally have dealt.

None of it succeeded in blotting out the one spectre crowding her mind.

On the Friday she told Ida by telephone that they would not be accepting the weekend luncheon invitation, not positively lying but allowing the inference of doing something else with Reimann, even surer now than she had been in avoiding the midweek encounter that she could not have sustained several hours with her sister without a blurted, tearful confession.

'Definitely next Saturday!' Ida insisted. 'Horst has got some new story ideas he wants to discuss with Otto. And we haven't talked for ages.'

So far the Australian payments had enabled them to repay Elke twenty thousand Deutschmarks against the original loan. 'If we possibly can,' Elke agreed. She didn't want to contemplate what there could be to talk about by the following weekend.

'Everything still OK between you two?'

'Fine,' said Elke. I'm soon going to find out, she thought.

'I've got something to tell you,' said Ida, circumspectly. 'About a friend.'

Elke tried to sound interested, which she normally would have been, but it was hard for her. She guessed there were other people in the house at Bad Godesberg whom Ida did not want to overhear. Safe at her end Elke said: 'About Kurt?'

'Yes.'

'You've finished it?' demanded Elke, hopefully.

'Wait until we meet,' Ida refused.

The awareness that for the first time in her life she didn't *want* to meet Ida, not yet, not now, burst in upon Elke as she replaced the receiver. She became physically hot, without bothering to seek out which of all the jumbled-up emotions brought that particular feeling. Her mind, every interrupted reflection, *was* jumbled, and from the mêlée came a phrase, and not just the words but the tone of voice in which they'd been spoken to her. *Stop feeling so sorry for yourself . . . so full of self-pity.* It was Ida's recollected voice, although Elke wasn't sure if the words were precisely accurate: wasn't sure of the actual occasion or reason, except that she believed the accusation had been comparatively recent. Not important, not when or how. But the warning was important. That *was* what was happening: she was letting herself be sucked down yet again into a swamp of sorrowful self-pity. She'd stopped letting that happen, months ago: and it had to remain stopped, never permitted back. OK, the mental highs and lows of the past days (what highs?) had been understandable, permissible, but she had to accept that the days were just that, past. Now she had to consider the future. Make plans. Make a list, even. Numbered, maybe: first priority, second priority, third priority and so on.

What was the first priority? To find out, she answered herself at once. To make an appointment with a gynaecologist and explain how careful they'd been, always, but that this had suddenly arisen so she'd thought it best to consult a specialist. (*Very wise, but I can assure you there's nothing*

293

for you to worry about . . . quite natural . . . just take this medication, as prescribed.) Monday: she'd talk to her general practitioner and get a recommendation and on Monday make an appointment. No reason to delay. She couldn't go on as she had been doing, pretending and making excuses. How long would this diagnosis take? Not long: it hadn't taken a full day to learn she was pregnant with Ursula, and from an ordinary doctor then, not a specialist. What if it wasn't the placating prognosis for which, still faintly, she hoped? Confront the situation, fully, properly. She wouldn't need any help, any support, from Ida to tell Otto. Just the simple, straight, unambiguous announcement. And hear in return his simple, straight, unambiguous reply. *I'm so happy, my darling: so pleased. We'll choose names and plan a nursery and have the wedding just as you want and be so happy, the four of us, you, me, the baby and Ursula . . .* And after that she'd tell Ida: the very next weekend, when Ida imagined she had announcements of her own to make to her!

Elke acknowledged how ridiculous she had been, letting herself slide as she had: she had to try to remember to say sorry to Otto, when everything else had been explained and they'd kissed and laughed and made their plans. She should be delighted, ecstatic, not buried in black depression. It was going to be wonderful, she determined, allowing herself the word: everything was going to be wonderful.

It was an impulsive decision that Saturday morning to re-weave old patterns, although Elke recognized before she set out that it would not be quite the same because there had been so many changes: Poppi wasn't with her any more, for a start. She still felt the desire for nostalgia, a reminder of an empty past to put against a full future. Elke drove carefully into the centre of Bonn and by incredible coincidence found a parking meter in Engeltalstrasse, where she'd parked the day Reimann's stolen car had been crashed into her Volkswagen. There was even a similarity in how crowded the main market and the adjoining flower square were, on her way to the Bonner Café. Clara was still there, and greeted Elke with reserved warmth, and her luck continued because the table that had always been hers on a Saturday morning was vacant, waiting for her. The apple cake was superb, not burned at all: Elke refused cream or custard with it but took cream with the coffee.

So lucky, Elke decided, her spirits completely restored, all her apprehensions firmly controlled at last: she was so incredibly, contentedly happy. Caught by the word, she tried to recall another time she'd felt like this. Andernach, she decided instantly. That beautiful, perfect day at Andernach, the first time he'd taken her, when he'd stumbled and couldn't openly say he loved her: the day, at the end, when they'd *made* love, for the very first time. Close, judged Elke: close but not a perfect comparison because in absolute honesty she believed she had been slightly happier that day at Andernach.

Elke felt comforted, warmed, by the nostalgia and didn't want it to stop. It didn't have to, she decided, indulging herself. She could fill part of the day by retracing the river cruise to Andernach. Not to their hidden valley, not by herself. Just to the tiny town, possibly. She could have lunch there and still be back in Bonn by the afternoon: she didn't want to be away from Kaufmannstrasse too late. Otto might call.

To avoid his being seen at Nord-Stadt the plan was for Jutta to pick him up in her car closer in to town, outside the Schlosspark Hotel on Kurfürstenstrasse. It was a glorious day and Reimann decided to walk: he guessed how long it would take and arrived early. Jutta was on time to the minute and he stepped forward on the pavement at the sight of the approaching grey Audi.

'I've been looking forward to today,' she said.

'So have I,' said Reimann. What would Elke be doing?

Chapter Thirty-Seven

When they started to go along the river road Reimann realized that although he had been early and Jutta had been prompt they had mistimed their arrival, forgetting the car. All the obvious parks were full and they couldn't immediately find spaces in any of the bordering roads. Jutta grew increasingly angry and several times said 'Shit!' and hit her hand against the wheel in frustration, like a child whose special outing was endangered. She drove too quickly and too far along Rathenauufer before turning back on herself, returning towards the bridge. It was practically departure time when they located a place in a small sidestreet off Zweite Fährgasse: he ran ahead to get the tickets, leaving Jutta to feed the meter. Reimann was at the jetty, waiting impatiently, when she panted up. The ferry cast off the moment they boarded.

'Did it!' said Jutta, triumphant with small successes.

'Why was *this* ferry so important?'

'It just was.' Jutta knew the reply was illogical but she didn't care: nothing was in its proper place any more. Otto had superseded her, taken over. She wished she could enjoy being told what to do by a man, as other women enjoyed it.

The ferry was already packed, but he managed two seats outside on a starboard deck, the side upon which they'd boarded. They were jammed tightly together, touching from calf to shoulder. With the weather as hot as it was he found the closeness uncomfortable.

'I told you I wanted to say something,' said Jutta.

Reimann had forgotten. 'Yes?' he said.

'I want to apologize.' She *had* to learn to accept it.

'What for?'

'How I've been. For a long time.'

Reimann frowned, looking directly at her.

'I didn't mean it,' Jutta continued, before he could speak, hoping the explanation came out as she wanted. 'Not intentionally . . . But I realize what it must have been like . . . It just meant a lot to me, I suppose . . . do you understand what I'm saying. . . ?'

'I'm not sure,' said Reimann, doubtfully. Subservience was uncomfortable for her.

296

'. . . I didn't treat you correctly . . . regard you as I should have done . . .' Jutta struggled to a halt. She wouldn't – couldn't – tell him she'd regarded him as her intellectual inferior. Which he clearly wasn't, not any more, anyway. She said: 'It was a mistake and I'm sincerely sorry. And I'm sorry about that nonsense of following you to the restaurant, too. It was . . . I wanted to see what she looked like, that's all. I was . . . I *needed* to. It won't happen again. None of it.'

'Stop it, Jutta,' said Reimann, gently. 'I *do* understand.' He realized that she was mentally prostrating herself before him: he should feel something. So why didn't he?

'Forgive me?'

'There's nothing to forgive.' At least the operation hadn't been endangered. He wasn't sure about anything else.

'I love you. I want you to know that: know that I love you.'

She'd expect a matching reassurance. 'I love you, too.'

'I won't let it happen again . . . in the future . . .'

'Let's forget it.' Was it too late? he wondered. He had to change the subject, talk about something else. He didn't want to analyse their personal relationship. 'How's the flat-hunting?' It was the best he could manage.

Jutta seemed as relieved as he was to move on to something else. 'I've seen something at Niederdollendorf. An old property, not purpose-built. It's got an extra bedroom to what I've got at Nord-Stadt, but it's the same price as I'm paying at the moment.'

'Are you going to take it?' Niederdollendorf would mean further for him to go for their meetings.

'I've put down a three-hundred-mark holding deposit to keep it for a fortnight,' disclosed Jutta. 'As you said before, I'd better get formal permission.'

Reimann wondered if the Russians would refuse. It was a possibility if they'd gone to a lot of trouble wiring Nord-Stadt. 'What if they say you have to stay where you are?'

She'd had her head on his shoulder. She pulled away, to look at him, and Reimann was glad the warmth of her closeness was eased temporarily. Worriedly she said: 'Why should they? There was no insistence at the beginning.'

'It was just a thought.' There were too many people – most certainly too many yelling, scurrying children – on the boat. They had to sit with their legs tightly withdrawn to allow a constant stream of aimless wanderers to pass in front. Reimann thought it was like being on a

297

cattle barge, although he was not sure cattle were transported up and down the Rhine by barge. Everything else seemed to be.

'I'd argue about it,' Jutta insisted. 'I don't want to stay at Nord-Stadt any longer. I want to get out.'

Try harder, Reimann told himself: he had to try much harder to show he was interested. He said: 'Tell them it's my idea, as much as yours: more my idea than yours, if you like. Say I'm concerned there might be curiosity at my coming there too frequently.'

Jutta tugged at his arm, putting her head back on his shoulder, which he wished she hadn't, and said: 'Wonderful, darling! I'll do that.'

Wonderful, isolated Reimann: Elke's word. *I mustn't use wonderful any more. I mustn't do anything to bore him.* Reimann let the reflection run. Elke didn't bore him. He'd thought she would – expected that she would – because of her insular, enclosed life, but it hadn't turned out like that at all. Although he had to remain constantly alert, for all the obvious reasons, at the same time he never felt pressured or on demand with her: never, particularly, on those recent, do-as-you-want nights together at Rochusplatz. He'd felt very contented then: just being there together, doing nothing, needing nothing, often not talking, which he privately acknowledged to be a professional failing on his part. It was unfortunate her periods were becoming difficult. He'd have to keep on until she went to a gynaecologist to get the problem sorted out. 'What?' Jutta had been speaking but he hadn't heard what she said.

'Do you think they will object?' Jutta repeated.

'I don't know,' said Reimann. 'It was just something that crossed my mind.' Even sardines were packed in cans with more room!

'What are we going to do in Koblenz?' asked Jutta, eagerly.

God knows, he thought: during conversations with journalists in their Joachimstrasse bar there'd been talk of an excellent inn, but he couldn't recall its name. And then, abruptly, he did. Weinhaus Hubertus. Very old and full of hunting trophies. But they'd get to the city too late for lunch. 'Look around. Have a drink. Shop,' said Reimann, emptily. Why in Christ's name was he bothering with her? 'Definitely shop!' he insisted, pushing some feeling into his voice. 'We'll shop and I'll buy you a present!'

Jutta pulled away again, allowing some welcome coolness to come between them. 'What?'

'What do you want? Think of something you want more than anything else in the world!'

'You to be . . .' started Jutta and stopped, looking away from him, waiting for the rebuke. When he didn't make one she said: 'I don't know! I can't think!'

'You've got time,' he said. Hours, he thought. Although they were shaded from the direct sunlight by the jut of an overhanging deck above, he was too hot. They *would* arrive at Koblenz long after any proper lunchtime. He jerked his head over his shoulder, towards the mid-deck bar and restaurant. 'If we went in now we would be ahead of the rush. We could have a peaceful drink.'

'We'd probably lose our seats here,' Jutta warned.

'I'd be glad to,' said Reimann, pulling his legs tighter in to allow the passage of a raucous school group herded by a strained-eyed teacher.

'You're making the decisions,' Jutta accepted.

She got up and followed him into the enclosed part of the steamer. The restaurant was virtually empty, the tablecloths unmarked, the posies of decorative flowers intact in their vases, shining cutlery regimented in stand-to-attention lines. They got a table set just for two, still on the starboard side. Making the effort, Reimann ordered a bottle of sparkling wine. 'To celebrate our having a whole day together.'

Jutta's face clouded, which he hadn't expected. 'What about tomorrow?' she demanded.

It was a consideration Reimann had been putting off, although he'd known the question would arise sometime during the day. He said: 'I hadn't got as far as tomorrow yet.' It was a lie! An easy, callous lie! Of course he'd thought about tomorrow. He'd thought of telephoning ahead and getting back to Kaufmannstrasse in time to drive Elke to Marienfels, and letting the day develop however it did after that.

'Think about it,' said Jutta. Instantly, hurried, she said: 'I didn't mean it like that! I meant please!'

Pressured and on demand, thought Reimann. 'We'll have all day together tomorrow,' he surrendered, knowing he had to. He'd have to call Elke: they'd made no positive arrangements but he imagined she'd expected him back. The excuse of being delayed by the assignment would be acceptable enough.

Jutta was smiling over the table to him. She looked around, needlessly, and said: 'Is there anything to tell me today that I should pass on?'

Elke had seemed more forthcoming during the previous week, but it was an impression without any supportive facts. Why should he try to impress the bastards after the way they'd demeaned him at the last meeting? He said: 'Not yet. We'll talk again before you go.'

'Something special!' announced Jutta, momentarily obtuse,

reaching across the table for him. 'That's what I want as a present. Something special. Like a ring or a brooch or a bracelet!'

Not a ring, Reimann decided at once. He took her hand familiarly between both of his and, despising himself for the theatricality of the gesture, pressed it against his face to kiss it.

Which was how Elke saw them.

With her habitual precision, Elke had arrived at the ferry terminal by the Kennedy Bridge well ahead of time, the Volkswagen safe in a protective car-park, and had been one of the first to board. Knowing from the earlier trips with Reimann how to judge the sun, she got a seat on the port side, out of its direct glare, and for the first part of the journey sat looking out at the now well-known landmarks, smiling contentedly to herself as she let Reimann's voice echo in her head with his mocking commentary. And she'd decided, too, that it would be better to get into the restaurant ahead of the main throng. Which was why she'd turned, to see how full it already was.

She'd known she was mistaken at first. What else could she be but mistaken? There was the slightly distorted reflection from the window glass to be allowed for. And Otto was away from Bonn, working. So it had to be someone very like him; a look-alike, just as he was similar to someone else she'd known before. Except that it wasn't. It was Otto – *her* Otto – and he was sitting intimately holding between both of his the hand of a beautiful, immaculately groomed woman, gazing at her across a table with sparkling wine already opened, oblivious to anyone else.

There was an announcement of a stopping point, although Elke did not hear the name. She was not even, at first, aware of moving. She stumbled up, blindly, pushing frantically against the block of people which at first wouldn't part to let her through, her mind gouged of thought or reason or understanding, wanting only to get away; to get through these people and away from the horror of what she'd seen. She couldn't run, although she wanted to, along the narrow gangway: when she reached the jetty she continued on, not looking back, shuddering against what she was leaving behind.

She was well into the arrival area before she focused on the destination board.

She was at Andernach: *their* Andernach.

Chapter Thirty-Eight

Long afterwards, when she tried to recall it, Elke found there were long periods of that stumbled arrival at Andernach that she could never bring to mind, no matter how hard she tried. It was as if she had lapsed in and out of consciousness – which she decided to be the most accurate description – sometimes with half awareness, other times totally blank. She could remember the signpost and her thought of what the town and its hidden valley had meant to her. People. Too many people, as there'd been too many people on the ferry, getting in her way when she didn't want to be crowded by anyone: when all she wanted was to be away somewhere, in the open, with no one around her. A shout and maybe a car horn, she wasn't sure, not where she'd carelessly crossed a road but where she'd stopped, suddenly unable to move, in the middle of a street. A hand on her shoulder there, words she couldn't hear. Then she was at a café, at an outside table: a waitress, not polite like Clara, but impatiently demanding what she wanted when she didn't know, couldn't think. Walking, trying to get away again although she didn't know where. Quiet at last. A near-empty street and a building she didn't recognize at first, needing time to realize that it was a church. The memories became better, more coherent, now. There'd been the instinctive movement, to go in, just as quickly halted. The first positive thought. *There's nothing inside a church for me: no help. Never has been.* Looking around, trying to find herself. She'd been climbing a hill, the tiny township displayed for approval below her, tied with the sparkling ribbon of the Rhine. Another positive, repeated thought. Their place: it had been *their* place. Not any more. What was theirs, any more?

The second café was quite clear in her mind. Pink tablecloths and lights supposed to be candles which weren't, and a strutting, look-at-me teenage waiter with a ring like a skull on one finger. She drank brandy, which she rarely did. Two. And thought.

She felt empty, hollowed out. And remembered, immediately and bitterly, that she was anything but that. Which added to the hopeless despair. She didn't think, at that time, she'd ever fully be able to comprehend the betrayal, the depth of deceit. Wasn't truly able, much later, after so many other things had happened, some of which she was never to learn. Wouldn't have wanted to learn. He hadn't had to tell her

301

he loved her: make her sincerely believe it. Make her love him, too, with all her heart and all her being. It was all she had ever wanted, ever dreamed of. Being loved. And loving back. Having someone, always. Being safe. Which she wasn't, not any more. He'd cheated. Lied. Humiliated her. He hadn't meant any of it – couldn't have meant it – not the caresses or the tenderness or the kindness. Had he laughed at her, amusing himself, thinking how pitiful she was? Had he said the same, cheated the same, lied the same, with the other woman? Had he fucked (*our word, darling: don't be shy. Say it*) her the same? Taught her all the tricks, all the excitements, made her want it every time and made her come every time? Made her pregnant?

What was she going to do? She didn't know, couldn't think, not about that. She could look backwards, with all the recriminations, but not forward, not yet. Still too much to absorb, fully to understand. Why had he done it? *How* could he have done it? She hadn't cheated or lied to him. Humiliated him. She would never have done anything to hurt him, to cause him pain. All she'd ever wanted to do was please him. And she was sure she had. She'd never argued to defeat him: just sometimes to express a contrary point of view, trying to help and guide so he wouldn't get letters threatening him with dismissal. She'd always let him make the decisions, content to follow. Never objected to any innovation or experiment in bed, although at first she hadn't liked or enjoyed some of them, not the way she did now. *Had* liked and enjoyed, she qualified. So *why*? There was nothing more she could have done, no way she knew that could have made him happier. *Why?*

The strutting teenager approached inquiringly, looking at her empty glass, and Elke thought: he thinks I'm a lonely but hopeful woman, out for adventure. Lonely, certainly. Again. But not looking for adventure. Not hopeful, either. Not any longer. She shook her head against a third brandy (why had she ordered it at all: she didn't even like brandy!), paid, and began descending the hill towards the town. To where? she asked herself. Not to any river craft. She didn't know what they were doing or where they were going, but she couldn't board any steamer or hydrofoil upon which they might be returning to Bonn, still hand-in-hand, eyes still held, love still obvious between them. So how was she going to get back herself? There was probably a train. Undoubtedly a train. But there were people on trains. Crowds. She didn't want crowds. How far was Andernach, from Bonn? Elke didn't know, only that it was obviously a long way. So a taxi would be expensive. But she'd be alone in a taxi, apart from the driver.

The man queried the destination and said it would probably cost more than a hundred marks. Elke said she didn't care. At the outset he tried to talk, offering professional companionship, but abandoned the effort when she ignored the attempt, scarcely answering.

Soon after they cleared the town Elke considered foreshortening the journey just slightly to stop at Bad Godesberg and throw herself upon Ida. That was the actual word that came into her head – throw – and it went towards her immediately changing her mind. She might need Ida's help with the other thing – to locate a good and discreet clinic in Cologne – but that was all. She determined, with sudden, even surprising resolve, that she had finished throwing herself at anyone. For help. Or for anything else. Whatever she had to do – decided to do – it would be by herself. Just herself. Alone. As she'd always been. Where then? She'd simply asked to go to Bonn, without a specific address. The car-park where she'd left the Volkswagen, she supposed: the Volkswagen that had brought them together in the first place. Then back to Kaufmannstrasse. Where else? There *was* nowhere else. Poppi wouldn't be there to greet her, not like he'd once been. No one. More alone than ever.

The ornate and castellated Schloss Marienfels was easily visible from the river highway. Elke strained beyond, trying to see the home in which Ursula would be, protected and secure, but the tree line was thick. If she could see the river from the institution, why couldn't she see the institution from the river? An inconsequential thought, she recognized: her brain was trying to ease the pain by intruding inconsequential thoughts. She didn't want her pain eased. She wanted to confront it, feel it, dissect it, understand it: to answer the recurring question. Why?

Not good enough, she told herself, attempting just such an answer. Although she'd thought she was doing everything right, everything he wanted her to do, the explanation had to be that she was not good enough: that she was inadequate. Hadn't she always feared that – known that – in her personal life? She was inadequate and so he'd gone elsewhere, to get what he couldn't find in her. But *what*? Why hadn't he talked to her? She'd have done it, whatever it was. All he would have had to do was to tell her! That's all.

She *wasn't* inadequate! How the hell could she be, elevated to the position she held, trusted and respected as she was? Known and acknowledged by the absolute leaders of her country when possibly her country was the most important – definitely a leader – in the world.

How else could she attempt to rationalize it, to comprehend? By more self-critically examining their relationship, perhaps? She and

Otto *weren't* engaged: hadn't discussed marriage, ever. So there was no commitment between them: no absolute loyalty he had to observe. He might have conveyed the impression that there was an understanding – misled her, which wasn't as bad as outright lying – but he still hadn't been bound to her, by a promise or a betrothal. Where was this avenue leading? To a choice? Elke's examination deepened. If Otto was undecided – trying to choose – then surely she was the favourite! Didn't he spend more time with her, during the week and at weekends, apart from the two most recent ones? Unquestionably. And some of his absences *had* to be genuine assignments. Lessening the other woman further. Elke didn't like the idea of his choosing, of his making a constant comparison between herself and somebody else, but there was a surging reassurance in the speculation. It would mean, if it was correct, that she hadn't lost him, not completely. Just that he wasn't sure. That didn't satisfy her completely, either, because he'd categorically said he loved her, but she could accept it. Learn to forgive him, if that was all it was – nothing more than a last-minute uncertainty.

The counter-balance fell upon her, so heavily that it was like a weight she could feel, pressing down upon her. How could she? How could she think as she had been thinking, criticize as she had been criticizing, even come close to contemplating the change from love to hatred! What about her? What about her having an illegitimate child by a man who had abandoned her? What possible grounds did she have, to sit in judgement upon Otto? She had complete recall of that night, which had begun so dreadfully – so dreadfully in her frightened mind – and ended so wonderfully. *I have a baby . . . no . . . a daughter . . . wasn't married . . .* Maybe she'd missed out some of the stumbling words. It wasn't important. What was important was how he'd reacted. Elke had the greatest clarity of all about that. *Oh, my darling. My poor frightened, innocent darling! Did you really think it would mean something? Upset me or offend me even . . .* And more, so much, so beautifully more. *You want to know how I feel? I feel angry, that a man could have treated you like that. And sad, because Ursula is as ill as she is. But happy: selfishly happy, because if you'd got married then we probably wouldn't have met. And I think meeting you is one of the most important things that's ever happened for me . . . I love you, Elke. I love you very much.*

How could she doubt – criticize or even imagine hating – a man who could say things like that, respond instantly like that? Elke hunched in the back of the speeding taxi, overwhelmed as quickly as most of her emotions had come that day by a feeling of shame. She had a right to be upset. To be hurt. But no cause – no justification yet – to be as devastated as she'd been, seeing them as they were. So he wasn't sure. She could accept that: better he allay his uncertainty now than later. She was still the favourite: still the one he spent most time with. With a further mental contortion, a gymnastic backward somersault of a waverer seeking conviction, she assured herself she was positively glad at the discovery of another woman. Now she *knew*: she knew she had competition and that she had to fight it. And win. It was natural for any man to be unsure about marriage: one unsure man had even run out on her before. But she would win this time. She'd fight, do whatever she had to do, however she had to do it, to keep him. Wasn't inadequate. Maybe she had been, once. Not any more. She'd grown to be in charge of herself. Confident. Sure of what she was doing, where she was going. Sure what she was going to do. *I don't intend letting anyone else have him. Not ever.* To whom had she made that insistence? Ida. And she'd meant it: meant it more deeply, more strongly, than she'd ever meant anything in her life before. She couldn't lose: not again. She could be hard enough, when the situation demanded: very hard, quite relentless. There was a momentary dip, a flutter, in her conviction. She wished so fervently he hadn't done it: that he hadn't presented her, unknowingly, with something for which to forgive him. Before he had been perfect but now he wasn't.

The taxi began entering the familiarly small streets of the familiarly small capital, and Elke came forward in her seat, explaining at last that she had a car to collect and directing the driver to the park. The fare came to a hundred and sixty marks and Elke gave him a fifteen-mark tip, which only left her with twenty marks. She got into the Volkswagen but made no attempt to start it, held by a further consideration. In Andernach, badly shocked (and maybe affected by the brandy) the possibility of seeing them together again had been anathema, utterly impossible. But after the reflection and conclusions in the homecoming taxi her attitude switched completely. She *wanted* to see them again: to see them together, to try to gauge their feelings. Old romance, new romance? Close or distant? Loving or bored? And to see her, the woman. There *had* been a backwards reflection from the ferry window, distorting any detailed impression. Sophisticated: a grey or possibly green V-necked sweater. Long fingers – fingers that had been held between his. But that was all. So she needed to look again. She needed to be able to guess an age. And whether she was truly beautiful, big-busted, trim-figured or sagging. How she walked. How she held herself. And other things she couldn't think of, not at that precise moment.

305

Elke left the car where it was, walking once more to the KD German Rhine kiosk below the bridge to get a timetable of the cruiser and hydrofoil service, to plan her amateur observation, which appeared to her to be quite simple. There was a high and walled park area directly adjacent to the river edge. She climbed the steep steps and realized, as soon as she reached the top, that it gave her a vantage point she hadn't at first imagined, a high elevation from which she could see far down the river, spotting the vessels long before they pulled alongside, giving her more than sufficient warning.

It proved to be a long and frustrating wait. Elke checked four crowded, bustled arrivals, straining for just two people, and became worried when the light began to dull that it might become dark and make her identification difficult, if not impossible. It wasn't. She picked out Otto Reimann, a figure she knew so well, long before the steamer even pulled against the jetty. Tightly alongside, clinging proprietorially to his arm, was the woman, uninterested in anything around her, gazing up at him with absolute concentration. As Elke watched the woman said something and laughed, her hand on a brooch at her left shoulder, and Reimann laughed back. The woman held up her face, so that her neck was stretched taut, and Reimann bent slightly to kiss her.

Now that it had happened, now that she had seen them, Elke didn't know what to do next. She remained staring down, experiencing a different sensation from that first sight on the ferry, but something very similar: the same tingling-skinned numbness and some clinging disbelief, but mostly hurt, terrible hurt, because there was the confirmation of everything displayed down there directly in front of her eyes. She couldn't remember any of the calmer reasoning or objective resolve that had seemed so sensible in the taxi on the way from Andernach.

Far below, Reimann and the woman disembarked and began walking slowly – the slow walk of long-time lovers – parallel to the river. There was another automatic movement from Elke, as there had been on the steamer. Without positive awareness she found herself going quickly out of the grassed area and down the steps, towards the river. When she reached the bottom, entering the throng of disembarking passengers, she was just able to pick out Reimann far along the road. Unaware of the concealment the other people might provide, not ever considering the possibility of Reimann turning and maybe recognizing her, Elke set out in pursuit. Was she pursuing them? The conscious thought entered her mind, with another quick to follow. What would he do if she caught up and confronted them? Would he remain composed, as he always seemed composed? Introduce the woman and explain? Or become confused, flustered? Composed, decided Elke: she couldn't imagine Reimann ever losing control of himself. What about her? What would she do, if she confronted them? What *could* she do? No engagement, no understanding, no commitment, she reminded herself again. So there were no demands she could make, no explanation she could insist upon. Elke shook her head, actually making the gesture as she continued on: she couldn't pursue or confront.

Ahead of her they went out of sight as they turned into Zweite Fährgasse. Elke missed their doing so and tried to go even faster, unsure what had happened. She got to the junction in time to see Reimann and the woman go into the minor street and stop at a dirty grey Audi car. Elke halted too, still on the river road and protected, although she still didn't consider the advantage, by the passing people and a clump of ornamental trees. She saw the woman take something from the windscreen and wave it, laughing still, at Reimann. A parking ticket, Elke guessed. The woman made as if to throw it away, but Reimann called out something and instead she put it carefully into her handbag. She appeared to have difficulty unlocking the car door and Reimann went around, doing it for her. As he did so, the woman offered her face again and Reimann kissed her once more. Inside the car he sat with his arm around the back of her seat. Absurdly the Bonn registration of the Audi – BN-278 – seemed like a taunt to her: without knowing why she was doing it, Elke scribbled the number on the back of her chequebook, looking up in time to see the vehicle take a far corner and disappear.

So what were the answers to her earlier questions? An old romance, she decided: settled, comfortable, each sure of the other. Close then. Loving. Everything she hadn't wanted to see: hadn't wanted to infer. *Won't* lose, she determined once more: *couldn't* lose. She could be hard, if she had to be: harder than anyone would ever guess.

Elke never really bothered to calculate how long it took her to work things out (or hopefully begin to work things out), because periods of time didn't seem important. The ideas came disjointedly, hardly ideas at all: just bits, floating driftwood she snatched at to try to keep afloat. It was a fitting analogy, because several times that first night her chest became tight and she had a panicked, suffocating sensation that she imagined to be just like drowning. Once, succumbing to the self-pity she was trying constantly to avoid, she decided that if she had been drowning she would have let herself go, *to* drown.

307

Discovering who the other woman was became important to her, although the desire wasn't accompanied by any reason or intention beyond finding an identity. Briefly – too briefly – she became excited at the thought that the name might show the woman to be a relation, a sister perhaps, until she remembered Reimann didn't have any surviving family and the driftwood sank beneath her. Elke couldn't think of a way to find the name and then believed she could: it would mean meetings she'd wanted to avoid, but the importance of one outweighed the disadvantage of the other and she was sure she could carry it off, just for one encounter. She'd already decided to tell Ida soon about the missed period, after all.

Ida sounded vaguely surprised on the telephone but agreed at once to her calling in to Bad Godesberg the following day, on her way back from Marienfels.

'You *and* Otto?' queried Ida.

'No!' said Elke, regretting both the quickness and the tone of the rejection.

'Oh?' said Ida, at once. 'Something wrong?'

Damn! She'd have to do better than that: far better, because it wasn't just Ida who had to believe she was still idyllically content. Elke said: 'No, nothing's wrong! Otto's away: working.'

'Just you then,' accepted Ida, reassured. 'The kids will look forward to it.'

For most of that night, except perhaps for a couple of hours when she fell into a half-sleep, Elke lay open-eyed in the darkness, her hand frequently straying to that side of the bed where he normally lay, the reflections jumbled and confused. Why didn't she tell Ida tomorrow: there didn't really seem any purpose in waiting for a doctor's confirmation. Quite simple. *You're not going to believe this, but it's happened again!* Too glib, as if it didn't matter. Get it sorted out this time. Quickly, no nonsense. Have to fix leave from the Chancellery this week. Not definite dates: necessary to make the clinic reservation first. But warn Günther she wanted time off. Say she was sorry if it was inconvenient but she had to have it. All over in a month. Sooner, if it were possible. Where had they gone, the woman and Reimann? Not Andernach, certainly. But did he know another hidden valley, at another stop, where he'd served quails' eggs and champagne? Bastard! Elke blinked in the darkness, shocked at the word, which had been a long time coming. Was that how she really felt about him? Yes, she decided. He'd cheated and lied so he was a bastard: whether there was

308

an understanding or commitment between them didn't come into it. Bastard. He shouldn't have done it.

Elke had bathed but not dressed when the telephone rang, startling her. Elke stare at it, not answering. It could be Ida, of course, but she doubted it. She could always check, from Marienfels. She didn't want to speak to the only other person it could be, not yet. She remained huddled in her robe, arms tight across herself, gazing at the receiver until finally the ringing stopped. She ignored it a second time, when she was almost ready to leave. Before setting out, she copied the car registration from her chequebook note.

At Marienfels she went impatiently through the greeting formalities with Dr Schiller, standing today before an overflowing vase of white and yellow lilies, which Elke didn't like because she always associated such flowers with mourning.

She didn't hurry or show any impatience with Ursula. The child was as Dr Schiller had warned, deeply enclosed, although she allowed Elke to take and hold her hand. Elke guessed that she would have been amenable to going out into the grounds, too, but Elke didn't try, not wanting to go out herself.

'Mummy's upset, darling,' Elke told the unhearing girl, the monologue beginning. 'We thought he was nice, didn't we? But he isn't, you know: not as nice as we believed. But don't worry. I'm going to think of something. I'm not going to let him abandon me, not like Daddy. Not again. Can't lose again: can't lose twice. That wouldn't be fair, would it? Not right. Mummy's going to work it out: think of something. You see.'

Elke left Marienfels slightly earlier than usual, and got to Ida's house by mid-afternoon. Ida had already arranged the chairs in the garden and Georg and Doris clustered around and kissed her, though she guessed they were disappointed Reimann wasn't with her. Georg openly said he'd got a book on American baseball rules, and Elke promised to tell Otto and suggest they try to play a game the next weekend.

'Where's Horst?' asked Elke.

'The dutiful writer is at his desk,' said Ida, disdainful as usual. 'He was disappointed Otto hadn't come. He wants to see you.'

And I want to see him, thought Elke. She said: 'Let's not disturb him yet.' The children were at the far side of the overgrown garden, well beyond hearing. 'What's the big news about Kurt?'

'We've decided not to see each other.'

The announcement was obviously contrived. Elke said: 'That doesn't sound right.'

'For a trial period,' Ida admitted.

'Then?'

'He's talking of leaving his wife. Wants me to leave Horst. To go away together permanently.'

Elke sighed. At the beginning of the year a declaration like that would have frightened her. She sought a response now; all she felt was irritation. 'Are you going to?' she asked. 'It's been a pretty long-running saga: you must have made your mind up by now.'

Ida frowned across the narrow gap between their lounging chairs. 'That wasn't quite what I expected you to say.'

It *was* a long-running saga and Elke was bored by it: bored and uninterested, although she was concerned about the children. But that was all: only the children. She said: 'All right, what do you want me to say?'

'You don't sound . . . well, not very sympathetic.'

'Sympathetic! What the hell are you talking about? You let a man grope your crotch, you fuck for most of the year, agonize around and around in circles about what to do, yet you still don't know what to do and I'm supposed to be sympathetic!'

'I'm sorry!' said Ida, tightly but loud-voiced.

'So am I, if I'm not saying what you want me to. I don't know what *to* say.'

'What's wrong? You're really angry!'

And not about you or Horst or Kurt or the children, conceded Elke. 'We've talked it all through before. You know how I feel.' She hadn't telephoned from Marienfels, Elke remembered. She said: 'Did you call me this morning, around nine?' There was an abrupt stab of pain, a definite jab, deep down in her stomach, and Elke winced.

Ida wasn't looking directly across the space between them and she missed the grimace. She frowned to herself, further confused. 'No. Why?'

'There was a call. I was in the bath.'

'Wasn't it Otto?'

'It might have been,' she said. Honestly she added: 'I don't know where he is: I couldn't call, to find out.' Had he been at Rochusplatz, with the other woman? Playing? Inventing?

'Are you all right?'

'Of course I'm all right! Why shouldn't I be?' Too defensive, too sharp, for a second time.

'You just don't seem . . . oh, forget it . . . it's not important.'

If only you knew, thought Elke. She'd apologize later: when she told

310

Ida and asked for her help. Elke felt a quick sweep of shame, at her hypocrisy. The pain came again, as sharp as before: she'd been lucky with the physical discomfort, apart from that one morning's sickness. She'd *felt* sick but hadn't *been* sick, not since. Elke said: 'It isn't such a difficult choice, is it? If Kurt means more to you than Horst – which he probably does – and the children, about which I don't know, then go away with him. Chuck it all up and go away and live on a desert island or a single room or wherever it is you think you are going to be happy.' She'd started out intending to be kind, but knew she had ended wrongly.

'You missed someone out of the equation,' said Ida.

'Who?'

'You.'

Elke shook her head, refusing the involvement. 'I don't feature in this; never have. Of course I'd be upset: miss you. But I'm not part of any consideration or doubt. Don't try to impose any responsibility upon me!' Wouldn't she miss Ida: wouldn't she miss the reassurance of her sister always being readily to hand? Those familiar demands: except that this time her reaction wasn't familiar. It was quite different, quite new. Always before she had been frightened: frightened of not having Ida, not being able to depend upon her. Elke didn't have that apprehension any more. She felt she could survive quite successfully on her own. And *really* on her own: not even with Otto, if she didn't have to. Not that she wanted to try: didn't intend to try. Just *if*, she recognized. No self-pity! She was strong enough now to resist any self-pity: strong enough now to be independent of anyone.

'Is that what you think I'm trying to do? Build up so much responsibility that I shan't be able to go?' demanded Ida.

'I haven't thought about it so analytically,' said Elke. 'Maybe that's what you're trying to do. And if you are then it means you don't *want* to go, not truly: that you're just trying to ease your own conscience when you make the final decision and tell Kurt it's all over.' Elke was utterly indifferent to the conversation: for the first time ever she realized she couldn't give a damn about Ida or any of Ida's problems. All she wanted to do was to persuade Horst to help her and get back to Kaufmannstrasse. Would the telephone ring tonight? The stomach pain came again, several short snatches. And then the nausea, rising like a belch. Elke realized that she couldn't remember the last time she'd eaten. Not yesterday – that awful yesterday – apart from the morning apple cake at the Bonner. Nor today, either. She wasn't hungry; didn't think she could have eaten anything.

'You despise me, don't you?' challenged Ida, suddenly.

Don't! thought Elke: please don't! She said: 'I despise the agonized prevarication.'

'Didn't you prevaricate, once?' said Ida, with rare venom, wanting to wound.

Elke didn't feel wounded. 'Once,' she admitted. 'Not again. *Never* again.'

'I hope you don't have to go back on that,' said Ida, bitterly.

'Yes,' conceded Elke, in complete and firm control of herself. 'I hope I don't, either.'

A chilling silence, like a block, descended between them. Like so much else it would have upset Elke a few months ago: that afternoon there wasn't the slightest discomfort. The children called and waved: neither Ida nor Elke heard the words. They waved back. Ida said: 'They know, about Horst and me. That we don't get on.'

'Good,' said Elke. 'It won't be so much of a shock for them if you decide to run off with Kurt, will it?'

'You have something to tell me?' demanded Ida, presciently.

'No.' The denial came out at once, quite definitely. 'Why?'

'You don't seem yourself.'

'I'm fine.' That was a lie that was going to be exposed in a very few days. Elke became anxious to get away. 'You said Horst wants to see me?'

'I'll call him.'

'Don't bother. I'll go up. And then I think I'll go.'

'Yes,' Ida accepted, making no effort to detain her.

Elke shouted her goodbyes to the children as she went into the house, shouting again to warn Kissel that she was on her way as she climbed the tattered, frayed stairway. He was at the bedroom door to meet her, gesturing her inside. The table at which he obviously worked looked as if it had just settled after an explosion.

'I was hoping Otto would come today,' announced Kissel.

'He's away, working.'

'I've finished another story I wanted to give him. Could you let him have it?'

A favour for a favour, thought Elke. She said: 'Of course.'

Kissel handed her an unsealed envelope and said: 'I think it's one of my best. They've accepted every one, you know?'

Elke did, from the regularity of the loan repayments. 'So I understand.'

'You'll see he gets it soon, won't you?'

312

'As quickly as possible.' Then she said: 'And I'd like you to do something for me.' She offered Kissel the paper on which she'd copied the Audi registration, from the scribbled note on the back of her chequebook. 'Could you find out the owner of that car? It's an Audi. Grey. I don't know the year of manufacture.'

The man frowned. 'I don't have any connection with vehicle registration,' he protested.

'But you must know people who have at the national traffic registration office in Flensburg,' persisted Elke, determinedly. 'You *could* find out, as a favour, couldn't you? It wouldn't take more than a telephone call to a friend you could ask.'

'Why do you want it?'

'A very minor traffic thing,' she evaded easily. 'Not a drama, like before.' She spoke looking down at the envelope containing Kissel's latest story, an obvious reminder of his indebtedness.

'It would be strictly against regulations,' said Kissel.

'I haven't told Ida I'm asking you. Or Otto. It would just be between the two of us.' She didn't want to remind him of the money.

'Couldn't you get it through the Chancellery?'

I don't want to be personally connected with the inquiry, you stupid bastard! She said: 'I thought you would know better than me how to go about it.'

'I'll try,' undertook Kissel, grudgingly.

'It's really quite important to me.'

'I'll call you tomorrow.'

Elke indicated the telephone number also on the paper she had given him. 'That's my Chancellery number: call me there during the day.'

She drove slowly back to Bonn, the stomach pain and sickness more persistent. At Kaufmannstrasse she swallowd some analgesics, wondering if she could keep them down, relieved when it appeared she could. She should eat something, she told herself. Elke actually opened the refrigerator, frowning in, attracted towards nothing. She was closing it again when she saw the opened bottle, in the door recess. She poured herself a glass, carrying it back into the main room. The envelope she had collected from Horst lay on the coffee table where she'd tossed it as she entered. She picked it up, put it down and picked it up again. It wasn't a private communication, something that was none of her business. If it hadn't been for her, Horst would not have met Otto and developed the extra source of income in the first place. The envelope was unsealed, even. And didn't he intend it to be read by thousands of people when it was published? Elke read intently, not hurrying, carefully replacing the pages one on top of the other as she completed them, her wine forgotten.

She was so absorbed, in her impressions as much as in the story, that at first, incredibly, she did not realize what was happening. It was the worst pain of all, pulling her forward in the chair, that was her first awareness, and then she felt the wetness, a lot of wetness. Elke groped upright, still bent forward by the pain, and staggered tight-legged towards the bathroom, suspecting the mess she was making. She was haemorrhaging badly by the time she got there, her skirt and underclothing deeply stained. For a long time she crouched over the toilet bowl, whimpering at the pain but most of all at the fear, not sure if she should try to get back to the telephone to call a doctor. Slowly she stripped her clothing off where she sat, seeing it was all ruined, dampening a small hand towel from the wash-basin alongside to try to clean herself. She wasn't very successful but it was better.

Gradually, too gradually, the pain began to ease and the flooding too, although for a long time that was imperceptible as well, so she remained where she was, too frightened to move. She felt very weak, her legs trembling under her weight, when she finally tried to get up. She did so only briefly, just to get a tampon from the cabinet. She had to clean herself again after even that little movement, and realized a tampon wasn't going to do it. Sitting once more, she fashioned a thick pad from a larger towel, holding it to herself until she could put on fresh underwear to keep it in place. She wrapped the already stained clothes in the earlier towel and bundled them into the corner of the bathroom, to be disposed of the following morning. Whimpering again, this time from the sheer effort, Elke swabbed clean the floor in the living-room and bathroom: she had to stop frequently, staying kneeling as she was, when dizziness swirled around her. Once she recovered to find she had toppled sideways, and supposed she had momentarily lost consciousness. Her stomach still ached but there was no nausea. She decided against calling a doctor: she could manage by herself.

She was laying another towel over the bedsheet, for additional protection, when the telephone rang. Elke hesitated and then groped towards it.

'Where have you been? I've been worried as hell! I called several times today when I thought you would be home!'

'I left early for Marienfels. Then I called in to see Ida.'

'Your voice doesn't sound right. What's wrong?'

'I'd already gone to bed: was almost asleep. My period's very bad this time.' The contradiction screamed in her head. Not my period! I've just miscarried: miscarried your child while you were fucking someone else!

'Would you like me to come round?'

'No!' The weakness of her voice took away the force of the rejection.

'Tomorrow?'

'I'll come to you, at Rochusplatz.'

'You're sure I can't do anything?'

'Positive.'

In bed Elke curled practically in an ironic foetal position, because it made the pain better. And cried. There was no specific reason: no one thing that filled her mind, for her to focus on. It was everything: she cried bitterly, uncontrollably, about everything. Everything and nothing. Maybe nothing – having nothing – most of all.

The following afternoon a subdued Horst Kissel called Elke's Chancellery number and said the grey Audi, number BN-278, was registered in the name of Ms Jutta Sneider. The address was in a block of apartments in the Nord-Stadt district.

'It wasn't easy,' Kissel complained.

'But you did it, didn't you?' said Elke. She believed she could understand her sister's indifference to the man.

Chapter Thirty-Nine

He'd always prepared, made her think for months that every time they met was special, but she had the feeling tonight that he'd prepared more carefully – tried harder – than before. The glasses were out, the wine opened, the flowers displayed, a soft, beguiling orchestral movement already playing. All so welcoming: welcoming and loving and intimate. All so false. Reimann held her close to him – although careful again, not too tightly – and she made herself hold him close in return. She made herself kiss him back, too, with the same fervency. He kept an arm around her shoulders, walked her to a chair and settled her. As he did so he knelt at her side, which Elke considered to be taking the supposed attentiveness too far. He retained her hand, as well. He'd held the hand of a woman called Jutta Sneider like this, Elke thought. With which of them did he practise?

'You should have let me come last night.' He'd wanted to – almost insisted upon doing so – because of the way she'd sounded. And he should have done, ignoring her refusal. She appeared wan, pale-faced: unsteady on her feet, even. He didn't like her to be as frail as this. The feeling wasn't professional.

'I didn't want you to.' She'd expected to be more repelled, more resistant to any contact with him than she was. She'd actually enjoyed his touch, wanting it. Wouldn't lose, she reminded herself.

'I've been with you before when it's happened. A lot of times. I could have looked after you.'

Elke refused the conversation. Instead, things arranged in her own mind, she said: 'How was your trip?'

Reimann got up from his kneeling position, shrugging. 'All right.'

'Are you worried you didn't get what you wanted?' It was a serious question, but cynically Elke recognized the ambiguity.

The opening he should take, Reimann recognized: curiously, inexplicably, he was reluctant to seize it. He did so, however, but with effort. 'It's still not complete: I've got the financial figures and statistics but I'm still short of the political background to fit it all together.' He'd told her he was going to Frankfurt, to investigate the financial pressures and uncertainties caused by the changes in the East.

'Where did you stay?' asked Elke, another rehearsed question.

'The Steigenberger,' replied Reimann, at once. She looked positively ill, which she hadn't at other times, no matter how bad her period.

'You didn't tell me, before you left. I could have called you. Just to talk.' She could expose his lie, by checking with the hotel. But why should she waste a telephone call? She knew already that he was lying.

'I didn't think: I'd hoped it wouldn't take me as long as it did. And I did try to call you.'

So Jutta Sneider was a good fuck, worth staying with. Elke said: 'We shouldn't do that again. I'd like to talk to you, when you are away.'

'You're right,' Reimann accepted. He'd find an escape, when the moment came. But he didn't want to do that, either. Not cut himself off from her. The reflection unsettled him because it wasn't the sort of reflection he should have had.

'Did you have a good time?' It was a question Elke had particularly planned, and she asked it intent upon his reaction.

'A good time!' echoed Reimann, bemused. He nevertheless considered the question, answering it for his own satisfaction. No, he decided. He hadn't had a good time: the entire weekend had been an ordeal, from beginning to end. He'd feigned and faked everything: affection, interest, consideration, sex. His only interest had been how quickly time would pass, so that he could leave. Aware of Elke's attention upon him, Reimann said: 'I was working, all the time. I ate – not very well – and worked and slept.'

'And you come back to find me like this!' tempted Elke.

'I've come back to find you unwell and it worries me,' said Reimann. 'I was thinking, while I was away. If it's going to be as bad as this we should get some professional advice. I don't want it to go on: I want it fixed.'

'It won't be as bad again,' said Elke. Like everything else, she'd worked that out. He was good at seeming genuinely concerned.

'You can't possibly know that,' argued Reimann.

'Let's see what happens next month,' said Elke. 'I'm not going to waste the time of a doctor or specialist unnecessarily.'

'Just one more month,' he insisted. He poured the wine at last, handing her a glass. Close to her again he said, sincerely: 'I missed you. I missed you like hell and could hardly wait to get back.' That remark wasn't professional either.

Maybe Jutta Sneider hadn't been such a good fuck after all. Elke said: 'I was lonely, too.' He was a superb actor, she decided. Or a superb liar. Obviously a combination of both.

He said: 'I guessed you wouldn't want to go out tonight.'

'No,' said Elke, quickly. Appearing to remember, she said: 'I saw

317

Horst yesterday. He gave me another story to pass on.' She took it from her handbag and gave it to him.

Reimann accepted the envelope without interest, carrying it across to his desk. It was cluttered, but in the manner of someone who worked, not like Kissel's, carefully arranged into chaos. 'I'll send it on tomorrow. He's becoming quite popular.'

'Have you got any here? Ones that have been published?' Elke asked him, knowing of the back copies stacked in a pile beside the desk.

As if responding to a cue, Reimann gestured towards the heap. 'Help yourself while I make us something to eat. It's trout. I didn't know how you'd feel so I took a chance with trout.'

'Trout's fine,' Elke accepted. A lot of things were working out fine.

By the time Reimann announced that the meal was ready, Elke had read five back copies. All had included articles under Reimann's byline, as well as Kissel's fiction. As always the meal was perfect, and she ate without any feeling of sickness, positively hungry. Reimann hovered constantly, trying to anticipate whatever she wanted. Elke decided against going back to the desk and the magazines afterwards, although she wanted to. Instead she sat on the voluminous leather couch while Reimann cleared away.

'Are you going to stay tonight?' he asked, returning.

'I didn't know if you'd want me to, as I . . .'

'. . . I could become irritated by your thinking that,' he cut in. 'I very much want you to stay.'

There were still some prepared questions. Elke said: 'Will you be going away again soon?'

'I don't know. I hope not,' said Reimann. He put out his arm, invitingly, and Elke settled into his shoulder. Again she enjoyed the physical contact.

'Any more rude letters? Or cables?'

He had to respond professionally, Reimann told himself, remaining reluctant to do so. 'Not yet,' he said. 'I'm frightened there will be if I can't provide the material they want.'

'You'll tell me if the pressure starts, won't you?' urged Elke. 'You never know. I might be able to help.'

'Help!' seized Reimann instantly. He was almost over the final barrier. All she had to do was part with one item – it wasn't really necessary on the first occasion for it to be particularly important – and the flow would start like water finding its way through a crack in a dam.

'Not by doing anything I shouldn't,' said Elke, in apparent correction. 'I mean we could discuss things, like we have in the past.'

That wasn't what she'd meant, Reimann gauged: Elke was drawing back from an over-commitment. He said: 'That would be helpful: I've found it extremely useful when we've done that.'

Was Jutta Sneider employed in any section of the government, Elke wondered. It was the source of substantial employment in the city, so it was a possibility. She said: 'So we'll talk if you've got a problem.'

'Definitely,' he promised.

Elke was glad, as usual at such times of the month, that he considerately let her go into the bedroom ahead of him to undress and put on a nightgown. She still needed the additional protection of a pad – a proper one she had bought that day – and as well as a supporting belt she wore underwear.

Reimann got into bed beside her, sighing with genuine contentment, stretching out a gentle arm to embrace her. 'It's so good, just being here next to you. I love you very much.'

Had he used such sentimentality upon Jutta Sneider, like everything else? wondered Elke. She decided he'd told several other lies that night: how many more would there be that she could isolate?

'Remember, I don't want her becoming suspicious.'

'She won't,' Turev assured Sorokin. 'Don't overlook her need to be the person in charge. She'll be flattered.'

'You're ready to wind up everything else?'

'Within hours of her arriving here in Moscow. A day after we've got her here there won't be a trace of Jutta Sneider ever having been in Bonn.'

'I hope you're right about Reimann's reaction.'

'I've timed his arrival in East Berlin to follow immediately.'

Chapter Forty

Elke was in a hurry to get all her decisions settled and established, although there was no definite cause for urgency in any of those plans. A meeting of the special committee was rescheduled for the Friday, with its inevitably increased workload, so she got a telephone recommendation from her regular physician and made an appointment with the gynaecologist early in the week. He was an urbane, grey-haired man with a pink polished face and the affectation of making towers with his fingers, which he collapsed at the end of sentences, to emphasize the finality of what he said. He listened to her account of increased difficulty with her periods and asked whether she was involved in a sexual relationship: without any of the awkwardness she would have shown so very recently Elke admitted, almost proudly, that she was. Under further, gently uncritical questioning she conceded that the relationship was extremely active, that she enjoyed it, but that it came after many years of total abstinence. When she said that, the man's fingers collapsed even though he wasn't talking himself. Elke insisted, again without any embarrassment, that there had not been any pregnancy alarms, reflecting as she did how easy it was becoming to lie. The consultation took an hour and concluded with her being prescribed a birth control pill which the gynaecologist assured her would ease the period difficulties in addition to providing the protection she obviously needed.

When she returned to the Chancellery Elke found waiting for her a letter of appreciation from the counter-intelligence department, praising her creation of a referencing system that had enabled their inquiries to be concluded so quickly and so satisfactorily. A copy was marked for Günther Werle, and attached to her original security letter was a copy of a personal commendation from Werle that was being recorded on her work file. When Elke thanked him, at their winding-up session for the day, the Cabinet Secretary said it was nothing less than she deserved to mark the efficiency with which she ran the entire Secretariat.

Among the other things waiting for her when she had returned from the gynaecologist was a message from the personnel directorate that there was no Jutta Sneider listed on any of the government employment records.

It had been Elke's insistence that they spend the second night at Rochusplatz, although not because of the continuing period discomfort which she let Reimann infer. Elke reached Nord-Stadt quite quickly, although it was more difficult locating the address she had for Jutta Sneider. The identification was helped by the Audi parked outside. Elke's impressions, at seeing the apartment block, were mixed. There were vaguely formed thoughts of the woman being outside and an idea of confrontation (instantly dismissed as foolish), but over-all it was a bizarre feeling of disappointment, which was more foolish than a confrontation. The block was cheap and tawdry, a crumbling place for crumbling people. Jutta Sneider hadn't looked cheap and tawdry during that snatched sight on the ferry, and later, walking along the river path. Elke waited, hopefully, for almost an hour but the woman didn't emerge. Elke didn't know what she would have done if Jutta Sneider *had* come out. Nothing, she supposed. What could she have done?

Reimann's greeting was as solicitous as she expected, and although Elke no longer had either discomfort or weakness she allowed him to prepare the promised meal. He ushered her towards the couch, but she went instead back to the desk, intent upon the magazines she hadn't got around to studying the previous night. This time she actually sat at the desk, the pages spread before her. Once, coming into the room from the kitchen, he asked her what she thought, and Elke, scarcely bothering to look up, insisted she was impressed. She'd read all she wanted by the time he announced dinner.

Towards its end, casually, he said: 'We're becoming quite a domesticated couple, aren't we?'

Elke hesitated and then, with her new-found attitude, became irked by her own uncertainty. 'I always thought to be domesticated people had to be married?' She spoke looking directly at him, holding his eyes for a change.

'Yes,' he said, returning the gaze unwaveringly. 'I suppose that's how it has to be.'

Why not go on? Elke thought; she'd never know now what, if anything, she had to lose. She said: 'And we're not married.'

'I know. Which seems quite wrong, don't you think?' What was he doing, saying? How could he encourage such a meaningless conversation? He was forgetting everything: professionalism, training, common sense, everything. It was madness! Stark, raving madness!

Elke regarded him warily across the table, searching for the right response. Was he telling her, clumsily but still telling her, what she

321

wanted to hear? That he'd been undecided, unable to make a choice, but now he had, and that he'd chosen her? That the previous weekend had not, in fact, been anything like it had appeared to be? That it had been the end of a competing affair, not a continuation of it? Cautiously Elke said: 'Maybe wrong isn't the way to think about it. Too protracted seems better.'

He couldn't retreat now, endangering everything. It was only words: always an escape. 'You're right,' he said. 'Too protracted.'

'So!' demanded Elke, unashamedly bold.

Reimann decided, anxiously, that he had to give himself time – space – but not for the one moment risk her guessing his avoidance. Training! he thought, summoning the proper reminders to mind at last. Training *and* professionalism. He had to use it, hide behind it. He said: 'I wouldn't – couldn't – consider asking anyone to marry me with all the uncertainty going on in Australia. That wouldn't be fair: not fair to you.'

'Shouldn't I be the judge of that?'

'No!' he said, forcefully, fully recovered. 'That's never the way it's going to be. I'll make the decisions, always.'

Surely he'd said it! But not properly. Determined now, Elke demanded: 'Are you asking me to marry you?'

Reimann sat utterly without expression or reply for several moments, so long that Elke began to regret her insistence. At last he said: 'Yes, I think I am. But when I say so: when I think it's right – safe – to do so.'

Safe, picked out Elke: the word that used to be so important to her. She felt momentarily lifted – exalted, as she sometimes had before with him – by the way the conversation had gone. He *had* chosen: he'd chosen her. Anxiously agreeing she said: 'All right. When you say so.'

Reimann smiled at her across the table, enjoying the moment despite its true emptiness. 'Is that an acceptance?'

'Yes,' said Elke. 'It's a very proud and grateful acceptance.' If he married her she could forgive everything: learn to forget all the unpleasantness in time.

Reimann was aware how Elke felt, so for a long time he let the evening drift, not wanting to spoil the mood he had created by announcing another absence, this time a genuine one. Turev's summons, through Rome, had arrived that morning. It was not until just before they went to bed that he said he had to go away again, hurrying the assurance that it did not have to be until after the weekend. They could go to Ida's on

322

Saturday if she wanted. And he wanted to go with her to Marienfels on the Sunday.

'How long away this time?' asked Elke, dully.

'Just a day,' Reimann promised. He couldn't guess the reason for being called yet again to East Berlin, but he was so accustomed to the trips by now that he knew he could get there and back without having to stay overnight.

'But we'll have the rest of the week together?' Elke pressed.

'I can't see you tomorrow night,' he evaded. 'I've got a column to write.' Jutta was leaving the day after tomorrow for Vienna: she could take with her his belief that Elke was about to cross the final divide with a provably official document.

Like so much else, Elke was never able, later, to find an explanation for what she did. So much about it was illogical. Coincidental, too: it made her hate coincidence. She was at Nord-Stadt by five-thirty the following evening, going there directly from the Chancellery. His Mercedes was already there, parked directly behind the Audi. Elke waited, her fragile, recovered happiness withering inside her, until midnight. The Mercedes was still there when she finally drove away.

She'd wanted to believe him: begged to believe him. But it had been another lie: the worst so far. And now she didn't regard Jutta Sneider as the only one. Who, Elke wondered, had sent the postcard from Rome that she'd read the previous night, discarded on the desk at Rochusplatz? The one that said *Looking forward to meeting again.*

Chapter Forty-One

Jutta had been off-balanced by the announcement, but pleasantly so, and now she was excited, impatient to get to Moscow, straining through the aircraft window for the first sight of the countryside below that she would know to be Russia. The fat man overflowed from the seat beside her, his arms and legs intruding into her space, and she was inhaling as much cigarette smoke as he was, which were further reasons for her wanting the journey to be over. There was never enough room in Aeroflot jets.

She looked towards the man and said: 'You must have some idea!' She'd shown the same insistence several times since they'd met, only a few hours before, in the glass-fronted café of the Sacher, in Vienna.

Turev shook his head. 'Just that you are to be given more responsibility: that things need to improve, as they did when you ran the operation more completely in West Berlin.'

Jutta identified the implied criticism of her husband. Loyally she said: 'It can't be easy . . .' She looked around the crowded aircraft. '. . . and I have some encouraging news, later.'

'That's good,' said Turev. He was relieved it had gone as smoothly as it had, without the slightest difficulty. He'd taken the precaution of having a well briefed four-man snatch squad close at hand in Vienna, not just to be ready there but to escort him unseen to the aircraft upon which they were travelling back to Moscow – here they were spread around the immediately adjacent seats. But there hadn't been any need for them and he was confident one wouldn't arise now. The silly bitch had reacted exactly as he'd anticipated, with the immediate conceited acceptance that there was some function for which she was indispensable. It wasn't going to take much longer for her to realize just how dispensable she really was.

'I assume I shall be remaining in Bonn?' asked Jutta.

'I really don't know. I told you: it's being handled at a higher responsibility than mine.'

'I want to change apartments,' she declared. 'I intended discussing it with you today, in Vienna. There won't be any objection, will there?'

'What's wrong with the one we found for you?'

'It's not safe,' insisted Jutta, the argument prepared. 'The walls are

324

too thin. And the complex isn't big enough: everyone comes to know everyone else. Otto doesn't think it's wise for me to stay any longer. We've talked about it and he told me to tell you.'

Turev nodded, glancing at his watch: they'd be landing in under an hour. Playing out the charade, the Russian said: 'Have you found anywhere else?'

'It's further out of the city than where I am now,' said Jutta, eagerly. 'On the other side of the river. It's bigger but the rent is the same.'

Turev realized, suddenly, that there was a reason to pursue the conversation: nothing could be left unresolved behind her. 'Have you entered into any contract? Made any definite arrangements?'

Jutta shook her head. 'I've just put down a small deposit, to hold it until I had a chance to talk about it with you today.'

No problem, Turev decided: she'd simply become a prospective tenant who'd changed her mind. Keep her happy for just a little while longer. 'I can't imagine there being any objections.'

Jutta looked down at the brooch Reimann had bought her in Koblenz, smiling at the recollection. It had been a perfect day, and he'd promised they could do something like it again, very soon. She was glad she had made the apology to Otto: settled their relationship on a better footing. How stupid she'd been, imagining any threat from someone like Elke Meyer, simply because the woman wasn't dowdy or unattractive. She'd get the move to Niederdollendorf arranged the moment she got back to Bonn: tomorrow if possible. She was sure she could do it in days.

The seatbelt sign came on simultaneously with the pilot's warning, and Jutta gazed through the torn clouds on the final descent. The countryside looked flat and grey and unwelcoming in the fading light of the day: it would probably look more attractive under a snow carpet. She'd obviously have to stay overnight. It was too much to expect that the opulent apartment on the Neglinnaya Ulitza would be made available, just for herself.

The arrangements were in place for their arrival at Sheremet'yevo. Turev led Jutta off ahead of everyone else, directly through a small building separate from the main airport terminals, and by so doing dispensed with any arrival formalities. Two of the Vienna escorts caught up with them as they entered the building, but Jutta did not recognize either of them from the flight. Having reluctantly imagined herself relegated to a secondary role, she was impressed – and encouraged – by this preferential treatment.

The curtained Zil was drawn up waiting when they exited on the other side of the building. Turev gestured her into the rear, following behind. There was a back-up car, although smaller, for the escorts.

'Are we going straight to a meeting?' Jutta inquired.

'Yes.'

The limousine gained the peripheral motorway that encircles Moscow and increased speed with the unrestricted freedom of an official car. Jutta sat with her hand nonchalantly through the courtesy strap beside her seat. If she was being accorded the luxury of a vehicle like this, then Neglinnaya Ulitza was certainly a possibility. She frowned at the sudden slowing, and then at the vast, modern building bordering the motorway into which they began to turn.

'Where is this?' she asked.

'Where the meeting is to be,' said Turev. Sure of his way through the huge building he controlled, he waddled urgently along a ground floor corridor, anxious to end everything: he'd got her back without any eruption of suspicion, but he'd felt himself under strain the entire time.

From long-standard design, the door outside which Turev halted seemed quite ordinary, with no indication of the steel lining or multi-locking securing mechanisms considered necessary for an interrogation room. Only when she was well across the threshold and Turev had come in behind her, sealing the door after them, did Jutta jerk to a stop, properly aware of the interior. There was only one window, high and barred, the opaque glass beyond wire-meshed and utterly without functional purpose, because daylight scarcely penetrated. Illumination, so whitely harsh that it was necessary for anyone inside to screw up their eyes against its glare, came from lights recessed fully into the ceiling behind glass again wire-meshed and unbreakable. Much of that ceiling and all four walls – again from standard psychological design – were white-tiled, and the floor was of white tiles, too, although slightly larger. The intentional effect was of a sterile, impersonal operating theatre: a place where men anonymous behind gowns and masks might carry out whatever exploration or experiment they considered necessary. There was a starkly functional table, again like an operating slab, in the middle of the room: to the left of the table was a tape recorder. Sorokin was already sitting on one chair: Turev went by her, to occupy the only other one, slightly to the side, leaving Jutta to stand.

' ... I don't ... this isn't ...' stumbled Jutta, completely bewildered.

Sorokin thrust out an impatient hand, starting the recording. The volume was tuned deliberately high, so the room was filled with the

326

argument between her and Reimann after she'd followed him to the Maternus.

Jutta gazed uncomprehendingly at the machine, unable in the first few moments fully to absorb all it meant. Then she said: 'You've had the apartment bugged, all this time!'

Sorokin ignored her awareness. 'Never go near them,' came his quiet voice. 'Those were your instructions. Never put yourself in any direct contact.'

'This isn't fair . . . not right!'

'No, it wasn't right,' Sorokin seized. 'Where was the discipline? Why?'

Jutta didn't respond to the question. 'There was no harm.'

Sorokin had the tape carefully marked. When he pressed the play button, the room echoed with Jutta's remark about wishing the Bonn operation were over. 'What's that mean?'

'It was a casual remark . . . nothing . . .' She came to a halt and then repeated: 'No harm.'

'Not that time. What about the next?'

'There won't be a next time!'

'I know,' said Sorokin. 'We're not going to allow you the opportunity. You became emotionally involved. Which could have put everything at risk. An operation of the highest importance: one that has taken months, years, to establish. All jeopardized.'

'That's not true! . . . it's ridiculous.'

'You've become an uncertainty. We can't allow any uncertainties.'

'What's going to happen to me?' For the first time there was fear in her voice.

'You'll be kept here, in Moscow, until we decide otherwise. We can't trust you anywhere else, certainly not until the Bonn operation is completed. Some function will be found, in one of the Directorates. Or a ministry, maybe.'

'I want to see Otto!' said the woman, with forced defiance.

'Don't be ridiculous.'

'He'll refuse to work, without me!'

'We'll see.'

'I love him! That's why I wanted to see her . . . I love him!'

Sorokin appeared genuinely surprised. 'What the hell has love got to do with anything?'

*

'We had to preserve the operation,' said Turev, in near apology, snapping the cassette from the recorder.

'Yes.' Reimann stared around the familiar room in the East Berlin safe house, waiting to experience some emotion. Nothing came. But why should it? He'd known they would hear: made no effort to get Jutta out of the apartment. He hadn't expected them to withdraw her, though. Or had he? 'I don't think she endangered anything.'

'She disobeyed a specific instruction. We can't take the risk.'

'I suppose not.'

'We expected more. We're surprised.'

'What will happen to her now?'

'She'll be given some work in Moscow.'

Virtual arrest, Reimann accepted. No need for bars or warders. 'How long will she stay here?'

'For as long as we consider necessary.'

'I see.'

Turev hesitated. 'Arrangements could be made, for you to see her. Not immediately: not today. But sometime in the future.'

What would there be for them to talk about? 'Thank you,' he said. He tried to identify the feeling and decided it was pure relief: he wouldn't have the perpetual challenge of Jutta any more: the nagging awareness of responsibility for her, the constant need to make excuses to get away and be with her. From now on it would just be himself and Elke. And the job he had to fulfil, of course, he reminded himself hurriedly; he shouldn't forget the job. He said: 'What about liaison, from now on?'

'Direct links between the two of us,' ordered Turev. 'It was a mistake to have included your wife at all.'

The fat Russian remained in the East Berlin house after Reimann left, waiting to be joined by Panin, who had witnessed and heard the entire exchange over the monitoring equipment.

'I thought there *might* have been a stronger reaction,' said Turev, although he allowed the doubt into his voice.

'I didn't,' said the psychologist. 'Otto Reimann behaved exactly as I expected. He's become the professional his wife used to be but isn't any longer. We were mistaken about her.'

'It's the only mistake we've made,' said Turev. 'And we've recovered from it completely.'

Chapter Forty-Two

Elke Meyer provided a document exactly one week after Reimann's East Berlin visit. And as she was handing it to him Reimann felt a surge of regret, absurdly wishing at the moment of his achieving his complete goal that she hadn't finally capitulated. Something of his reaction was visibly obvious, because Elke regarded him curiously and said she thought it was what he'd wanted to see, the precise layout and composition of a memorandum from the special Cabinet committee to guide his article on the interlocking of the two Germanys. Reimann had to call upon every ounce of inculcated expertise to cover his lapse. He assured her that it was *exactly* the guidance he needed to satisfy his demanding, dismissal-threatening editors, and promised that he would never utilize the contents so as to embarrass her, but would merely refer accurately to the format. It was a one-sheet paper, marked as a second copy for Cabinet Secretariat retention, and the moment he looked at it – moving his head to give the impression of being more interested in its layout than its brief contents – the bubble formed in Reimann's stomach at his immediate realization that it was sensational.

The memorandum was headed Eyes Only, which he knew to be the top security classification. It was entitled Future Intention on Unification/Federation, dated the previous week – while he had actually been in East Berlin – and was listed for circulation to all members of the special committee, each of whose names the Russians had already identified.

In full it read:

Options to be decided from previous private discussions and contacts with German Democratic Republic:
1   To support acceptance of GDR within European Economic Community as separate member state.
2   To support acceptance within European Economic Community of Poland, Czechoslovakia, Hungary and Romania.
3   To oppose acceptance into European Economic Community of GDR, Poland, Czechoslovakia, Hungary and Romania in favour of these countries becoming linked as separate trading partners.

329

4   To resolve, by whatever protocol necessary, the military presence and requirements of a united Germany within NATO.

'Will that help?' Elke pressed.

'Very much,' said Reimann. The fourth point itemized was *precisely* what he had been ordered to discover. And was electrifying: nowhere, before, had there been any mention of protocols.

'If you continue getting guidance like this, there won't be any danger of your being transferred from Bonn?' she asked, needing the answer. *I don't intend letting anyone else have him.*

Reimann stared directly back at her, but not for the usual reasons. Had she *really* guessed? Was this an invitation for him to declare himself completely, as she had committed herself completely by disclosing such a Top-Secret document? He had an overwhelming urge to tell her, to admit the truth so that he wouldn't be deceiving her any more, but again the expertise won. He couldn't take a chance like that based on just one, possibly ambiguous question, and a particular look on her face when she asked it. Later, perhaps, but not yet. Going as far as he felt able, Reimann said: 'If I go on getting guidance like this there'll be no possibility of my being transferred.' And then he waited.

So did Elke, for a moment. 'That's what I wanted to hear,' she smiled. She nodded towards the memorandum he still held. 'I have to return it in the morning.'

'I know,' Reimann accepted, unsure if he had handled the exchange as he should have done. That night, waiting until he was quite certain she was deeply asleep, he used the long-neglected Nikon camera with its copying lens for the first time.

The memorandum was greeted by the Soviets with the alarm Reimann anticipated. Sorokin travelled from Moscow to the East Berlin meeting following the one at which Reimann handed over the film. After quick congratulations came the fervent demand that Reimann obtain more: Sorokin actually admitted that policy decisions at the highest level were being formulated on the material that Reimann was now obtaining.

'It can only indicate *secret* protocols!' Sorokin said.

'I think so too,' said Reimann. 'This is the first indication.'

'We must have *everything*! Every negotiation we are having hinges on this information!'

'I realize that,' said Reimann. 'I'll get it.'

Sorokin hesitated. 'Your wife has been found work, in a Ministry.

We don't want you away from Bonn, not at a time like this. But you'll be permitted to visit her, soon.'

'Thank you,' said Reimann, mechanically. He'd loved Jutta once, he reflected. Or thought he had. But not any more. His attitude towards her was the attitude he would have had about a friend he'd once been close to and whose company he had enjoyed, but from whom he had drifted apart – someone he rarely thought about any more. Making himself confront his own behaviour, he recognized that he could have avoided what had happened to Jutta if he'd challenged her away from her apartment. It was pointless now, to recriminate. He *had* openly challenged her. Now there was nothing he could do to help her. She had never relied upon him, after all. Never depended upon him. Never included him – not *properly* included – in either her professional life or their married life. Friend, he thought again. That was absolutely what Jutta had been. They had been friends, not husband and wife.

'It will only be a temporary parting,' Sorokin assured.

'Of course.'

'We don't expect it to have any effect or influence at all upon what you're doing.'

'It won't have,' came Reimann's own assurance.

Life in Bonn with Elke actually settled – when they thought about it – into a pattern which satisfied them both. She spent more time with him at Rochusplatz than he did at Kaufmannstrasse. On the weekend of his return from the hand-shakes and congratulations, Reimann suggested alternating the habitual lunch, so Ida and the family came to eat with them. On that very first Saturday, while the men were across the other side of the room with a fresh contribution from Kissel, Ida volunteered quietly: 'I said no to Kurt. When it came to it, I couldn't abandon the children. But I'm not happy about it. In fact I'm downright fucking miserable, with nothing to look forward to except boredom.'

Elke wasn't happy about it either, not as she should have been after all the preaching. Just relieved, for Doris and Georg, who were also Ida's excuse. Elke decided that Ida was submerged in self-pity now. Everything had turned the complete circle: on the roundabout, off the roundabout, on – off, on – off. The thing to remember was never to become giddy: never to lose your head.

Despite the regular – *very* regular – absences, Reimann became even more attentive, which Elke had hardly imagined possible. There were always presents; flowers every week, music tapes she only had once to mention she would like, tickets for concerts or theatre productions she might have commented upon from advance publicity. Staying in –

usually at Rochusplatz – became settled as a preference, but they also went out, visiting every recommended restaurant not just in Bonn but in Cologne: the Maternus remained their favourite. Elke still carefully preserved that first-night rose within the pages of a poetry book.

They did not go to Marienfels every Sunday, as Elke had once done. The visits averaged once a fortnight, although there were occasionally longer gaps, but whenever Elke went Reimann accompanied her. Ursula appeared to recognize him, and was usually more amenable and easier to control in his presence. Once, at Reimann's suggestion, they tried to have her home at Kaufmannstrasse for an entire weekend, beginning on the Friday evening. The error, they later decided, was to include Ida and the family for Saturday lunch. Unlike the birthday party, so many people disorientated the child, confusing her. Despite the soothing, continuous tape music and Reimann's hours-long attempts to placate her, Ursula grew angry, resistant to everything, and particularly to sleeping on the Saturday night in the apartment. They did stay there, but no one had any sleep and Ursula suddenly began to cry, which was something she rarely did, whatever her mood. Early on the Sunday morning, because of her distress, they took her back to Marienfels. Reimann broke their silent return to apologize: it had been his idea and it had been a mistake. Elke told him not to be silly, that it was no one's fault. It was just the way Ursula was: would always be.

And the leaking of documents continued: increased, after that first time, and grew more sensational with each disclosure. There appeared to emerge a Cabinet committee concern to allay any Soviet objection or suspicion of a united Germany while at the same time continuing as an active NATO participant. Two documents actually referred to suggested protocols as secret. Five successive memoranda that Elke smuggled from the Chancellery were predominantly concerned with military planning. The last was an actual framework for the covert protocol. It recommended the presentation to NATO Foreign Ministers of a never-to-be-revealed proposal for the retention on German soil of all existing short-range nuclear missiles, together with the upgraded missiles being urged upon the Alliance by Washington. All the missiles were to be housed, however, in mobile transporters belonging to the armed forces of those other NATO countries, allowing a united Germany to claim that it had no knowledge of the transporters' contents.

An unspoken, unarranged understanding arose between Elke and Reimann. Always, after what he knew to be the day of a Cabinet special committee meeting, he would suggest staying in for the evening at Rochusplatz. Always Elke would agree. She would produce the papers, talking with intentional vagueness of guidance. He would read through whatever she offered, never showing excessive interest. That night he would keep awake, far into the night, until she slept. Only with the framework document did the photography take him longer than a few minutes. Within two days of copying the documents he would operate within the required time schedule and warn Elke that he had an out-of-town assignment to work on. Sometimes he did the round trip to Berlin within the day, leaving early in the morning and returning by mid-evening, so they did not have to be apart even for a night.

The regularity extended beyond his situation with Elke, to include his encounters with the increasingly frantic Russians. Never any longer was it a meeting with just the fat one. The balding, bearded man attended every time now, always demanding more, always insisting on the final, positive decision on the secret protocol which still, from what they understood, amounted only to a suggested proposal.

It was almost three months after Elke had first provided a document that the idea began to germinate in Reimann's mind. At first he considered it with positive amusement, seeing the nonsense of it, self-critical that so smoothly and so easily was everything finally working that his very reasoning was being affected, tilted off balance just as he had tried, so long ago now, to tilt Elke's reasoning and emotions off balance. But then he began seriously to reflect, although not upon all of it. Just the important parts, the parts that could – and should – be resolved. Jutta particularly. There was no purpose – and certainly no reason – for them to remain officially married. So why didn't he divorce her? He supposed it would be complicated, because of the particular and even bizarre circumstances, but the Russian authorities who were prepared to grant him any favour could sort that out: decide jurisdiction and arrange the formalities. He told himself at once that Elke Meyer formed no part of his consideration. All he was contemplating was tidying up a situation that needed tidying: sensibly freeing himself from an unnecessary, unwanted encumbrance. But not just like that: he wouldn't do it *in absentia*. He'd tell Jutta to her face.

At the meeting with Sorokin and Turev at which he delivered the paper suggesting consultation with NATO Foreign Ministers on keeping missiles in Germany, Reimann said: 'I'd like to talk soon about myself and Jutta.'

'We've other things to talk about first,' refused Sorokin

Chapter Forty-Three

'I never believed it,' said Sorokin, distantly. 'Despite all the expectations that there would be some subterfuge, I never really thought they
would do it!' He sat gazing down at the single-sheet document that
Reimann had produced, lost in thought. But they had to believe it, of
course. From the never acted upon but provably genuine Vienna
material they knew that everything that Reimann had provided was
authentic. The format of the Gerda Pohl documents, their creation and
even the wording accorded absolutely with the material leaked by Elke
Meyer: everything from Bonn was now being forwarded directly to the
President, with the impressions that Reimann gained from his
conversations with Elke forming a separate file.

'It's still only a recommendation,' warned Turev, cautiously. 'No
decision has positively been made, by full Cabinet.'

'Will it be?' Sorokin demanded of Reimann.

Reimann rarely hesitated any more, when asked an opinion.
'Inevitably, I would think,' he said. 'I'm sure of getting the decision,
when it's reached.'

'You've actually asked the woman?' Turev pressed.

'Not in any specific words,' sighed Reimann. 'I thought I made it
clear that's not how I work her. We've talked in general terms, and I
asked if this was a genuine proposal, or was Bonn trying to take a
stance, to impress the other NATO members? She says it isn't a stance.
And we know, from all the other material we have seen, that posturing
isn't the way the sub-committee operate. They're serious: they leave
the politicking to Bundestag debates.'

Sorokin smiled, nodding across the desk. 'I trust and believe you. I
think you have performed brilliantly.'

'Thank you,' said Reimann, too quickly, so that he cut the other man
off.

Sorokin was unoffended. '. . . Which has been recognized,' he
continued. 'I am authorized to inform you that you have been
promoted to the rank of colonel, within the Soviet service.'

'That's . . .' tried Reimann and stopped, not able to complete the
sentence. 'Thank you . . . I'm honoured. Gratified,' he finished,
inadequately. Why was it so difficult for him to feel any emotion about

anything these days? This was everything he'd ever dreamed about, from the days of being Jutta's dutiful subordinate – or had it been servant? – in West Berlin. This was the moment he achieved the proper recognition in his own right: his acceptance as a superbly professional intelligence officer.

Sorokin's smile dimmed, to become as near as the man could ever achieve to a sympathetic expression. 'And we can now start thinking of your making a visit to Moscow, to see your wife.'

'I would like that,' said Reimann, quickly. 'I've decided to divorce her. It's right that she should hear it from me.'

Sorokin's face changed completely, into a frown of curiosity. 'Why?' he demanded, shortly.

'It was never a completely successful marriage,' Reimann told him. 'There doesn't seem any purpose in continuing it.'

'That must be your decision,' said the Russian, still doubtfully.

'Do you have any official objection?'

'None,' said the man.

After Reimann had left, Turev said: 'It would seem we went to a lot of trouble for very little, trying to keep them together.'

'There was the point, in initially distancing any Soviet involvement,' reminded Sorokin. 'It doesn't matter, anyway. It's all worked out magnificently.'

Always, before, Sorokin and Cherny had met with members of the Politburo or of the Presidential Secretariat, but for this meeting the President himself took the chair and every member of the Presidential Council attended, as well.

'So we are being tricked!' the President accepted. 'But I don't want any miscalculation. Throughout the time this man has been in place in Bonn, obtaining this material, how many times has he been wrong?'

Confronted with the need for a positive statement, Cherny deferred to the KGB deputy. 'Never,' said Sorokin. 'Until we started getting actual copies of documents, the information has sometimes been incomplete. There was the need to interpret. But what has come from him has always been totally reliable.'

'So we can challenge them: defeat them! Would these transporters be difficult to monitor?'

It was a military question, posed to Cherny. The soldier shifted, uncomfortably. 'They shouldn't be: mobile missile carriers are tracked: highly visible from satellite reconnaissance. We could be positive, if we negotiated on-site inspection.'

335

'We can put NATO into complete disarray,' declared the President. 'And put a unified Germany in disarray, too.'

The move was made within a week. The Soviet Union dropped its demand for any Warsaw Pact link with NATO, and pledged within six months to withdraw all Russian military forces from the former Warsaw Pact countries, most particularly from East Germany. Such a gesture, the statement insisted, made quite unnecessary the continued existence of NATO and the need for US missiles or troops to remain anywhere in Western Europe. Therefore, every concession being offered by Moscow was conditional upon there being on-site inspection of any weaponry remaining in Germany. Timed to coincide precisely with the declaration was a further Russian statement at the Vienna Conventional Arms Conference of substantial across-the-board cuts in the Soviet Union's conventional weapons arsenal.

'We've given away nothing!' declared the President, at a full meeting of the Politburo. 'Whenever we choose we can disclose our knowledge of the secret protocol and show the West to be the aggressors. And keep our troops where we like and abandon any conventional weapon agreement.'

The same day Dimitri Sorokin was appointed chairman of the KGB. Nikolai Turev was confirmed as deputy. Anticipating the ironic comments about General Cherny's appointment as Minister of Defence in a supposed climate of demilitarization, a statement was added that Cherny's promotion was regarded by the Kremlin as being more political than military.

The NATO reaction was bewildered confusion, which had been Moscow's intention.

Elke Meyer attended the specially convened Cabinet session from which, at Washington's urging, no public communiqué was afterwards issued.

'Moscow are behaving as if they have knowledge that no one else has,' said Werle, after the meeting.

Chapter Forty-Four

It had been the conversation with the Russians that had made Reimann finally confront how he *did* feel about Elke Meyer. He'd known, he supposed, for several weeks: maybe several months. But there'd been a hundred different reasons to avoid even considering the absurdity of it: indeed, his initial feeling at the half-formed, shadowy possibility was one of positive astonishment that he could even be *thinking* like that. *Love* never entered the training or indoctrination of a raven. There wasn't a word powerful enough fully to express the nonsense of it. Despite which, despite all the self-warnings, he accepted at last that he deeply and sincerely loved her.

Reimann knew the precise moment when the recognition came to him: when he eventually let himself think the unthinkable. He was on his way home (which was how he now always regarded that part of the journey, returning to Bonn) from Berlin, looking down from about 25,000 feet at the scattered lights of unknown towns and villages of West Germany after the meeting at which he had disclosed the NATO decision. And began, logically enough, with his reflections about Jutta. There *was* no purpose in seeking any legal dissolution of his marriage: it was practically laughable for him, in intelligence parlance referred to as much as an illegal as a raven, to consider something legal! What he'd had – what little he'd had – with Jutta was over. Finished. He was a free man. Unencumbered, as he'd already decided.

Except that, still being legally married to Jutta, he couldn't legally marry Elke. After all the shadowy half-thoughts and avoidance the awareness – the true awareness that had set everything in motion in the beginning – came to mind suddenly and complete. He still tried to argue with himself, to produce more excuses and more avoidance. They *could* marry, of course. It had been little more than instinct to dodge the Russian's question. So well established was he with them now that it would be simple to argue that he would get more from her if he did go through the ceremony.

So did he want to?

Certainly – admitting it finally – he loved her. And she loved him. She'd never know the deceit at the beginning; the falseness with which everything had started, so there would never be the danger of her being hurt. They were virtually living together all the time, although they retained separate apartments. What were the professional dangers of their being together permanently in a situation where she was likely to become aware of things happening around her? There were the postcards from Rome, demanding contact. That could be simply resolved with a new meeting system: he could establish specific meeting dates and times and merely keep the card summons as the device with which to alert the Russians if he wanted to see them. What else? Nothing, Reimann told himself, positively.

So accustomed was he by now to the arrival procedure at Cologne that Reimann passed through with scarcely any consciousness of his surroundings, his concentration still absolute upon himself and Elke.

What about Elke? Every speculation, every consideration, had so far been from his viewpoint. If he cared for her so much, shouldn't he look from the other side, from Elke's side?

Reimann guessed she would move in with him permanently if he asked her, because she did whatever he wanted now. But he knew for them to live together wasn't what Elke really hoped for: what she really expected was for them to get properly, officially married. Which they couldn't do. Not properly. It would always be a bigamous union. But it wouldn't be the sort of deceit that he'd been showing, all these months. This was *for* Elke. For himself, as well, but it would make her happy, make everything perfect, for her as well. It could work, he determined, happily. *Would* work.

Or would it? Reimann was sure he could settle with Elke and create a home with her, and live without the lies he couldn't avoid becoming a barrier between them. And she would never know, never guess. But what about the time when the Russians decided, as they inevitably would at some stage in the future, that his usefulness – her usefulness – was over? Reimann didn't believe they would let him go: thank him for work well done in the past, accord him his colonel's pension to live upon, and let him retire contentedly in Bonn. They'd move him on. Or maybe take him protectively back to the dreary greyness of Moscow: back, even, to Jutta. What was he expected to do then, simply turn his back and abandon Elke?

No, decided Reimann, with even more adamant determination. Whether they were married or not he would never abandon Elke. He couldn't. Something else high on the list of unthinkables. So what was the alternative? There wasn't one. He *wasn't* his own master, able to decide his own actions and his own future. He couldn't be, never again.

He was a threadbare monkey on their organ grinder's box, dancing to a tune he couldn't choose.

There *was* a choice he could make. A nerve-stretching, gut-churning, frightening choice: the most inconceivably absurd fantasy of all. It would mean, eventually, his having to confess everything to Elke. To admit that he'd cheated her in the beginning, beg her forgiveness and convince her that he loved her and wanted to be with her forever. And then convince her further to quit the Chancellery and run with him, going somewhere where they'd assume false identities and false lives and hope the Russians would never find them to inflict the retribution they always did upon defectors. No, thought Reimann again, in another adamant decision. He could never ask Elke to do that: he could never expose her to that sort of physical danger, a danger far worse at every stage than that to which he had already put her by seducing her into doing what she was for him at the moment. And there was another preventing factor. How could she run – how could he ask her to run – with Ursula to care for? Elke would never do that: he wouldn't expect her to do that. Inexplicably Reimann felt his chest contracting, so that he had to force his breathing, like a poor swimmer suddenly out of his depth.

It had been a day of truthful acceptances, and at that moment Reimann objectively accepted the most gut-churning truth of all. He was trapped. Hopelessly and inextricably trapped. There was room to move, to exist – so there wasn't any cause to feel claustrophobic – but he was still incarcerated in a set of circumstances, a prisonlike maze, from which he couldn't possibly escape, desperate though he was to do so. And to think he'd once doodled Elke's name into the centre of a maze! The only real question he had to decide was how much further could he selfishly inveigle Elke into a maze from which there was no exit? Which automatically created another. Just how sincerely did he love her? Just how much did he want to protect and guard her?

Reimann telephoned the moment he got to Rochusplatz. 'Do you want me to come to you?' So very few months ago that would never have been a question; always she would have had to come to him.

'It's better at your apartment,' said Elke.

After she arrived, they'd kissed, and she'd said the piece of Meissen pottery was beautiful but that he shouldn't always buy her presents, Elke remarked casually: 'I was thinking today. If I'd had a key I could have already been here, waiting for you, couldn't I?'

She *wanted* to live with him. No professional danger, he thought again. Presenting another gift he detached a spare apartment key from his master ring. 'I want you always to be here when I get back.'

339

Elke tried to convince herself she *had* to have preference over the other woman if he was prepared to allow her access to Rochusplatz whenever she wanted. The others couldn't be permitted there at all, in fact. There were her spare clothes, always in the closet. And he surely wouldn't risk her unexpectedly entering if there was another woman there. Jutta Sneider didn't seem to be at Nord-Stadt any more. Elke had driven curiously by a total of five times now, looking for the tell-tale Audi: sometimes stopping for as long as an hour when she imagined the woman returning from whatever work she did. Jutta Sneider had never appeared. Neither had the Audi been there. Elke said: 'That's what I'll always be: here when you want me.'

'Which is all the time,' Reimann repeated. He'd never believed he could feel like this about anyone. It had certainly never been the feeling he'd known about Jutta.

'You wanted to know about the secret protocol,' said Elke. 'It's been adopted. I've brought it with me.'

It wasn't as difficult that night as it had sometimes been for Reimann to remain awake long enough to ensure that Elke was deeply asleep. He was glad he had eventually allowed the thoughts about their future: angry that he hadn't faced the reality of how he felt before now. It had been ridiculous, pretending for so long – and entirely for his own pointless benefit – that such reality didn't exist. He wasn't sure – didn't have a logical, reasoning clue, in fact – where the realization was going to lead. Everything was still far too confused and mixed up in his mind, point and counter-point. But he would sort it out. Not completely, perhaps. There were too many imponderables, too many difficulties, for his ever to resolve his life with Elke with complete satisfaction. But better than it had been, up to now. In a way to please her more; to make her feel more secure. And she *was* secure. He had to convince her of that, whatever happened. From now on, somehow, some way, he was always going to look after her. She was never going to be alone again.

Reimann did not hurry, knowing that he wasn't going to sleep that night and quite unworried about it. It was past three when he eventually, gently, slipped from Elke's side to walk soundlessly back into the main room. The Cabinet document was in her handbag. Reimann worked quickly, well practised by now with the Nikon and its special lenses, which for so long had remained unused in the drawer until these last few weeks. He smoothed the single sheet out on the desk beneath a pair of paperweights and a heavy stapler, to iron away the creases for as clear a negative as possible, then positioned and

340

illuminated the desk lamp directly overhead, not needing any more light because of the speed of the film he was using. He made six exposures, barely altering his stance because there was no need for a range of shots: all they wanted were the official words, printed out before him in a simple, five-sentence paragraph.

Satisfied, Reimann put out the lamp and before disassembling the camera replaced the copied document in Elke's handbag. He was back at the desk, putting the proxile lenses back in their protective boxes, when Elke spoke from the bedroom door.

'What are you doing?'

Reimann jumped, but decided at once that it didn't matter if she had seen the physical movement: it was understandable that she would have startled him. 'I couldn't sleep. I decided to get up in case my moving about in bed disturbed you.'

'What are you doing with the camera?'

'Putting the bits and pieces away, after the trip. I got some pictures of the people I interviewed. I have to get them developed tomorrow.' Dear God, he'd been lucky! Minutes earlier she would have caught him without any possible explanation.

Elke came further into the room, holding the robe around her. 'I didn't know what had happened when I woke up and you weren't there.'

Reimann was grateful that with the desk lamp turned off the sheen of perspiration would not be visible in the soft-lighted room. Striving for a casual reply he said: 'I could hardly have woken you up and said I was going, could I?'

Elke didn't smile, as he'd hoped. Well within the room she appeared uncertain what to do, finally sitting on an easy chair from which she could look up sideways at him. She sat bent forward, arms around her knees. From Reimann she looked obviously at the handbag containing the replaced document and then back again.

Hurriedly he said: 'Can I get you something? A hot drink, maybe?'

'No.'

'Are you all right?'

'Why do you ask?'

'You seem . . .' Reimann shrugged, feeling the perspiration worsen. '. . . tense. As if something's wrong.'

'No,' said Elke. 'Nothing's wrong.'

'You should get back to bed. You'll be tired tomorrow – later today – if you don't get more sleep.'

'I don't feel tired any more,' said Elke. 'Just like you.'

Reimann used the excuse of completing the protective closure of the camera to turn his back to her. Convinced she couldn't see, he wiped the sweat from his face before twisting again to walk towards her. 'Should have done that before,' he said, conscious of how false his voice sounded when he spoke.

'What are you?' There was no emotion, no feeling at all, in her question. Neither was it any sort of challenge: just three, flat, expressionless words.

'What?'

'I think you heard what I said.'

It was the opportunity if he chose to take it. Here, at her bidding, was the moment for him at last to be honest with her – as he wanted to be honest – but try at the moment of absolute confession to make her see it on his terms, the different shelves upon which he had arranged it in his own head. But he was frightened. More than frightened. Reimann was suddenly terrified he *wouldn't* be able to make her understand and that he would drive her away, destroying what there was. Later, he told himself: later when he'd assembled all the arguments and persuasions. He said: 'You know what I am!'

'Do I?'

'You know you do!' How to escape? He had to deflect her, turn aside the tunnelled curiosity.

'I'm not sure,' Elke persisted. 'I can't ever lose the impression that there's something I don't understand. That I should know but which I don't, because you won't tell me.'

'That's four o'clock in the morning talk,' Reimann said. What was the way? Where was the way?

'You do love me? More than anyone else, don't you?'

Reimann saw the welcoming path opening before him. He came to the couch adjacent to where she was sitting so that he could take the hands she still had tightly clasped about her knees. 'There *is* no one else,' he insisted, honestly. 'There's only you. And will only ever be you . . .' Should he say it? Make the promise. It *would* be the way to deflect her and he had to do that. He went on: 'I was thinking about us, coming back on the plane today.'

'What about us?'

'The decision I promised to make: about the time to get married.'

Elke blinked at him, clearly astonished. 'You *really* mean that?' She'd been convinced it was a lie, before: just another lie.

'We talked about it,' he reminded her. 'I think it's time we properly settled down, don't you?'

'I suppose . . . I don't know . . .'

Reimann was astonished. 'Don't you want us to be married?'

'I . . .' she began, and stopped. Then she said: 'I suppose that's what I'd hoped, yes. I guess I need time to think.'

Reimann remained surprised. 'I thought you'd feel differently than this! I thought you'd be excited!'

'I am . . . it's just . . .' Elke humped her shoulders. 'It *is* four o'clock in the morning!' Would being married make any difference? Or would there still be svelte women in grey Audis and others who sent missing-you cards from Italy? She said: 'If we got married would you still have to go away so much?'

'Sometimes,' said Reimann cautiously. 'I'd try to cut it down as much as possible.' If he insisted upon regularizing the contact meetings with the Russians he *could* reduce the frequency: once a month would be sufficient. And there could be another insistence, that they were held somewhere closer to Bonn to avoid the occasional need for him to remain overnight.

'There's something . . .' started Elke and stopped again.

'What?'

She shook her head. 'Nothing.' She smiled, fleetingly. 'When? When can we get married?'

'Whenever you like! As soon as you like! It's all going to be marvellous!' He could live with the lie: he could live with any lie, so long as it enabled him to be with her.

'Yes,' said Elke. 'Marvellous.'

Chapter Forty-Five

It was a grey, overcast day: when he'd boarded the plane it had been raining heavily. Reimann hoped it would have stopped by the time he reached Berlin. It was a long walk into the East, and he couldn't risk a taxi to the safe house. Strictly according to operational instructions he shouldn't have flown direct from Cologne, but he was impatient with circuitous routes after so long. Flying above the clouds it was impossible to look down at the towns and hamlets as he had the previous week, returning from East Berlin. Reimann knew he'd be able to get back that night, hopefully on an early flight. To hand over the confirming film roll would only take minutes, and he'd decided against discussing his marrying Elke. Better to build up a series of untrue difficulties with her to make the idea acceptable.

He'd agree to a church wedding if Elke wanted it. She'd probably have Ida as an attendant. Maybe Doris, as well. What about Ursula? She wasn't capable of acting as a bridesmaid, but there was no reason why the child couldn't be brought out of the home for the occasion. It was something he would have to discuss with Elke. There were, in fact, a lot of things he had to discuss with Elke. He was surprised she wasn't more excited. The last few days it had always been he who'd had to initiate any conversation, and he had been sure she would have talked and planned with Ida the previous weekend. In the event she'd said nothing and asked him not to, either, as they drove to Bad Godesberg. *I don't want to make any announcement until we've fixed a date and made definite arrangements*, she'd said. He could accept – but only just – that she might be cautious after being abandoned once before, but he had hoped she trusted him more than that. What about himself? Should he have trusted her – believed in her – when she'd given him the chance? And it had been a chance, when she'd asked what he was. A pointless recrimination now. If it had been a chance, then he'd missed it. It could come later: a lot could come later. The important thing was to get the marriage settled. Everything else could follow: he'd handle the difficulties as they arose.

It wasn't raining in Berlin but the streets were wet. Reimann crossed directly, no longer interested in old landmarks or abandoned divisions.

Coming here was a chore now: dull, boring routine. The usual attendant opened the door at Johannisstrasse, but only Turev awaited him in their customary room. It stank, as things usually stank about the man.

'We're not staying,' announced Turev, urgently. 'Come!'

'What? . . . where?' Reimann was startled by the jarring break with routine.

'We think this house is compromised. There was no way we could warn you. That's what I'm doing now. Warning you. Come!'

'But tell me. . . ?'

'Later. It'll all be explained later.' The fat Russian waddled hurriedly across the room, leading the way out. Reimann followed, picking up the other man's agitation: his body was twitching, and as he was crossing the narrow distance from the house to a waiting car which Reimann hadn't seen when he'd entered, the Russian darted looks from side to side, as if he feared being challenged or arrested. There was a raised partition between the front and rear seats: the driver did not turn. As the doors closed behind them, the vehicle moved off. In the back Reimann said: 'Where are we going?'

'One of our own military installations is only a few kilometres out of town. We'll be safe there.' The man filled the car with smoke: the hand holding the cigarette was shaking.

'Who's identified the house? The Germans or someone else?'

'Maybe both.'

'We should have switched sooner,' said Reimann. They appeared to have got away unhindered, so the trembling concern was hardly justified. But then they'd always panicked, he remembered. They'd have to decide a new contact place. Maybe he would suggest Vienna: take over Jutta's venue. Vienna would be far preferable to the drabness of East Berlin.

The Russian didn't respond to the implied criticism, tensed forward on the seat, gazing directly ahead. He remained that way until they approached the army camp: not before the car passed through the guarded entrance did he show any relaxation, and then only to look sideways at Reimann, set-faced. Turev said: 'I've got you safely back on Russian territory.'

They pulled up in front of a low barrack block. There were uniformed men everywhere, most of them armed. As they got out of the car there was the fluttering noise of a camouflaged helicopter lifting off from a nearby pad, making any conversation impossible. The Russian jerked his hand, gesturing Reimann to follow. The barrack building appeared to be guarded by more armed men.

The room into which Reimann was led was larger than that at Johannisstrasse: a briefing chamber, he guessed. As he entered the balding, bearded man he'd expected to see earlier rose from behind a desk, supporting himself against it with both hands. Reimann's passing awareness was that this man was shaking, too.

'BASTARD!' Sorokin yelled, purple-faced, a vein pumping in his forehead. He'd needed the release, in his personal terror, but he at once regretted the outburst, wanting to appear controlled.

Reimann was momentarily speechless. 'What the. . . ?' he groped.

'Bastard!' repeated Sorokin, but quieter now, threateningly so. 'But you're going to tell me! You're going to be questioned by experts, and we're going to use every chemical we've got until you tell us.' The biggest political disaster for years, he thought: since the new thinking and the reforms of glasnost and perestroika. With its diplomatic but still unannounced agreement to on-site inspection in Germany, NATO had called Moscow's bluff. So they'd lost the demand for Warsaw inclusion. Had to withdraw the troops as undertaken and surrendered God knows how much conventional armaments. Sorokin knew he'd be stripped of his promotion. They all would. There would be other, worse punishment.

'Please!' said Reimann. He extended his arms, helplessly. There was an immediate noise behind him, and he turned and saw there were three armed Soviet soldiers inside the room: they'd started forward at his movement. Reimann blinked back to the still standing, puce-faced Sorokin and said: 'I don't understand . . . you must tell . . .'

'It's not going to work!' sneered Sorokin, mocking now. 'So who is it? The West Germans? The CIA? The British? Who? Who have you gone over to? Easy to see now why you felt able to object and argue as you did, about every order. Took so long. And why you weren't worried at the West German counter-intelligence investigation. Was that when they got to you? Turned you? But you mistimed everything. Let it run too long! So now we've got you! And how we've got you!'

Reimann shook his head, punch-drunk. 'You must tell me . . .' he tried again, desperately. 'I can't. . . ?'

Sorokin ignored him, consumed with rage, terrified for himself. The noise of another helicopter seemed to remind him. He nodded through the wired windows and said: 'That's how you're being taken back to Moscow. You thought you were safe, didn't you? Thought you could go on fooling us! Laughing at us! Not at any risk, coming here today! You're going to know just how much at risk you are! You'll go insane, you know! You're going to have so much pain you're going to lose your mind. In the end you'll beg to be killed. And you will be. I promise you that. But not until you've told me every secret and every trick. Everything that you've done. Bastard!'

'I DON'T KNOW WHAT'S GONE WRONG!' Reimann screamed back at the man.

'Take him,' Sorokin ordered the waiting guards.

Jutta stared down at the official communication on flimsy paper, but didn't see the words. 'Dead!' she said, echoing what the prison official had announced, handing it to her in her clerk's office of the Interior Ministry building in central Moscow.

'That's what it says.' The official's voice was hard, surly.

'How . . . it doesn't say . . .'

'That's all you're permitted to know. Just that he's dead.' No official document anywhere recorded that Otto Reimann had died in agony, under interrogation, still unable to answer the questions of the frantic Dimitri Sorokin.

'No!' wailed Jutta. The only hope to which she had clung, all these weeks, was that somehow Otto would find a way to get her reinstated.

'You have to sign the receipt,' the man insisted.

'What's going to happen to me?' said Jutta, echoing the plea she'd made to Sorokin.

'How do I know?' said the surly official.

Chapter Forty-Six

Everyone had been extremely kind: sympathetic. 'Everyone' didn't seem the right word. It indicated a lot of people and there weren't a lot of people. There never had been, even before Otto. Ida and the family, of course: always Ida. In a bizarre, illogical way Elke felt more embarrassed for Ida than she believed Ida was for her. In those first weeks poor Ida and even poorer Horst had gone through agonies trying to find the right phrase, until she'd become sure herself and told them they didn't have to try any more: that she knew Otto had left her, as Dietlef had left her before. As it always happened. There were still half-begun sentences that trailed away to nothing: blurted mentions of his name, gulped back, as if they were trying to swallow instead of saying it before Ida finally did say it, that she'd always thought there was something odd about him and never really trusted him. Elke was glad she hadn't talked to them about the wedding, as Reimann had urged. Just as she felt sorry for Ida, she felt pity for Horst, for losing his fiction market. And not just for Horst and his self-assurance and the extra money, although the man would never know what sort of escape he'd had. Elke was resigned to not getting the outstanding five thousand marks repaid, as she was resigned to so much else: resigned to everything.

Who else had been kind? Günther Werle, she supposed. Pleased, too, she knew. It had actually been he who raised it – *are you still friendly with the person you met through that accident?* – and within a fortnight started talking about a concert when she'd admitted that she wasn't. Elke supposed she would go with him, eventually. Like she might do other things, eventually. Werle wouldn't be able to fuck like Otto, but she'd come to like it so she probably would go to bed with him, if he tried hard enough. There wouldn't ever again be any danger, of course. Although at the moment she was completely celibate Elke was still taking the Pill and intended to go on doing so, although not specifically for sexual protection. Her periods *were* much easier, because of it. Elke reflected, with a cynicism that was practically permanent these days, that her less painful periods remained one of the minuscule benefits of ever having known Otto Reimann. She found it difficult to think of any others.

Elke turned on the windscreen wipers, fearing at first that it might be snow and glad when it wasn't. Not much longer, she estimated: only a week or two before hard winter. With German efficiency the autobahns were cleared very promptly, but Elke always allowed herself extra time to get to Marienfels in the winter. She'd have to remember to check her tyres, for roadworthiness in the snow. No she wouldn't, she corrected herself at once. Otto had had new tyres fitted, after the accident. Had it all happened in such short time, in less than a full year? It seemed difficult to believe.

Because the institution was high in the hills the wind howled through the trees, chilling Elke the moment she got out of the Volkswagen. Futilely clutching her coat around her, she hurried into the former mansion for the greeting ritual from Dr Schiller. Someone else who had been kind? Otto had come quite often to Marienfels, but the principal had never remarked upon his absence in these recent weeks. Yes, decided Elke, positively: someone else who had been kind. Still not enough to qualify for an embracing word like 'everyone'.

Ursula was huddled not on her chair but on the bed, and in a way that didn't look comfortable, but Elke made no attempt to get her off or resettle her because Dr Schiller had warned of a fractious mood: it was best she remained undisturbed. The predictable tape played softly; Chopin, Elke identified.

'Hello, darling. It's Mummy.'

Ursula didn't move: didn't hear.

Elke sat in the chair her daughter normally occupied, sighing at the familiarity of it all. Resigned, she told herself again; completely and utterly resigned. She felt out, touching Ursula's shoulder. The girl let the hand remain there, not aware of it.

'It's all finished,' declared Elke, setting out on a longer monologue than usual. 'That man you met: the one who was nice. He's gone. I hoped he wouldn't: didn't want him to. But he has. So we won't be seeing him again . . . I won't be seeing him . . .'

In its sealed container the tape clicked to a stop and whirred into rewind.

'. . .Of course I cried,' resumed Elke, as if she'd been asked a question. 'Didn't want at first to believe he wasn't coming back, not like it was with your Daddy. But not for too long: because I knew, you see. I'd found out . . .'

The music began softly playing again.

'. . . Even know her name, Sneider. Jutta Sneider. She was poised: attractive. They seemed very much in love. Used to each other. And there was another one. At least I think there was another one.

There were postcards, always with the same message . . . like a love message . . .'

Ursula moved, irritably, straightening herself slightly. Elke watched, not attempting to help, simply withdrawing her hand.

'. . . He was cheating me. That's what I hated . . . couldn't forgive, ever. That he was cheating me. He was sleeping with me and making love to me and telling me that he loved me and all the time he wanted other women. Even when he asked me properly to marry him and I asked him if he would still have to go away he said he would . . . that's what I couldn't forgive . . . couldn't accept . . .'

Ursula shifted again, going back into almost the same position as when Elke had entered the room.

'. . . And I could have accepted a lot,' Elke resumed, a conversation more than ever with herself. 'I knew what else he was. Suspected at first, before I really found out. He made a mistake, a long time ago. Tried to excuse it but I knew it was a lie because no one answers the telephones identifying the Cabinet Secretariat, which he tried to convince me they did. So he knew that was where I worked, long before I told him . . .'

Elke briefly looked up at the music complex, wishing for once she could turn it off. She realized she probably could if she studied it, but remembered Dr Schiller's warning and decided against it.

'. . . And there were the conversations: guidance, he called them. All he needed was guidance, to help him write the articles his magazine wanted. There were even complaints, supposedly from Australia. But you know what? He never wrote what I told him. When we were practically living together at Rochusplatz I read all the articles that appeared under his name and there was never once any indication of his writing what I told him, disguised as he promised it would be disguised to make it untraceable to me. Then I found out how he'd tricked poor, innocent Uncle Horst. I'll never know why. To ingratiate himself, I guess. He was commissioning stories from Uncle Horst, telling him he could write fiction. I read one original, you see. It was dreadful: silly and dreadful and sad. The stories that appeared in the magazines – and I read them all, in the end, at Rochusplatz – were quite different: the one I read in the original had hardly any connection with what eventually appeared . . . another trick.'

Ursula turned, jerkily, and smiled and Elke smiled back and said: 'Ursula!' The child's face cleared, into blankness.

'. . . Yes,' Elke started, as if answering another question. 'I really could have forgiven that: gone on telling him things, if it had meant our staying together; if it had meant he would be with me forever. But as I

350

said, it was the other woman. I think I hated him by the time he began asking for documents. I was having his baby then, you see: just like I had you. I was pregnant and he was with the other woman, kissing her and holding her close. I never took any risk, of course: not a personal risk. Poor Gerda Pohl . . . remember I told you about her . . . poor Gerda gave away little secrets . . . I saw how it was investigated and realized how easy it would be for me to do it. I couldn't have got into trouble, though: not like she did. I made everything up, you see. But in the proper way. Who knows better about the format and the style of the highest classified material than I do? So I invented the first document entirely. Not badly to affect him: I never intended that. Just to make things difficult, because of how he'd hurt me with other women. But he asked more and more about military things so I went on inventing, creating fake documents, saying the opposite to all the real Cabinet discussions about defence and NATO. I wanted him to question it: tell me the truth about himself, so I could have agreed to do what he really wanted . . .'

Far away in a distant part of the houses a luncheon bell sounded. Elke decided they could wait: there was always a rush at the beginning.

'. . . I saw him photographing them, of course. From the very beginning, with the first one I made up. I felt him get out of bed and go into the lounge and I looked through the gap in the door and saw him taking pictures. That was when I *really* knew, for certain, that Otto was a spy. I almost went in that night; almost went in and said I know what you are and it doesn't matter and I'll go on doing whatever you want, just as long as you don't have other women. And then finally I did. It was the last night, when I'd shown him the made-up paper saying the Cabinet had agreed a secret agreement to maintain missiles. I waited so I didn't really catch him but I went in and openly asked him who he was, wanting him to be honest at last. I waited for him to say it: just as I was waiting to say I wasn't shocked and didn't care and admit how I'd tricked him and how I wanted to correct everything: put it right. But he *wouldn't* tell me! He was so used to lying that he wouldn't tell me! He went on cheating, instead. Talked about us getting married and with what he thought was the last piece of paper he wanted he ran away . . . like they always run away . . . He could have got into trouble, of course. Moscow made a lot of concessions, so it's possible he got into trouble. Deserved it, if he did. He hurt me very badly . . .'

With a suddenness that surprised her Elke felt herself close to tears and fought against them. She *had* cried, as she'd admitted to the unlistening Ursula, but not for a long time.

351

'. . . I *did* love him,' said Elke. 'I didn't want anything, except him. That's why I would have willingly spied if he'd asked me: I don't give a damn for all these stupid politicians and their stupid discussions and stances, conceding this to gain that. And I *could* have done it so easily! No one would ever have suspected me. . . !'

Elke jerked to a stop at the door opening. An attendant said: 'Dr Schiller didn't think Ursula would want to come down into the dining hall today.'

'I don't think she does,' Elke confirmed.

'I'll bring something up later,' the woman promised. 'Why don't you let me know when you think she's ready?'

Elke nodded to the retreating nurse, looking back to her daughter. 'I know he's never coming back,' she went on. 'I used the Chancellery authority, to check the press office. There's been a letter from the Australian magazines, saying the accreditation has been withdrawn: that Otto Reimann resigned. I should have told security about the magazines, but that would have led them to me and I don't want that, do I? And I was very careful, about the apartment at Rochusplatz. He gave me a key in the end. So I collected all my clothes and went through all the drawers, in case there was anything incriminating that could be linked with me. There was a strange list, a lot of questions. It referred to "that woman", which I suppose was me. He'd asked me quite a lot of them, before I began giving him what he thought were genuine documents. I took the list: destroyed it, because it might have made people curious . . .' Elke leaned forward, kissing the unresponsive child. 'So there's only us again, darling. Everyone thinks it's just like it was before: that I've been abandoned . . .' Elke made a further pause. 'Which is what's happened, darling. We're abandoned again . . .'

Elke felt the tears about to return and gulped against them. 'I truly believed he loved me!' she said, plaintively. 'I truly believed this time that I was going to be happy, just as he promised we would be . . .' Elke smiled sadly across at her daughter. 'I've been a lot of times to the flat where I knew Jutta Sneider lived, but she's not there any more. I finally checked with the agent. He said she moved away, without warning: that lawyers settled everything for her. So that's where I suppose he is now. With her. Unless he's being punished, that is. As I said, he deserves to be punished . . .'

Elke got up, going to the door, deciding that today the nurse could feed Ursula. She turned back into the room. 'Next week, my darling,' she promised. 'I'll be here next week, as usual.'

On her way back to Bonn, Elke decided she'd have to start writing a diary again. She might get a dog, too. She missed Poppi. A dog would be a companion: someone to talk to at Kaufmannstrasse.